Chloe

charmz™

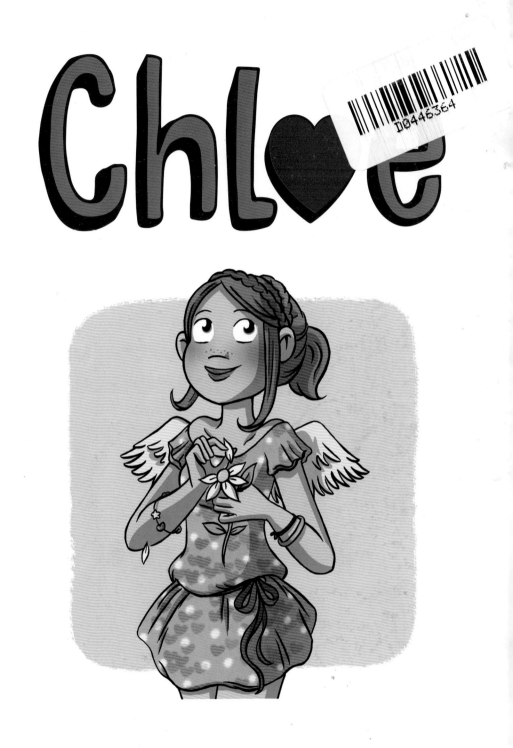

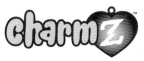

Chl♥e

RAINY DAY

Story by Greg Tessier
Art by Amandine

NEW YORK

A big thanks to all those kindly folks who, in daily life, manage to bring out smiles and serenity all around! Because family and Brittany have always gone well together. Thanks to the residents of Brittany, France who have always been there for me!
—*Greg*

Thanks to our adorable readers;
thanks for your encouragement, your kindhearted notes, and your awesome drawings!
Thanks, too, of course, to my dear family for their invaluable support and for ZouZou's astute advice that's now benefitting CHLOE! Thanks to Ali and Fabrice for being my friends during the studious summer hours! To Capu, my irreplaceable old friend! To our fantastic past vacations and those to come in Brittany and elsewhere!
And lastly, a huge thanks to Pierre for his irreplaceable coloring and culinary assistance!
—*Amandine*

Mistinguette [CHLOE] volume 7 "Un Peu...Beaucoup...Passionnement!" © Jungle! 2016 and
Mistinguette [CHLOE] volume 8 "Pagaille et Retrouvailles" © Jungle! 2017
www.editions-jungle.com. All rights reserved. Used under license.

English translation and all other editorial material © 2018 by Papercutz
All rights reserved.

CHLOE #4
"Rainy Day"

GREG TESSIER—Story
AMANDINE—Art and Color
JOE JOHNSON—Translation
BRYAN SENKA—Lettering
DAWN GUZZO—Production
JEFF WHITMAN—Editor
JIM SALICRUP
Editor-in-Chief

Charmz is an imprint of Papercutz.

PB ISBN: 978-1-5458-0010-2
HC ISBN: 978-1-5458-0011-9

Printed in China
May 2018

Charmz books may be purchased for business or promotional use.
For information on bulk purchases please contact Macmillan
Corporate and Premium Sales Department at
(800) 221-7945 x5442

Distributed by Macmillan
First Charmz Printing

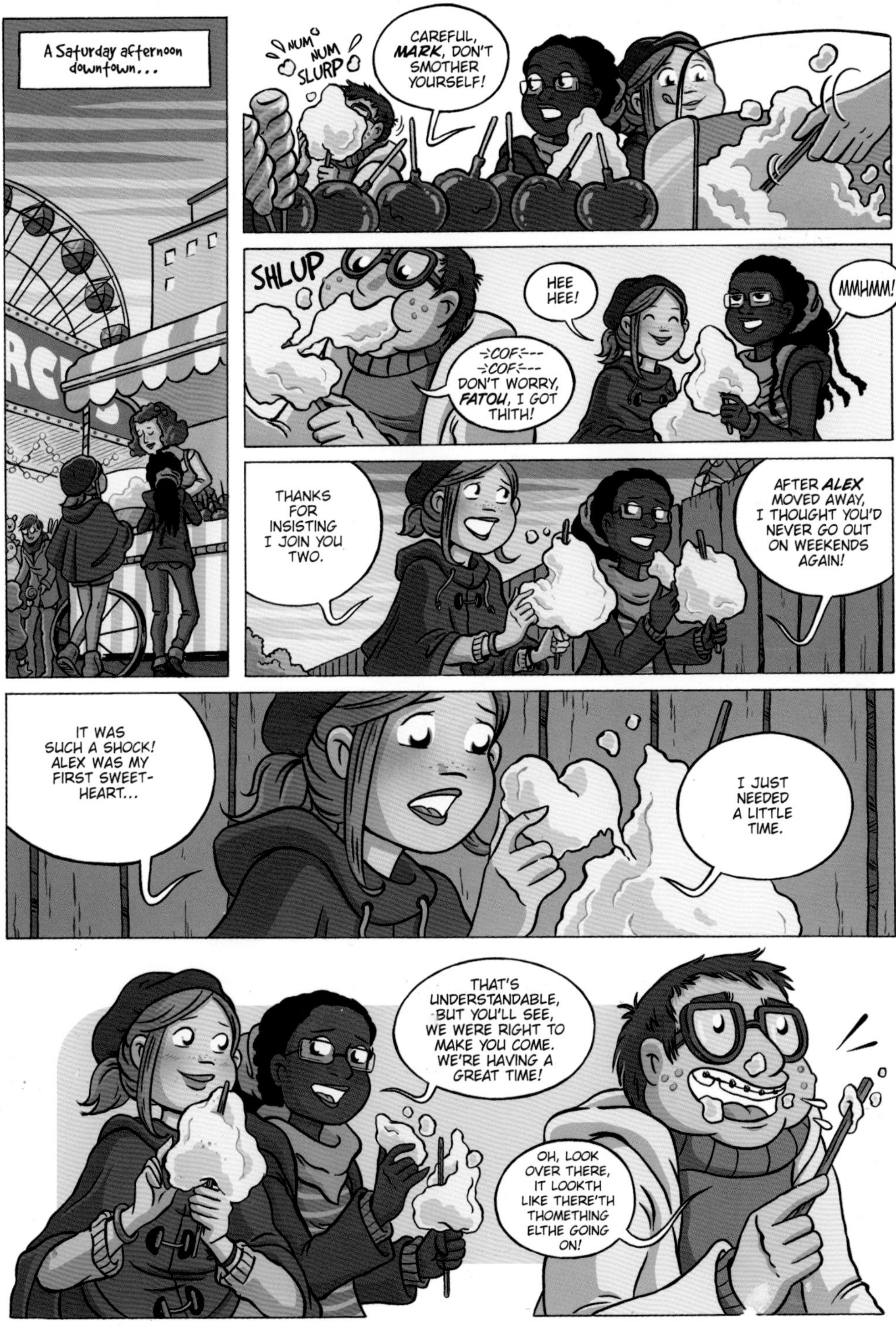
A Saturday afternoon downtown...
NUM NUM SLURP
CAREFUL, MARK, DON'T SMOTHER YOURSELF!
SHLUP
HEE HEE!
MMHMM!
COF COF DON'T WORRY, FATOU, I GOT THITH!
THANKS FOR INSISTING I JOIN YOU TWO.
AFTER ALEX MOVED AWAY, I THOUGHT YOU'D NEVER GO OUT ON WEEKENDS AGAIN!
IT WAS SUCH A SHOCK! ALEX WAS MY FIRST SWEET-HEART...
I JUST NEEDED A LITTLE TIME.
THAT'S UNDERSTANDABLE, BUT YOU'LL SEE, WE WERE RIGHT TO MAKE YOU COME. WE'RE HAVING A GREAT TIME!
OH, LOOK OVER THERE, IT LOOKTH LIKE THERE'TH THOMETHING ELTHE GOING ON!

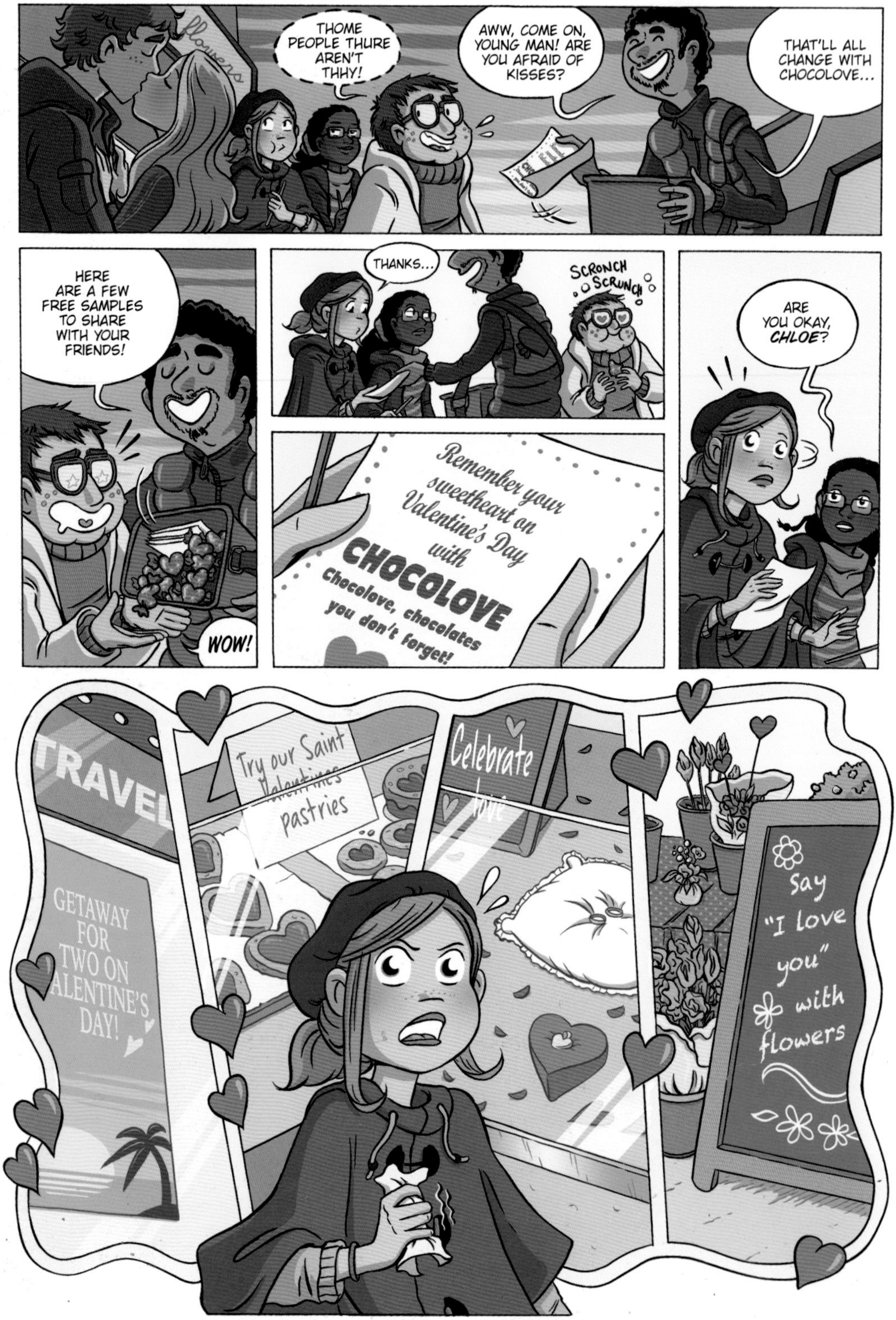
flowers
THOME PEOPLE THURE AREN'T THHY!
AWW, COME ON, YOUNG MAN! ARE YOU AFRAID OF KISSES?
THAT'LL ALL CHANGE WITH CHOCOLOVE...
HERE ARE A FEW FREE SAMPLES TO SHARE WITH YOUR FRIENDS!
WOW!
THANKS...
SCRONCH SCRUNCH
ARE YOU OKAY, CHLOE?
Remember your sweetheart on Valentine's Day with
CHOCOLOVE
Chocolove, chocolates you don't forget!
TRAVEL
GETAWAY FOR TWO ON ALENTINE'S DAY!
Try our Saint Valentine's pastries
Celebrate love
Say "I love you" with flowers

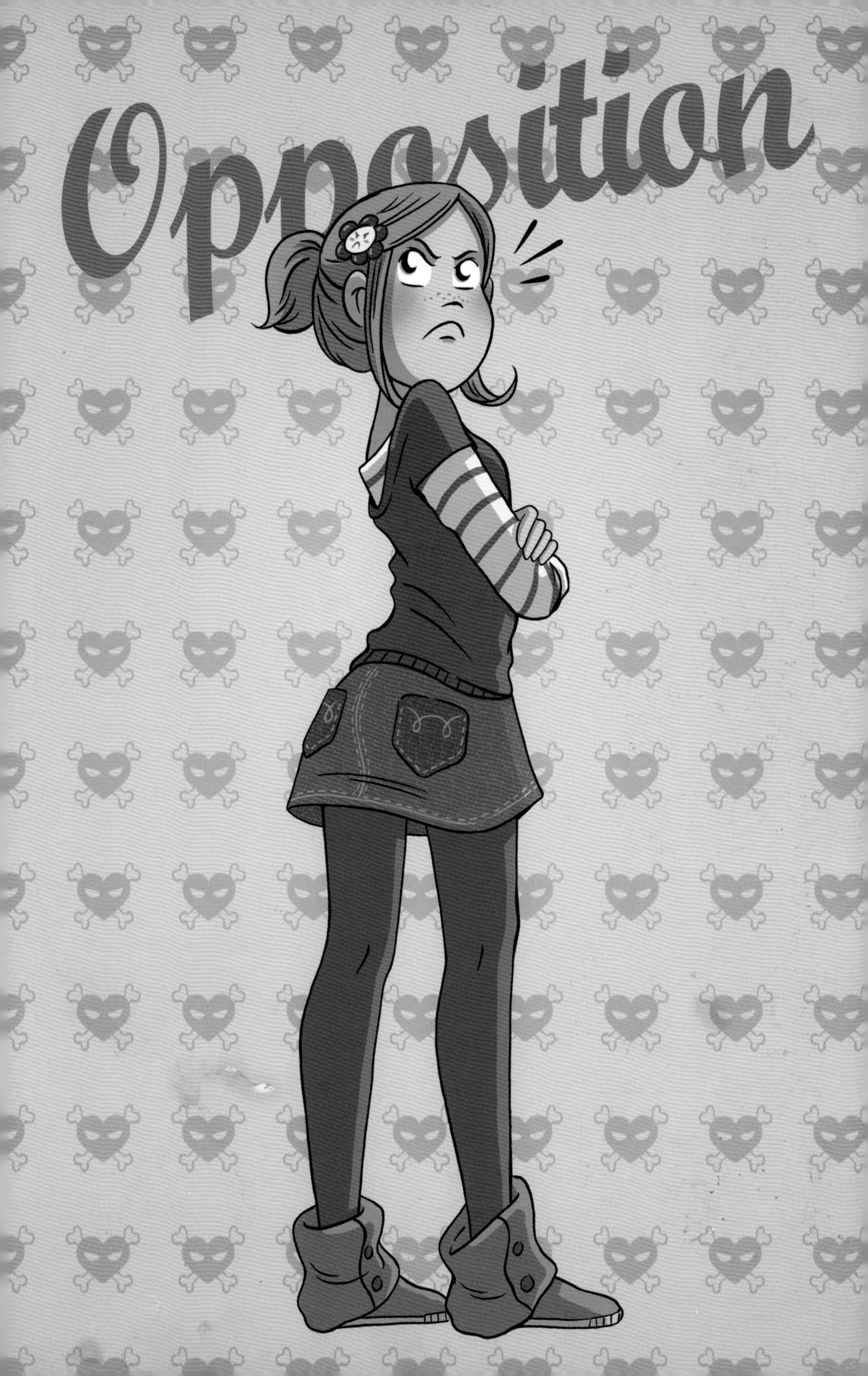
Opposition

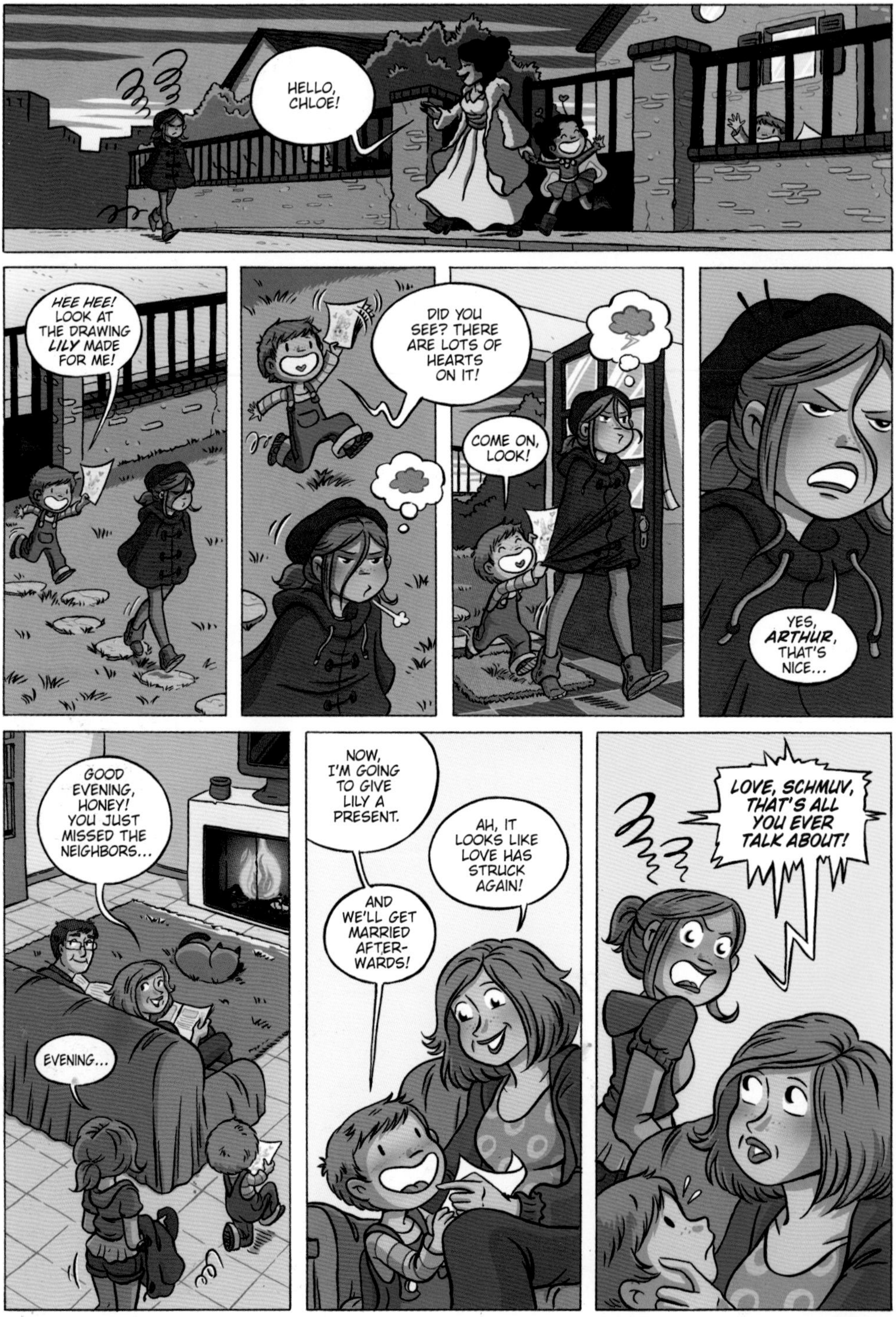
HELLO, CHLOE!
HEE HEE! LOOK AT THE DRAWING LILY MADE FOR ME!
DID YOU SEE? THERE ARE LOTS OF HEARTS ON IT!
COME ON, LOOK!
YES, ARTHUR, THAT'S NICE...
GOOD EVENING, HONEY! YOU JUST MISSED THE NEIGHBORS...
EVENING...
NOW, I'M GOING TO GIVE LILY A PRESENT.
AND WE'LL GET MARRIED AFTER-WARDS!
AH, IT LOOKS LIKE LOVE HAS STRUCK AGAIN!
LOVE, SCHMUV, THAT'S ALL YOU EVER TALK ABOUT!

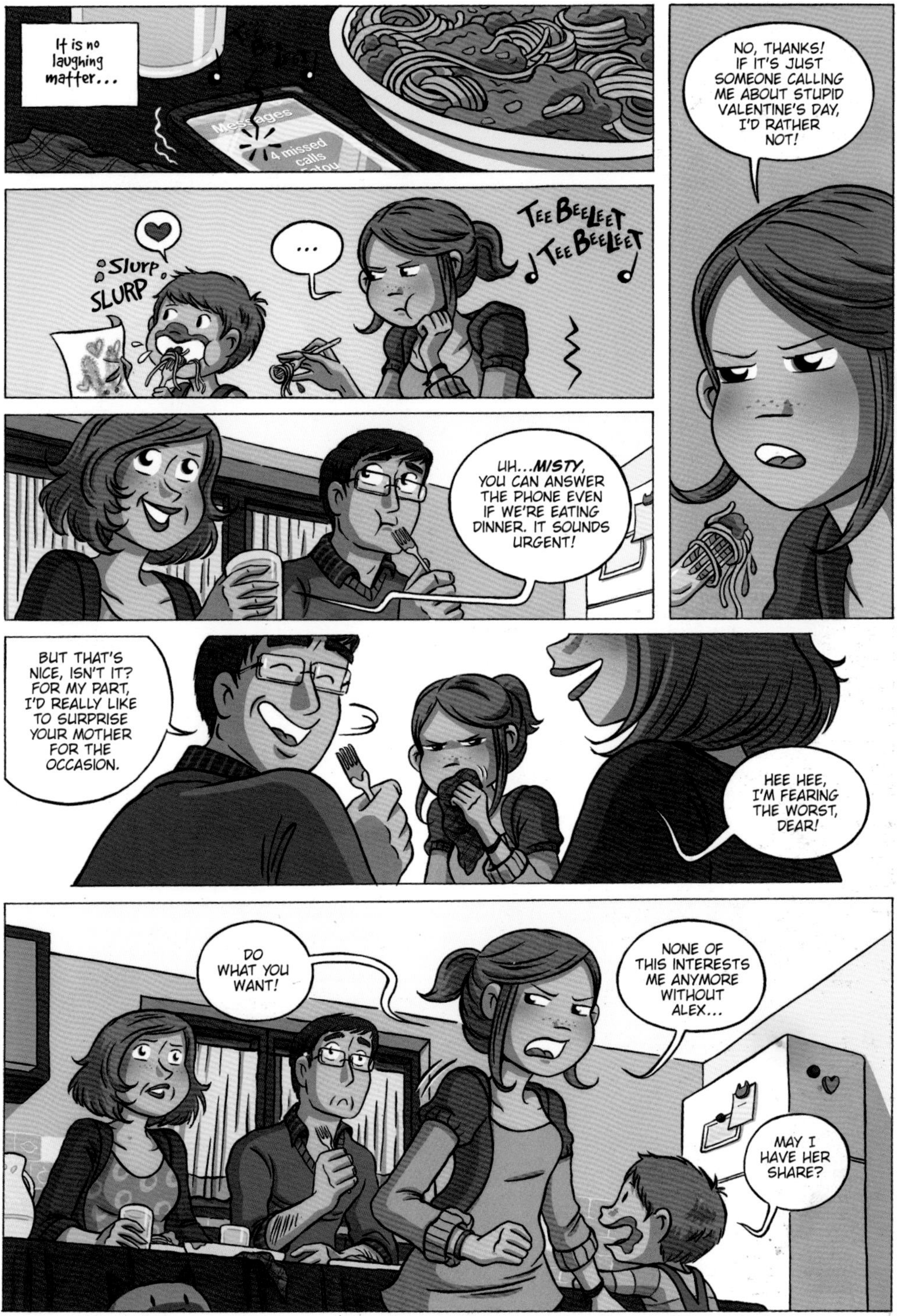
It is no laughing matter...
Messages
4 missed calls
NO, THANKS! IF IT'S JUST SOMEONE CALLING ME ABOUT STUPID VALENTINE'S DAY, I'D RATHER NOT!
SLURP
SLURP
...
TEE BEELEET
TEE BEELEET
UH... MISTY, YOU CAN ANSWER THE PHONE EVEN IF WE'RE EATING DINNER. IT SOUNDS URGENT!
BUT THAT'S NICE, ISN'T IT? FOR MY PART, I'D REALLY LIKE TO SURPRISE YOUR MOTHER FOR THE OCCASION.
HEE HEE, I'M FEARING THE WORST, DEAR!
DO WHAT YOU WANT!
NONE OF THIS INTERESTS ME ANYMORE WITHOUT ALEX...
MAY I HAVE HER SHARE?

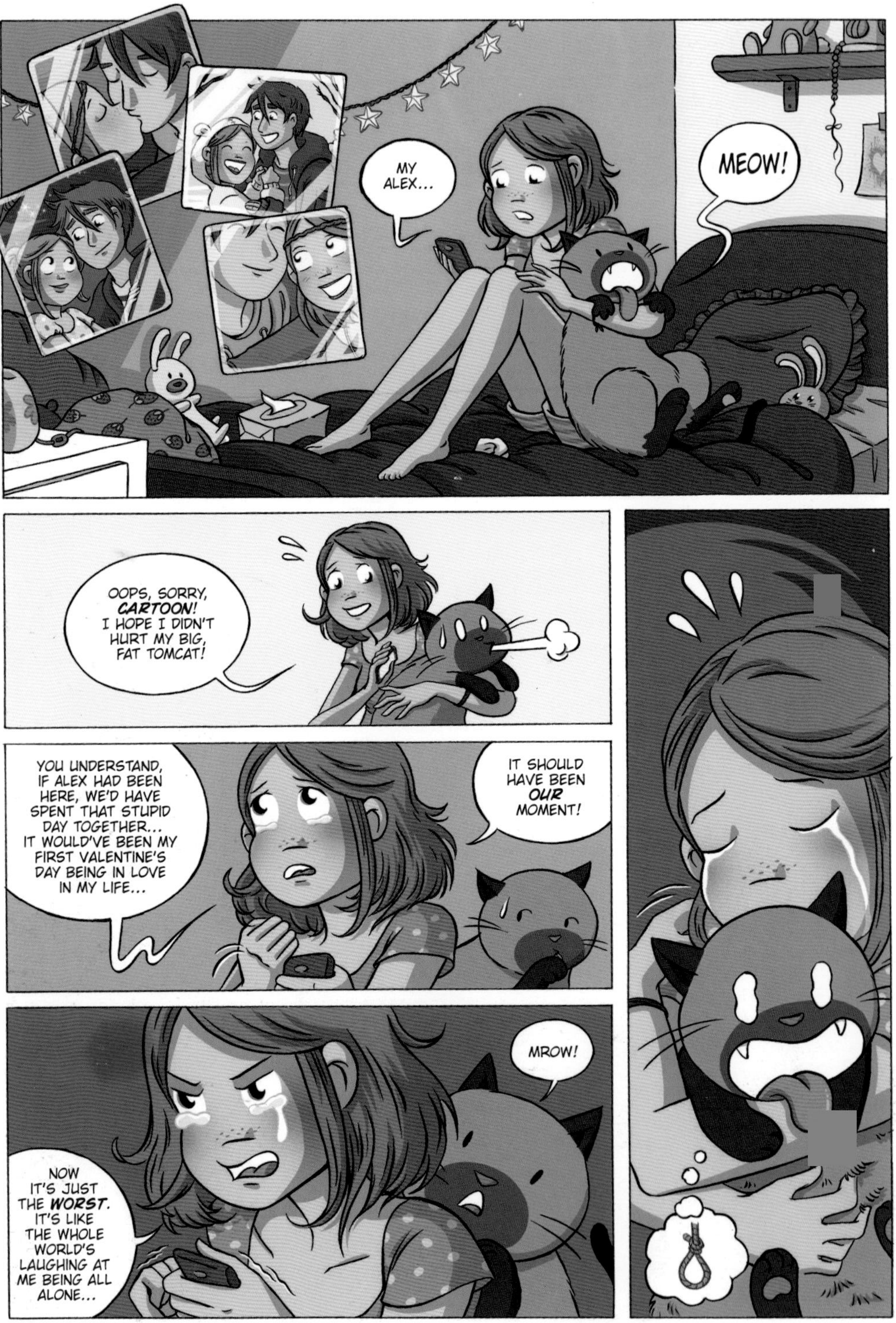

MY ALEX...
MEOW!
OOPS, SORRY, CARTOON! I HOPE I DIDN'T HURT MY BIG, FAT TOMCAT!
YOU UNDERSTAND, IF ALEX HAD BEEN HERE, WE'D HAVE SPENT THAT STUPID DAY TOGETHER... IT WOULD'VE BEEN MY FIRST VALENTINE'S DAY BEING IN LOVE IN MY LIFE...
IT SHOULD HAVE BEEN OUR MOMENT!
MROW!
NOW IT'S JUST THE WORST. IT'S LIKE THE WHOLE WORLD'S LAUGHING AT ME BEING ALL ALONE...

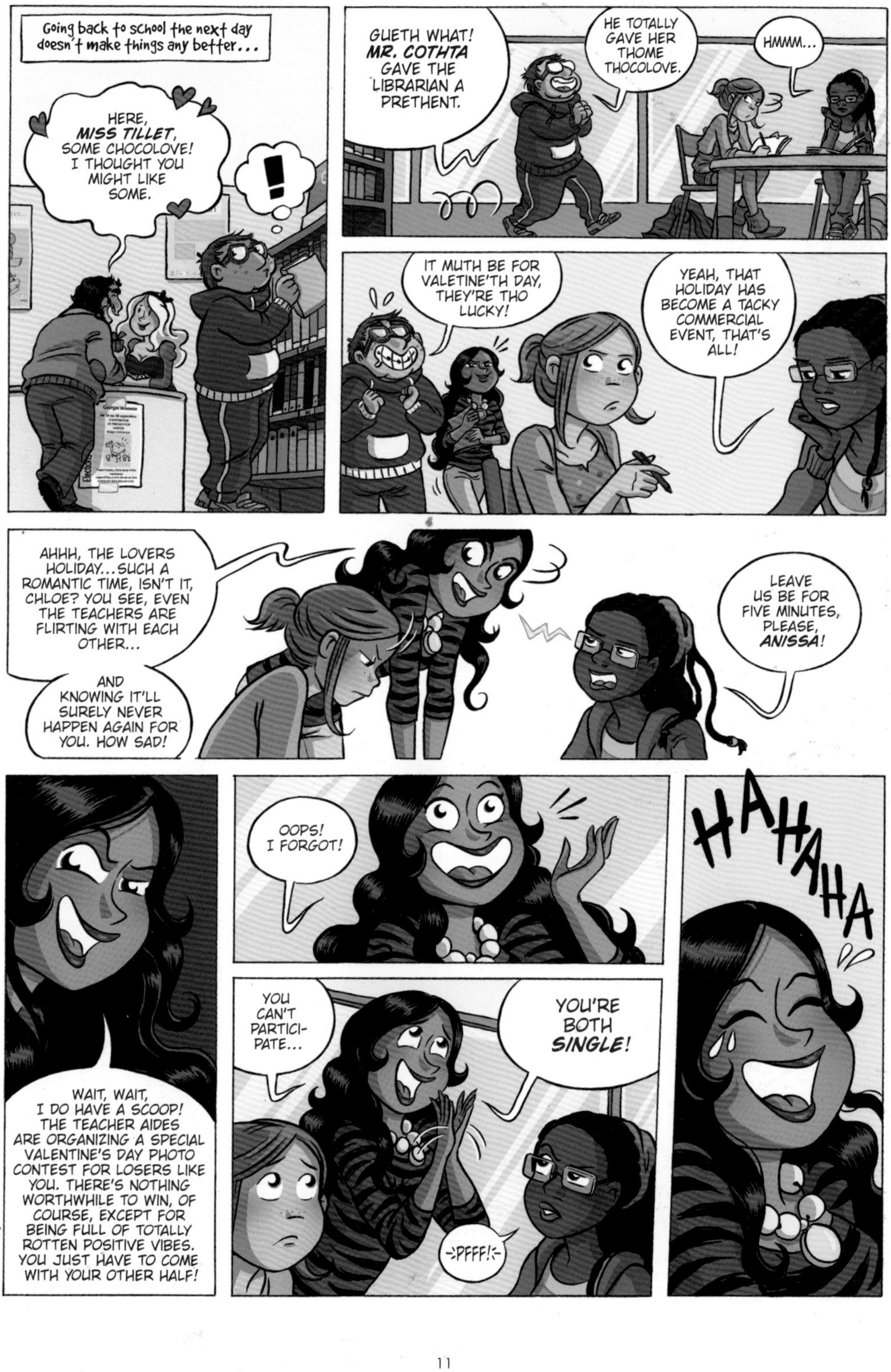
Going back to school the next day doesn't make things any better...
HERE, MISS TILLET, SOME CHOCOLOVE! I THOUGHT YOU MIGHT LIKE SOME.
!
GUETH WHAT! MR. COTHTA GAVE THE LIBRARIAN A PRETHENT.
HE TOTALLY GAVE HER THOME THOCOLOVE.
HMMM...
IT MUTH BE FOR VALETINE'TH DAY, THEY'RE THO LUCKY!
YEAH, THAT HOLIDAY HAS BECOME A TACKY COMMERCIAL EVENT, THAT'S ALL!
AHHH, THE LOVERS HOLIDAY...SUCH A ROMANTIC TIME, ISN'T IT, CHLOE? YOU SEE, EVEN THE TEACHERS ARE FLIRTING WITH EACH OTHER...
AND KNOWING IT'LL SURELY NEVER HAPPEN AGAIN FOR YOU. HOW SAD!
LEAVE US BE FOR FIVE MINUTES, PLEASE, ANISSA!
WAIT, WAIT, I DO HAVE A SCOOP! THE TEACHER AIDES ARE ORGANIZING A SPECIAL VALENTINE'S DAY PHOTO CONTEST FOR LOSERS LIKE YOU. THERE'S NOTHING WORTHWHILE TO WIN, OF COURSE, EXCEPT FOR BEING FULL OF TOTALLY ROTTEN POSITIVE VIBES. YOU JUST HAVE TO COME WITH YOUR OTHER HALF!
OOPS! I FORGOT!
YOU CAN'T PARTICI-PATE...
YOU'RE BOTH SINGLE!
-PFFF!-
HAHAHAHA

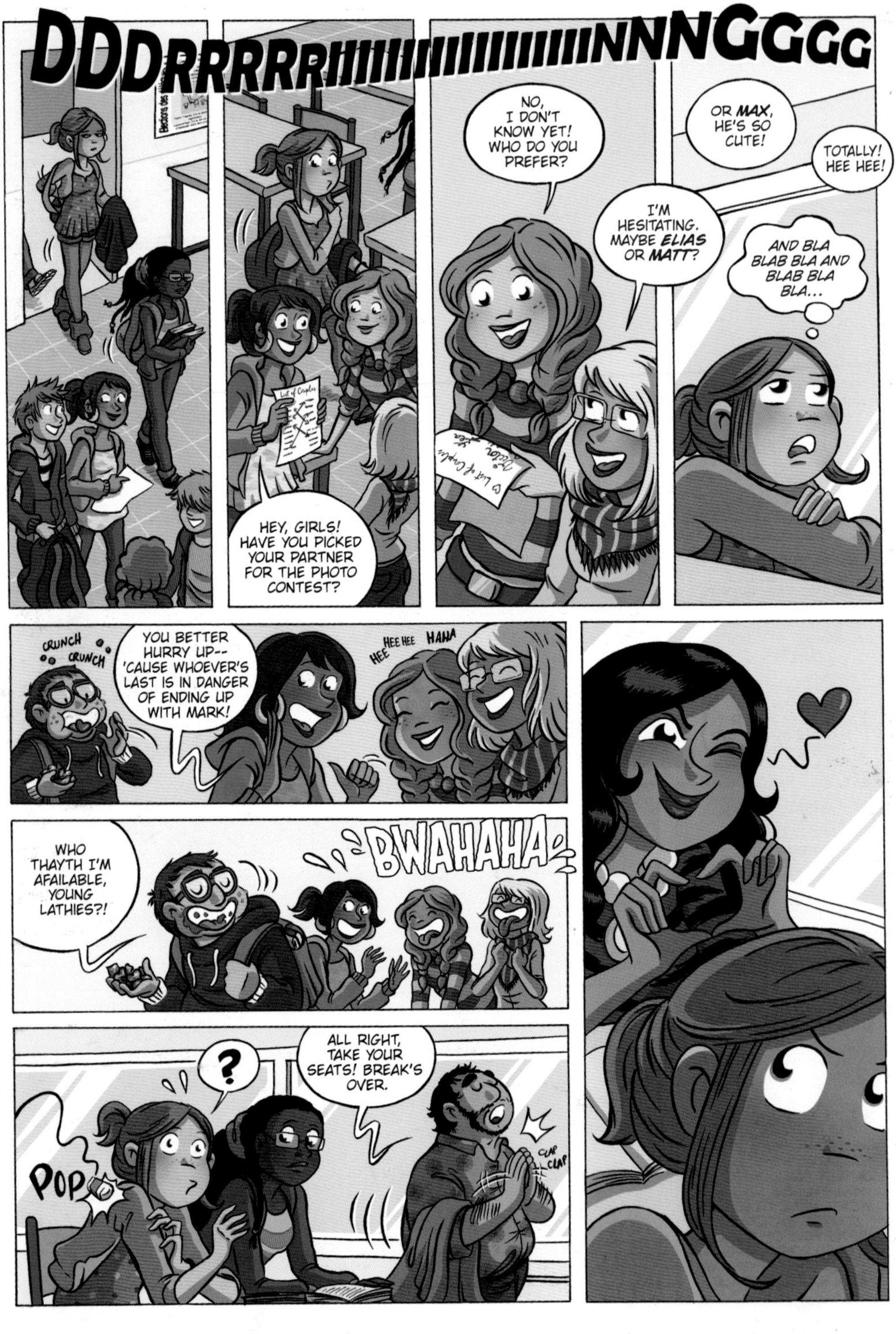
DDDRRRRRIIIIIIIIIIIIIIIIIIIIIIINNNGGGG
HEY, GIRLS! HAVE YOU PICKED YOUR PARTNER FOR THE PHOTO CONTEST?
List of Couples
NO, I DON'T KNOW YET! WHO DO YOU PREFER?
I'M HESITATING. MAYBE ELIAS OR MATT?
OR MAX, HE'S SO CUTE!
TOTALLY! HEE HEE!
AND BLA BLAB BLA AND BLAB BLA BLA...
CRUNCH CRUNCH
YOU BETTER HURRY UP-- 'CAUSE WHOEVER'S LAST IS IN DANGER OF ENDING UP WITH MARK!
HEE HEE HEE HAHA
WHO THAYTH I'M AFAILABLE, YOUNG LATHIES?!
BWAHAHA
?
ALL RIGHT, TAKE YOUR SEATS! BREAK'S OVER.
POP
CLAP CLAP

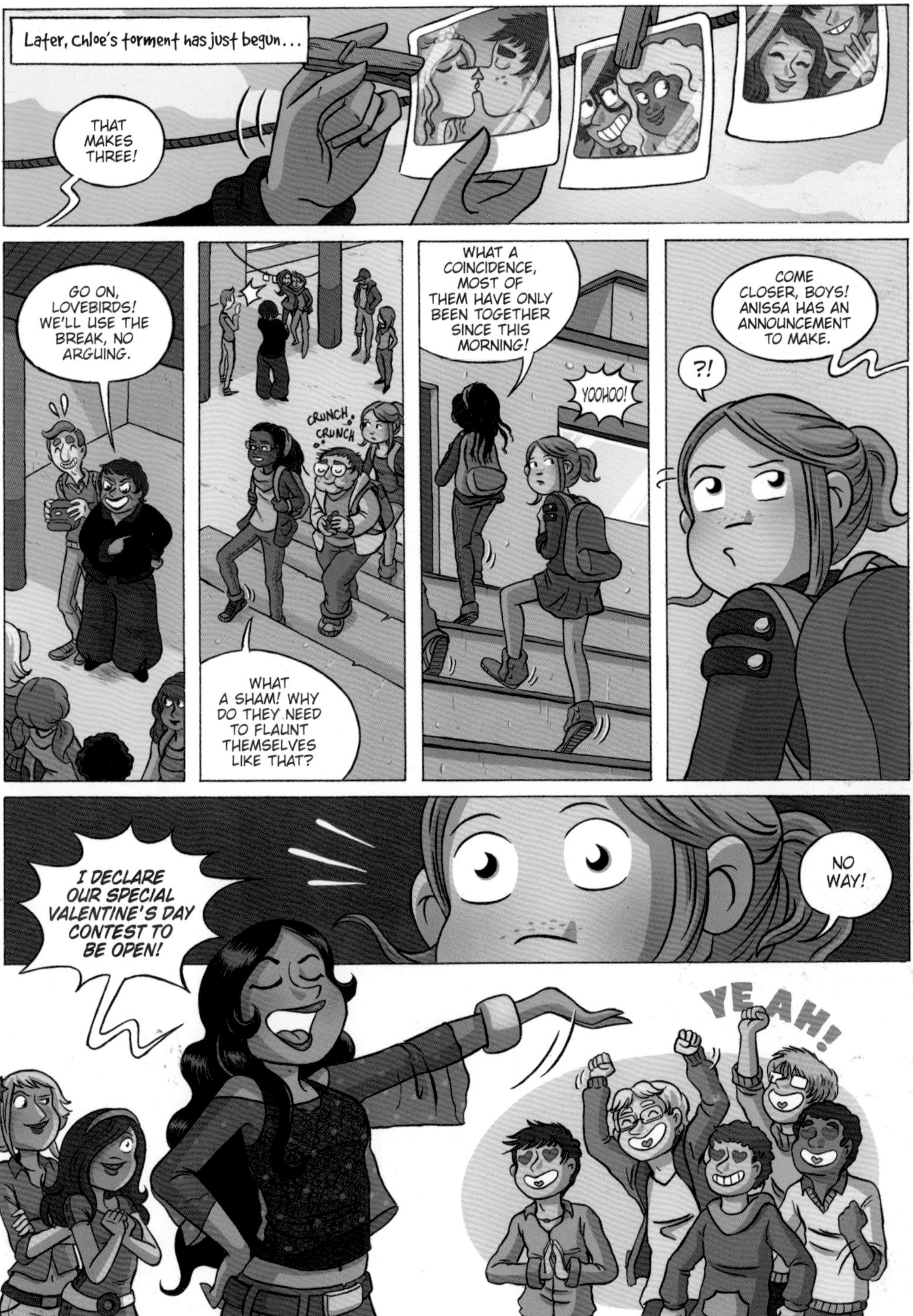
Later, chloe's torment has just begun...
THAT MAKES THREE!
GO ON, LOVEBIRDS! WE'LL USE THE BREAK, NO ARGUING.
CRUNCH CRUNCH
WHAT A SHAM! WHY DO THEY NEED TO FLAUNT THEMSELVES LIKE THAT?
WHAT A COINCIDENCE, MOST OF THEM HAVE ONLY BEEN TOGETHER SINCE THIS MORNING!
YOOHOO!
COME CLOSER, BOYS! ANISSA HAS AN ANNOUNCEMENT TO MAKE.
?!
NO WAY!
I DECLARE OUR SPECIAL VALENTINE'S DAY CONTEST TO BE OPEN!
YEAH!

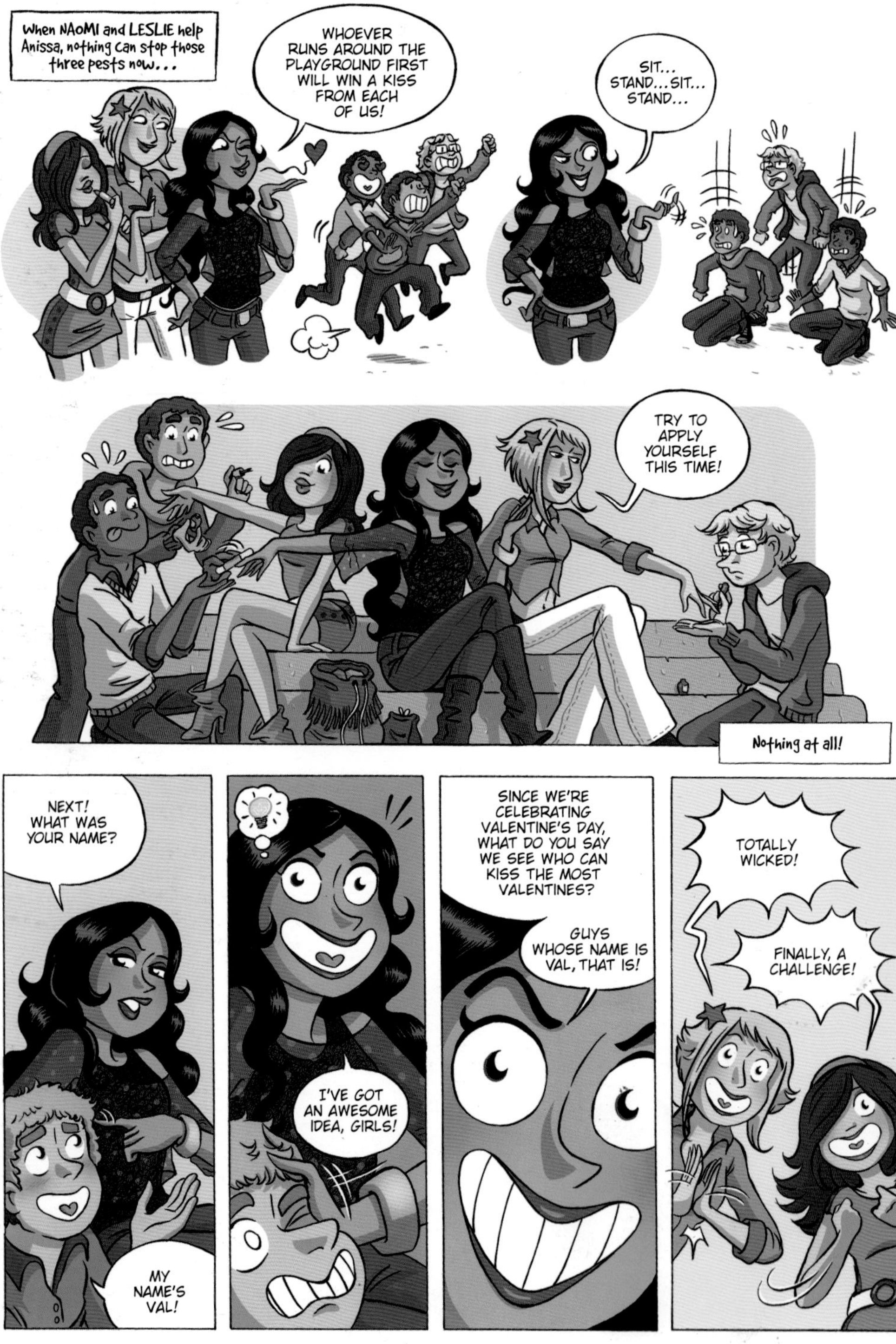
When NAOMI and LESLIE help Anissa, nothing can stop those three pests now...
WHOEVER RUNS AROUND THE PLAYGROUND FIRST WILL WIN A KISS FROM EACH OF US!
SIT... STAND...SIT... STAND...
TRY TO APPLY YOURSELF THIS TIME!
Nothing at all!
NEXT! WHAT WAS YOUR NAME?
MY NAME'S VAL!
I'VE GOT AN AWESOME IDEA, GIRLS!
SINCE WE'RE CELEBRATING VALENTINE'S DAY, WHAT DO YOU SAY WE SEE WHO CAN KISS THE MOST VALENTINES?
GUYS WHOSE NAME IS VAL, THAT IS!
TOTALLY WICKED!
FINALLY, A CHALLENGE!

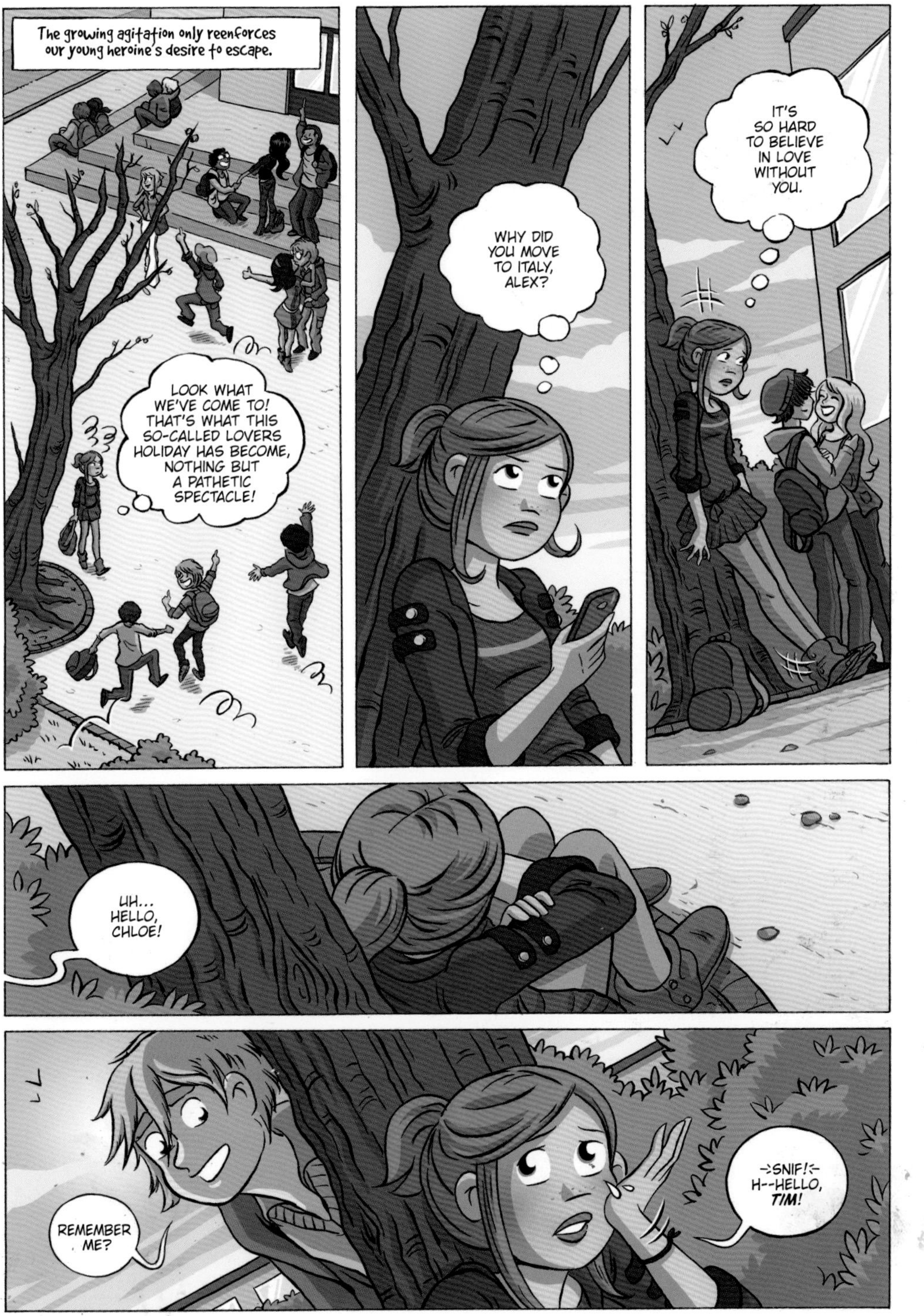
The growing agitation only reenforces our young heroine's desire to escape.
LOOK WHAT WE'VE COME TO! THAT'S WHAT THIS SO-CALLED LOVERS HOLIDAY HAS BECOME, NOTHING BUT A PATHETIC SPECTACLE!
WHY DID YOU MOVE TO ITALY, ALEX?
IT'S SO HARD TO BELIEVE IN LOVE WITHOUT YOU.
UH... HELLO, CHLOE!
REMEMBER ME?
-SNIF!- H--HELLO, TIM!

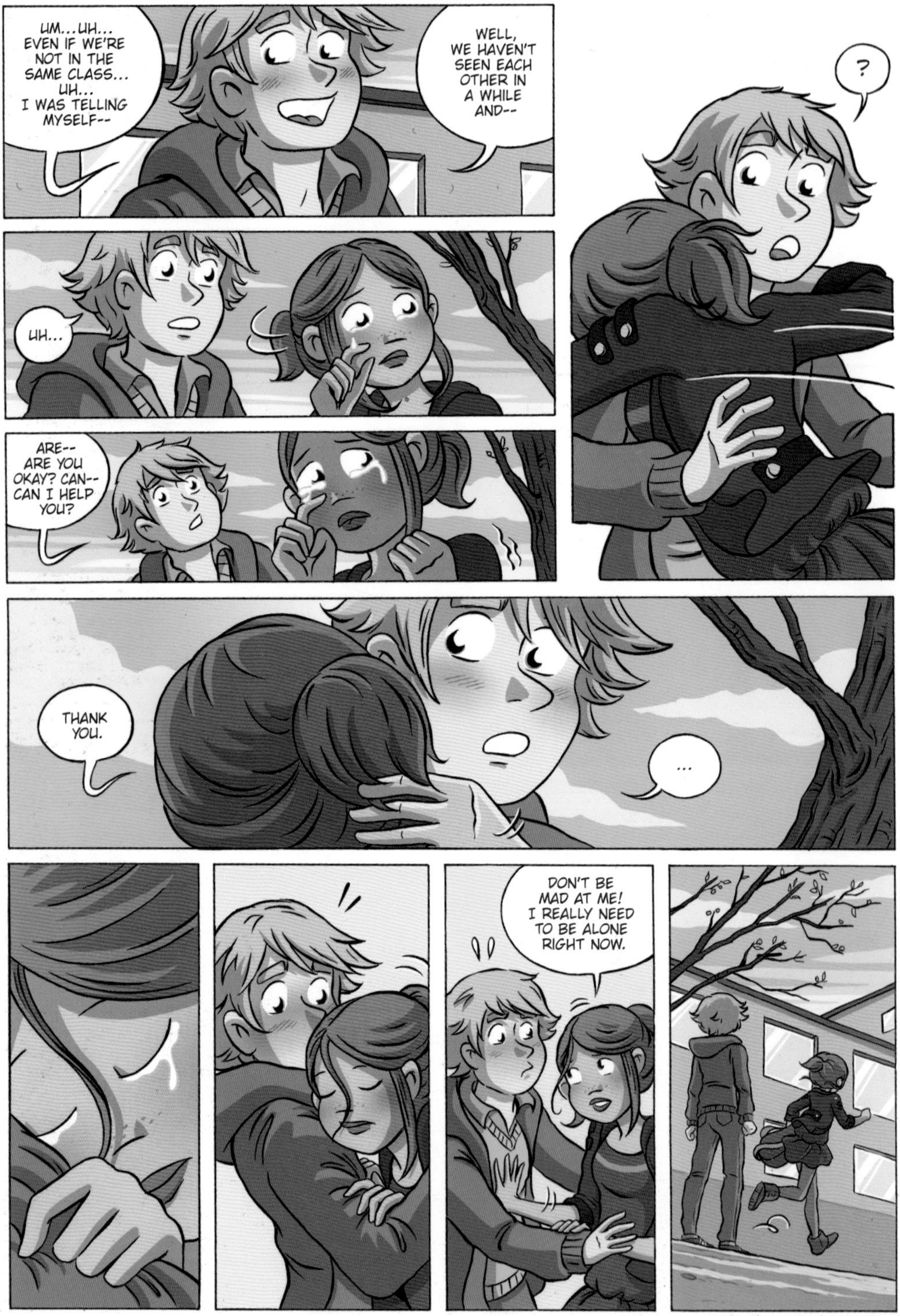
UM...UH... EVEN IF WE'RE NOT IN THE SAME CLASS... UH... I WAS TELLING MYSELF--
WELL, WE HAVEN'T SEEN EACH OTHER IN A WHILE AND--
?
UH...
ARE-- ARE YOU OKAY? CAN-- CAN I HELP YOU?
THANK YOU.
...
DON'T BE MAD AT ME! I REALLY NEED TO BE ALONE RIGHT NOW.

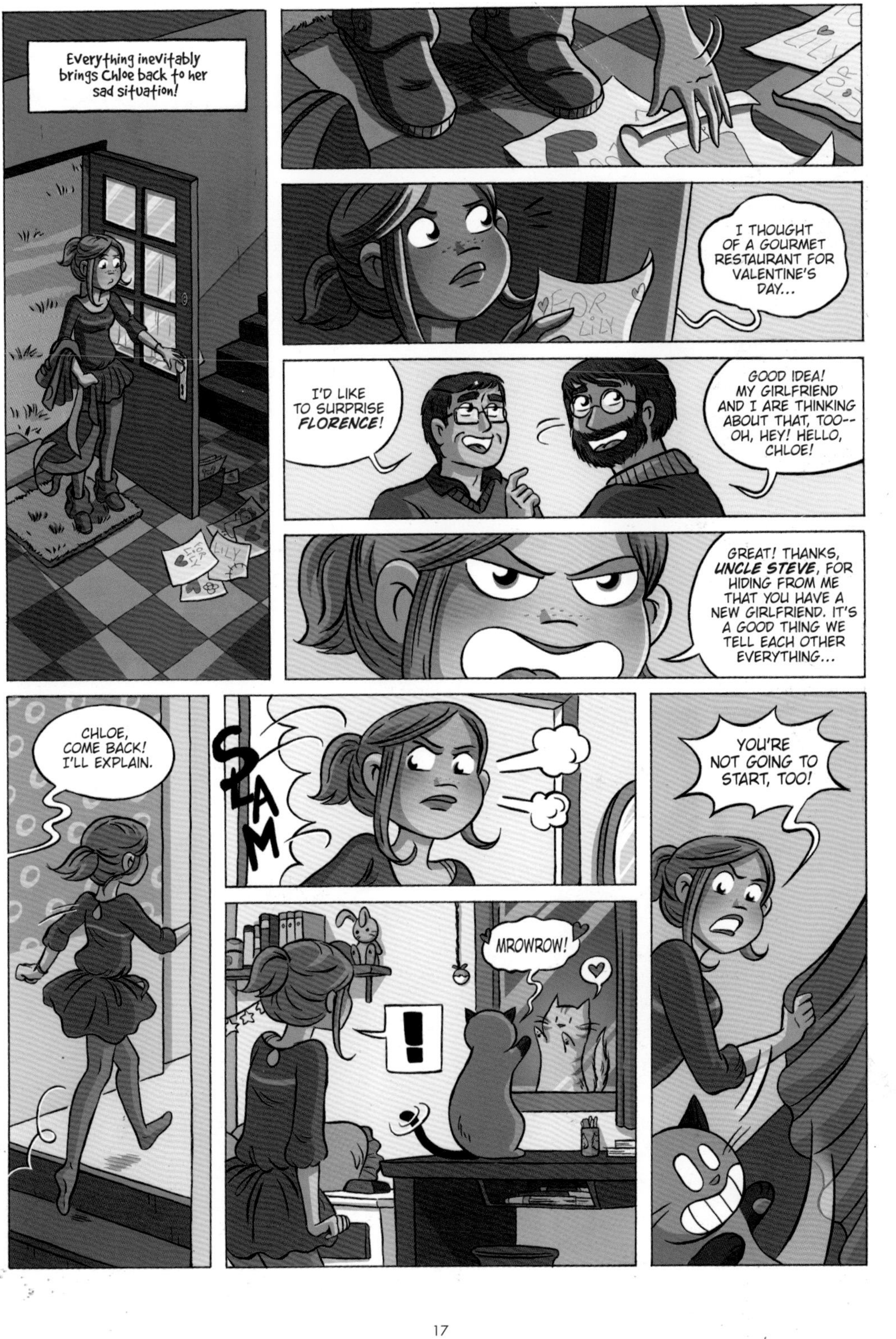
Everything inevitably brings Chloe back to her sad situation!
FOR LILY
I THOUGHT OF A GOURMET RESTAURANT FOR VALENTINE'S DAY...
I'D LIKE TO SURPRISE FLORENCE!
GOOD IDEA! MY GIRLFRIEND AND I ARE THINKING ABOUT THAT, TOO-- OH, HEY! HELLO, CHLOE!
GREAT! THANKS, UNCLE STEVE, FOR HIDING FROM ME THAT YOU HAVE A NEW GIRLFRIEND. IT'S A GOOD THING WE TELL EACH OTHER EVERYTHING...
CHLOE, COME BACK! I'LL EXPLAIN.
SLAM
MROWROW!
!
YOU'RE NOT GOING TO START, TOO!

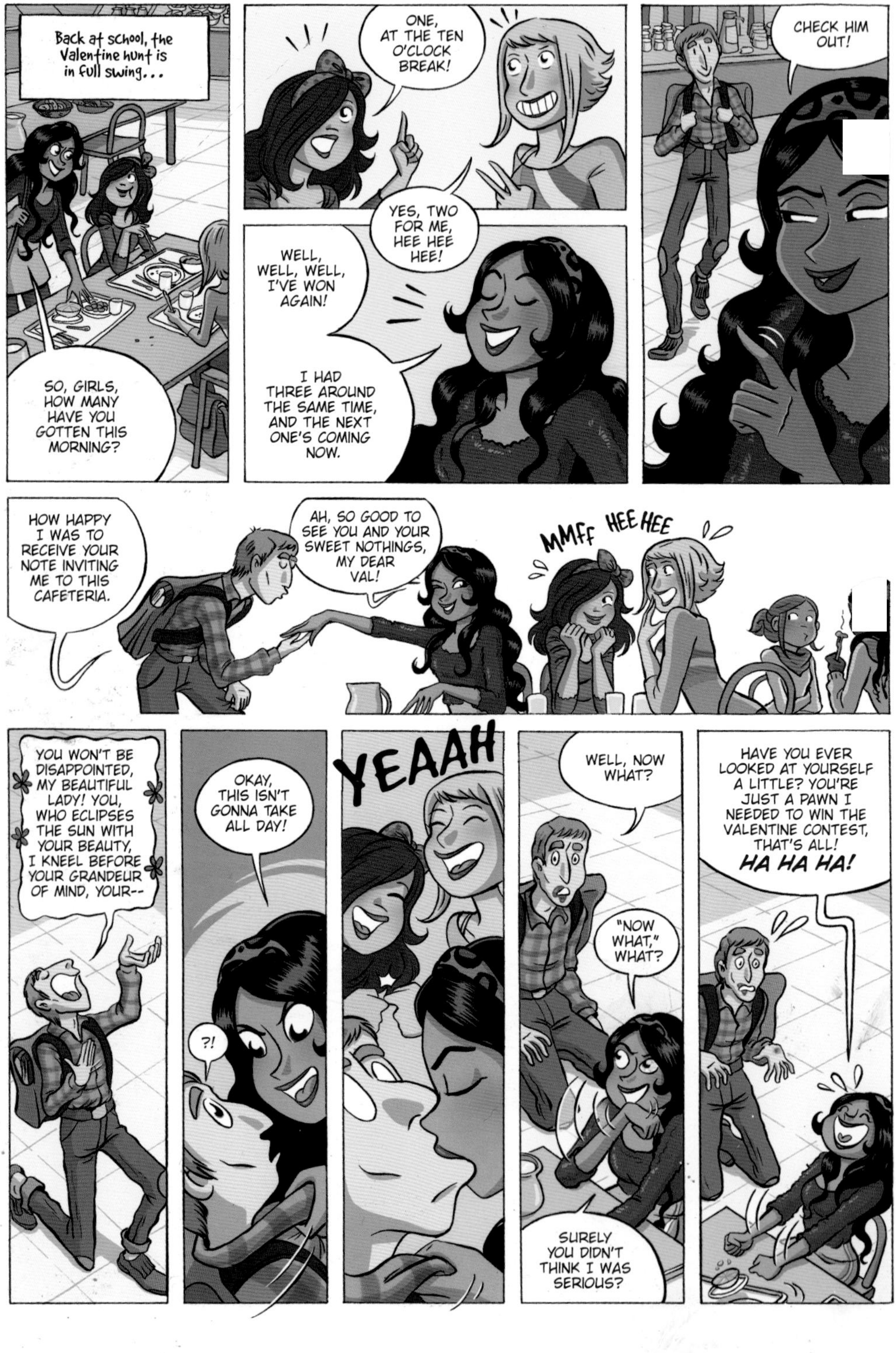

Back at school, the Valentine hunt is in full swing...
SO, GIRLS, HOW MANY HAVE YOU GOTTEN THIS MORNING?
ONE, AT THE TEN O'CLOCK BREAK!
YES, TWO FOR ME, HEE HEE HEE!
WELL, WELL, WELL, I'VE WON AGAIN!
I HAD THREE AROUND THE SAME TIME, AND THE NEXT ONE'S COMING NOW.
CHECK HIM OUT!
HOW HAPPY I WAS TO RECEIVE YOUR NOTE INVITING ME TO THIS CAFETERIA.
AH, SO GOOD TO SEE YOU AND YOUR SWEET NOTHINGS, MY DEAR VAL!
MMFF
HEE HEE
YOU WON'T BE DISAPPOINTED, MY BEAUTIFUL LADY! YOU, WHO ECLIPSES THE SUN WITH YOUR BEAUTY, I KNEEL BEFORE YOUR GRANDEUR OF MIND, YOUR--
OKAY, THIS ISN'T GONNA TAKE ALL DAY!
?!
YEAAH
WELL, NOW WHAT?
"NOW WHAT," WHAT?
SURELY YOU DIDN'T THINK I WAS SERIOUS?
HAVE YOU EVER LOOKED AT YOURSELF A LITTLE? YOU'RE JUST A PAWN I NEEDED TO WIN THE VALENTINE CONTEST, THAT'S ALL! HA HA HA!

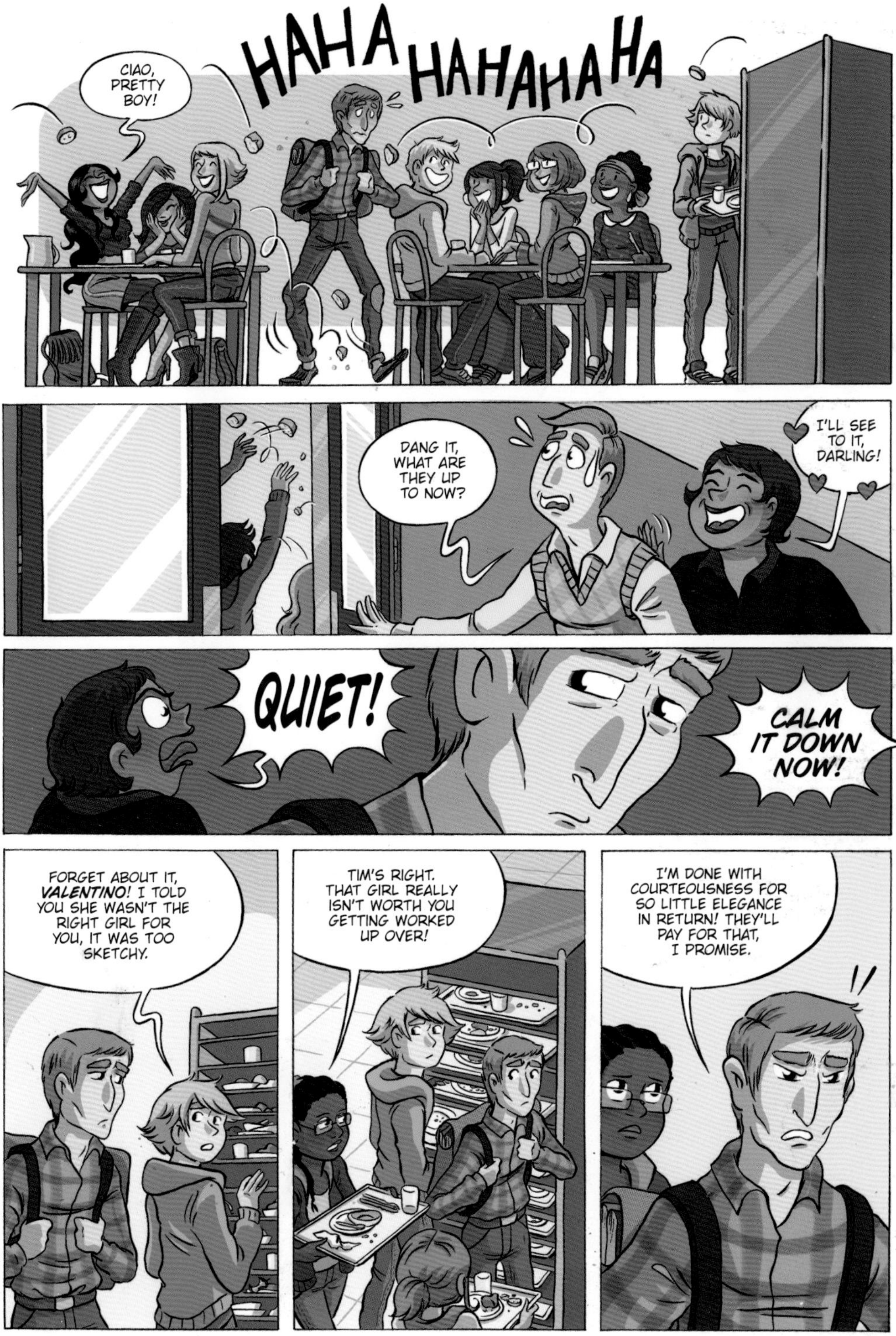
CIAO, PRETTY BOY!
HAHA HAHAHAHA
DANG IT, WHAT ARE THEY UP TO NOW?
I'LL SEE TO IT, DARLING!
QUIET!
CALM IT DOWN NOW!
FORGET ABOUT IT, VALENTINO! I TOLD YOU SHE WASN'T THE RIGHT GIRL FOR YOU, IT WAS TOO SKETCHY.
TIM'S RIGHT. THAT GIRL REALLY ISN'T WORTH YOU GETTING WORKED UP OVER!
I'M DONE WITH COURTEOUSNESS FOR SO LITTLE ELEGANCE IN RETURN! THEY'LL PAY FOR THAT, I PROMISE.
!!

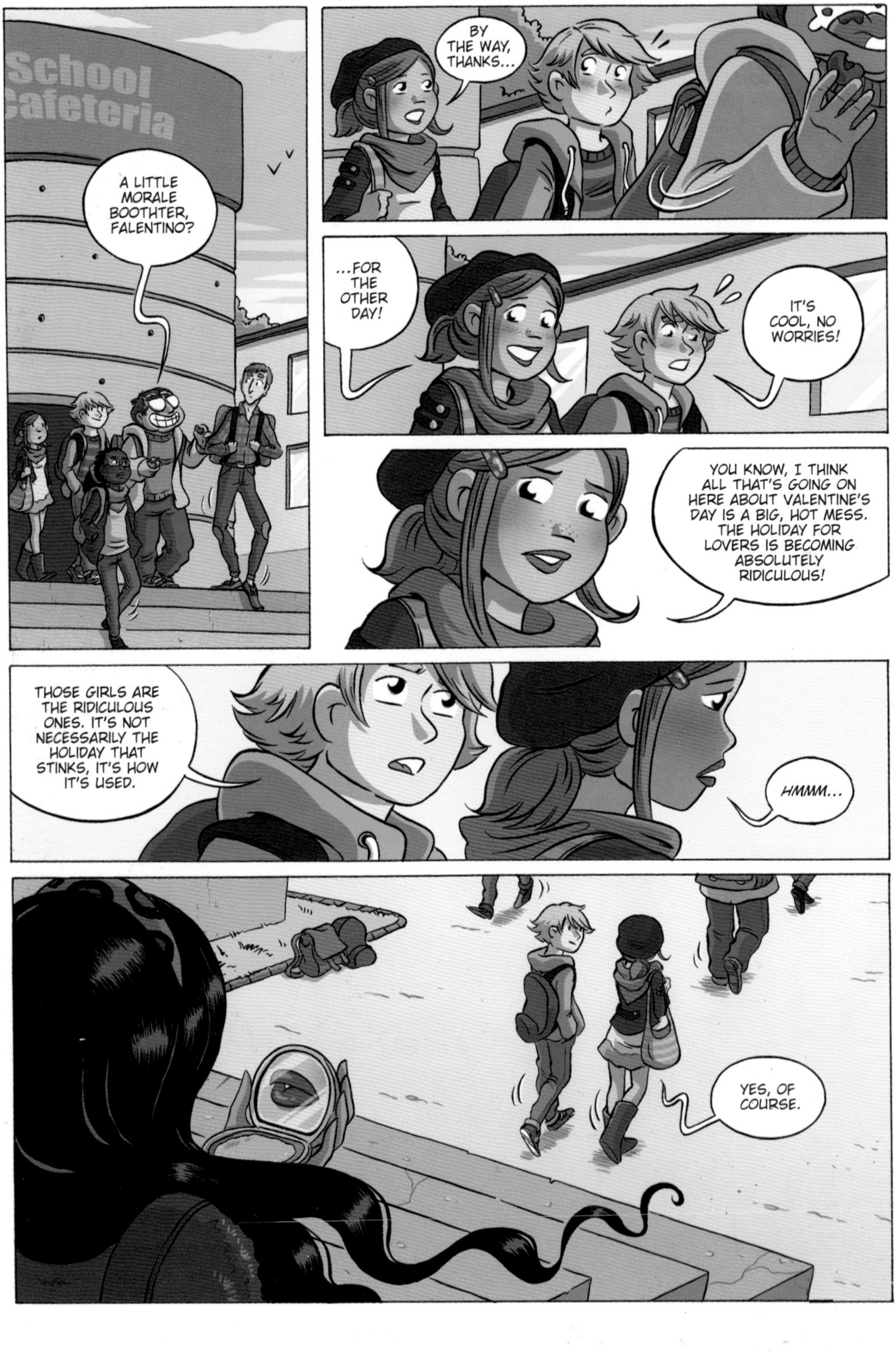
School Cafeteria
A LITTLE MORALE BOOTHTER, FALENTINO?
BY THE WAY, THANKS...
...FOR THE OTHER DAY!
IT'S COOL, NO WORRIES!
YOU KNOW, I THINK ALL THAT'S GOING ON HERE ABOUT VALENTINE'S DAY IS A BIG, HOT MESS. THE HOLIDAY FOR LOVERS IS BECOMING ABSOLUTELY RIDICULOUS!
THOSE GIRLS ARE THE RIDICULOUS ONES. IT'S NOT NECESSARILY THE HOLIDAY THAT STINKS, IT'S HOW IT'S USED.
HMMM...
YES, OF COURSE.

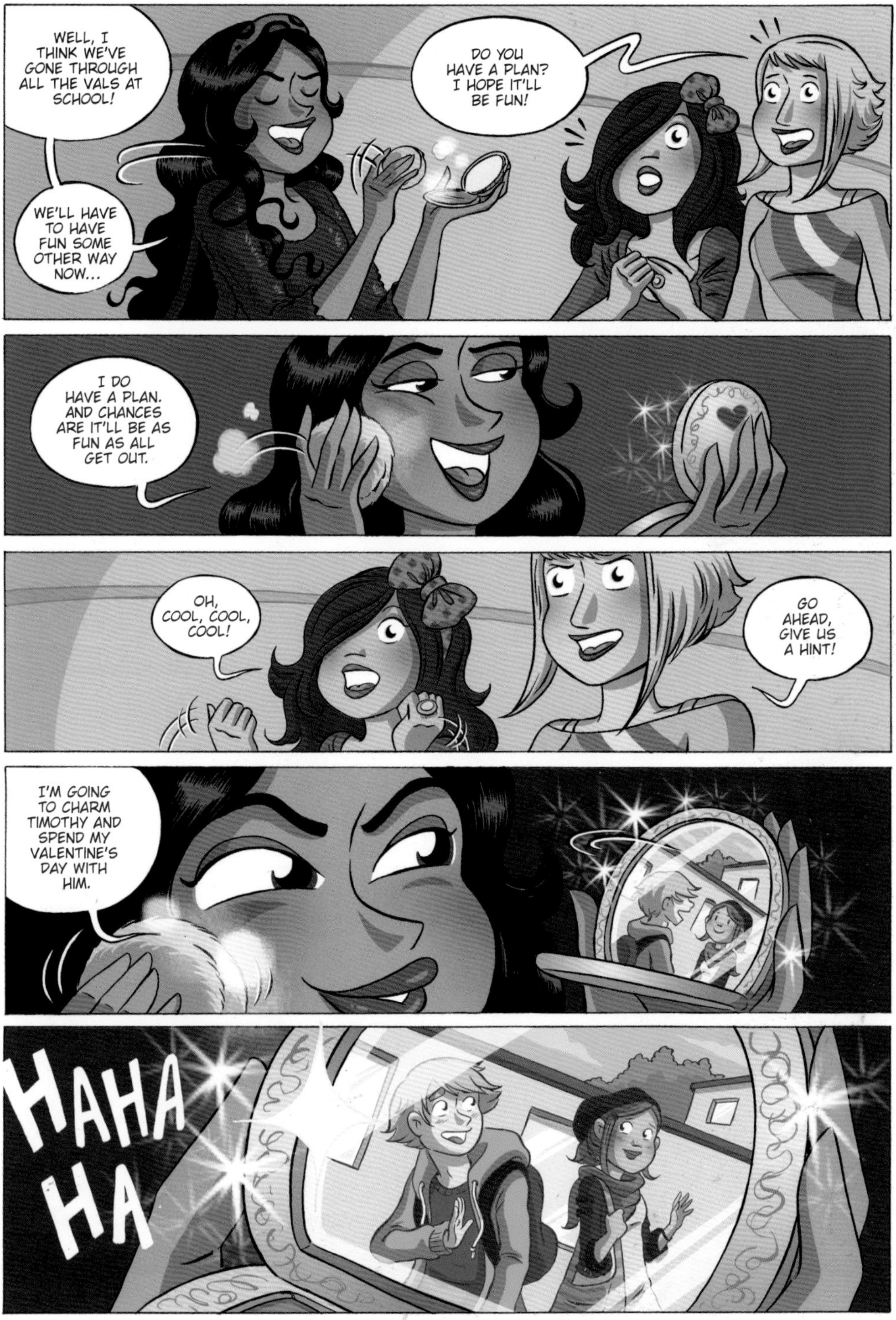
WELL, I THINK WE'VE GONE THROUGH ALL THE VALS AT SCHOOL!
WE'LL HAVE TO HAVE FUN SOME OTHER WAY NOW...
DO YOU HAVE A PLAN? I HOPE IT'LL BE FUN!
I DO HAVE A PLAN. AND CHANCES ARE IT'LL BE AS FUN AS ALL GET OUT.
OH, COOL, COOL, COOL!
GO AHEAD, GIVE US A HINT!
I'M GOING TO CHARM TIMOTHY AND SPEND MY VALENTINE'S DAY WITH HIM.
HAHA HA

Cupid News

Current Events

Creative businesses compete to celebrate Valentine's Day

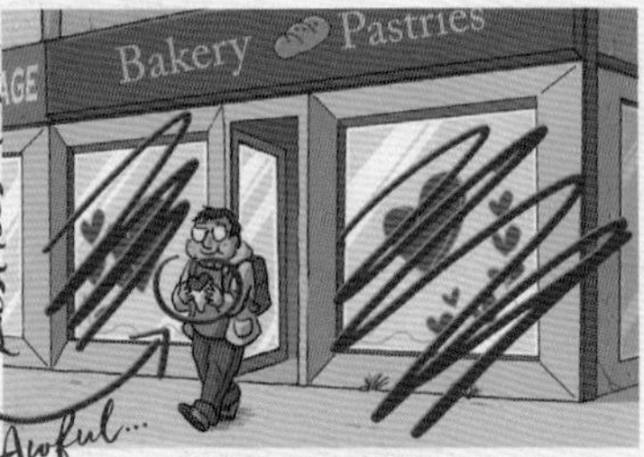

Bakery Pastries
So they're making pastries now?!
Awful...

Heart-shaped cakes are popular this year. PAGE 2

News Items

The Valentine Phenomenon

How horrible! And people say Valentine's Day ought to be a real holiday...

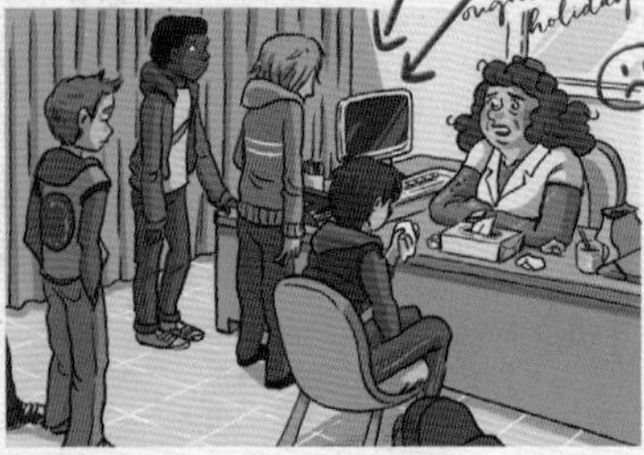

The nurse's office has recently been strangely overwhelmed with heartbroken Valentines PAGE 10

Weather Report from the Heart

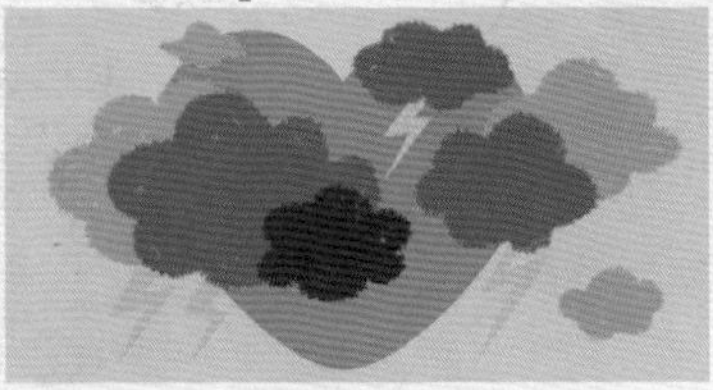

Miserable weather.
Sadness and non-stop thunderclaps.

Social Life

The young are full of ideas.

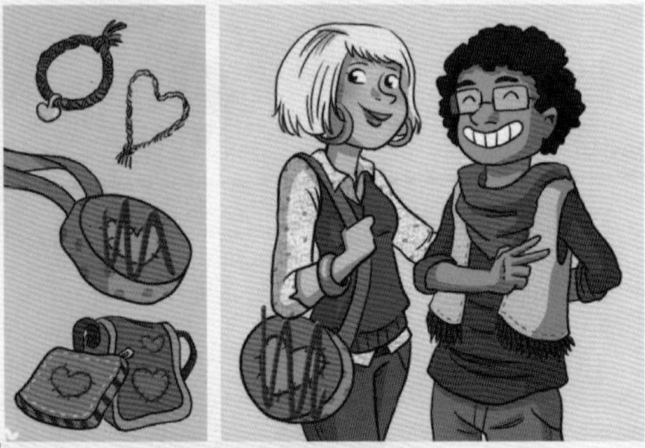

Creative seventh-graders Lucy Anne and ~~Alex~~ introduce their gift ideas fo~~r loved one~~s. PAGE 6

ESPECIALLY not that name, please!

Education

A love photo contest

More like a DISASTER contest!

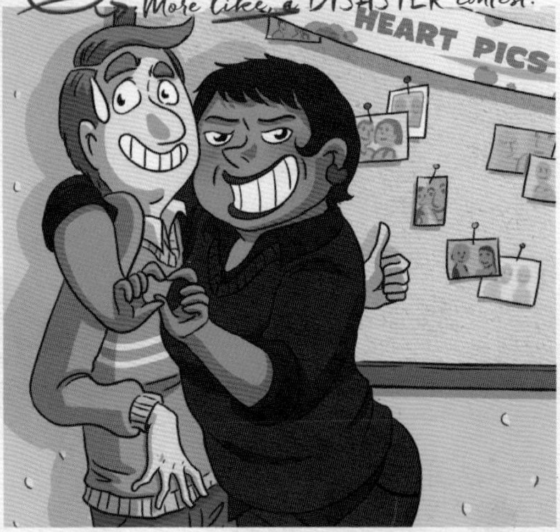

HEART PICS

The kind teacher-aides at Brassens J.H. suggest an original project. PAGE 14

Don't litter.

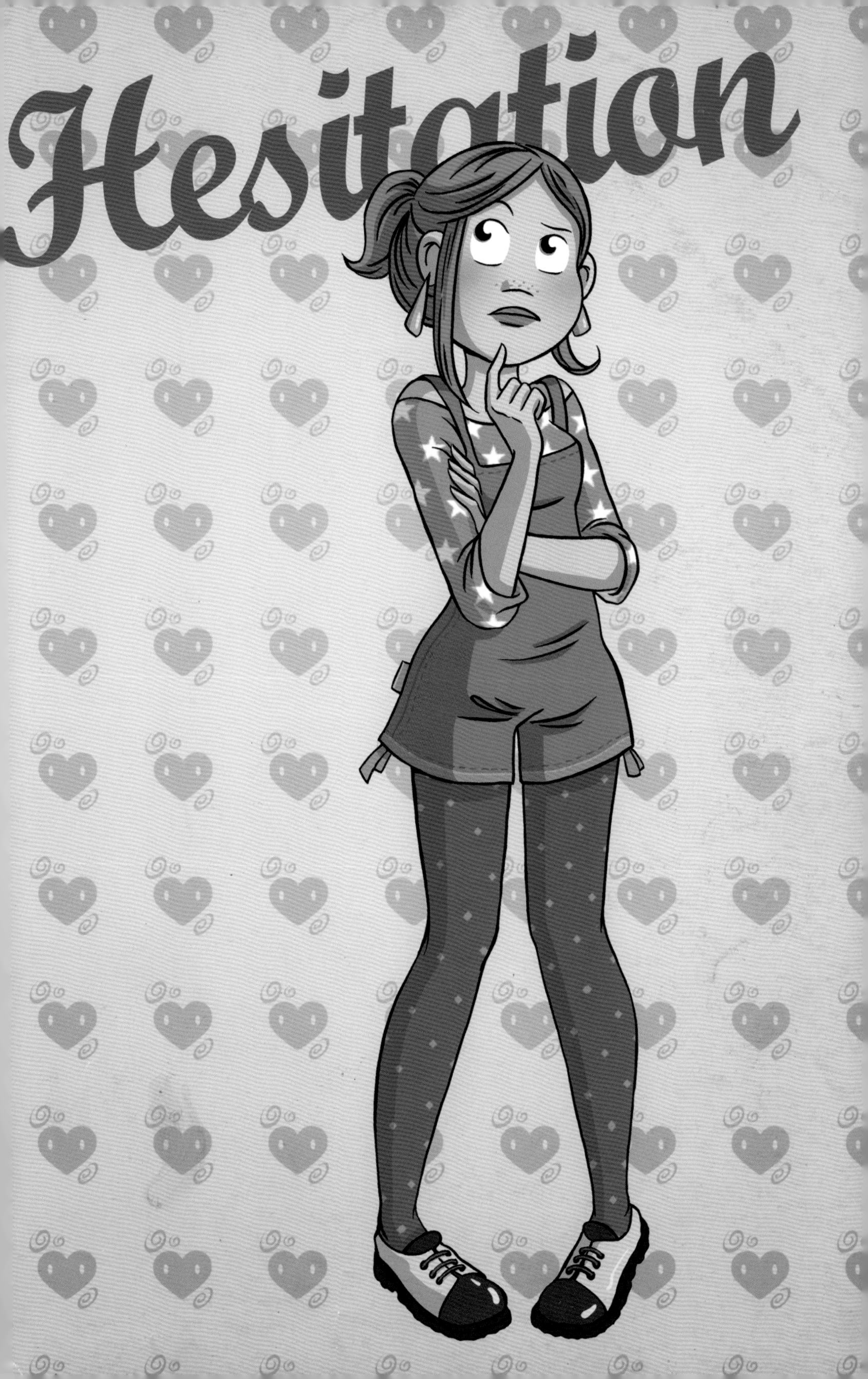
Hesitation

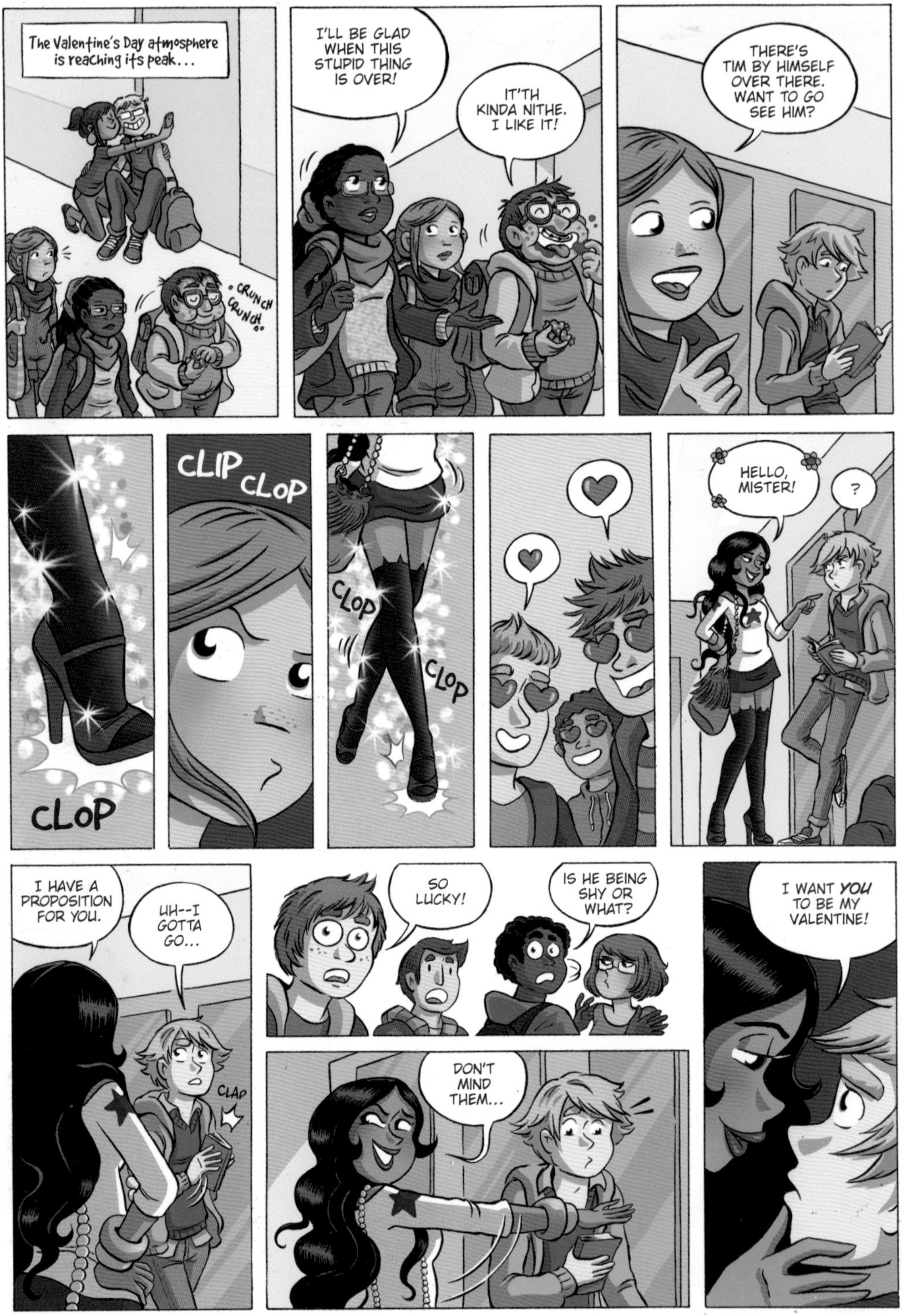
The Valentine's Day atmosphere is reaching its peak...
CRUNCH CRUNCH
I'LL BE GLAD WHEN THIS STUPID THING IS OVER!
IT'TH KINDA NITHE. I LIKE IT!
THERE'S TIM BY HIMSELF OVER THERE. WANT TO GO SEE HIM?
CLOP
CLIP CLOP
CLOP
CLOP
HELLO, MISTER!
?
I HAVE A PROPOSITION FOR YOU.
UH--I GOTTA GO...
CLAP
SO LUCKY!
IS HE BEING SHY OR WHAT?
DON'T MIND THEM...
I WANT YOU TO BE MY VALENTINE!

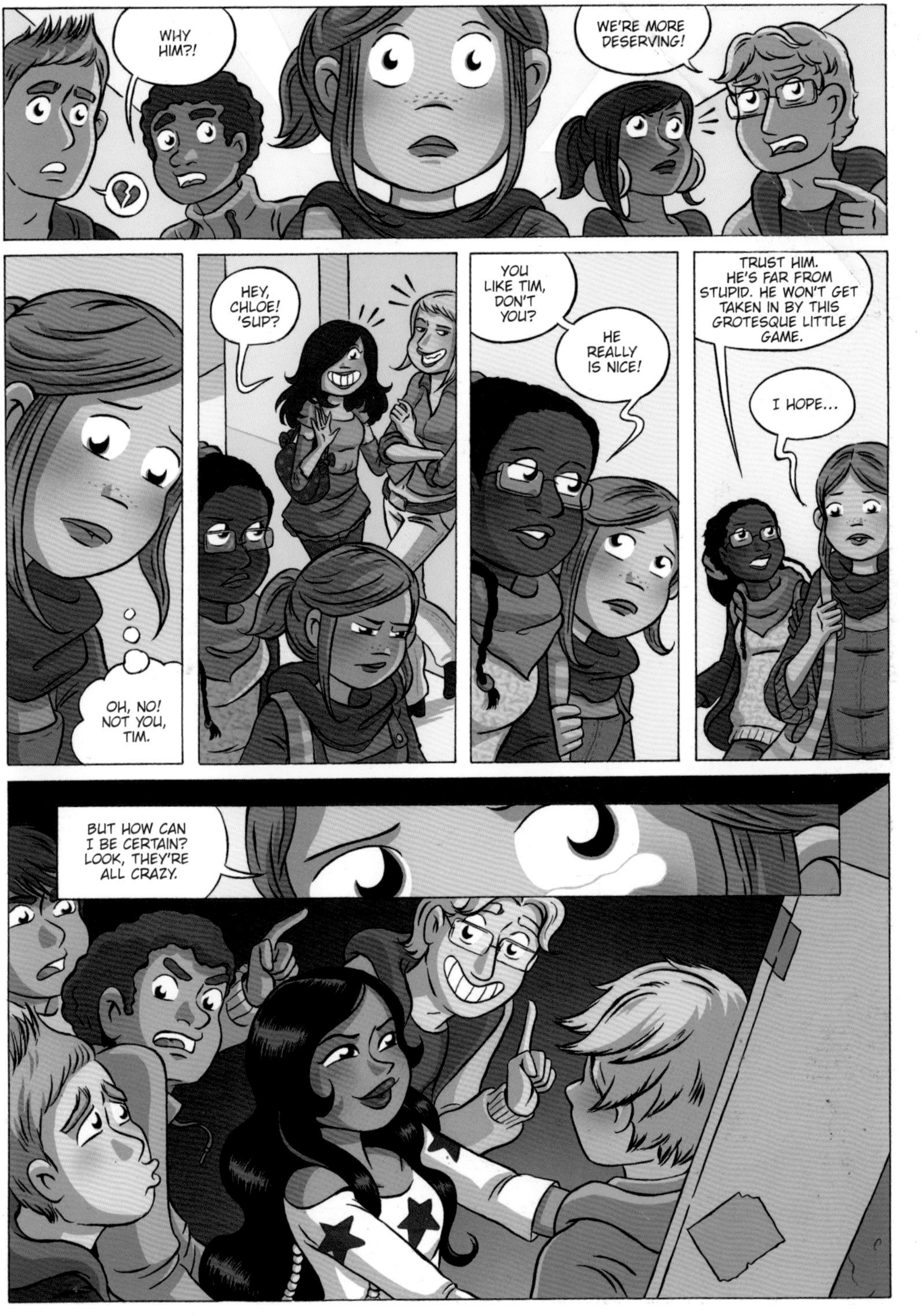
WHY HIM?!
WE'RE MORE DESERVING!
OH, NO! NOT YOU, TIM.
HEY, CHLOE! 'SUP?
YOU LIKE TIM, DON'T YOU?
HE REALLY IS NICE!
TRUST HIM. HE'S FAR FROM STUPID. HE WON'T GET TAKEN IN BY THIS GROTESQUE LITTLE GAME.
I HOPE...
BUT HOW CAN I BE CERTAIN? LOOK, THEY'RE ALL CRAZY.

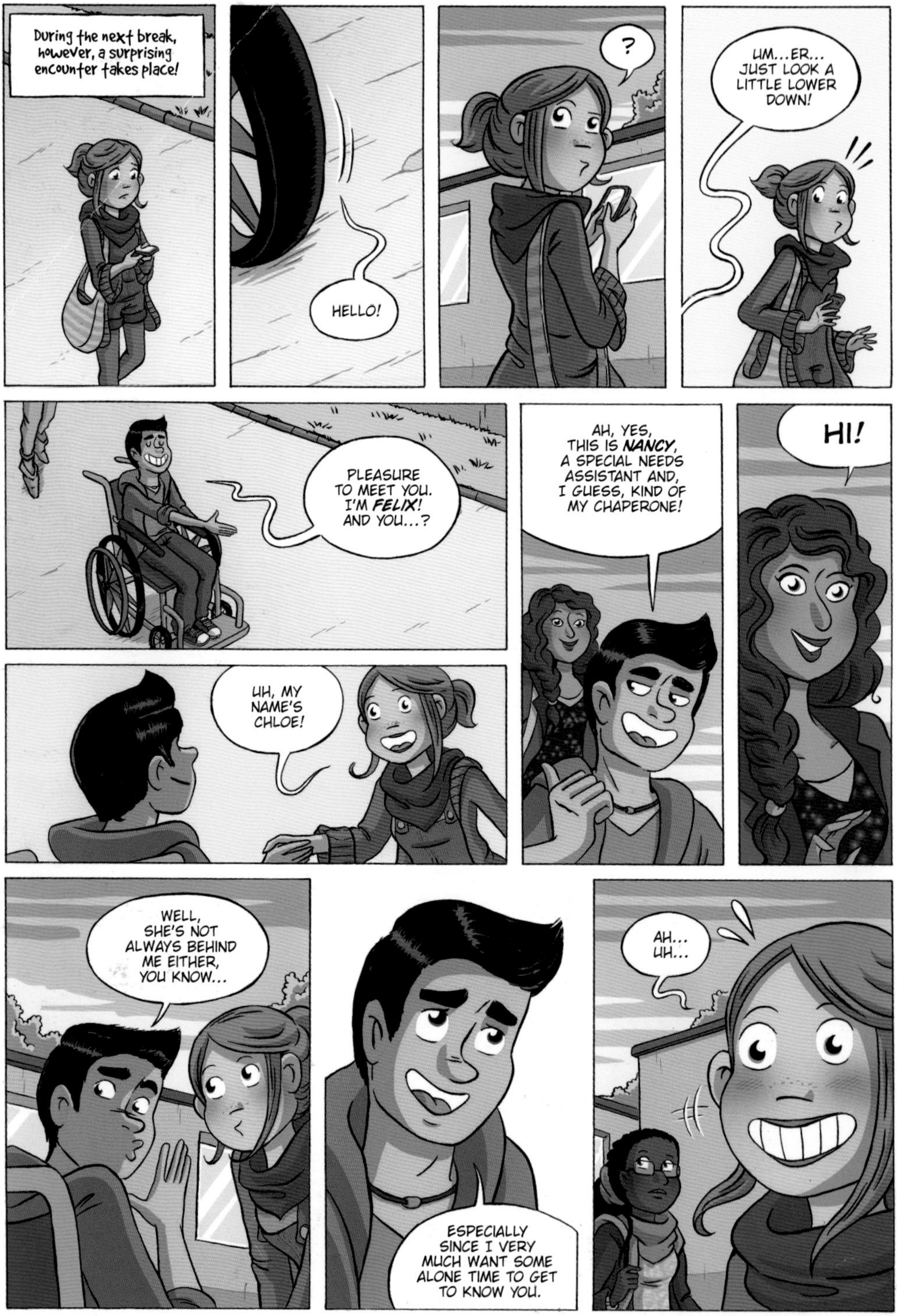
During the next break, however, a surprising encounter takes place!
HELLO!
?
UM...ER... JUST LOOK A LITTLE LOWER DOWN!
PLEASURE TO MEET YOU. I'M FELIX! AND YOU...?
UH, MY NAME'S CHLOE!
AH, YES, THIS IS NANCY, A SPECIAL NEEDS ASSISTANT AND, I GUESS, KIND OF MY CHAPERONE!
HI!
WELL, SHE'S NOT ALWAYS BEHIND ME EITHER, YOU KNOW...
ESPECIALLY SINCE I VERY MUCH WANT SOME ALONE TIME TO GET TO KNOW YOU.
AH... UH...

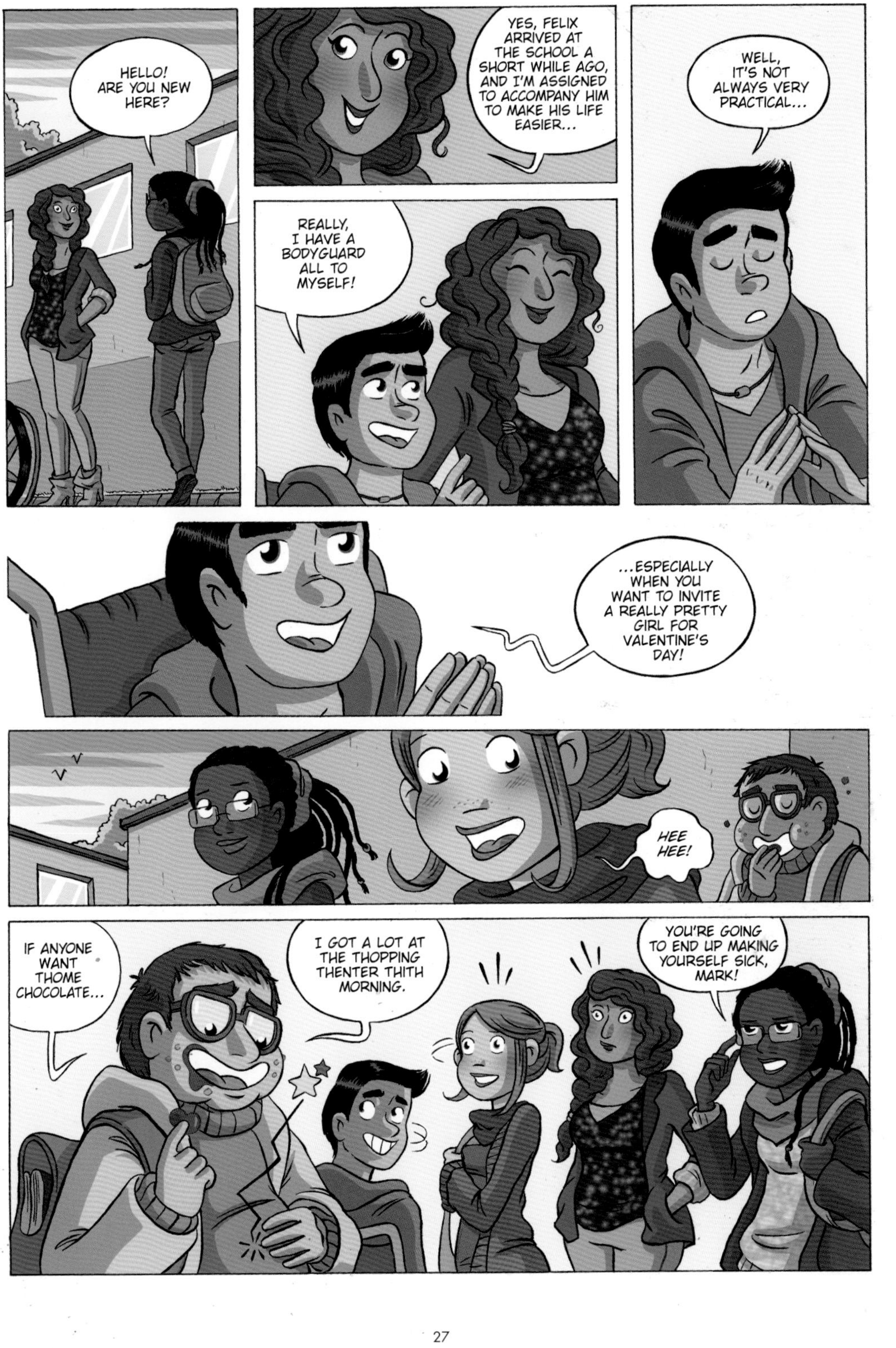
HELLO! ARE YOU NEW HERE?
YES, FELIX ARRIVED AT THE SCHOOL A SHORT WHILE AGO, AND I'M ASSIGNED TO ACCOMPANY HIM TO MAKE HIS LIFE EASIER...
REALLY, I HAVE A BODYGUARD ALL TO MYSELF!
WELL, IT'S NOT ALWAYS VERY PRACTICAL...
...ESPECIALLY WHEN YOU WANT TO INVITE A REALLY PRETTY GIRL FOR VALENTINE'S DAY!
HEE HEE!
IF ANYONE WANT THOME CHOCOLATE...
I GOT A LOT AT THE THOPPING THENTER THITH MORNING.
YOU'RE GOING TO END UP MAKING YOURSELF SICK, MARK!

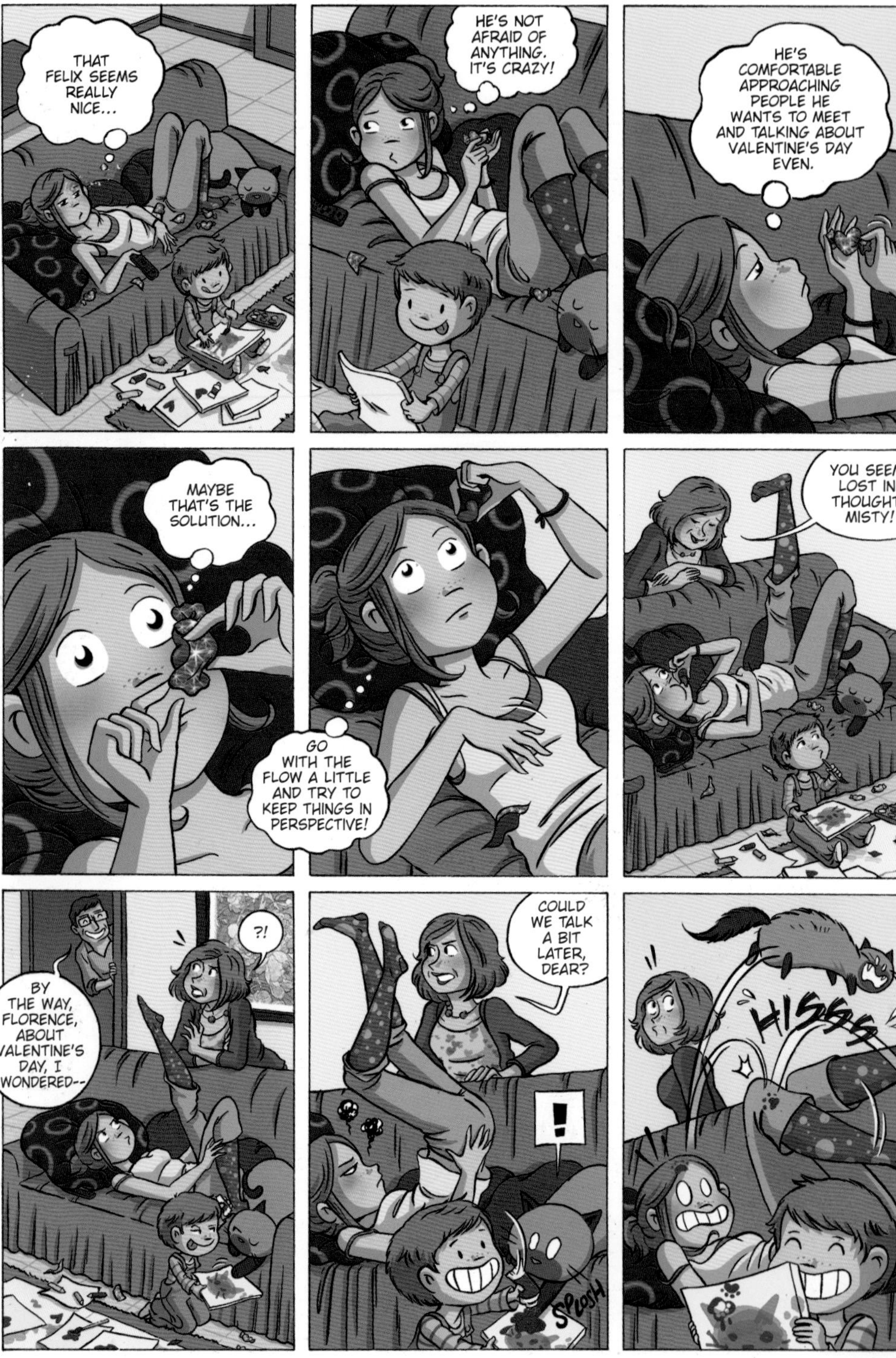
THAT FELIX SEEMS REALLY NICE...
HE'S NOT AFRAID OF ANYTHING. IT'S CRAZY!
HE'S COMFORTABLE APPROACHING PEOPLE HE WANTS TO MEET AND TALKING ABOUT VALENTINE'S DAY EVEN.
MAYBE THAT'S THE SOLUTION...
GO WITH THE FLOW A LITTLE AND TRY TO KEEP THINGS IN PERSPECTIVE!
YOU SEEM LOST IN THOUGHT, MISTY!
?!
BY THE WAY, FLORENCE, ABOUT VALENTINE'S DAY, I WONDERED--
COULD WE TALK A BIT LATER, DEAR?
!
SPLOSH
HISSSS

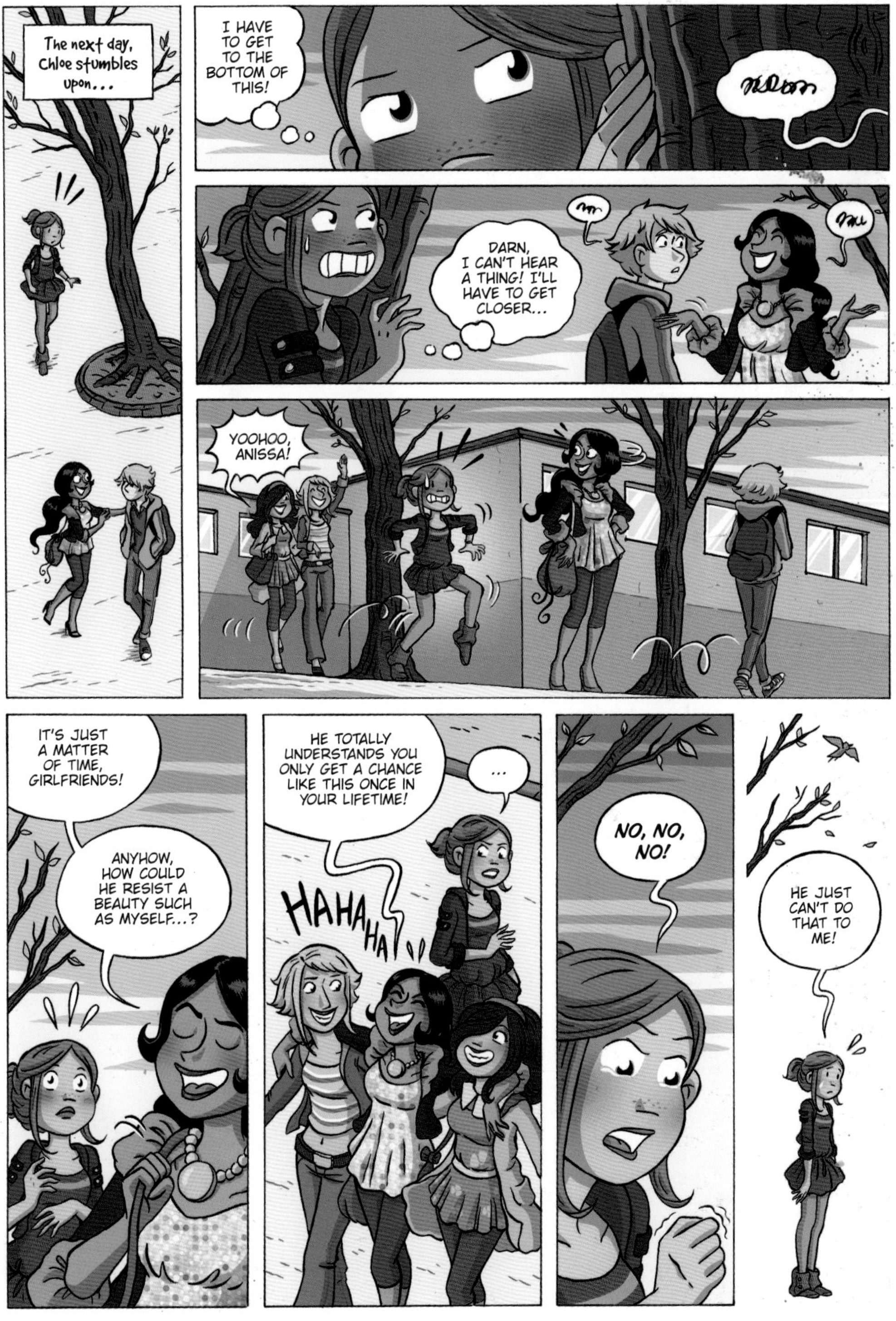
The next day, Chloe stumbles upon...
I HAVE TO GET TO THE BOTTOM OF THIS!
DARN, I CAN'T HEAR A THING! I'LL HAVE TO GET CLOSER...
YOOHOO, ANISSA!
IT'S JUST A MATTER OF TIME, GIRLFRIENDS!
ANYHOW, HOW COULD HE RESIST A BEAUTY SUCH AS MYSELF...?
HE TOTALLY UNDERSTANDS YOU ONLY GET A CHANCE LIKE THIS ONCE IN YOUR LIFETIME!
...
HAHAHA
NO, NO, NO!
HE JUST CAN'T DO THAT TO ME!

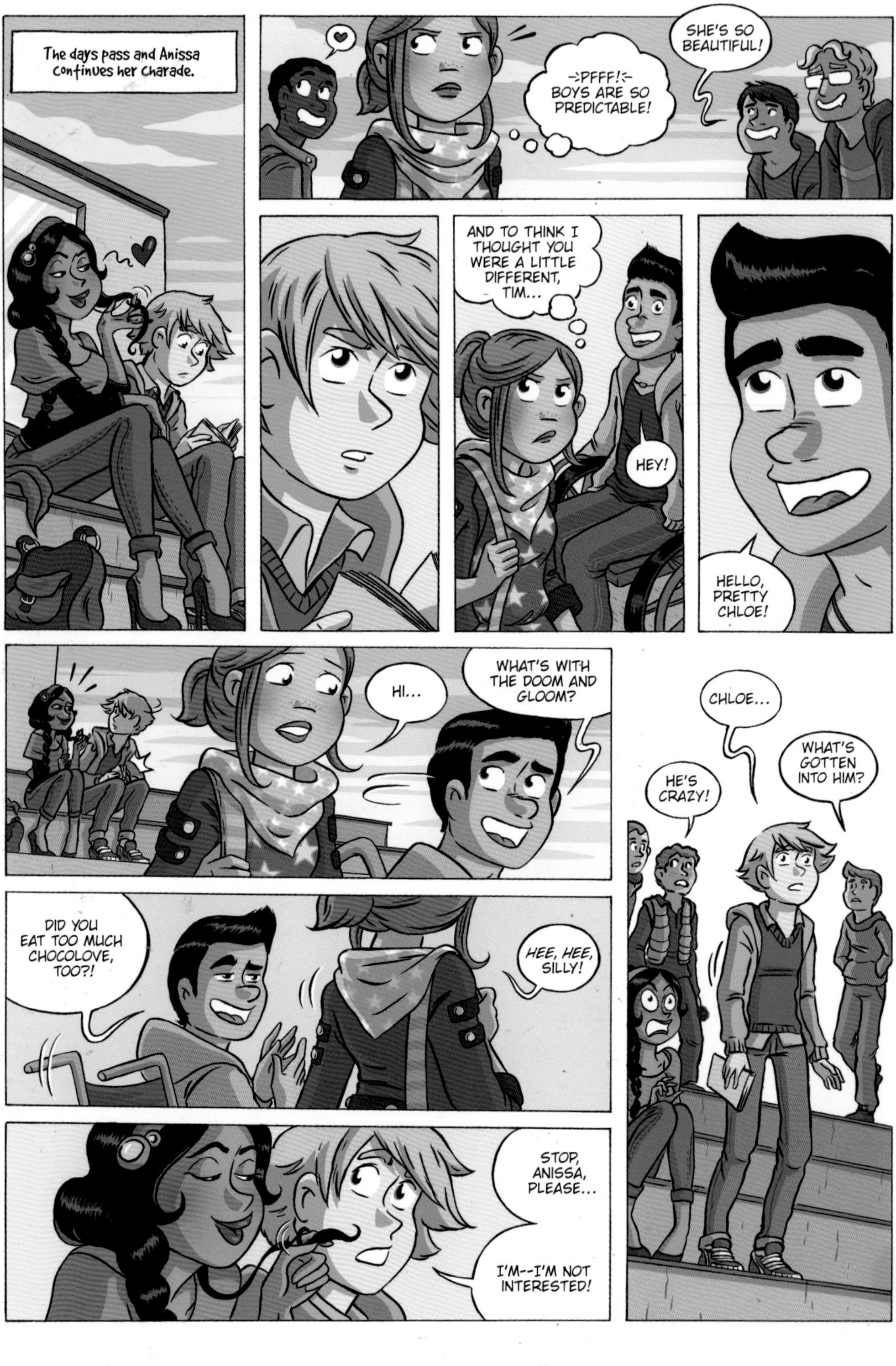
The days pass and Anissa continues her charade.
PFFF! BOYS ARE SO PREDICTABLE!
SHE'S SO BEAUTIFUL!
AND TO THINK I THOUGHT YOU WERE A LITTLE DIFFERENT, TIM...
HEY!
HELLO, PRETTY CHLOE!
HI...
WHAT'S WITH THE DOOM AND GLOOM?
DID YOU EAT TOO MUCH CHOCOLOVE, TOO?!
HEE, HEE, SILLY!
STOP, ANISSA, PLEASE...
I'M--I'M NOT INTERESTED!
CHLOE...
HE'S CRAZY!
WHAT'S GOTTEN INTO HIM?

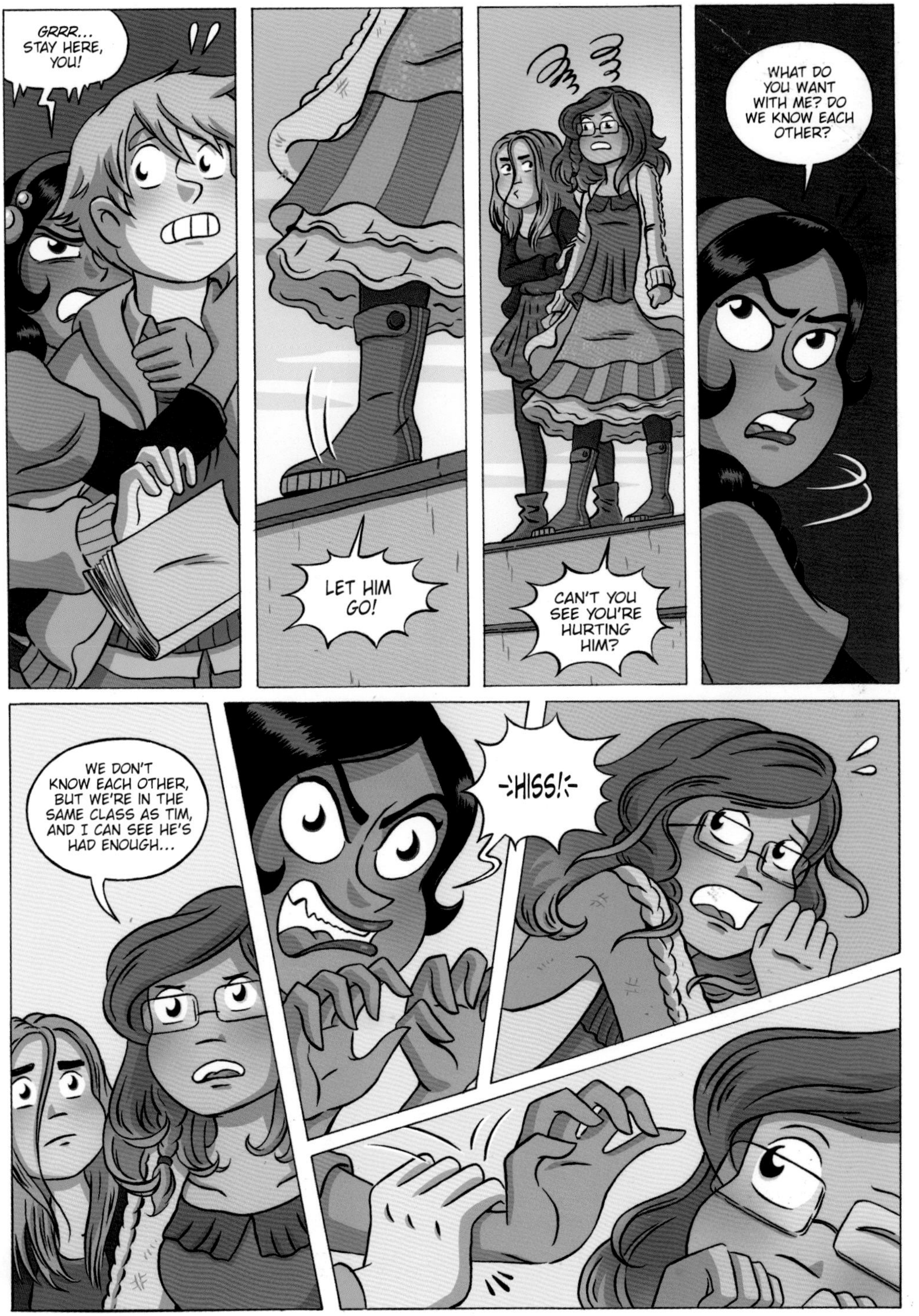
GRRR... STAY HERE, YOU!
LET HIM GO!
CAN'T YOU SEE YOU'RE HURTING HIM?
WHAT DO YOU WANT WITH ME? DO WE KNOW EACH OTHER?
WE DON'T KNOW EACH OTHER, BUT WE'RE IN THE SAME CLASS AS TIM, AND I CAN SEE HE'S HAD ENOUGH...
HISS!

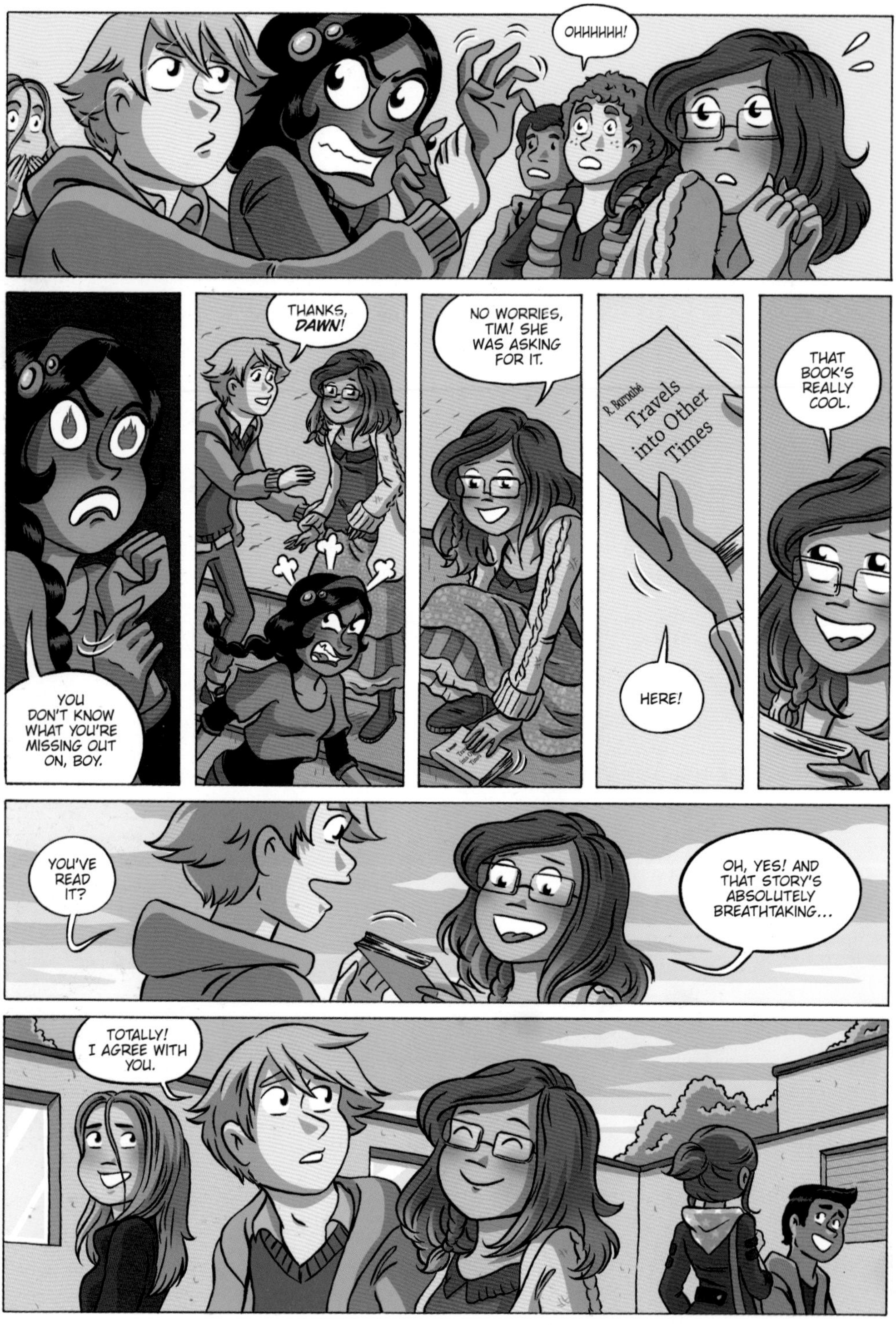
OHHHHHH!
YOU DON'T KNOW WHAT YOU'RE MISSING OUT ON, BOY.
THANKS, DAWN!
NO WORRIES, TIM! SHE WAS ASKING FOR IT.
R. Barnabé Travels into Other Times
HERE!
THAT BOOK'S REALLY COOL.
YOU'VE READ IT?
OH, YES! AND THAT STORY'S ABSOLUTELY BREATHTAKING...
TOTALLY! I AGREE WITH YOU.

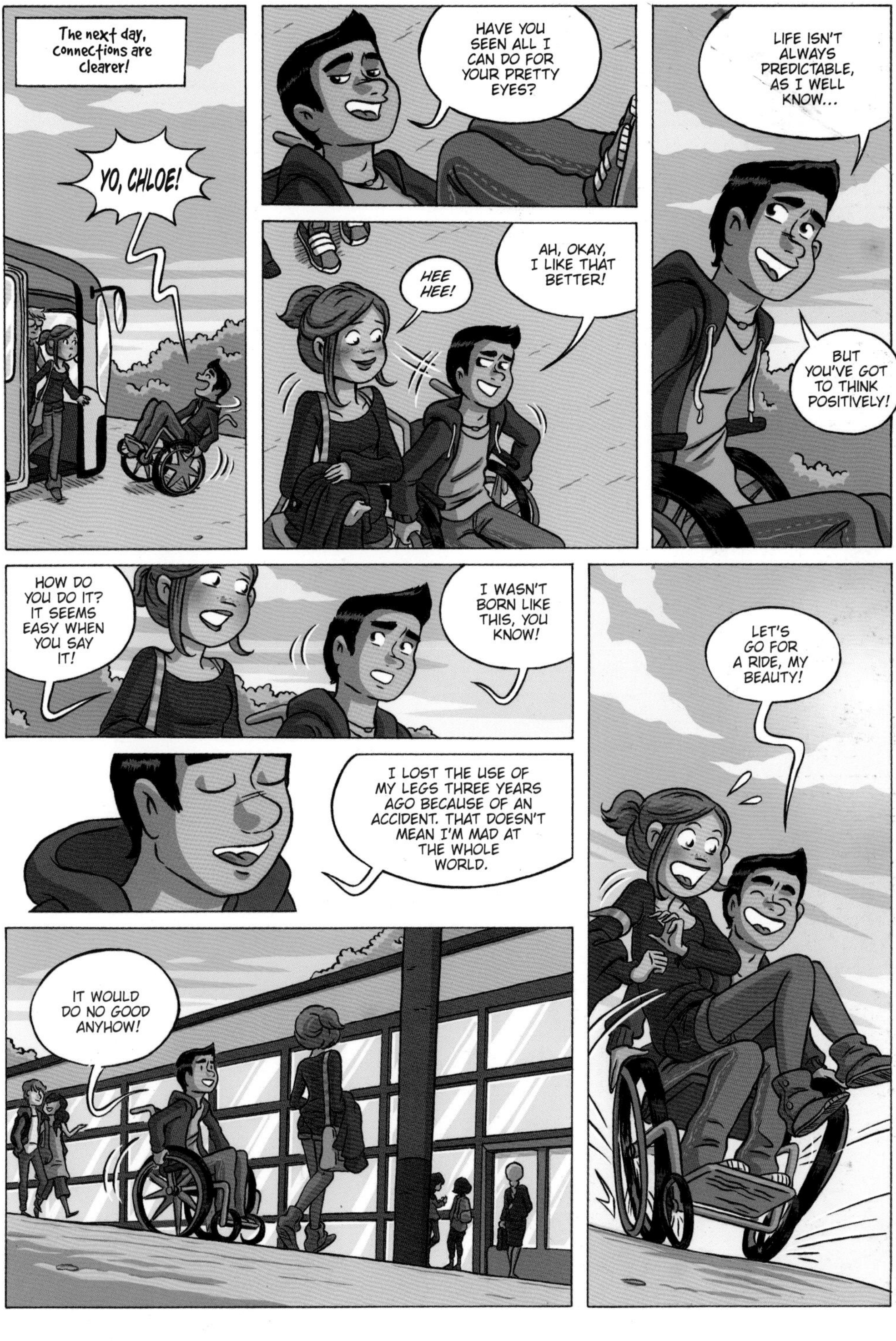
The next day, connections are clearer!
YO, CHLOE!
HAVE YOU SEEN ALL I CAN DO FOR YOUR PRETTY EYES?
HEE HEE!
AH, OKAY, I LIKE THAT BETTER!
LIFE ISN'T ALWAYS PREDICTABLE, AS I WELL KNOW...
BUT YOU'VE GOT TO THINK POSITIVELY!
HOW DO YOU DO IT? IT SEEMS EASY WHEN YOU SAY IT!
I WASN'T BORN LIKE THIS, YOU KNOW!
I LOST THE USE OF MY LEGS THREE YEARS AGO BECAUSE OF AN ACCIDENT. THAT DOESN'T MEAN I'M MAD AT THE WHOLE WORLD.
IT WOULD DO NO GOOD ANYHOW!
LET'S GO FOR A RIDE, MY BEAUTY!

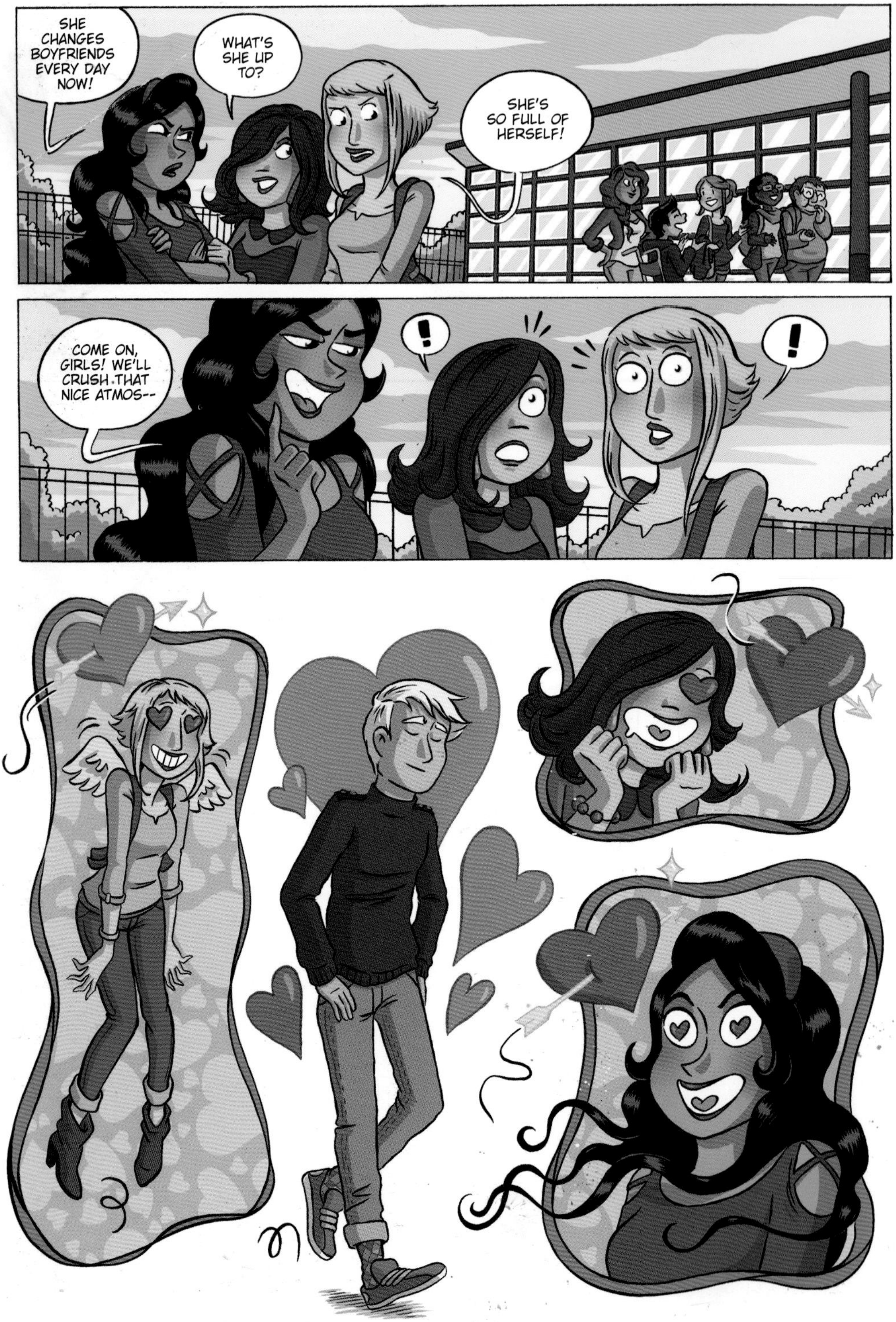
SHE CHANGES BOYFRIENDS EVERY DAY NOW!
WHAT'S SHE UP TO?
SHE'S SO FULL OF HERSELF!
COME ON, GIRLS! WE'LL CRUSH THAT NICE ATMOS--
!
!

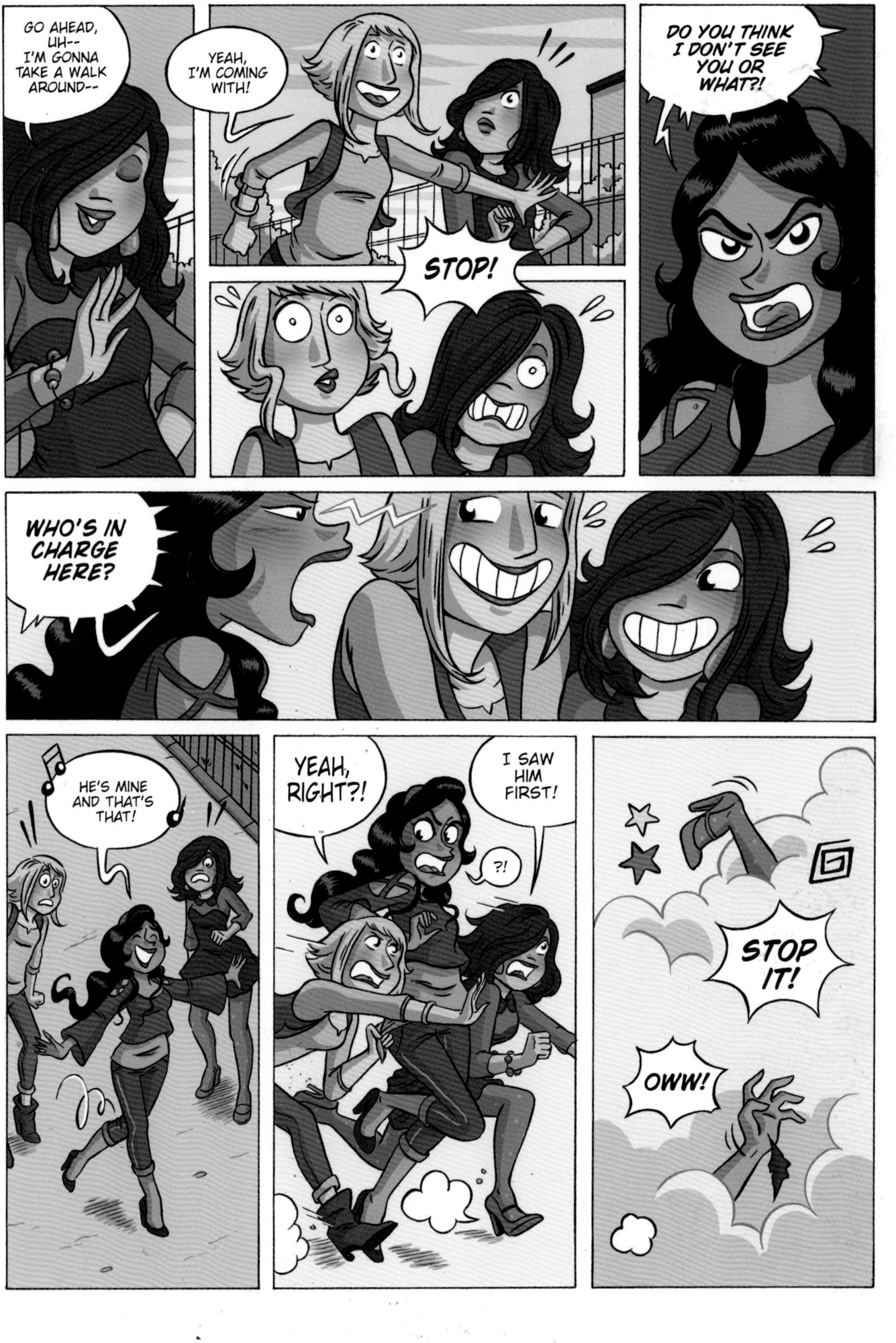
GO AHEAD, UH-- I'M GONNA TAKE A WALK AROUND--
YEAH, I'M COMING WITH!
STOP!
DO YOU THINK I DON'T SEE YOU OR WHAT?!
WHO'S IN CHARGE HERE?
HE'S MINE AND THAT'S THAT!
YEAH, RIGHT?!
I SAW HIM FIRST!
?!
STOP IT!
OWW!

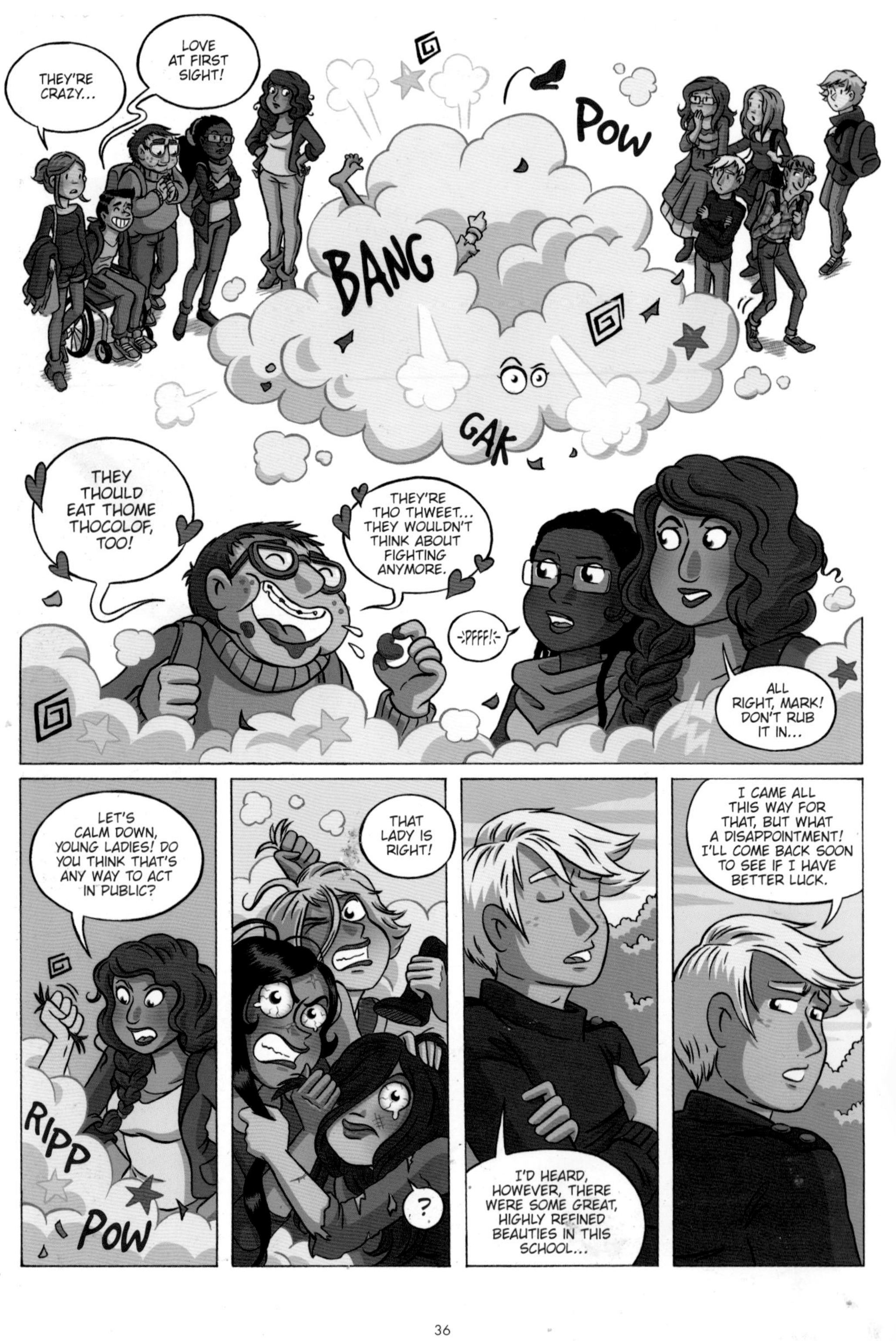
THEY'RE CRAZY...
LOVE AT FIRST SIGHT!
POW
BANG
GAK
THEY THOULD EAT THOME THOCOLOF, TOO!
THEY'RE THO THWEET... THEY WOULDN'T THINK ABOUT FIGHTING ANYMORE.
PFFF!
ALL RIGHT, MARK! DON'T RUB IT IN...
LET'S CALM DOWN, YOUNG LADIES! DO YOU THINK THAT'S ANY WAY TO ACT IN PUBLIC?
RIPP
POW
THAT LADY IS RIGHT!
?
I'D HEARD, HOWEVER, THERE WERE SOME GREAT, HIGHLY REFINED BEAUTIES IN THIS SCHOOL...
I CAME ALL THIS WAY FOR THAT, BUT WHAT A DISAPPOINTMENT! I'LL COME BACK SOON TO SEE IF I HAVE BETTER LUCK.

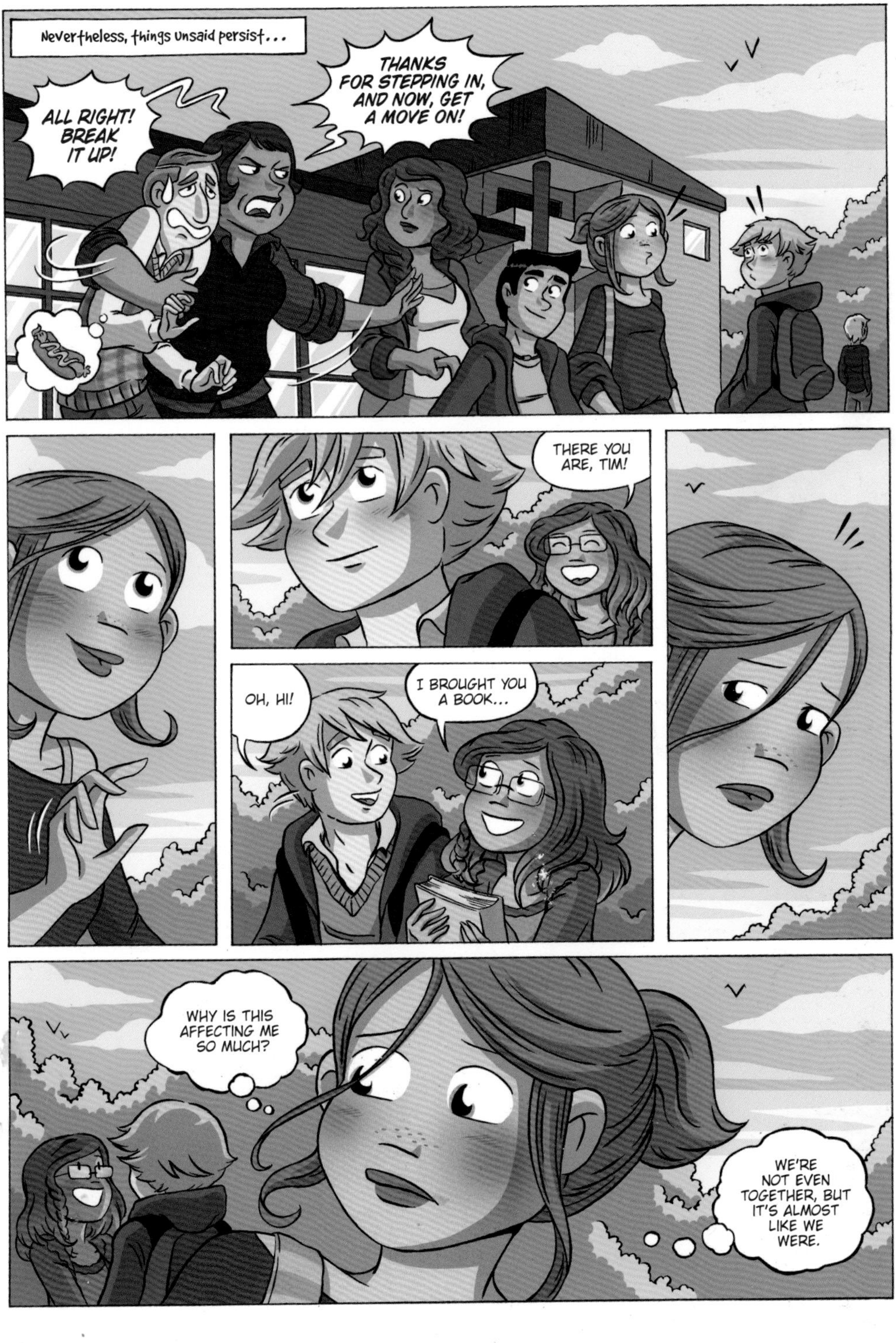
Nevertheless, things unsaid persist...
ALL RIGHT! BREAK IT UP!
THANKS FOR STEPPING IN, AND NOW, GET A MOVE ON!
THERE YOU ARE, TIM!
OH, HI!
I BROUGHT YOU A BOOK...
WHY IS THIS AFFECTING ME SO MUCH?
WE'RE NOT EVEN TOGETHER, BUT IT'S ALMOST LIKE WE WERE.

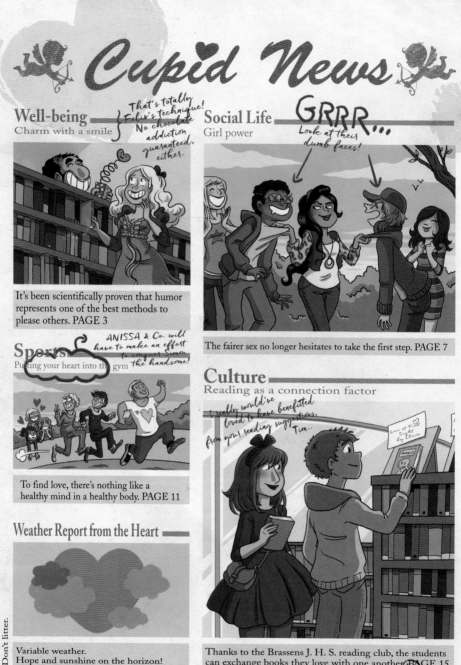

Cupid News

Well-being

Charm with a smile

That's totally Felix's technique! No chocolate addiction guaranteed, either.

It's been scientifically proven that humor represents one of the best methods to please others. PAGE 3

Social Life

Girl power

GRRR...

Look at their dumb faces!

The fairer sex no longer hesitates to take the first step. PAGE 7

Sports

Putting your heart into the gym

ANISSA & Co. will have to make an effort to conquer Simon the handsome!

To find love, there's nothing like a healthy mind in a healthy body. PAGE 11

Culture

Reading as a connection factor

I really would've loved to have benefitted from your reading suggestions, Tim...

Love at First Sight by Claire
ZOMBIES

Thanks to the Brassens J. H. S. reading club, the students can exchange books they love with one another. PAGE 15

I hope it's not too late!

Weather Report from the Heart

Variable weather.
Hope and sunshine on the horizon!

Don't litter.

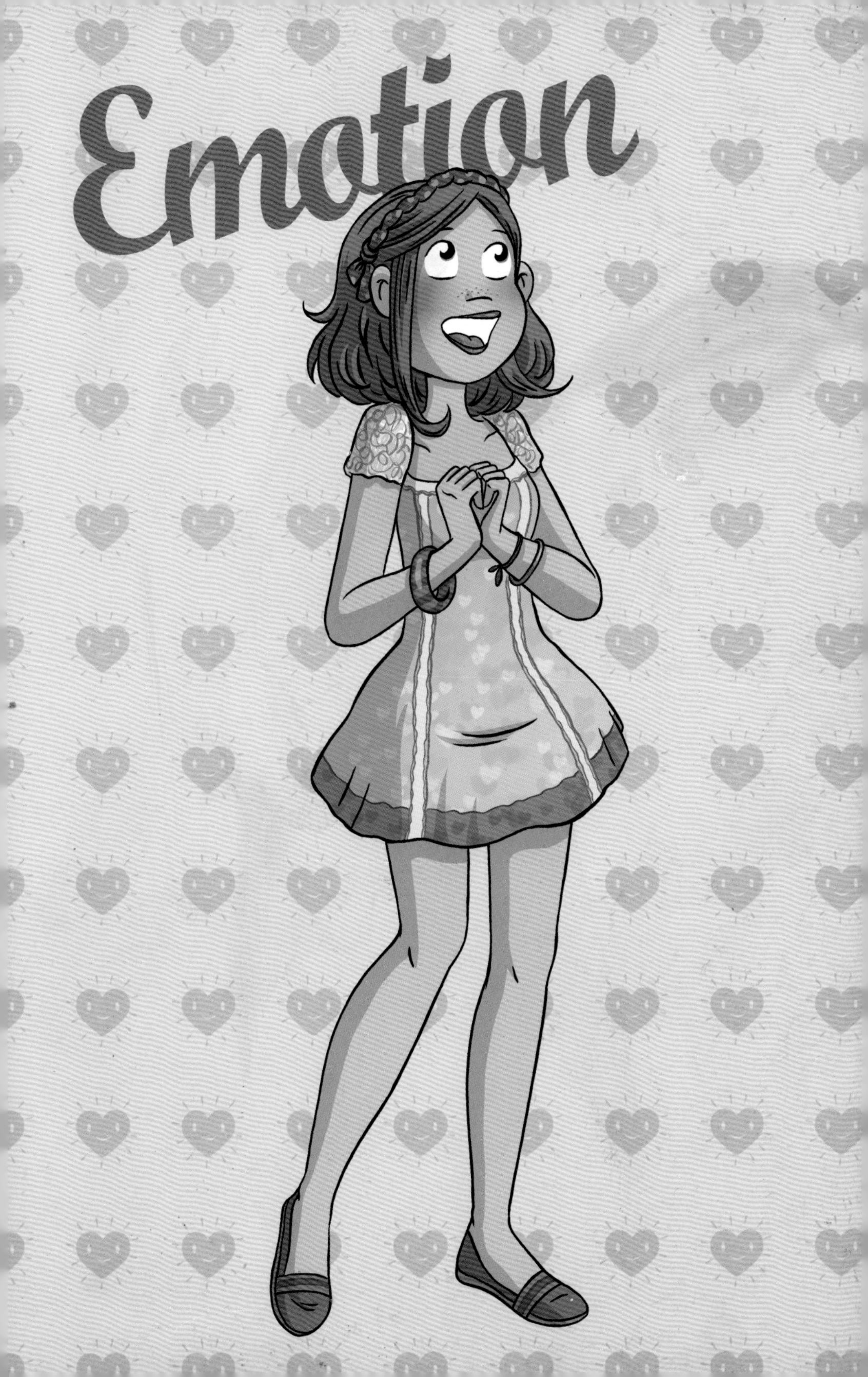
Emotion

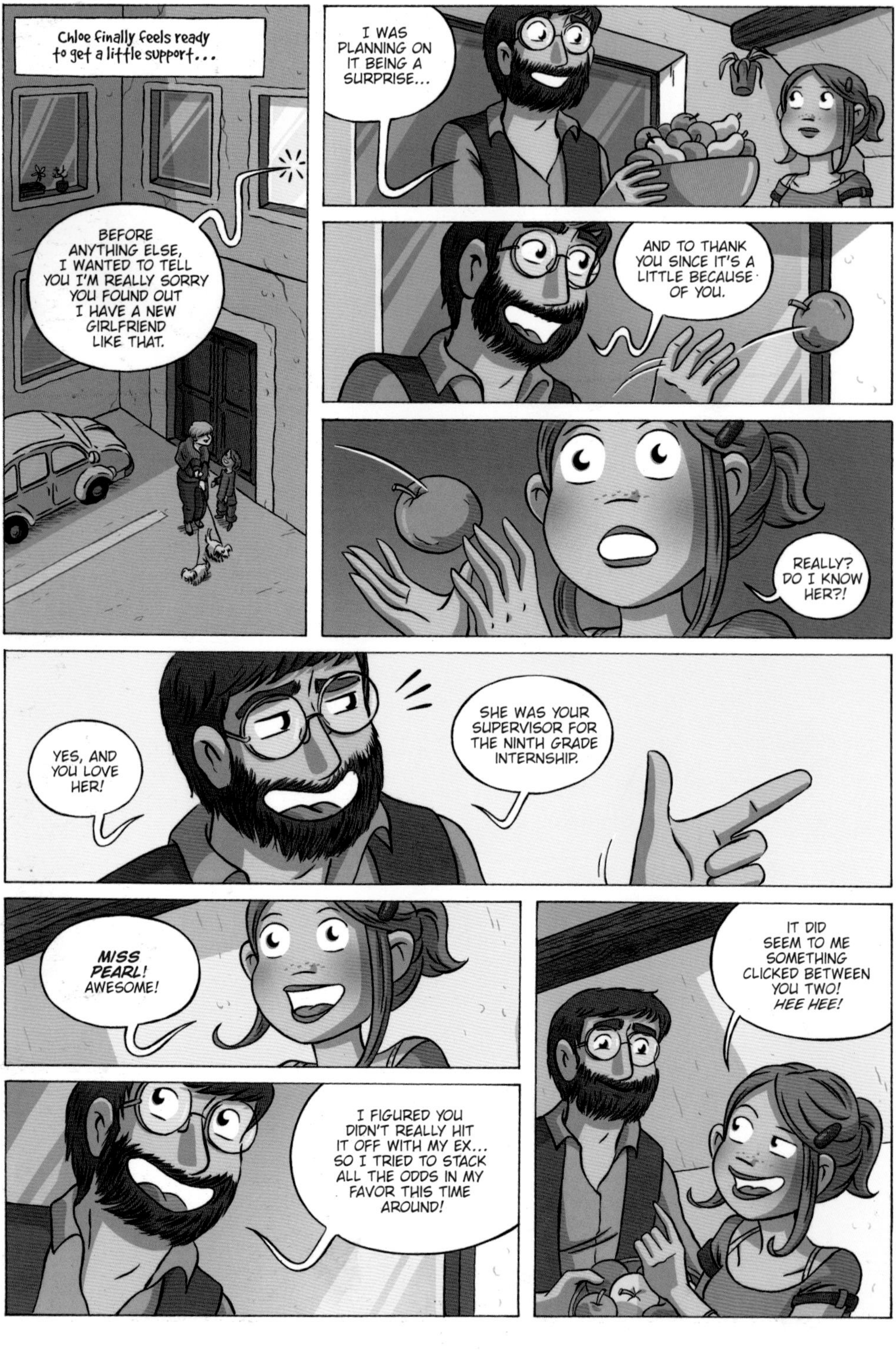
Chloe finally feels ready to get a little support...
BEFORE ANYTHING ELSE, I WANTED TO TELL YOU I'M REALLY SORRY YOU FOUND OUT I HAVE A NEW GIRLFRIEND LIKE THAT.
I WAS PLANNING ON IT BEING A SURPRISE...
AND TO THANK YOU SINCE IT'S A LITTLE BECAUSE OF YOU.
REALLY? DO I KNOW HER?!
YES, AND YOU LOVE HER!
SHE WAS YOUR SUPERVISOR FOR THE NINTH GRADE INTERNSHIP.
MISS PEARL! AWESOME!
I FIGURED YOU DIDN'T REALLY HIT IT OFF WITH MY EX... SO I TRIED TO STACK ALL THE ODDS IN MY FAVOR THIS TIME AROUND!
IT DID SEEM TO ME SOMETHING CLICKED BETWEEN YOU TWO! HEE HEE!

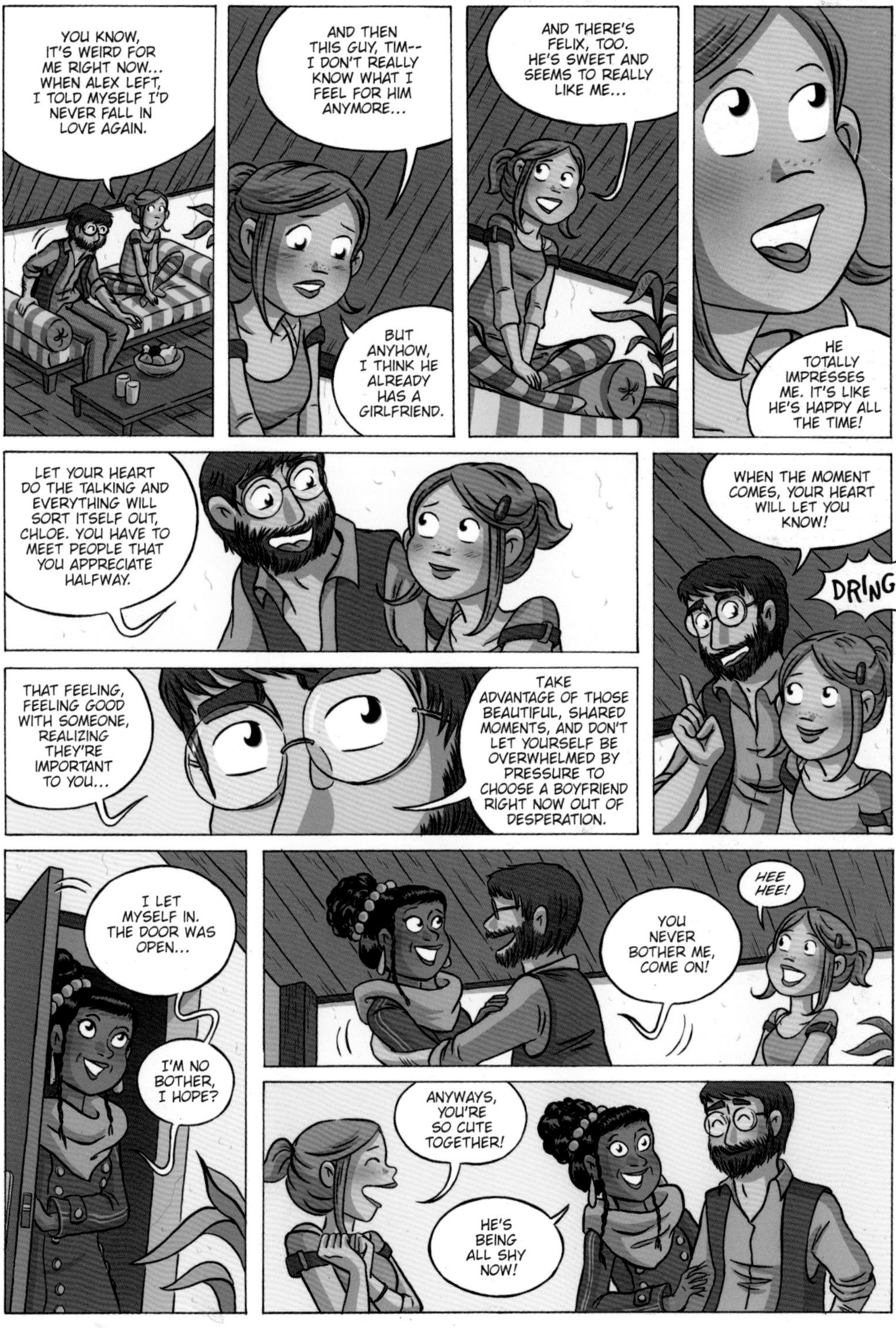
YOU KNOW, IT'S WEIRD FOR ME RIGHT NOW... WHEN ALEX LEFT, I TOLD MYSELF I'D NEVER FALL IN LOVE AGAIN.
AND THEN THIS GUY, TIM-- I DON'T REALLY KNOW WHAT I FEEL FOR HIM ANYMORE...
BUT ANYHOW, I THINK HE ALREADY HAS A GIRLFRIEND.
AND THERE'S FELIX, TOO. HE'S SWEET AND SEEMS TO REALLY LIKE ME...
HE TOTALLY IMPRESSES ME. IT'S LIKE HE'S HAPPY ALL THE TIME!
LET YOUR HEART DO THE TALKING AND EVERYTHING WILL SORT ITSELF OUT, CHLOE. YOU HAVE TO MEET PEOPLE THAT YOU APPRECIATE HALFWAY.
THAT FEELING, FEELING GOOD WITH SOMEONE, REALIZING THEY'RE IMPORTANT TO YOU...
TAKE ADVANTAGE OF THOSE BEAUTIFUL, SHARED MOMENTS, AND DON'T LET YOURSELF BE OVERWHELMED BY PRESSURE TO CHOOSE A BOYFRIEND RIGHT NOW OUT OF DESPERATION.
WHEN THE MOMENT COMES, YOUR HEART WILL LET YOU KNOW!
DRING
I LET MYSELF IN. THE DOOR WAS OPEN...
I'M NO BOTHER, I HOPE?
YOU NEVER BOTHER ME, COME ON!
HEE HEE!
ANYWAYS, YOU'RE SO CUTE TOGETHER!
HE'S BEING ALL SHY NOW!

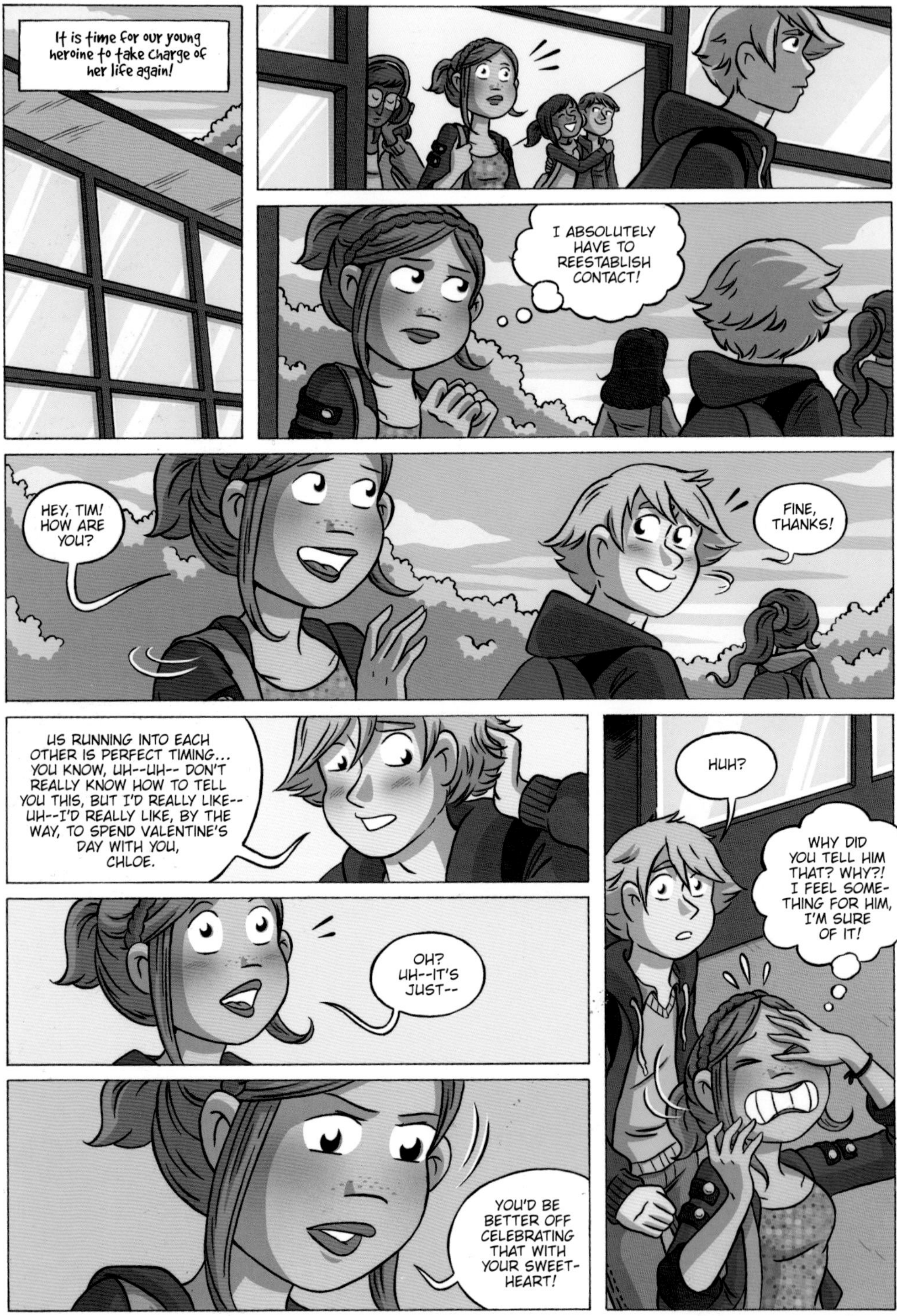
It is time for our young heroine to take charge of her life again!
I ABSOLUTELY HAVE TO REESTABLISH CONTACT!
HEY, TIM! HOW ARE YOU?
FINE, THANKS!
US RUNNING INTO EACH OTHER IS PERFECT TIMING... YOU KNOW, UH--UH-- DON'T REALLY KNOW HOW TO TELL YOU THIS, BUT I'D REALLY LIKE-- UH--I'D REALLY LIKE, BY THE WAY, TO SPEND VALENTINE'S DAY WITH YOU, CHLOE.
OH? UH--IT'S JUST--
YOU'D BE BETTER OFF CELEBRATING THAT WITH YOUR SWEET-HEART!
HUH?
WHY DID YOU TELL HIM THAT? WHY?! I FEEL SOME-THING FOR HIM, I'M SURE OF IT!

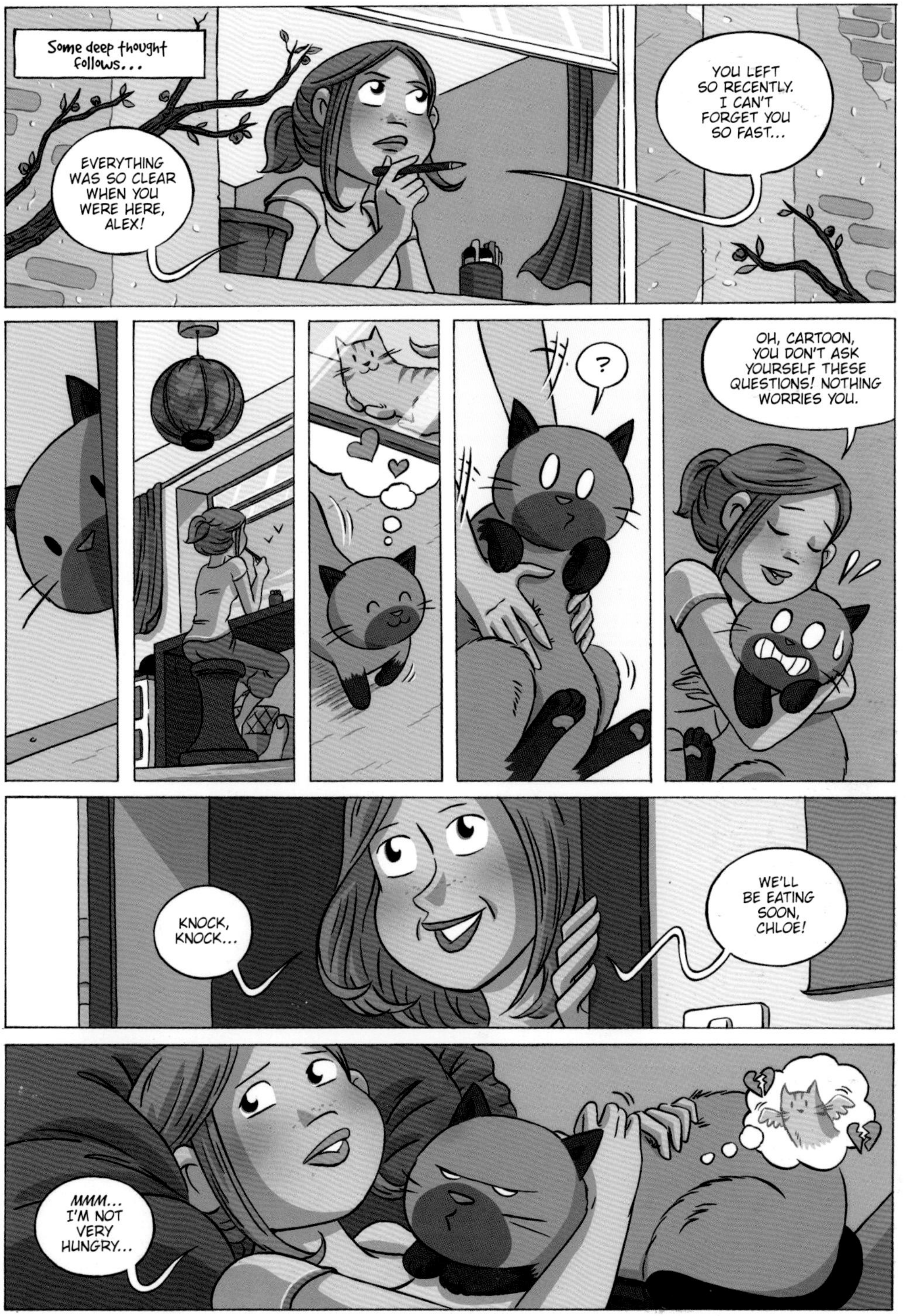
Some deep thought follows...
EVERYTHING WAS SO CLEAR WHEN YOU WERE HERE, ALEX!
YOU LEFT SO RECENTLY. I CAN'T FORGET YOU SO FAST...
?
OH, CARTOON, YOU DON'T ASK YOURSELF THESE QUESTIONS! NOTHING WORRIES YOU.
KNOCK, KNOCK...
WE'LL BE EATING SOON, CHLOE!
MMM... I'M NOT VERY HUNGRY...

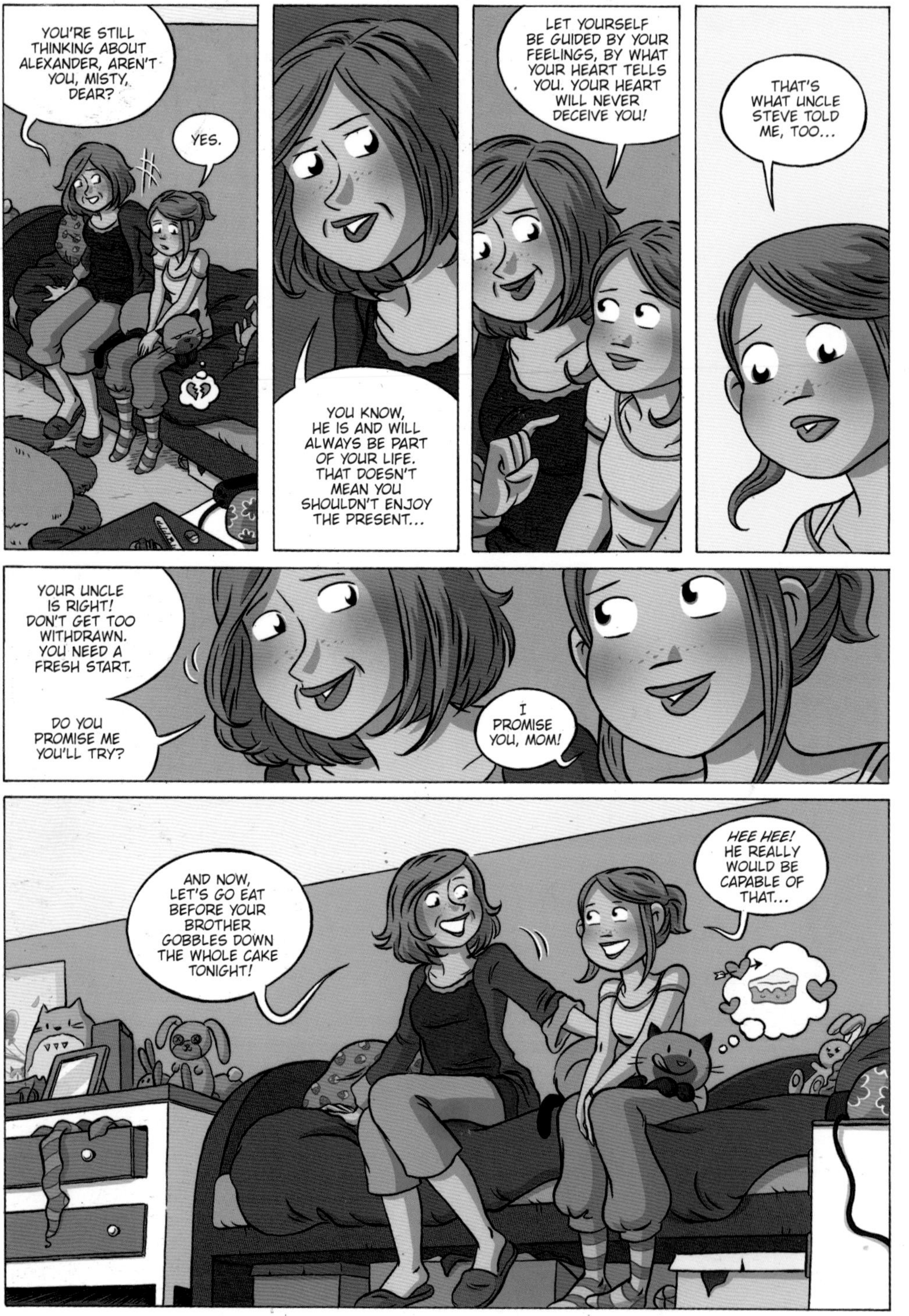
YOU'RE STILL THINKING ABOUT ALEXANDER, AREN'T YOU, MISTY, DEAR?
YES.
YOU KNOW, HE IS AND WILL ALWAYS BE PART OF YOUR LIFE. THAT DOESN'T MEAN YOU SHOULDN'T ENJOY THE PRESENT...
LET YOURSELF BE GUIDED BY YOUR FEELINGS, BY WHAT YOUR HEART TELLS YOU. YOUR HEART WILL NEVER DECEIVE YOU!
THAT'S WHAT UNCLE STEVE TOLD ME, TOO...
YOUR UNCLE IS RIGHT! DON'T GET TOO WITHDRAWN. YOU NEED A FRESH START.
DO YOU PROMISE ME YOU'LL TRY?
I PROMISE YOU, MOM!
AND NOW, LET'S GO EAT BEFORE YOUR BROTHER GOBBLES DOWN THE WHOLE CAKE TONIGHT!
HEE HEE! HE REALLY WOULD BE CAPABLE OF THAT...

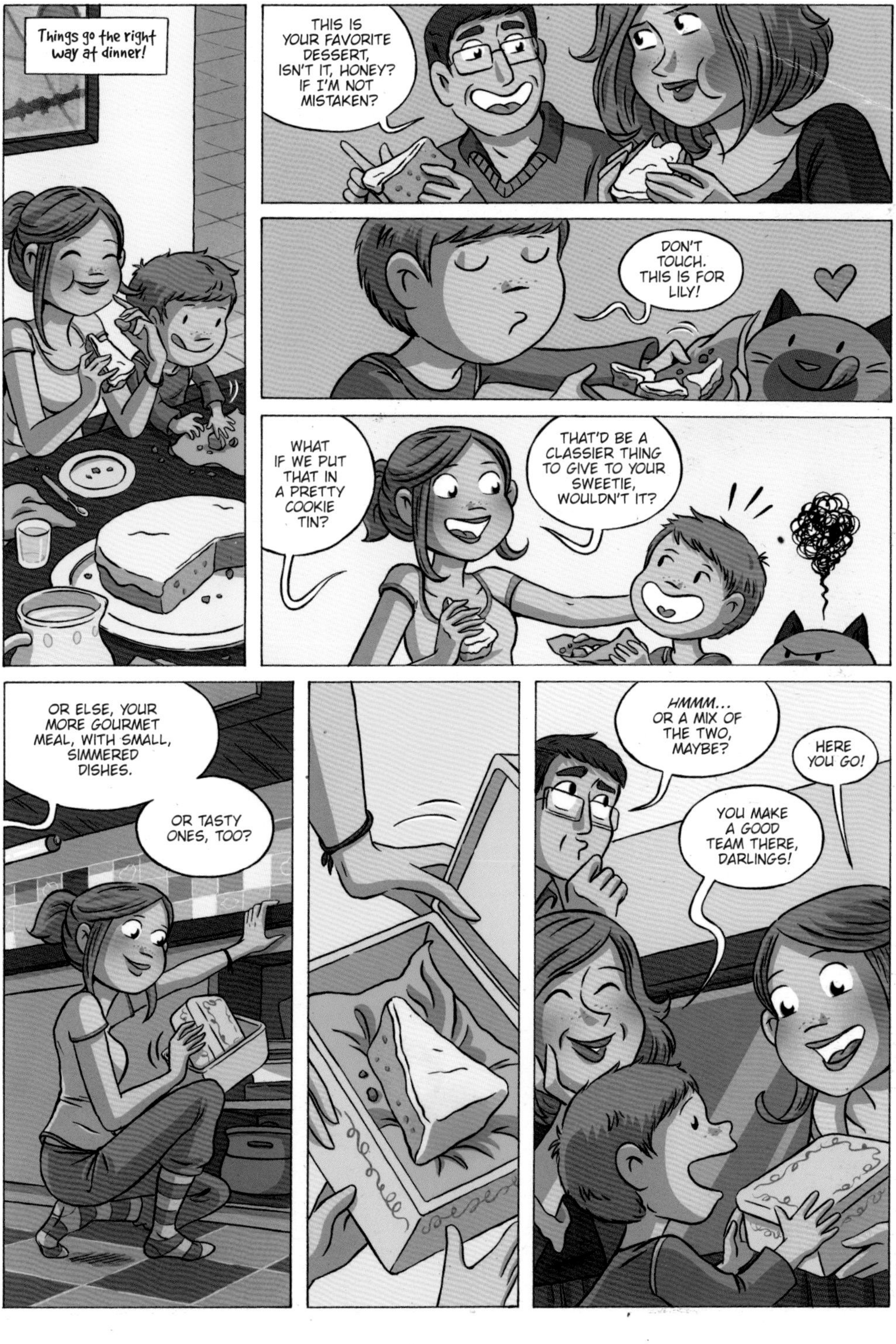
Things go the right way at dinner!
THIS IS YOUR FAVORITE DESSERT, ISN'T IT, HONEY? IF I'M NOT MISTAKEN?
DON'T TOUCH. THIS IS FOR LILY!
WHAT IF WE PUT THAT IN A PRETTY COOKIE TIN?
THAT'D BE A CLASSIER THING TO GIVE TO YOUR SWEETIE, WOULDN'T IT?
OR ELSE, YOUR MORE GOURMET MEAL, WITH SMALL, SIMMERED DISHES.
OR TASTY ONES, TOO?
HMMM... OR A MIX OF THE TWO, MAYBE?
HERE YOU GO!
YOU MAKE A GOOD TEAM THERE, DARLINGS!

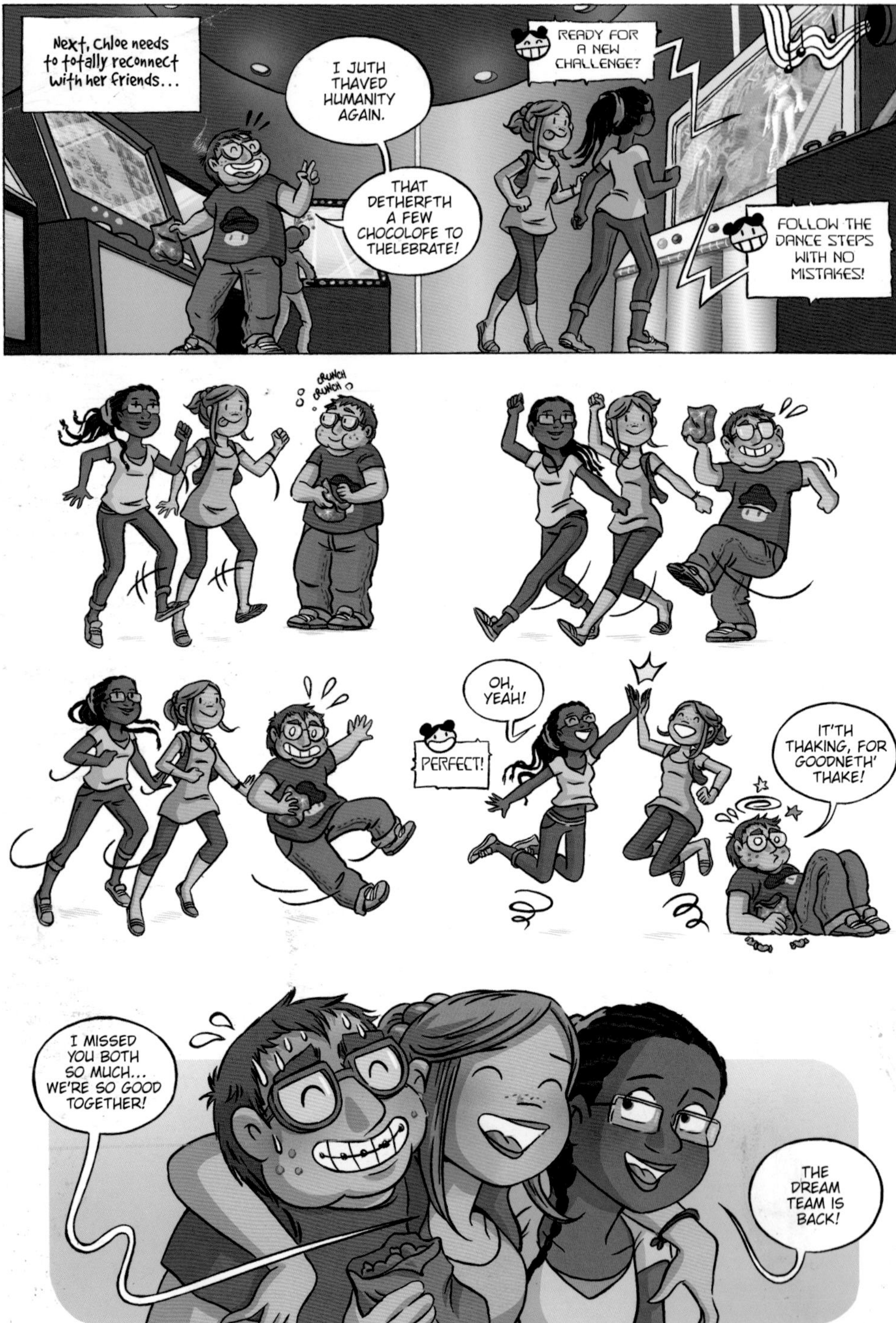
Next, Chloe needs to totally reconnect with her friends...
I JUTH THAVED HUMANITY AGAIN.
THAT DETHERFTH A FEW CHOCOLOFE TO THELEBRATE!
READY FOR A NEW CHALLENGE?
FOLLOW THE DANCE STEPS WITH NO MISTAKES!
CRUNCH CRUNCH
OH, YEAH!
PERFECT!
IT'TH THAKING, FOR GOODNETH' THAKE!
I MISSED YOU BOTH SO MUCH... WE'RE SO GOOD TOGETHER!
THE DREAM TEAM IS BACK!

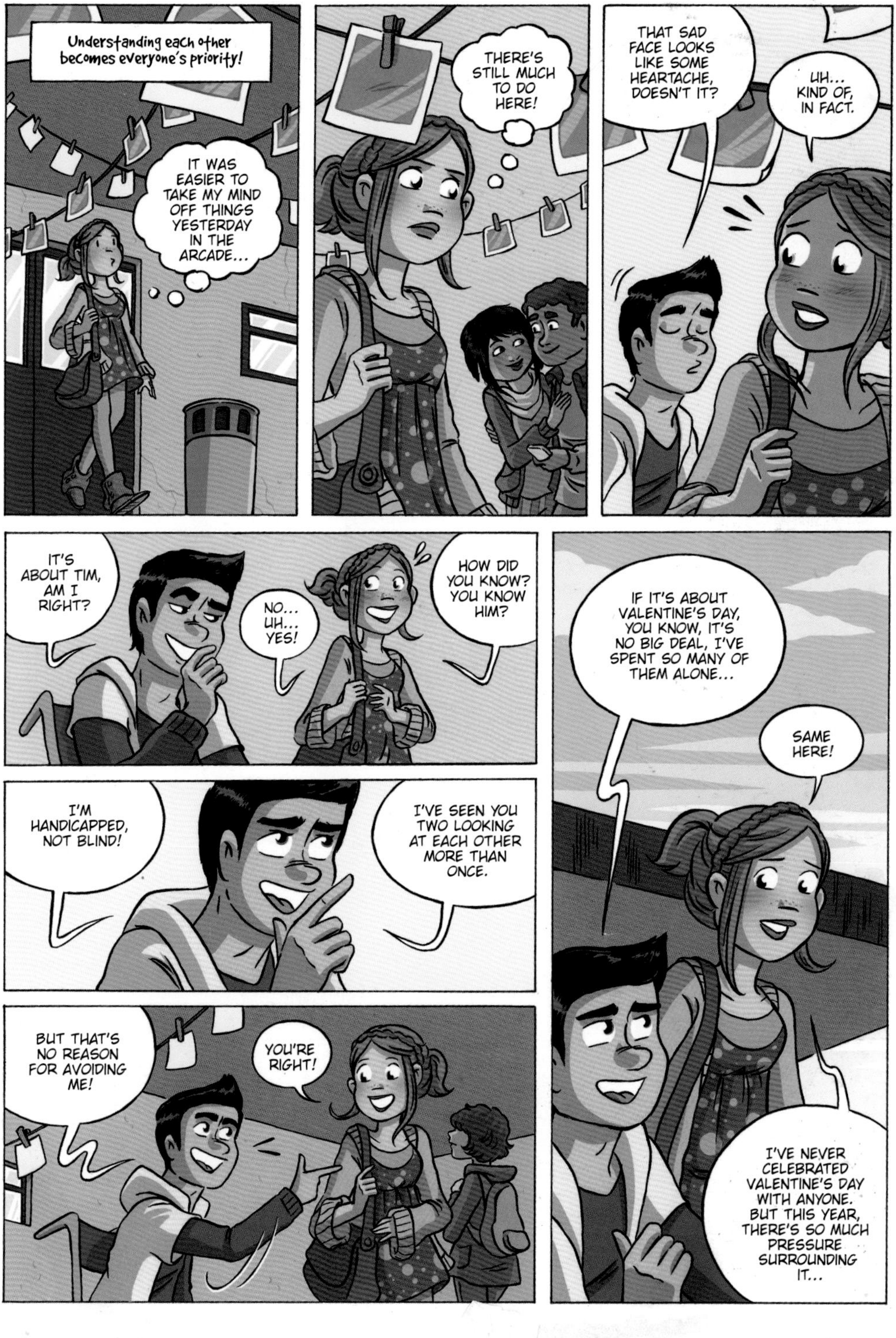

Understanding each other becomes everyone's priority!
IT WAS EASIER TO TAKE MY MIND OFF THINGS YESTERDAY IN THE ARCADE...
THERE'S STILL MUCH TO DO HERE!
THAT SAD FACE LOOKS LIKE SOME HEARTACHE, DOESN'T IT?
UH... KIND OF, IN FACT.
IT'S ABOUT TIM, AM I RIGHT?
NO... UH... YES!
HOW DID YOU KNOW? YOU KNOW HIM?
I'M HANDICAPPED, NOT BLIND!
I'VE SEEN YOU TWO LOOKING AT EACH OTHER MORE THAN ONCE.
BUT THAT'S NO REASON FOR AVOIDING ME!
YOU'RE RIGHT!
IF IT'S ABOUT VALENTINE'S DAY, YOU KNOW, IT'S NO BIG DEAL, I'VE SPENT SO MANY OF THEM ALONE...
SAME HERE!
I'VE NEVER CELEBRATED VALENTINE'S DAY WITH ANYONE. BUT THIS YEAR, THERE'S SO MUCH PRESSURE SURROUNDING IT...

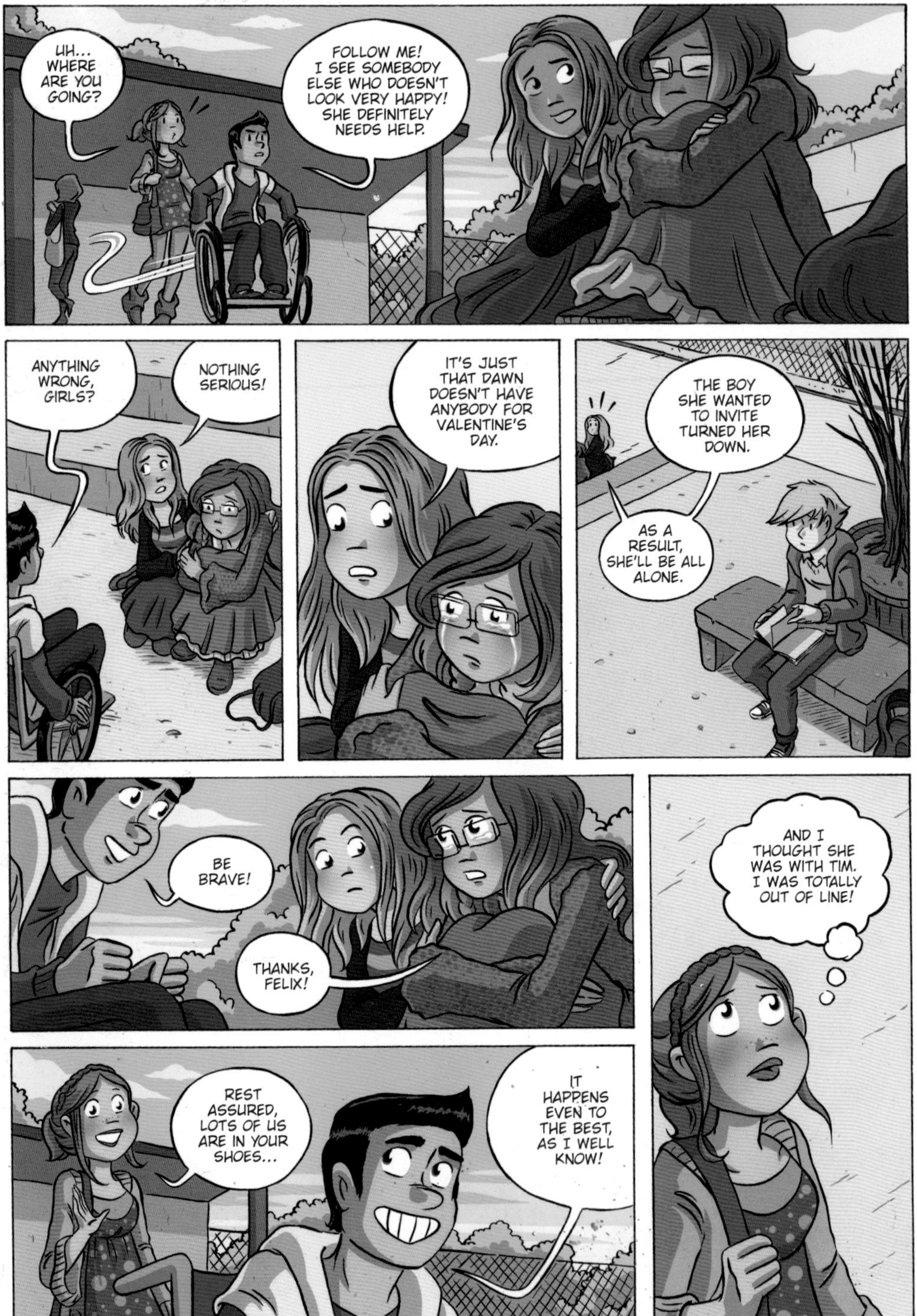
UH... WHERE ARE YOU GOING?
FOLLOW ME! I SEE SOMEBODY ELSE WHO DOESN'T LOOK VERY HAPPY! SHE DEFINITELY NEEDS HELP.
ANYTHING WRONG, GIRLS?
NOTHING SERIOUS!
IT'S JUST THAT DAWN DOESN'T HAVE ANYBODY FOR VALENTINE'S DAY.
THE BOY SHE WANTED TO INVITE TURNED HER DOWN.
AS A RESULT, SHE'LL BE ALL ALONE.
BE BRAVE!
THANKS, FELIX!
AND I THOUGHT SHE WAS WITH TIM. I WAS TOTALLY OUT OF LINE!
REST ASSURED, LOTS OF US ARE IN YOUR SHOES...
IT HAPPENS EVEN TO THE BEST, AS I WELL KNOW!

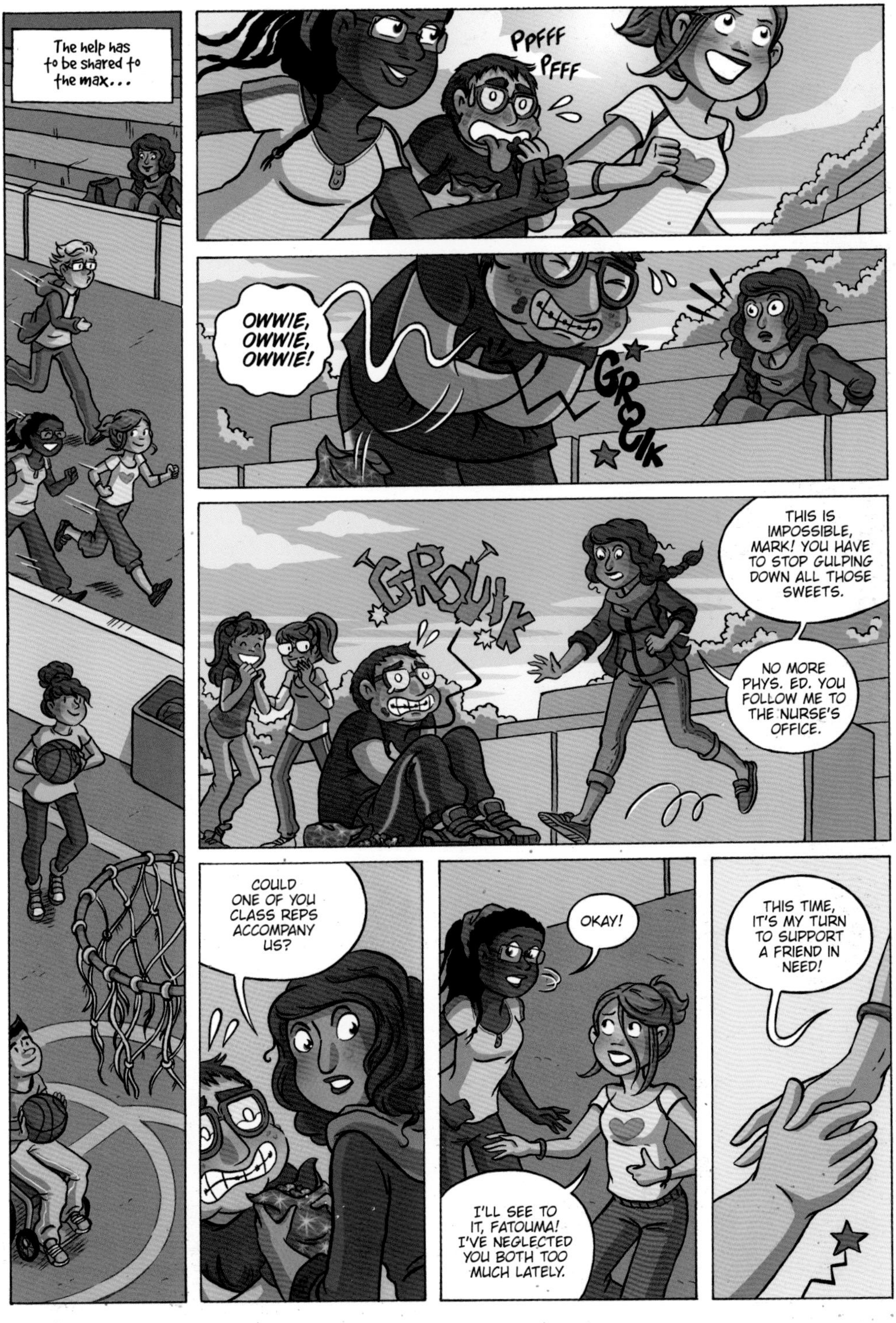

The help has to be shared to the max...
PPFFF PFFF
OWWIE, OWWIE, OWWIE!
GROUIK
GROUIK
THIS IS IMPOSSIBLE, MARK! YOU HAVE TO STOP GULPING DOWN ALL THOSE SWEETS.
NO MORE PHYS. ED. YOU FOLLOW ME TO THE NURSE'S OFFICE.
COULD ONE OF YOU CLASS REPS ACCOMPANY US?
OKAY!
I'LL SEE TO IT, FATOUMA! I'VE NEGLECTED YOU BOTH TOO MUCH LATELY.
THIS TIME, IT'S MY TURN TO SUPPORT A FRIEND IN NEED!

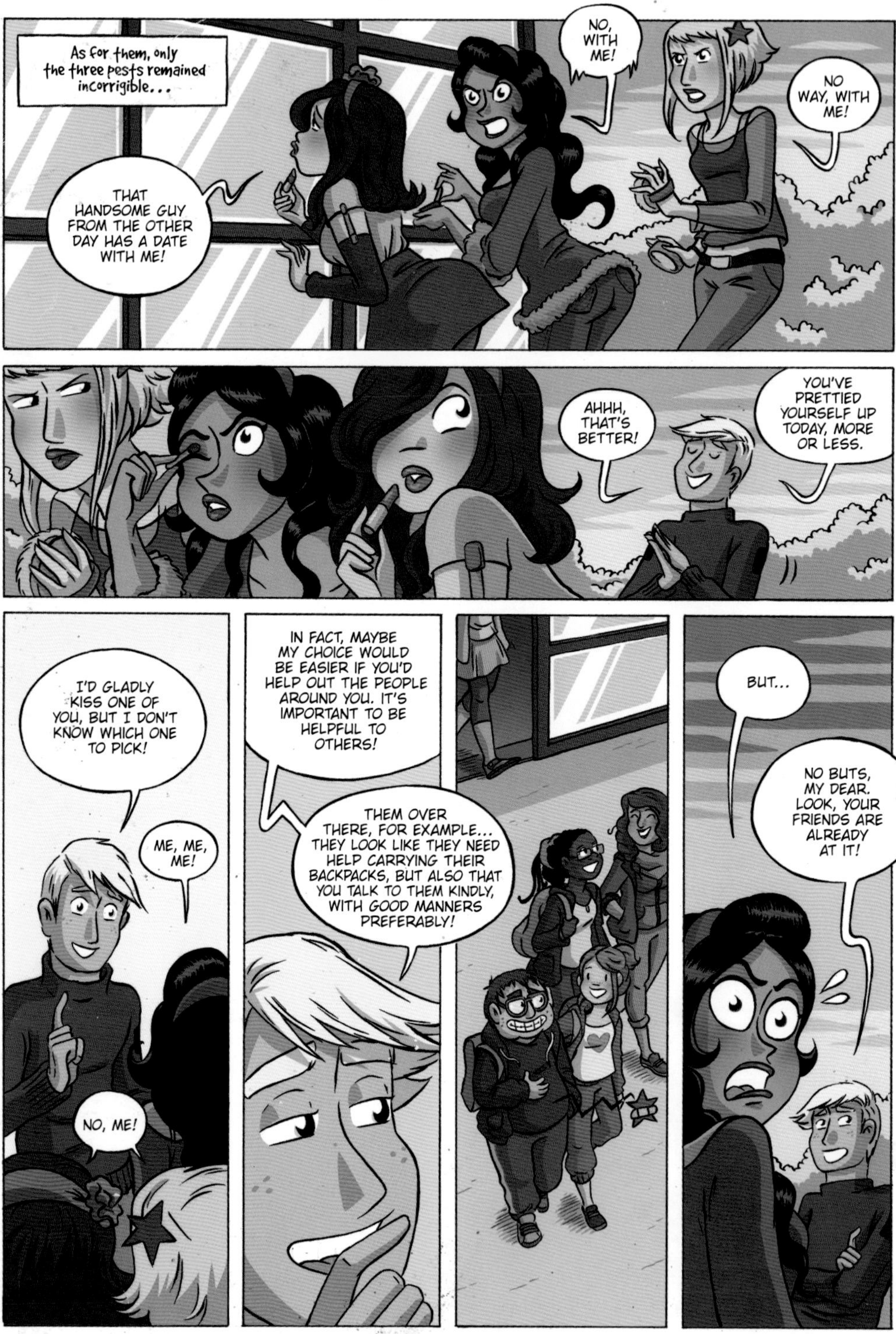

As for them, only the three pests remained incorrigible...
THAT HANDSOME GUY FROM THE OTHER DAY HAS A DATE WITH ME!
NO, WITH ME!
NO WAY, WITH ME!
AHHH, THAT'S BETTER!
YOU'VE PRETTIED YOURSELF UP TODAY, MORE OR LESS.
I'D GLADLY KISS ONE OF YOU, BUT I DON'T KNOW WHICH ONE TO PICK!
ME, ME, ME!
NO, ME!
IN FACT, MAYBE MY CHOICE WOULD BE EASIER IF YOU'D HELP OUT THE PEOPLE AROUND YOU. IT'S IMPORTANT TO BE HELPFUL TO OTHERS!
THEM OVER THERE, FOR EXAMPLE... THEY LOOK LIKE THEY NEED HELP CARRYING THEIR BACKPACKS, BUT ALSO THAT YOU TALK TO THEM KINDLY, WITH GOOD MANNERS PREFERABLY!
BUT...
NO BUTS, MY DEAR. LOOK, YOUR FRIENDS ARE ALREADY AT IT!

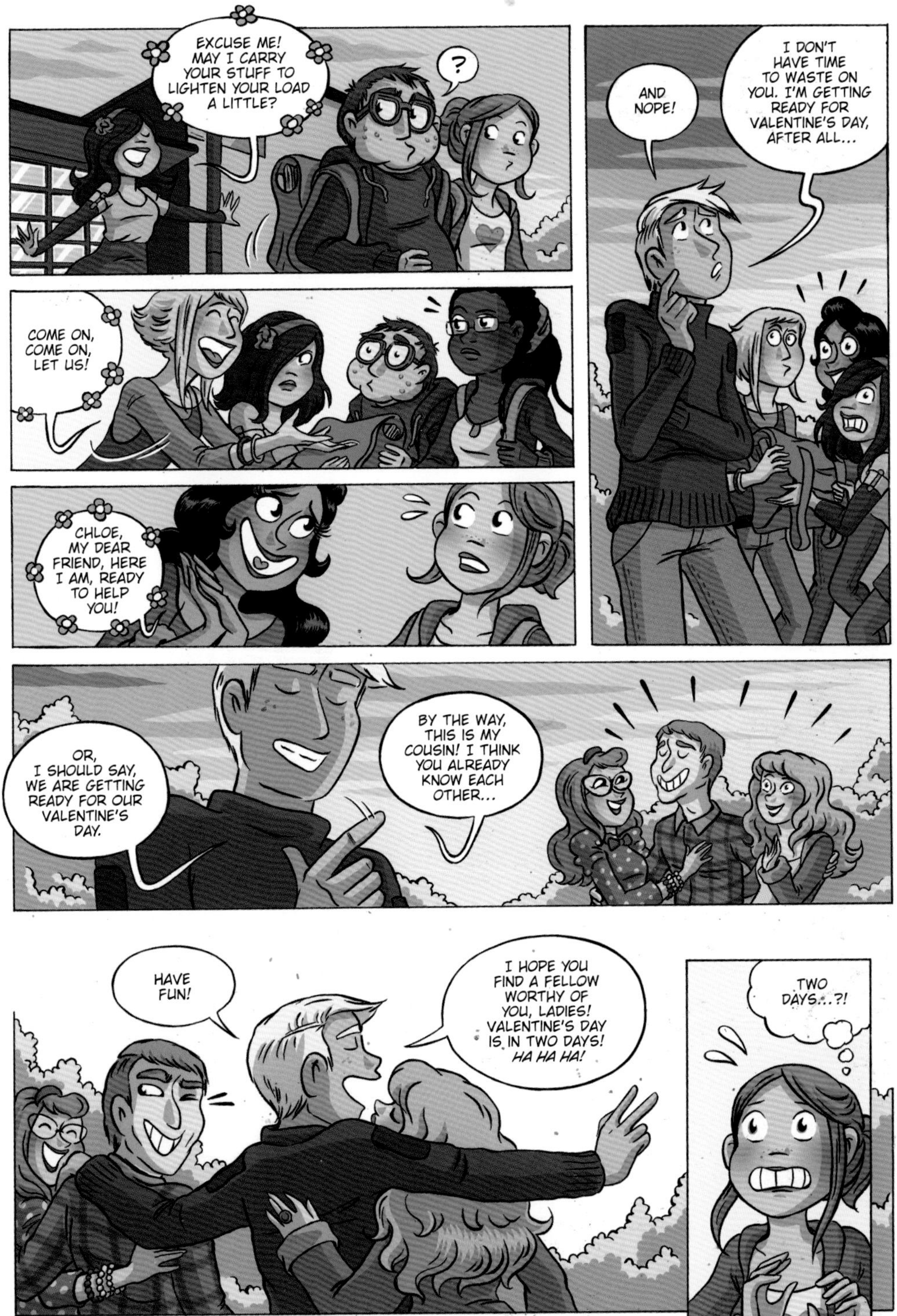
EXCUSE ME! MAY I CARRY YOUR STUFF TO LIGHTEN YOUR LOAD A LITTLE?
?
COME ON, COME ON, LET US!
CHLOE, MY DEAR FRIEND, HERE I AM, READY TO HELP YOU!
AND NOPE!
I DON'T HAVE TIME TO WASTE ON YOU. I'M GETTING READY FOR VALENTINE'S DAY, AFTER ALL...
OR, I SHOULD SAY, WE ARE GETTING READY FOR OUR VALENTINE'S DAY.
BY THE WAY, THIS IS MY COUSIN! I THINK YOU ALREADY KNOW EACH OTHER...
HAVE FUN!
I HOPE YOU FIND A FELLOW WORTHY OF YOU, LADIES! VALENTINE'S DAY IS IN TWO DAYS! *HA HA HA!*
TWO DAYS...?!

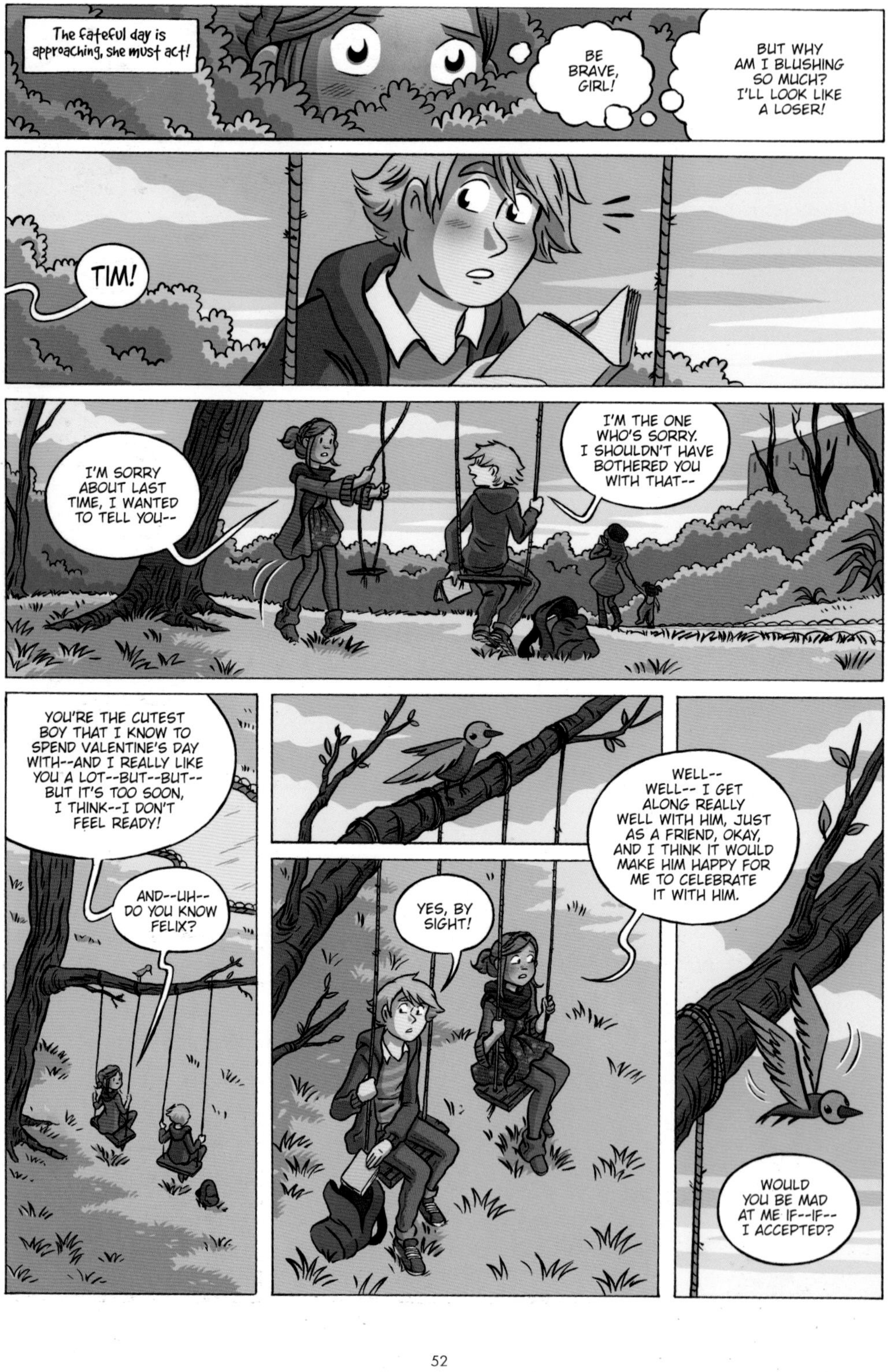
The fateful day is approaching, she must act!
BE BRAVE, GIRL!
BUT WHY AM I BLUSHING SO MUCH? I'LL LOOK LIKE A LOSER!
TIM!
I'M SORRY ABOUT LAST TIME, I WANTED TO TELL YOU--
I'M THE ONE WHO'S SORRY. I SHOULDN'T HAVE BOTHERED YOU WITH THAT--
YOU'RE THE CUTEST BOY THAT I KNOW TO SPEND VALENTINE'S DAY WITH--AND I REALLY LIKE YOU A LOT--BUT--BUT--BUT IT'S TOO SOON, I THINK--I DON'T FEEL READY!
AND--UH--DO YOU KNOW FELIX?
YES, BY SIGHT!
WELL-- WELL-- I GET ALONG REALLY WELL WITH HIM, JUST AS A FRIEND, OKAY, AND I THINK IT WOULD MAKE HIM HAPPY FOR ME TO CELEBRATE IT WITH HIM.
WOULD YOU BE MAD AT ME IF--IF--I ACCEPTED?

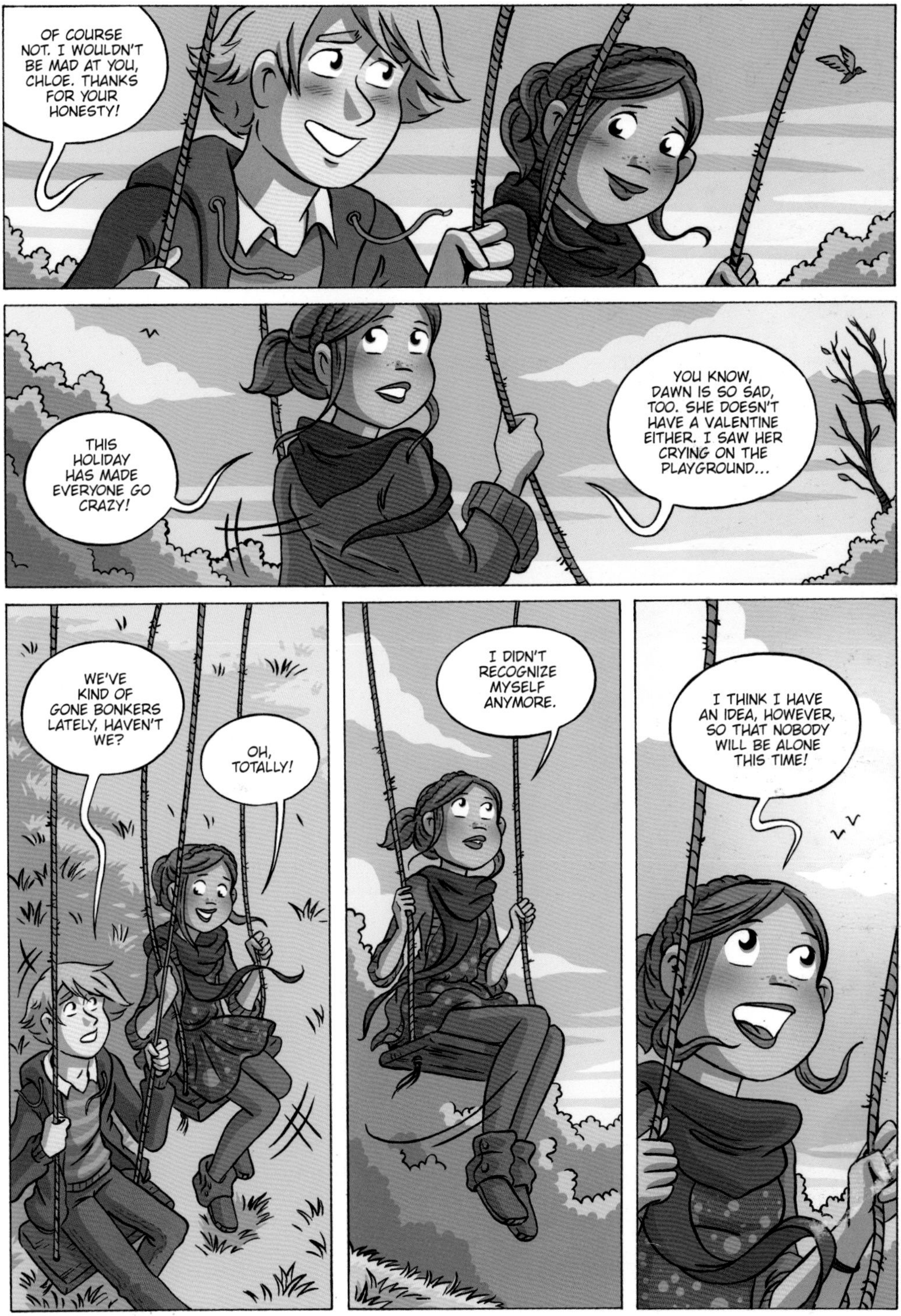
OF COURSE NOT. I WOULDN'T BE MAD AT YOU, CHLOE. THANKS FOR YOUR HONESTY!
THIS HOLIDAY HAS MADE EVERYONE GO CRAZY!
YOU KNOW, DAWN IS SO SAD, TOO. SHE DOESN'T HAVE A VALENTINE EITHER. I SAW HER CRYING ON THE PLAYGROUND...
WE'VE KIND OF GONE BONKERS LATELY, HAVEN'T WE?
OH, TOTALLY!
I DIDN'T RECOGNIZE MYSELF ANYMORE.
I THINK I HAVE AN IDEA, HOWEVER, SO THAT NOBODY WILL BE ALONE THIS TIME!

Cupid News

Animals
The Valentine Cat

(handwritten: The Valentine's honor is safe!)

(handwritten: Your turn, Cartoon!)

Animals also have their seasons of love. PAGE 4

Cooking

The success of "lovebirds special" recipes

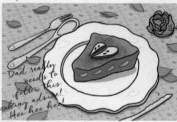

(handwritten: Dad really needs to follow his cooking advice! Hee hee hee)

The meal that will blow your sweetheart's socks off. PAGE 12

Weather Report from the Heart

Radiant weather. Sunshine finally on tap!

(sideways: Don't litter.)

Music
They're singing about love

(handwritten: My uncle's band is the BEST in the world!)

The rock group, "The Magical Lovers" back in town to give everyone a thrill. PAGE 8

Going out
An unforgettable weekend

(handwritten: it's gonna be unforgettable for sure!)

Valentine's Day is tomorrow already! To have an unforgettable night, follow our last-minute ideas. PAGE 16

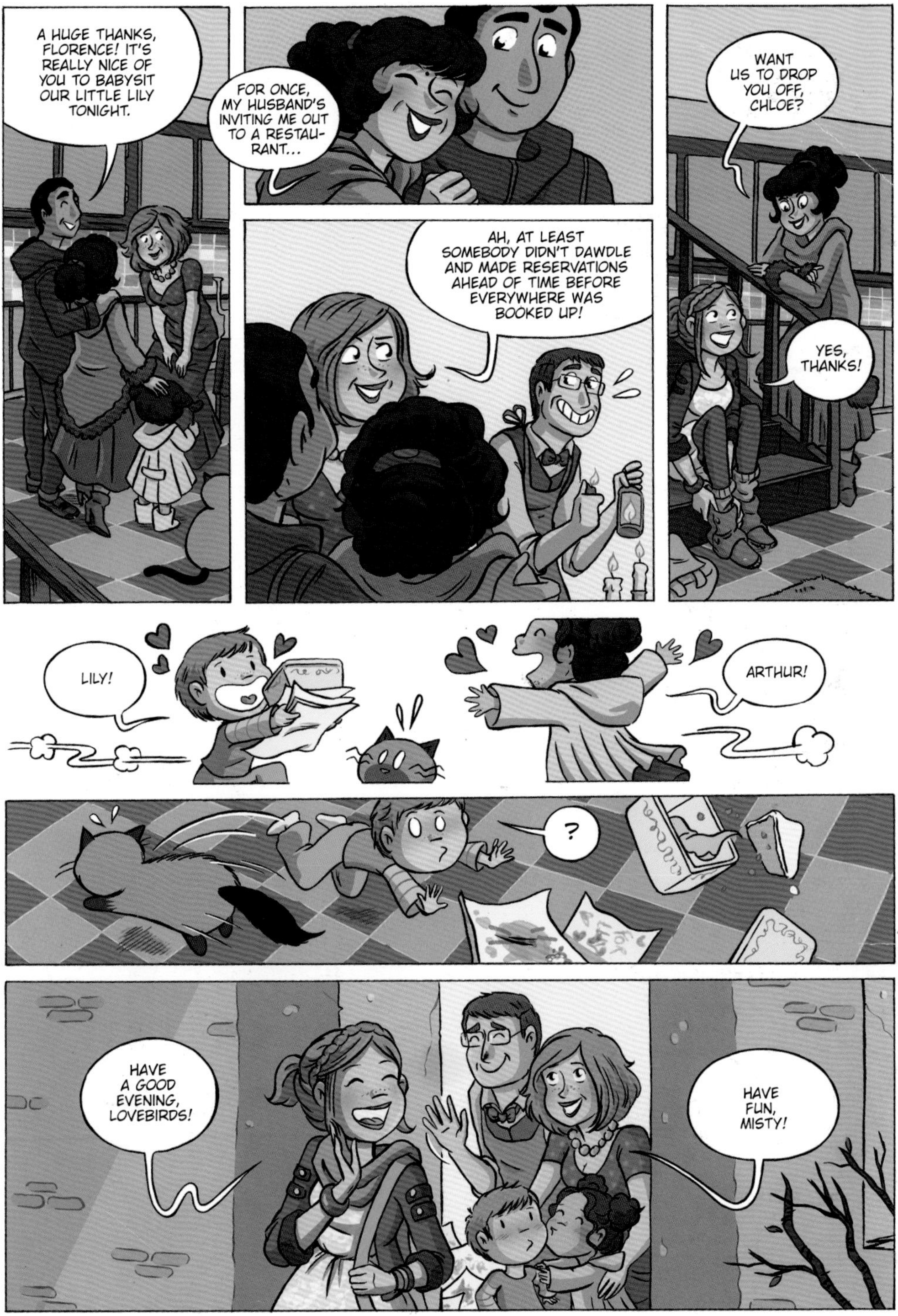

A HUGE THANKS, FLORENCE! IT'S REALLY NICE OF YOU TO BABYSIT OUR LITTLE LILY TONIGHT.
FOR ONCE, MY HUSBAND'S INVITING ME OUT TO A RESTAU-RANT...
AH, AT LEAST SOMEBODY DIDN'T DAWDLE AND MADE RESERVATIONS AHEAD OF TIME BEFORE EVERYWHERE WAS BOOKED UP!
WANT US TO DROP YOU OFF, CHLOE?
YES, THANKS!
LILY!
ARTHUR!
?
HAVE A GOOD EVENING, LOVEBIRDS!
HAVE FUN, MISTY!

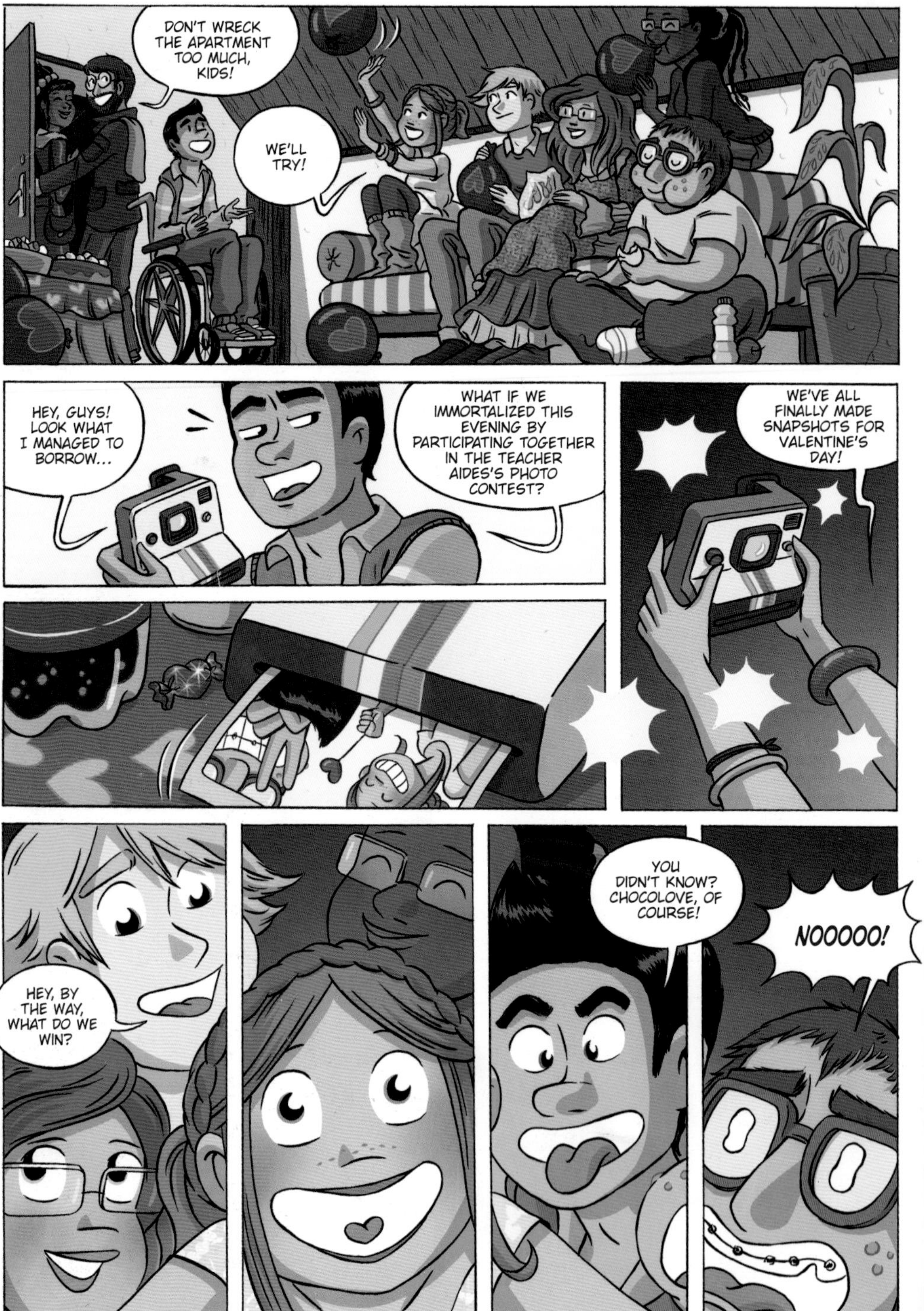
DON'T WRECK THE APARTMENT TOO MUCH, KIDS!
WE'LL TRY!
HEY, GUYS! LOOK WHAT I MANAGED TO BORROW...
WHAT IF WE IMMORTALIZED THIS EVENING BY PARTICIPATING TOGETHER IN THE TEACHER AIDES'S PHOTO CONTEST?
WE'VE ALL FINALLY MADE SNAPSHOTS FOR VALENTINE'S DAY!
HEY, BY THE WAY, WHAT DO WE WIN?
YOU DIDN'T KNOW? CHOCOLOVE, OF COURSE!
NOOOOO!

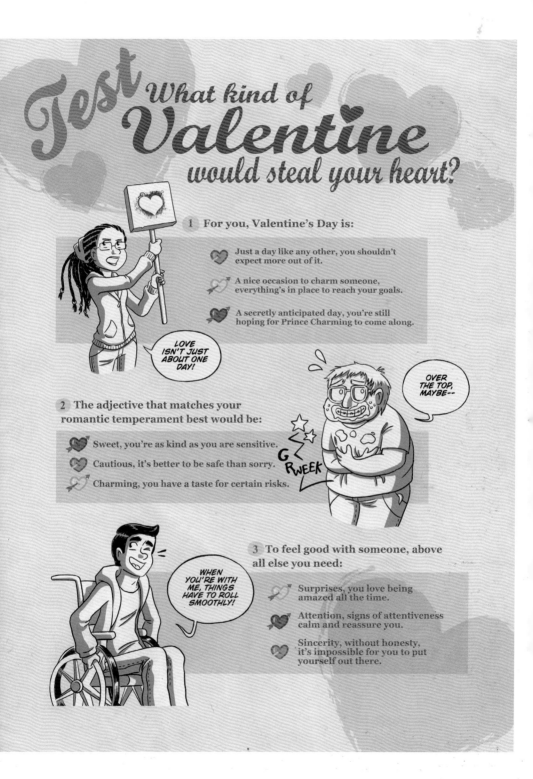

Test What kind of Valentine would steal your heart?

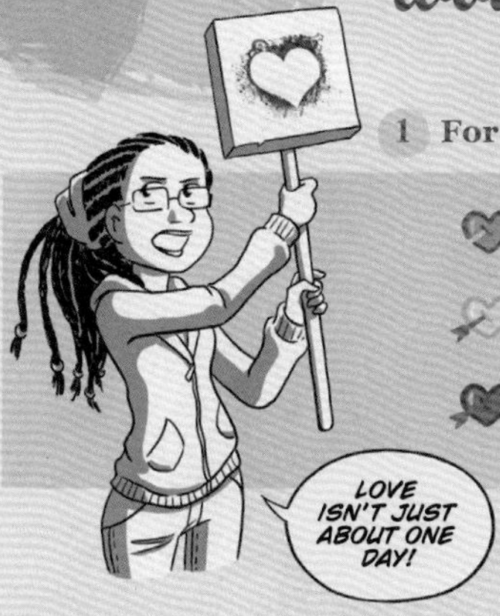
LOVE ISN'T JUST ABOUT ONE DAY!

1 For you, Valentine's Day is:

- Just a day like any other, you shouldn't expect more out of it.
- A nice occasion to charm someone, everything's in place to reach your goals.
- A secretly anticipated day, you're still hoping for Prince Charming to come along.

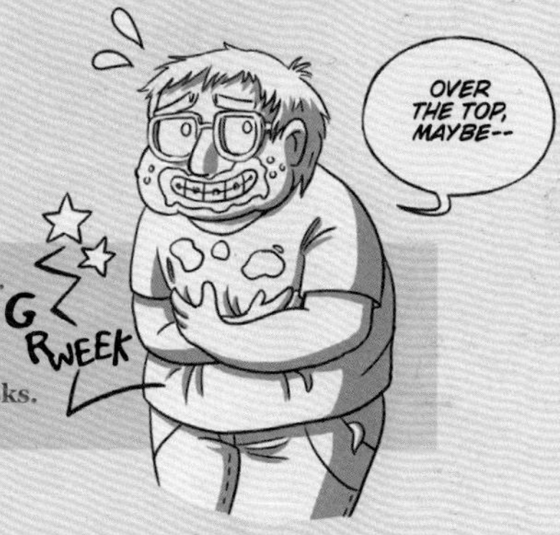
OVER THE TOP, MAYBE--
GRWEEK

2 The adjective that matches your romantic temperament best would be:

- Sweet, you're as kind as you are sensitive.
- Cautious, it's better to be safe than sorry.
- Charming, you have a taste for certain risks.

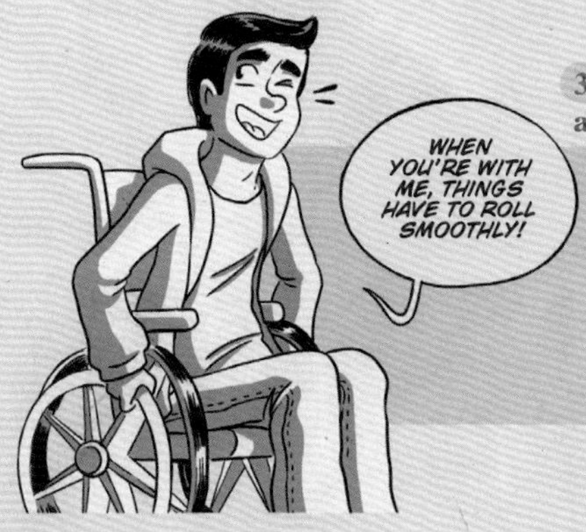
WHEN YOU'RE WITH ME, THINGS HAVE TO ROLL SMOOTHLY!

3 To feel good with someone, above all else you need:

- Surprises, you love being amazed all the time.
- Attention, signs of attentiveness calm and reassure you.
- Sincerity, without honesty, it's impossible for you to put yourself out there.

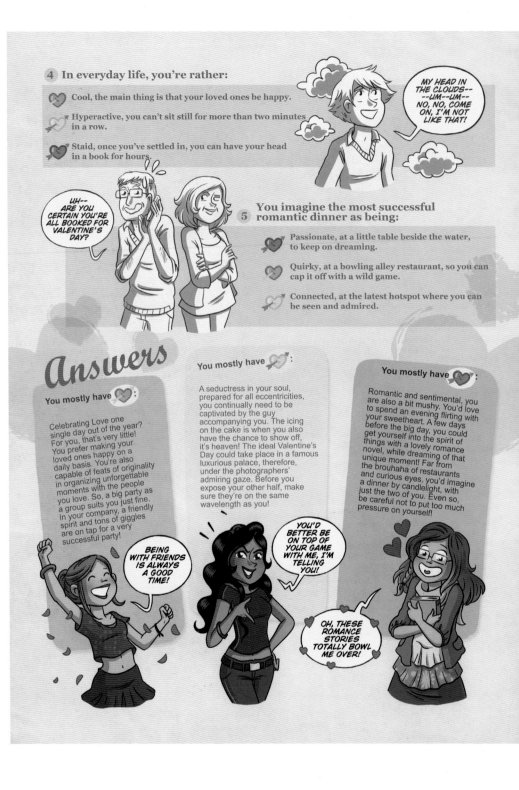

4 In everyday life, you're rather:

- Cool, the main thing is that your loved ones be happy.
- Hyperactive, you can't sit still for more than two minutes in a row.
- Staid, once you've settled in, you can have your head in a book for hours.

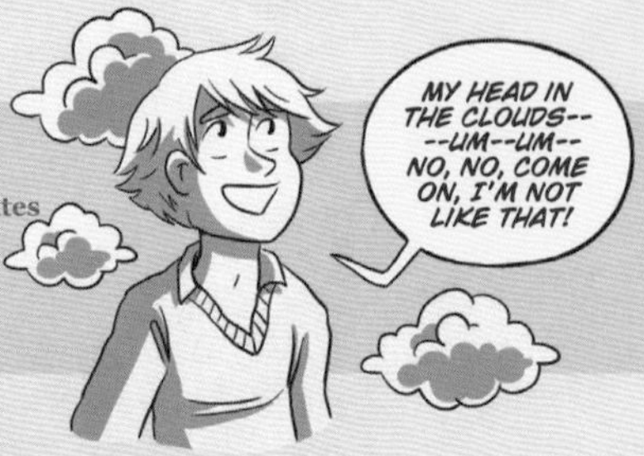
MY HEAD IN THE CLOUDS-- --UM--UM-- NO, NO, COME ON, I'M NOT LIKE THAT!

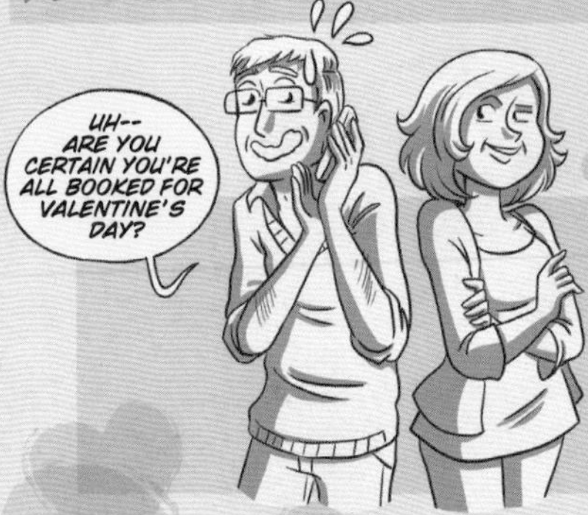
UH-- ARE YOU CERTAIN YOU'RE ALL BOOKED FOR VALENTINE'S DAY?

5 You imagine the most successful romantic dinner as being:

- Passionate, at a little table beside the water, to keep on dreaming.
- Quirky, at a bowling alley restaurant, so you can cap it off with a wild game.
- Connected, at the latest hotspot where you can be seen and admired.

Answers

You mostly have :

Celebrating Love one single day out of the year? For you, that's very little! You prefer making your loved ones happy on a daily basis. You're also capable of feats of originality in organizing unforgettable moments with the people you love. So, a big party as a group suits you just fine. In your company, a friendly spirit and tons of giggles are on tap for a very successful party!

You mostly have :

A seductress in your soul, prepared for all eccentricities, you continually need to be captivated by the guy accompanying you. The icing on the cake is when you also have the chance to show off, it's heaven! The ideal Valentine's Day could take place in a famous luxurious palace, therefore, under the photographers' admiring gaze. Before you expose your other half, make sure they're on the same wavelength as you!

You mostly have :

Romantic and sentimental, you are also a bit mushy. You'd love to spend an evening flirting with your sweetheart. A few days before the big day, you could get yourself into the spirit of things with a lovely romance novel, while dreaming of that unique moment! Far from the brouhaha of restaurants and curious eyes, you'd imagine a dinner by candlelight, with just the two of you. Even so, be careful not to put too much pressure on yourself!

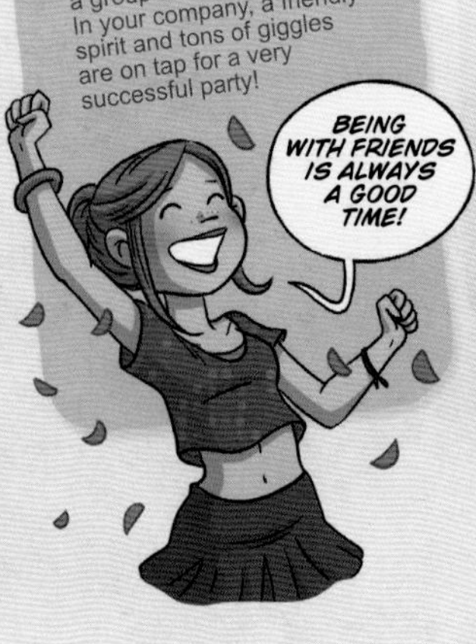
BEING WITH FRIENDS IS ALWAYS A GOOD TIME!

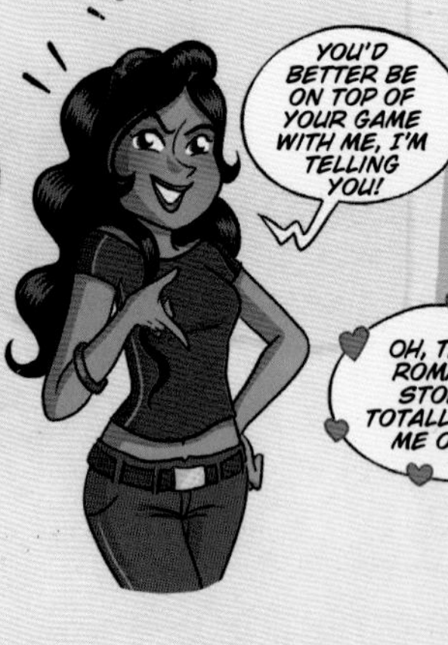
YOU'D BETTER BE ON TOP OF YOUR GAME WITH ME, I'M TELLING YOU!

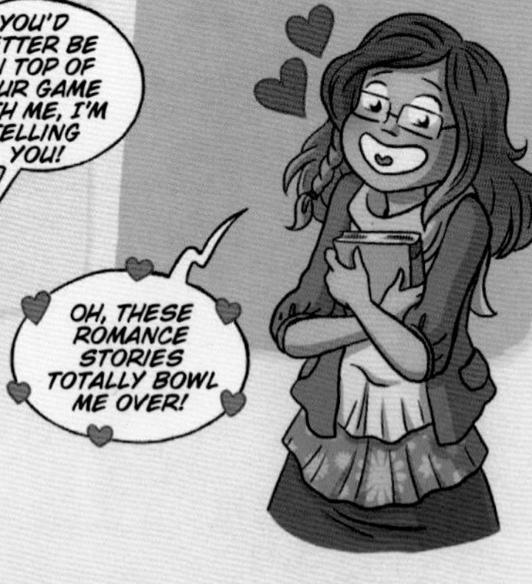
OH, THESE ROMANCE STORIES TOTALLY BOWL ME OVER!

MESSY HOMECOMING

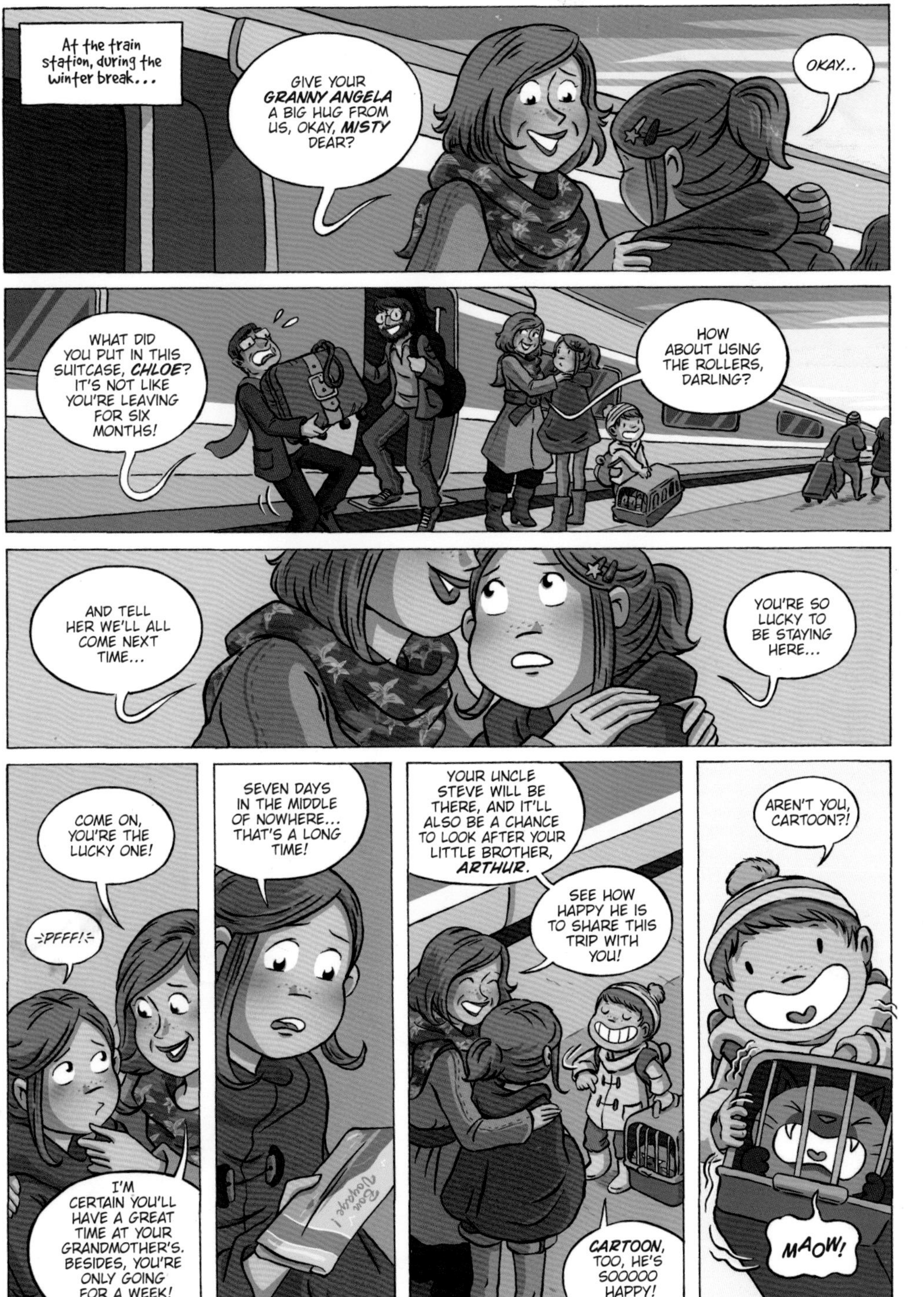
At the train station, during the winter break...
GIVE YOUR GRANNY ANGELA A BIG HUG FROM US, OKAY, MISTY DEAR?
OKAY...
WHAT DID YOU PUT IN THIS SUITCASE, CHLOE? IT'S NOT LIKE YOU'RE LEAVING FOR SIX MONTHS!
HOW ABOUT USING THE ROLLERS, DARLING?
AND TELL HER WE'LL ALL COME NEXT TIME...
YOU'RE SO LUCKY TO BE STAYING HERE...
COME ON, YOU'RE THE LUCKY ONE!
PFFF!
I'M CERTAIN YOU'LL HAVE A GREAT TIME AT YOUR GRANDMOTHER'S. BESIDES, YOU'RE ONLY GOING FOR A WEEK!
SEVEN DAYS IN THE MIDDLE OF NOWHERE... THAT'S A LONG TIME!
YOUR UNCLE STEVE WILL BE THERE, AND IT'LL ALSO BE A CHANCE TO LOOK AFTER YOUR LITTLE BROTHER, ARTHUR.
SEE HOW HAPPY HE IS TO SHARE THIS TRIP WITH YOU!
CARTOON, TOO, HE'S SOOOOO HAPPY!
AREN'T YOU, CARTOON?!
MAOW!

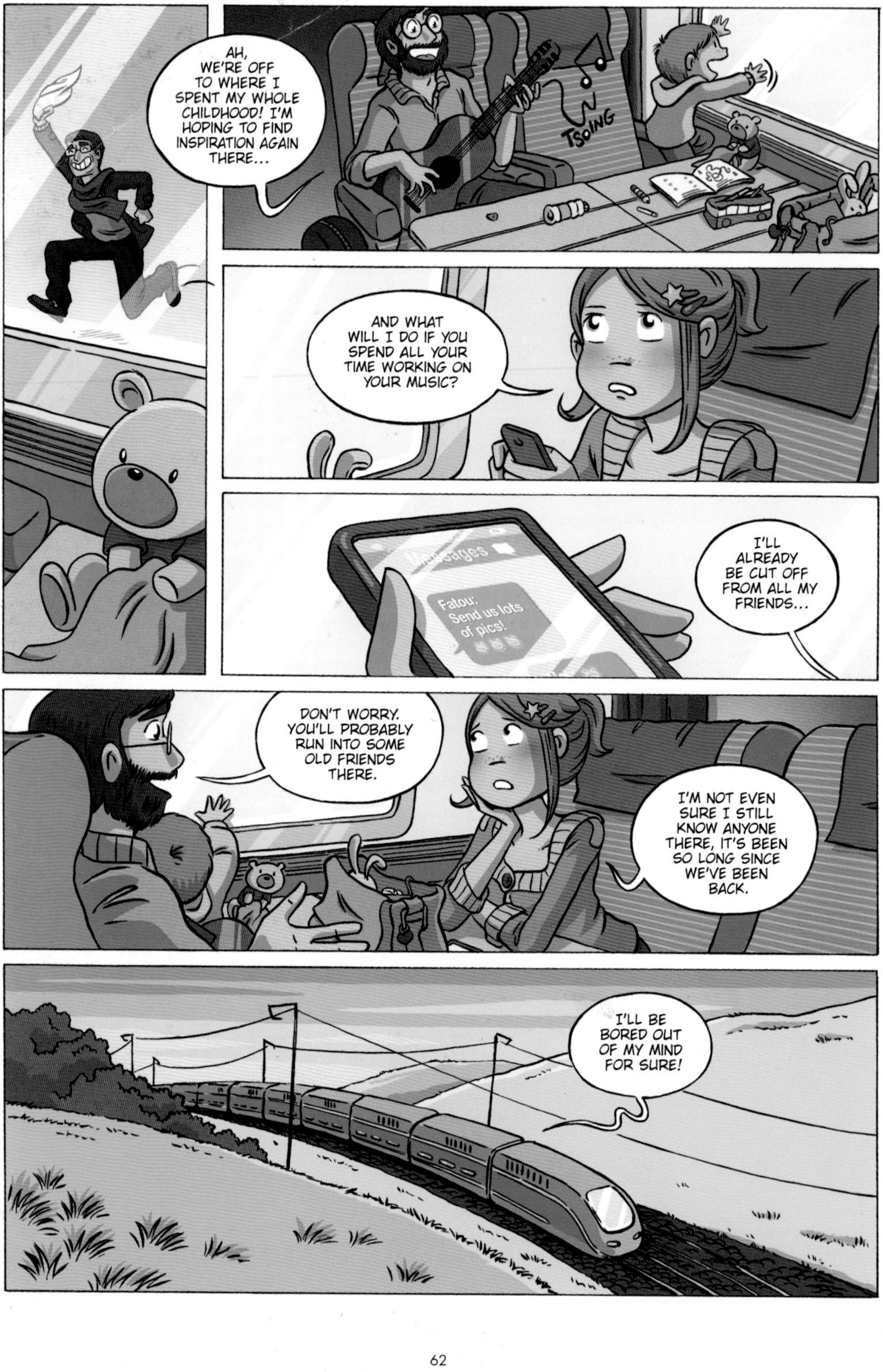
AH, WE'RE OFF TO WHERE I SPENT MY WHOLE CHILDHOOD! I'M HOPING TO FIND INSPIRATION AGAIN THERE...
TSOING
AND WHAT WILL I DO IF YOU SPEND ALL YOUR TIME WORKING ON YOUR MUSIC?
Messages
Fatou: Send us lots of pics!
I'LL ALREADY BE CUT OFF FROM ALL MY FRIENDS...
DON'T WORRY. YOU'LL PROBABLY RUN INTO SOME OLD FRIENDS THERE.
I'M NOT EVEN SURE I STILL KNOW ANYONE THERE, IT'S BEEN SO LONG SINCE WE'VE BEEN BACK.
I'LL BE BORED OUT OF MY MIND FOR SURE!

Remembering

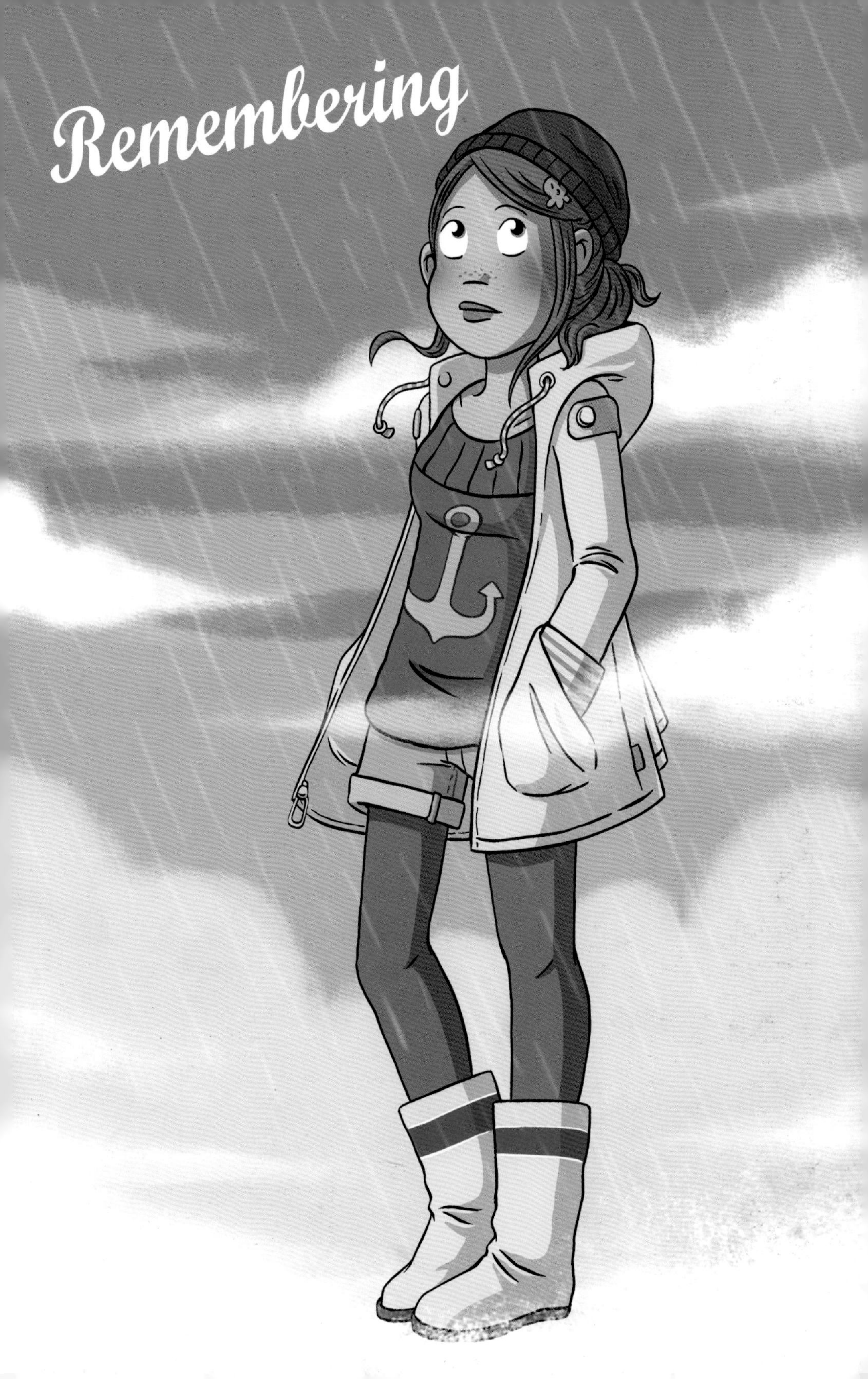

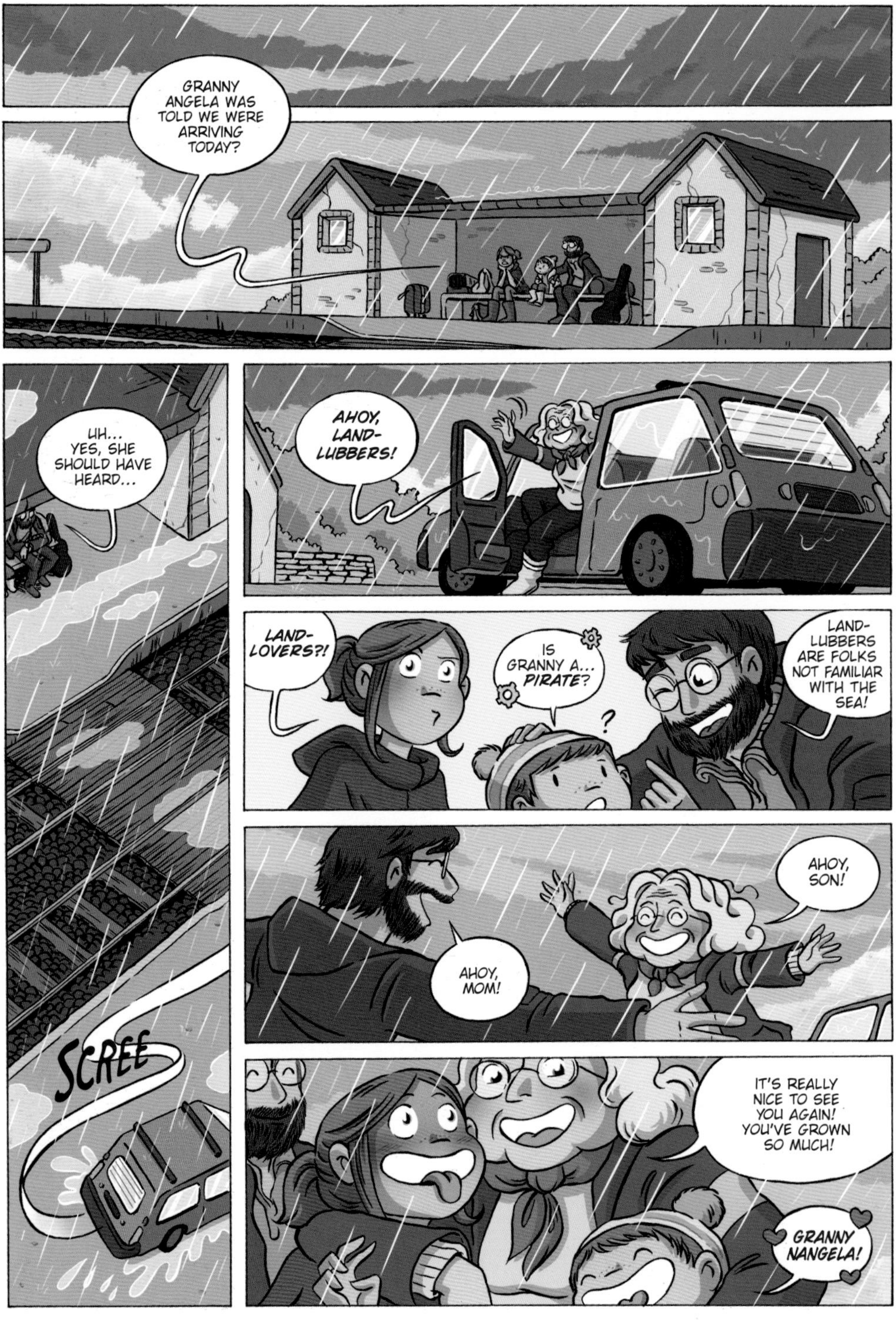
GRANNY ANGELA WAS TOLD WE WERE ARRIVING TODAY?
UH... YES, SHE SHOULD HAVE HEARD...
SCREE
AHOY, LAND-LUBBERS!
LAND-LOVERS?!
IS GRANNY A... PIRATE?
?
LAND-LUBBERS ARE FOLKS NOT FAMILIAR WITH THE SEA!
AHOY, SON!
AHOY, MOM!
IT'S REALLY NICE TO SEE YOU AGAIN! YOU'VE GROWN SO MUCH!
GRANNY NANGELA!

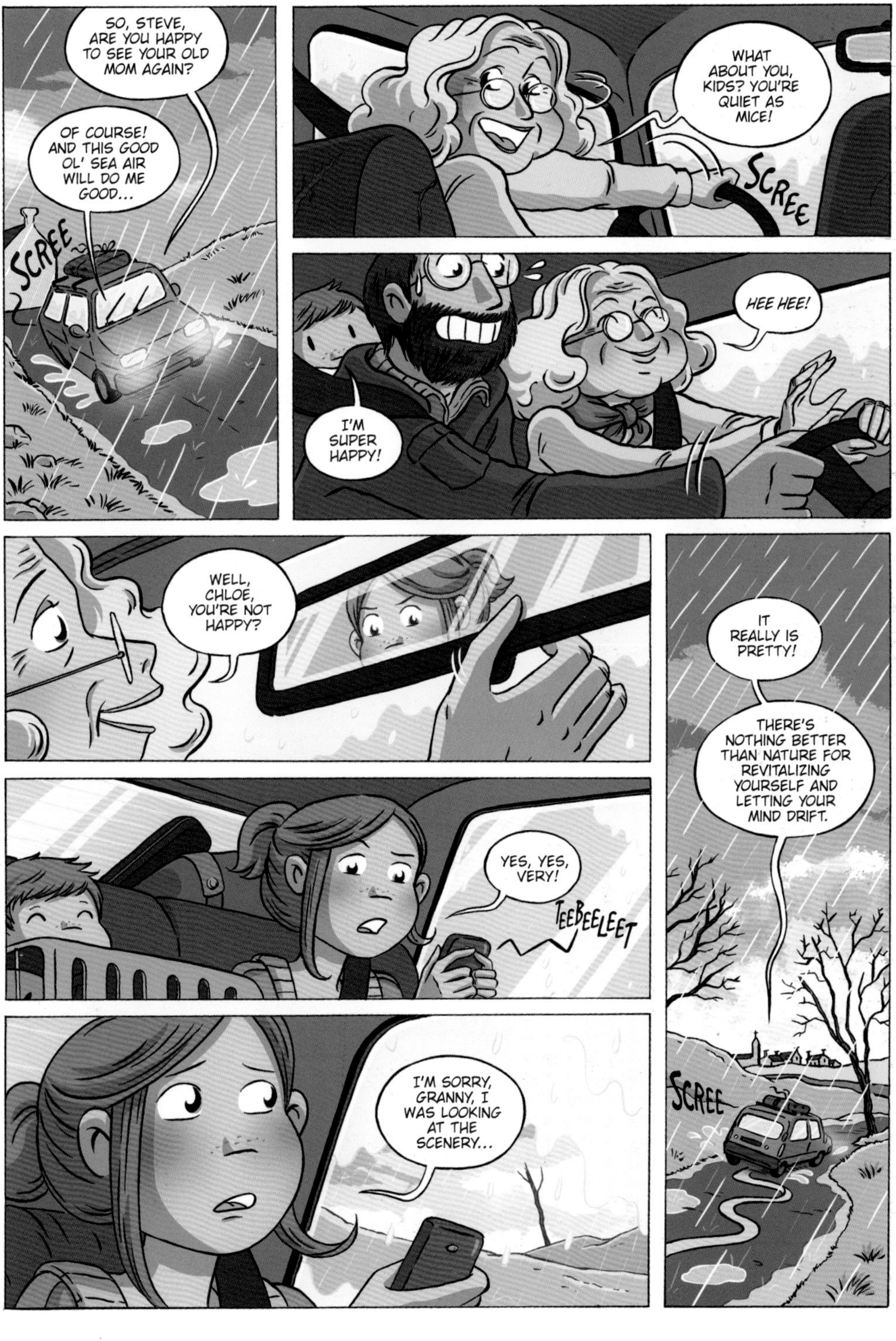
SO, STEVE, ARE YOU HAPPY TO SEE YOUR OLD MOM AGAIN?
OF COURSE! AND THIS GOOD OL' SEA AIR WILL DO ME GOOD...
SCREE
WHAT ABOUT YOU, KIDS? YOU'RE QUIET AS MICE!
SCREE
HEE HEE!
I'M SUPER HAPPY!
WELL, CHLOE, YOU'RE NOT HAPPY?
YES, YES, VERY!
TEEBEELEET
I'M SORRY, GRANNY, I WAS LOOKING AT THE SCENERY...
IT REALLY IS PRETTY!
THERE'S NOTHING BETTER THAN NATURE FOR REVITALIZING YOURSELF AND LETTING YOUR MIND DRIFT.
SCREE

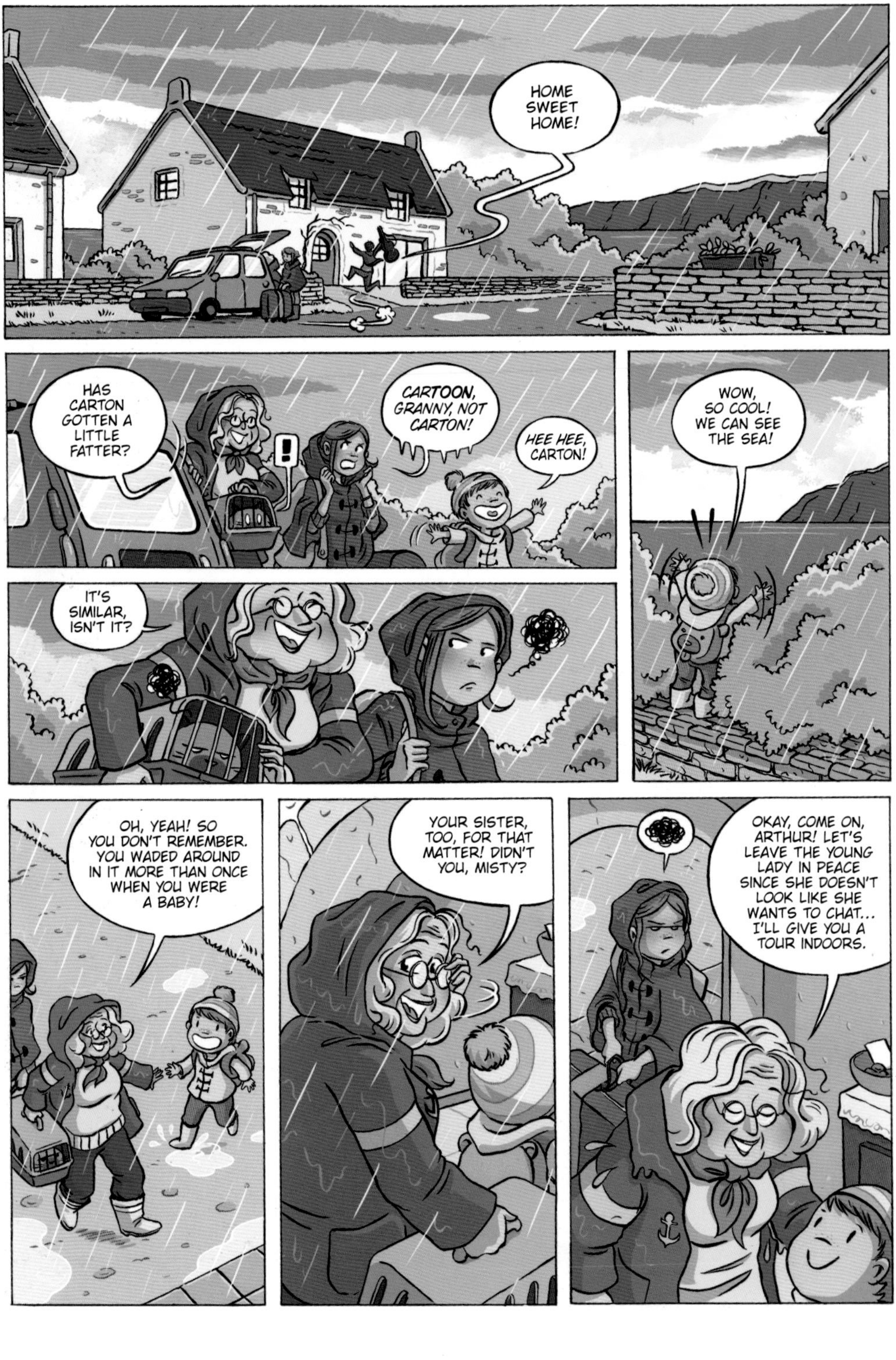
HOME SWEET HOME!
HAS CARTON GOTTEN A LITTLE FATTER?
!
CARTOON, GRANNY, NOT CARTON!
HEE HEE, CARTON!
WOW, SO COOL! WE CAN SEE THE SEA!
IT'S SIMILAR, ISN'T IT?
OH, YEAH! SO YOU DON'T REMEMBER. YOU WADED AROUND IN IT MORE THAN ONCE WHEN YOU WERE A BABY!
YOUR SISTER, TOO, FOR THAT MATTER! DIDN'T YOU, MISTY?
OKAY, COME ON, ARTHUR! LET'S LEAVE THE YOUNG LADY IN PEACE SINCE SHE DOESN'T LOOK LIKE SHE WANTS TO CHAT... I'LL GIVE YOU A TOUR INDOORS.

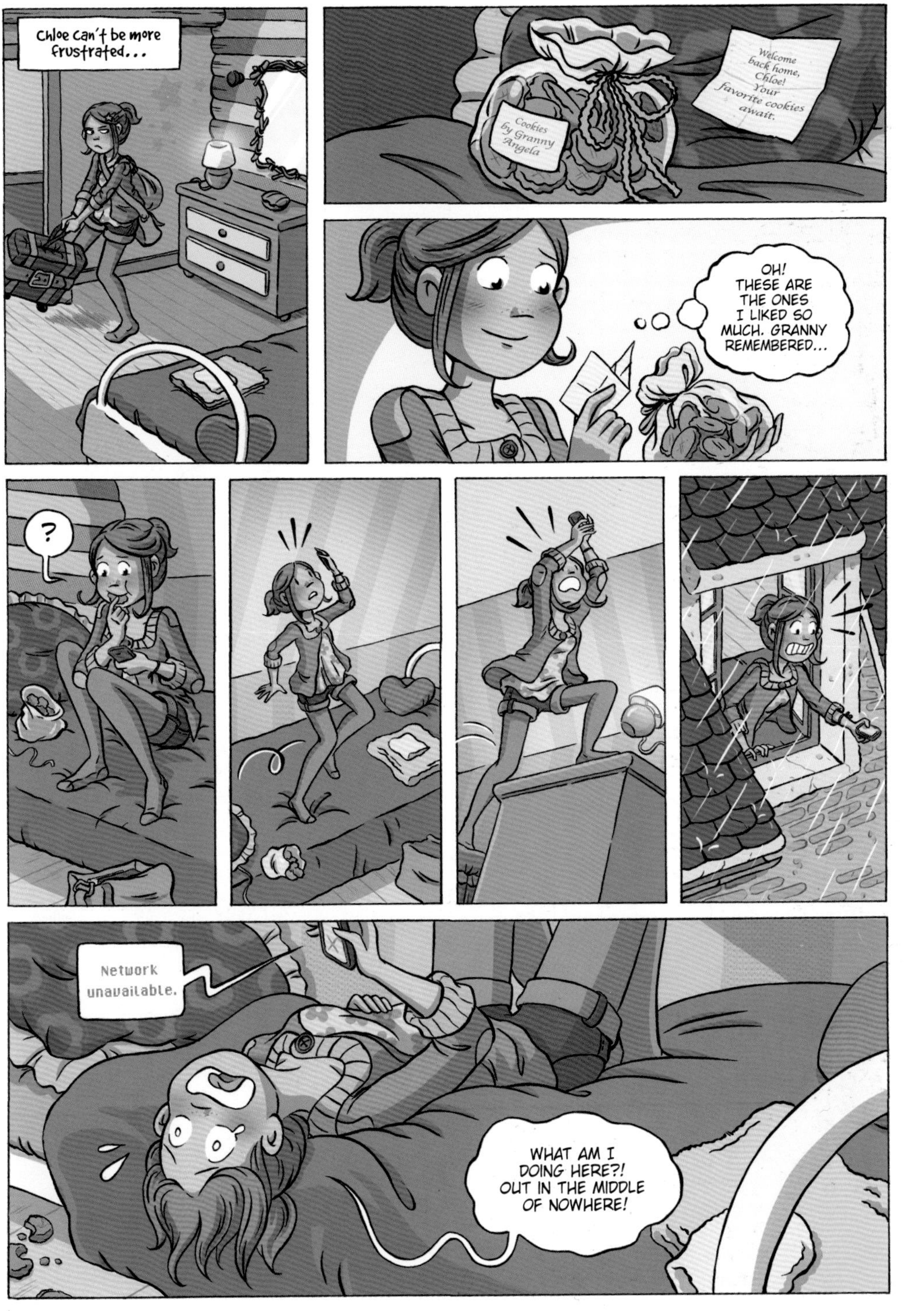
Chloe can't be more frustrated...
Cookies by Granny Angela
Welcome back home, Chloe! Your favorite cookies await.
OH! THESE ARE THE ONES I LIKED SO MUCH. GRANNY REMEMBERED...
?
Network unavailable.
WHAT AM I DOING HERE?! OUT IN THE MIDDLE OF NOWHERE!

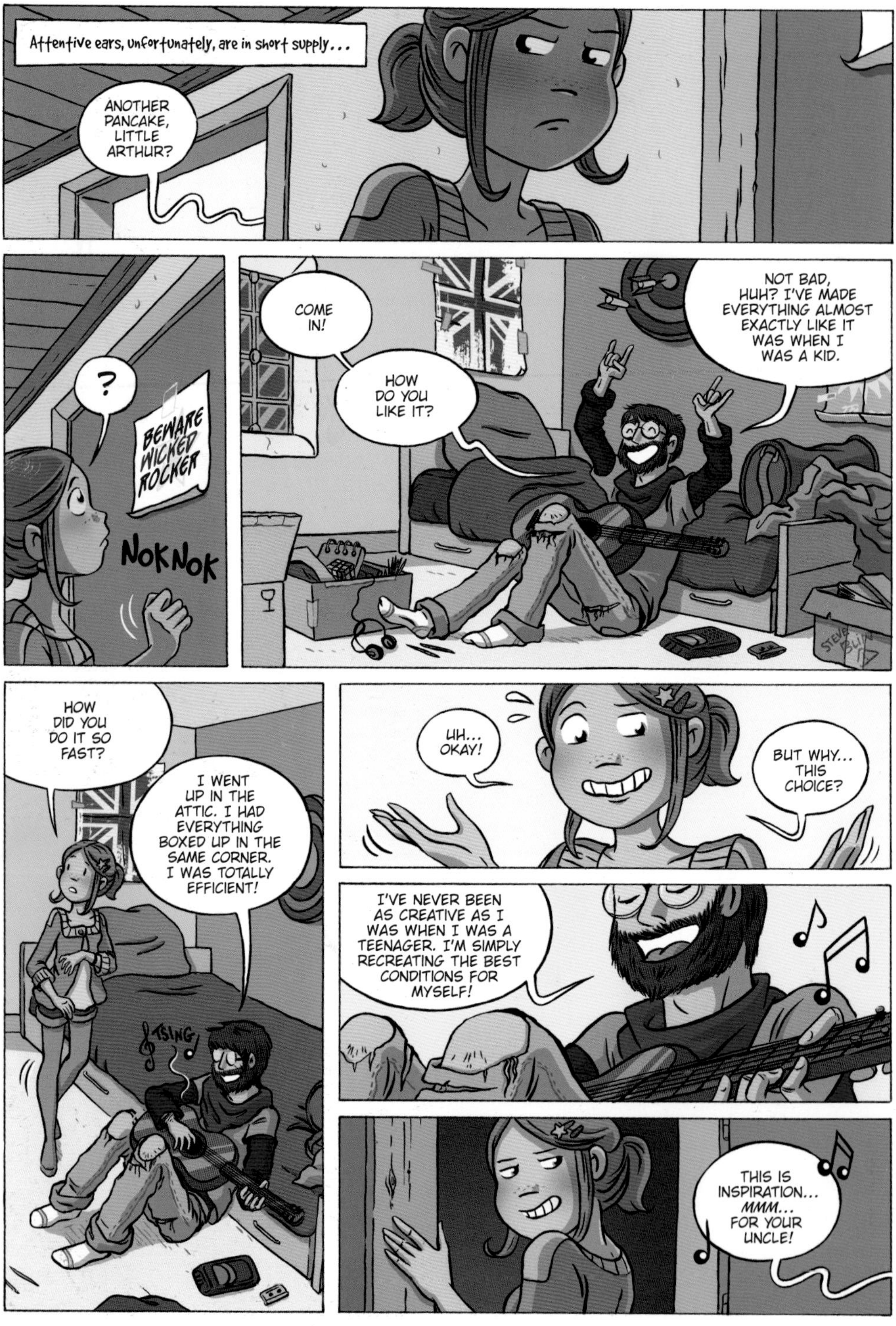
Attentive ears, unfortunately, are in short supply...
ANOTHER PANCAKE, LITTLE ARTHUR?
?
BEWARE WICKED ROCKER
NOKNOK
COME IN!
HOW DO YOU LIKE IT?
NOT BAD, HUH? I'VE MADE EVERYTHING ALMOST EXACTLY LIKE IT WAS WHEN I WAS A KID.
HOW DID YOU DO IT SO FAST?
I WENT UP IN THE ATTIC. I HAD EVERYTHING BOXED UP IN THE SAME CORNER. I WAS TOTALLY EFFICIENT!
TSING
UH... OKAY!
BUT WHY... THIS CHOICE?
I'VE NEVER BEEN AS CREATIVE AS I WAS WHEN I WAS A TEENAGER. I'M SIMPLY RECREATING THE BEST CONDITIONS FOR MYSELF!
THIS IS INSPIRATION... *MMM*... FOR YOUR UNCLE!

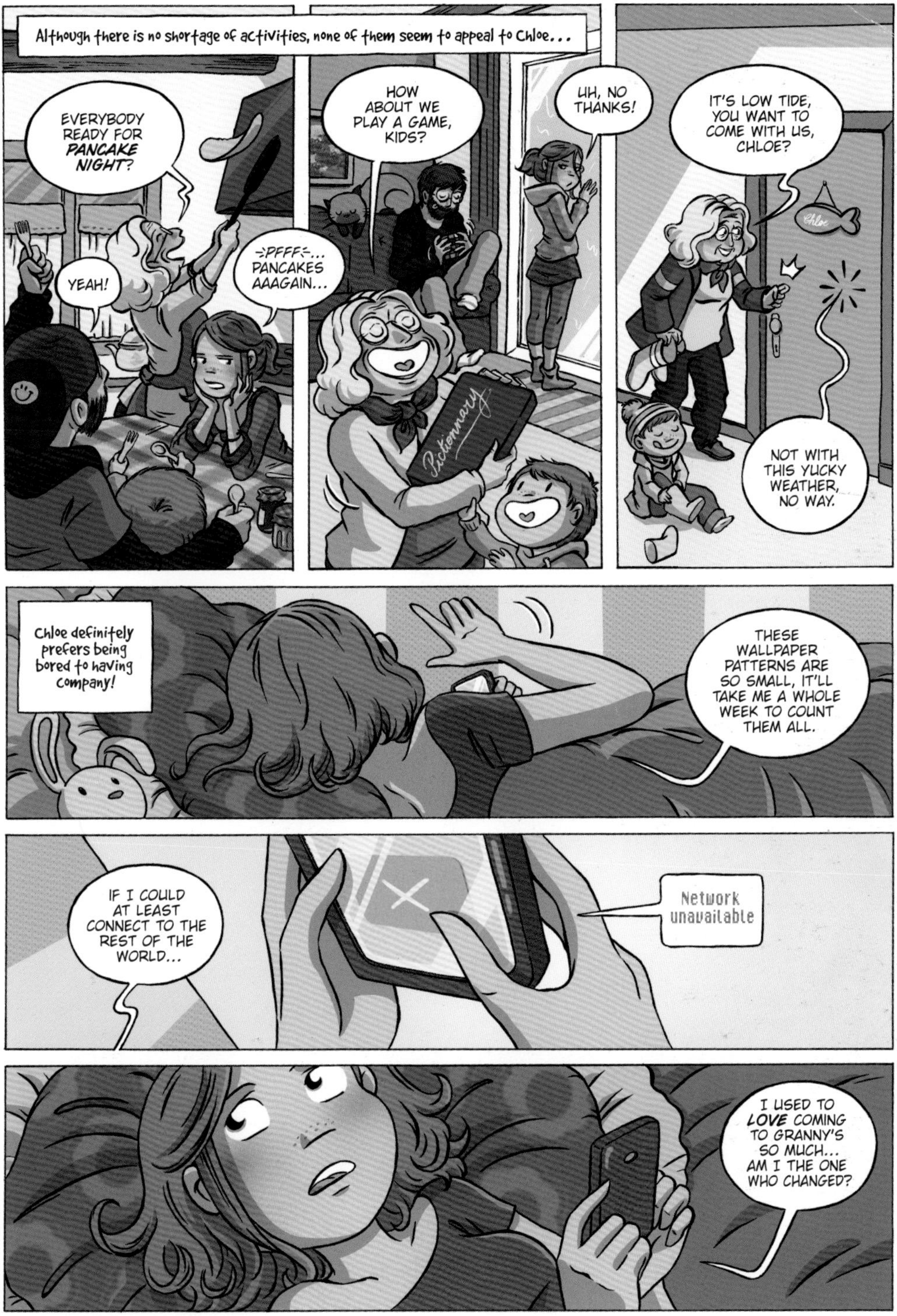
Although there is no shortage of activities, none of them seem to appeal to Chloe...
EVERYBODY READY FOR PANCAKE NIGHT?
YEAH!
≈PFFF≈... PANCAKES AAAGAIN...
HOW ABOUT WE PLAY A GAME, KIDS?
UH, NO THANKS!
Pictionnary
IT'S LOW TIDE, YOU WANT TO COME WITH US, CHLOE?
Chloe
NOT WITH THIS YUCKY WEATHER, NO WAY.
Chloe definitely prefers being bored to having company!
THESE WALLPAPER PATTERNS ARE SO SMALL, IT'LL TAKE ME A WHOLE WEEK TO COUNT THEM ALL.
IF I COULD AT LEAST CONNECT TO THE REST OF THE WORLD...
Network unavailable
I USED TO LOVE COMING TO GRANNY'S SO MUCH... AM I THE ONE WHO CHANGED?

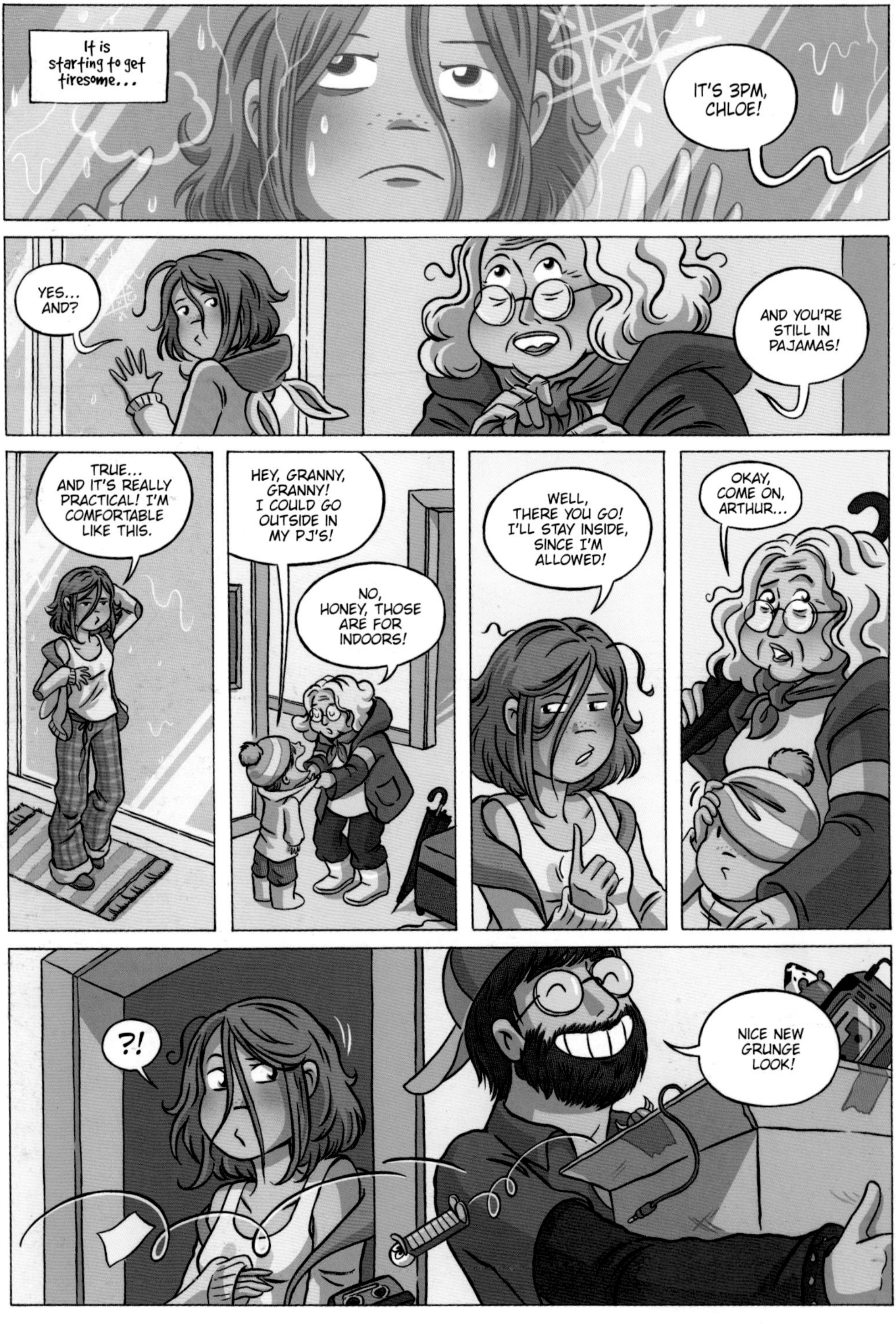
It is starting to get tiresome...
IT'S 3PM, CHLOE!
YES... AND?
AND YOU'RE STILL IN PAJAMAS!
TRUE... AND IT'S REALLY PRACTICAL! I'M COMFORTABLE LIKE THIS.
HEY, GRANNY, GRANNY! I COULD GO OUTSIDE IN MY PJ'S!
NO, HONEY, THOSE ARE FOR INDOORS!
WELL, THERE YOU GO! I'LL STAY INSIDE, SINCE I'M ALLOWED!
OKAY, COME ON, ARTHUR...
?!
NICE NEW GRUNGE LOOK!

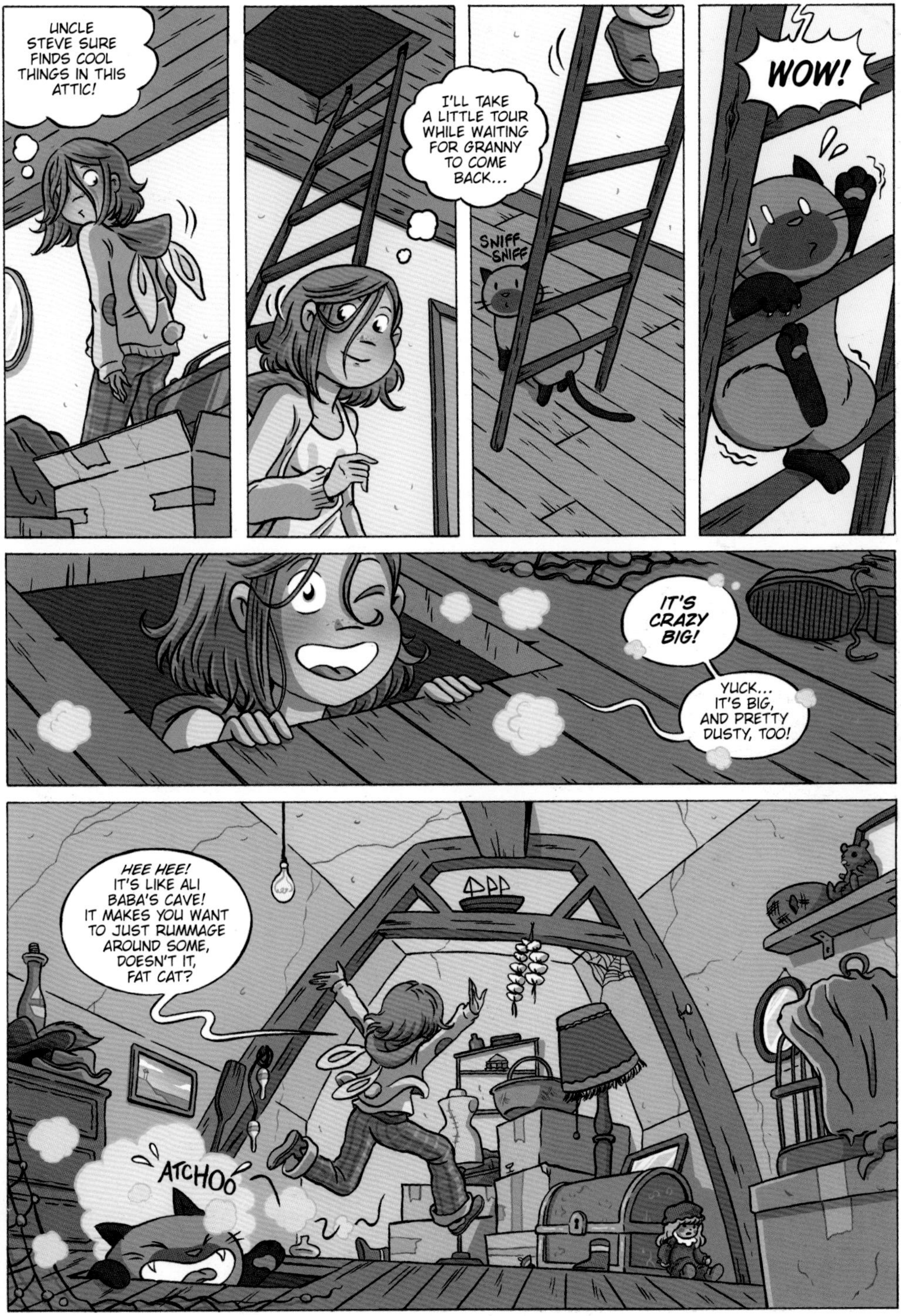
UNCLE STEVE SURE FINDS COOL THINGS IN THIS ATTIC!
I'LL TAKE A LITTLE TOUR WHILE WAITING FOR GRANNY TO COME BACK...
SNIFF SNIFF
WOW!
IT'S CRAZY BIG!
YUCK... IT'S BIG, AND PRETTY DUSTY, TOO!
HEE HEE! IT'S LIKE ALI BABA'S CAVE! IT MAKES YOU WANT TO JUST RUMMAGE AROUND SOME, DOESN'T IT, FAT CAT?
ATCHOO

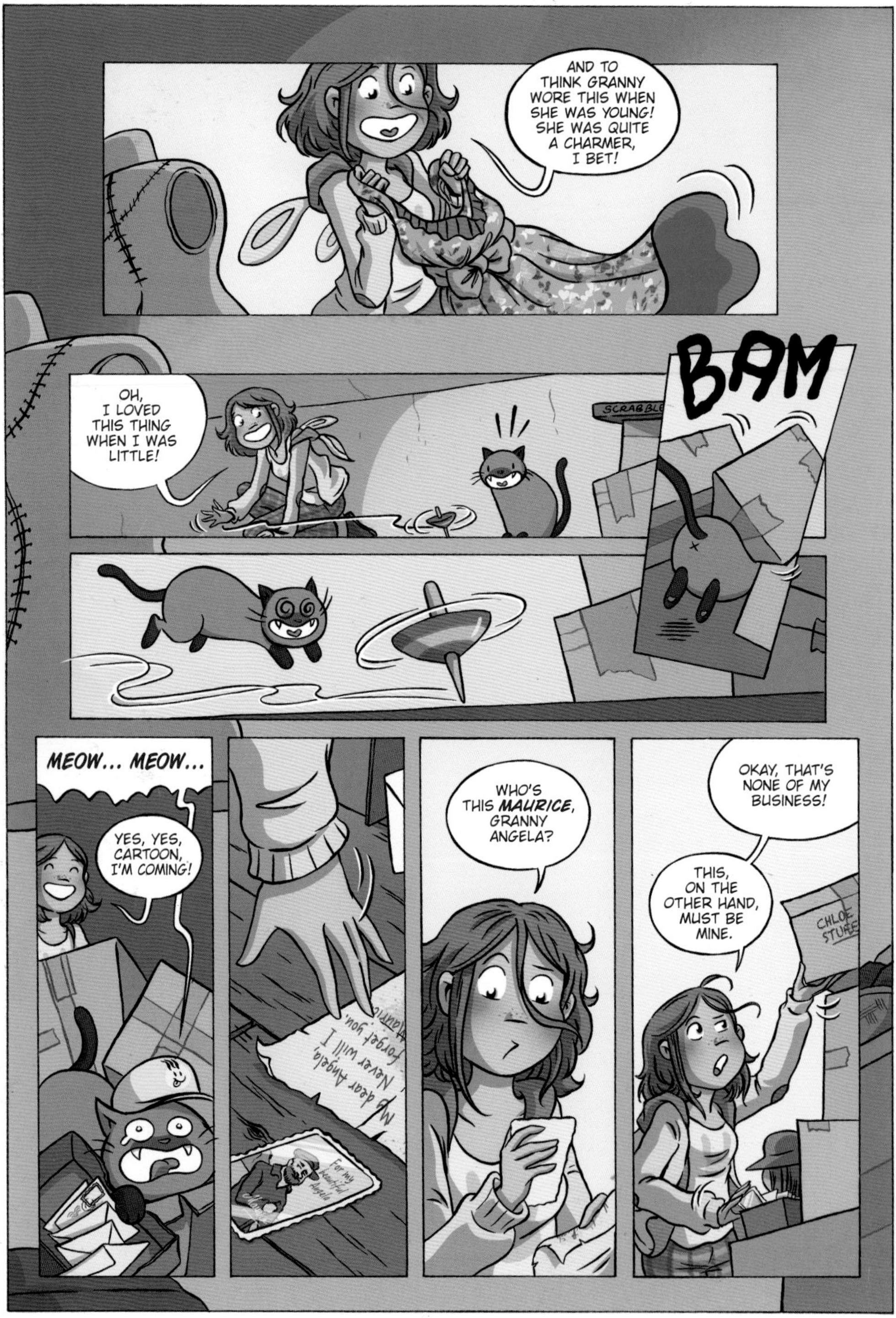
AND TO THINK GRANNY WORE THIS WHEN SHE WAS YOUNG! SHE WAS QUITE A CHARMER, I BET!
OH, I LOVED THIS THING WHEN I WAS LITTLE!
BAM
MEOW... MEOW...
YES, YES, CARTOON, I'M COMING!
My dear Angela, Never will I forget you. Maurice
For my beautiful Angela
WHO'S THIS MAURICE, GRANNY ANGELA?
OKAY, THAT'S NONE OF MY BUSINESS!
THIS, ON THE OTHER HAND, MUST BE MINE.

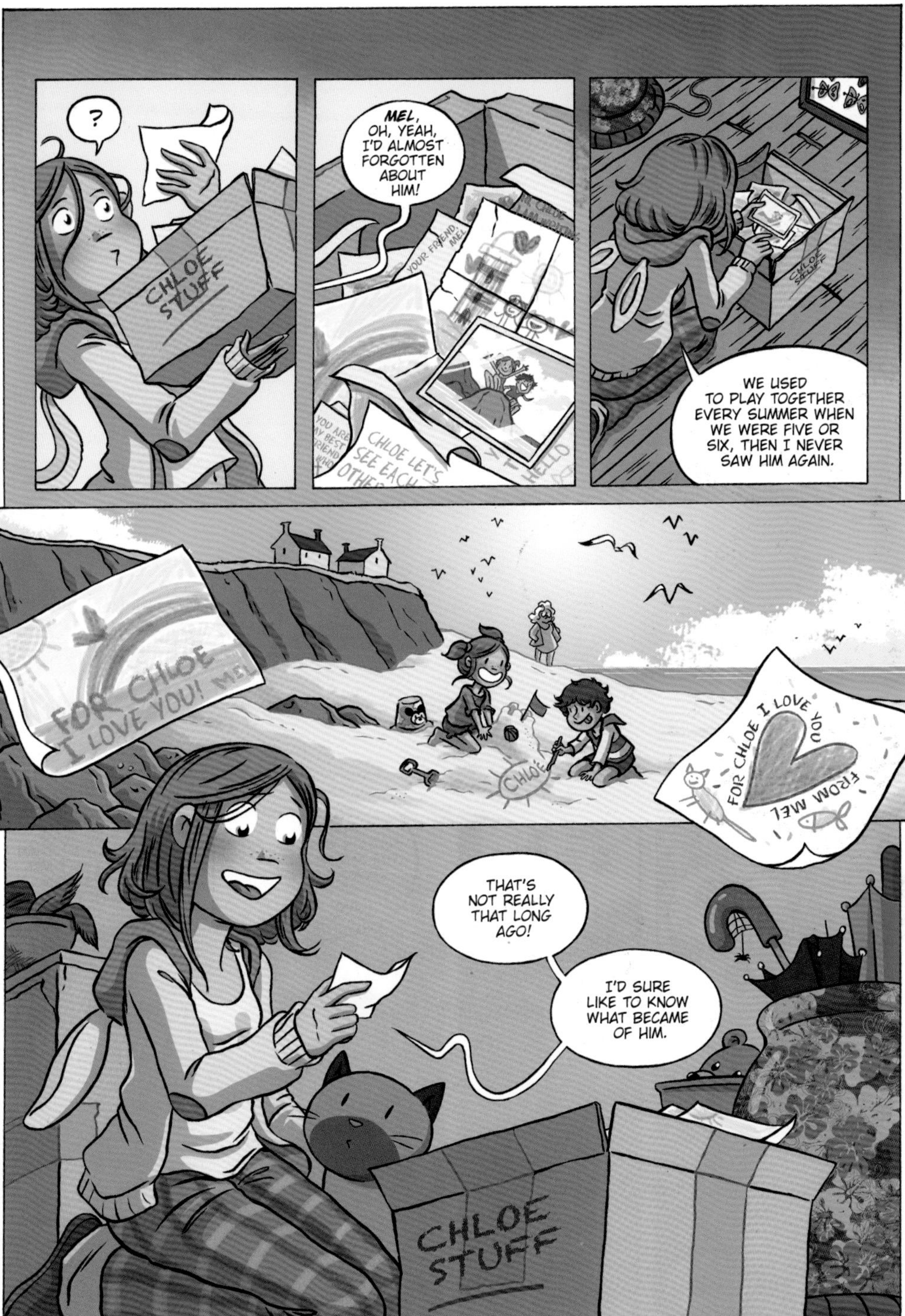
?
CHLOE STUFF
MEL, OH, YEAH, I'D ALMOST FORGOTTEN ABOUT HIM!
YOUR FRIEND, MEL
CHLOE LET'S SEE EACH OTHER
CHLOE STUFF
WE USED TO PLAY TOGETHER EVERY SUMMER WHEN WE WERE FIVE OR SIX, THEN I NEVER SAW HIM AGAIN.
FOR CHLOE I LOVE YOU! MEL
CHLOE
FOR CHLOE I LOVE YOU FROM MEL
THAT'S NOT REALLY THAT LONG AGO!
I'D SURE LIKE TO KNOW WHAT BECAME OF HIM.
CHLOE STUFF

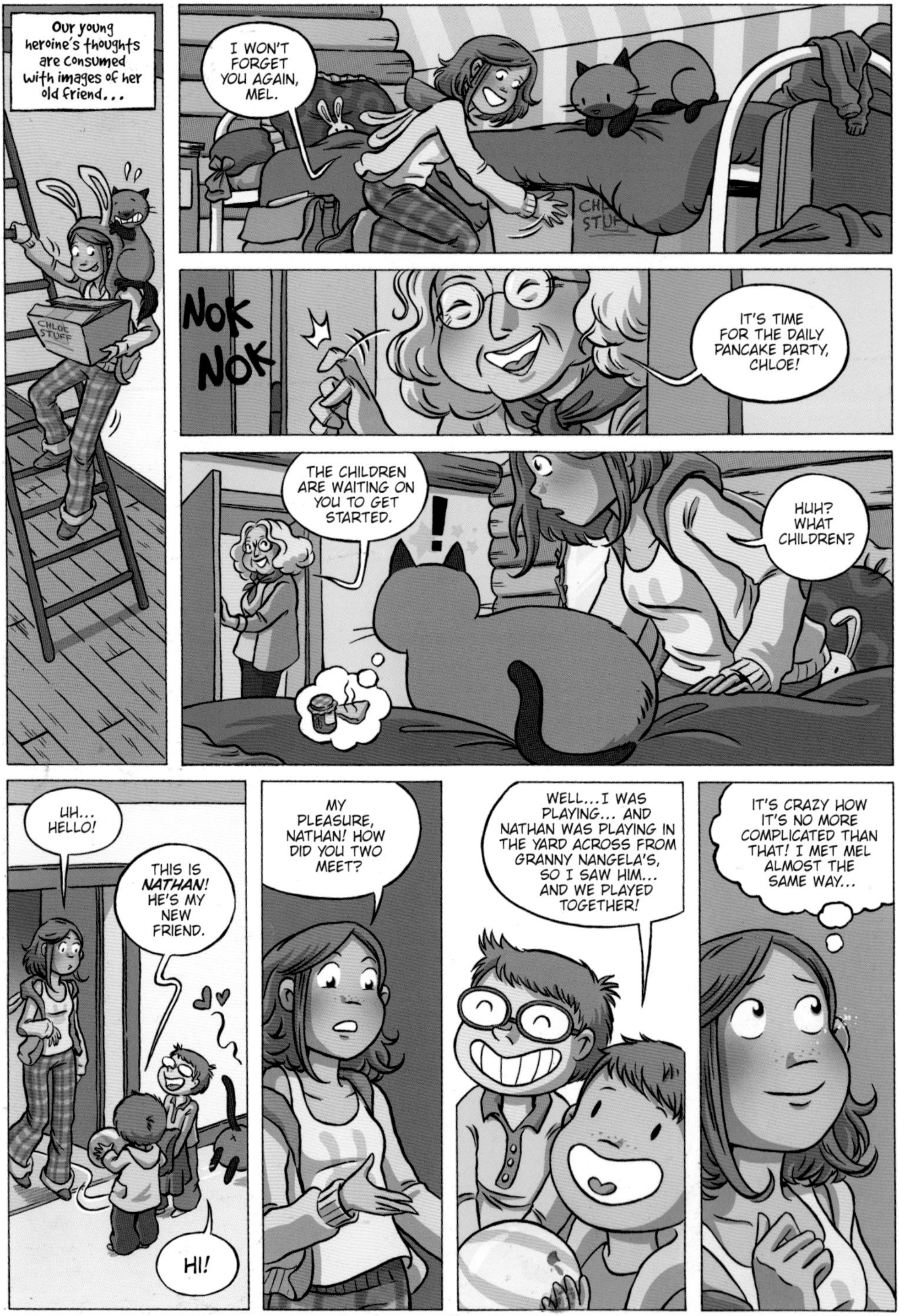

Our young heroine's thoughts are consumed with images of her old friend...
CHLOE STUFF
I WON'T FORGET YOU AGAIN, MEL.
NOK NOK
IT'S TIME FOR THE DAILY PANCAKE PARTY, CHLOE!
THE CHILDREN ARE WAITING ON YOU TO GET STARTED.
!
HUH? WHAT CHILDREN?
UH... HELLO!
THIS IS *NATHAN*! HE'S MY NEW FRIEND.
HI!
MY PLEASURE, NATHAN! HOW DID YOU TWO MEET?
WELL... I WAS PLAYING... AND NATHAN WAS PLAYING IN THE YARD ACROSS FROM GRANNY NANGELA'S, SO I SAW HIM... AND WE PLAYED TOGETHER!
IT'S CRAZY HOW IT'S NO MORE COMPLICATED THAN THAT! I MET MEL ALMOST THE SAME WAY...

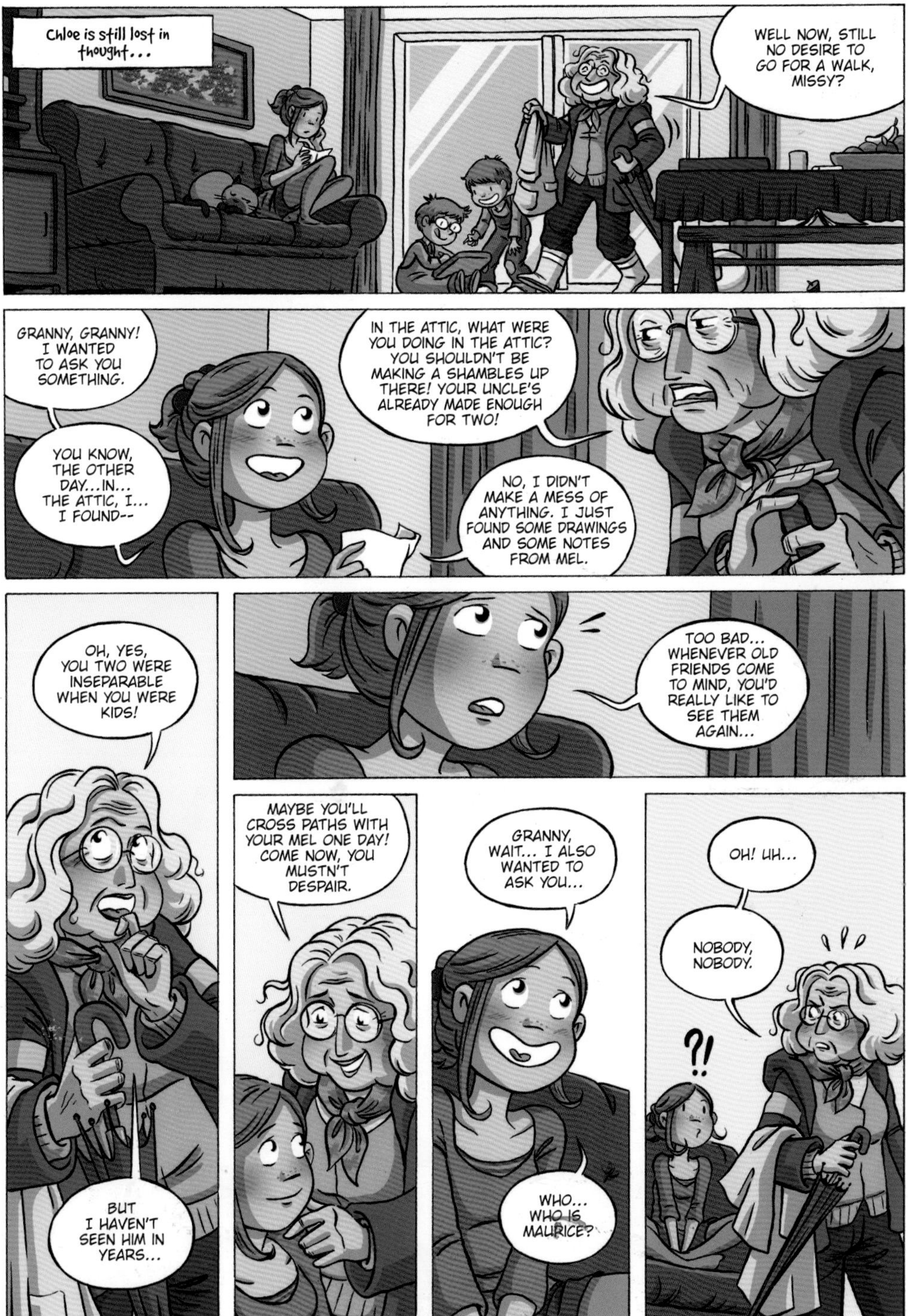

Chloe is still lost in thought...
WELL NOW, STILL NO DESIRE TO GO FOR A WALK, MISSY?
GRANNY, GRANNY! I WANTED TO ASK YOU SOMETHING.
YOU KNOW, THE OTHER DAY...IN... THE ATTIC, I... I FOUND--
IN THE ATTIC, WHAT WERE YOU DOING IN THE ATTIC? YOU SHOULDN'T BE MAKING A SHAMBLES UP THERE! YOUR UNCLE'S ALREADY MADE ENOUGH FOR TWO!
NO, I DIDN'T MAKE A MESS OF ANYTHING. I JUST FOUND SOME DRAWINGS AND SOME NOTES FROM MEL.
OH, YES, YOU TWO WERE INSEPARABLE WHEN YOU WERE KIDS!
BUT I HAVEN'T SEEN HIM IN YEARS...
TOO BAD... WHENEVER OLD FRIENDS COME TO MIND, YOU'D REALLY LIKE TO SEE THEM AGAIN...
MAYBE YOU'LL CROSS PATHS WITH YOUR MEL ONE DAY! COME NOW, YOU MUSTN'T DESPAIR.
GRANNY, WAIT... I ALSO WANTED TO ASK YOU...
WHO... WHO IS MAURICE?
OH! UH...
NOBODY, NOBODY.
?!

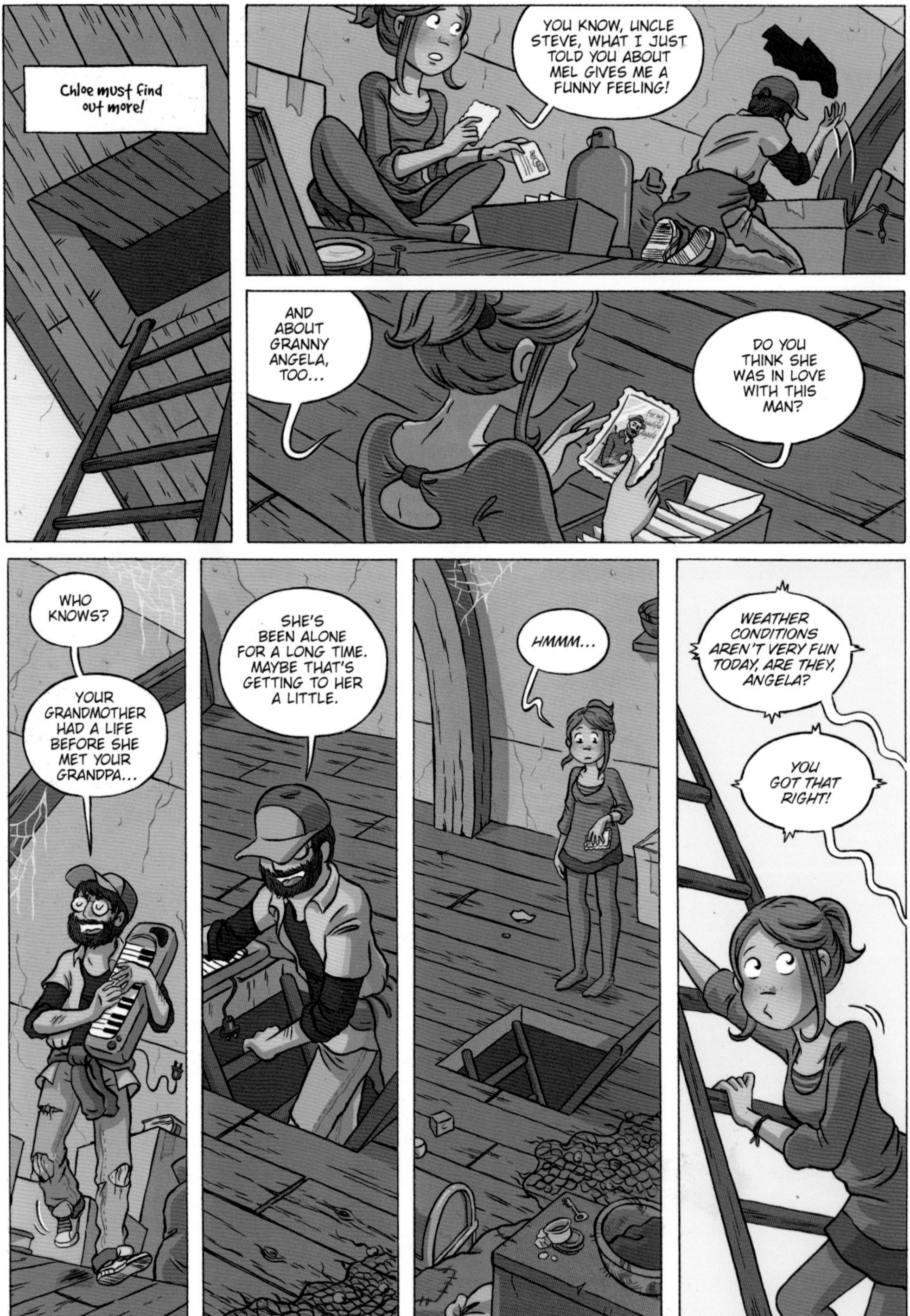
Chloe must find out more!
YOU KNOW, UNCLE STEVE, WHAT I JUST TOLD YOU ABOUT MEL GIVES ME A FUNNY FEELING!
AND ABOUT GRANNY ANGELA, TOO...
DO YOU THINK SHE WAS IN LOVE WITH THIS MAN?
WHO KNOWS?
YOUR GRANDMOTHER HAD A LIFE BEFORE SHE MET YOUR GRANDPA...
SHE'S BEEN ALONE FOR A LONG TIME. MAYBE THAT'S GETTING TO HER A LITTLE.
HMMM...
WEATHER CONDITIONS AREN'T VERY FUN TODAY, ARE THEY, ANGELA?
YOU GOT THAT RIGHT!

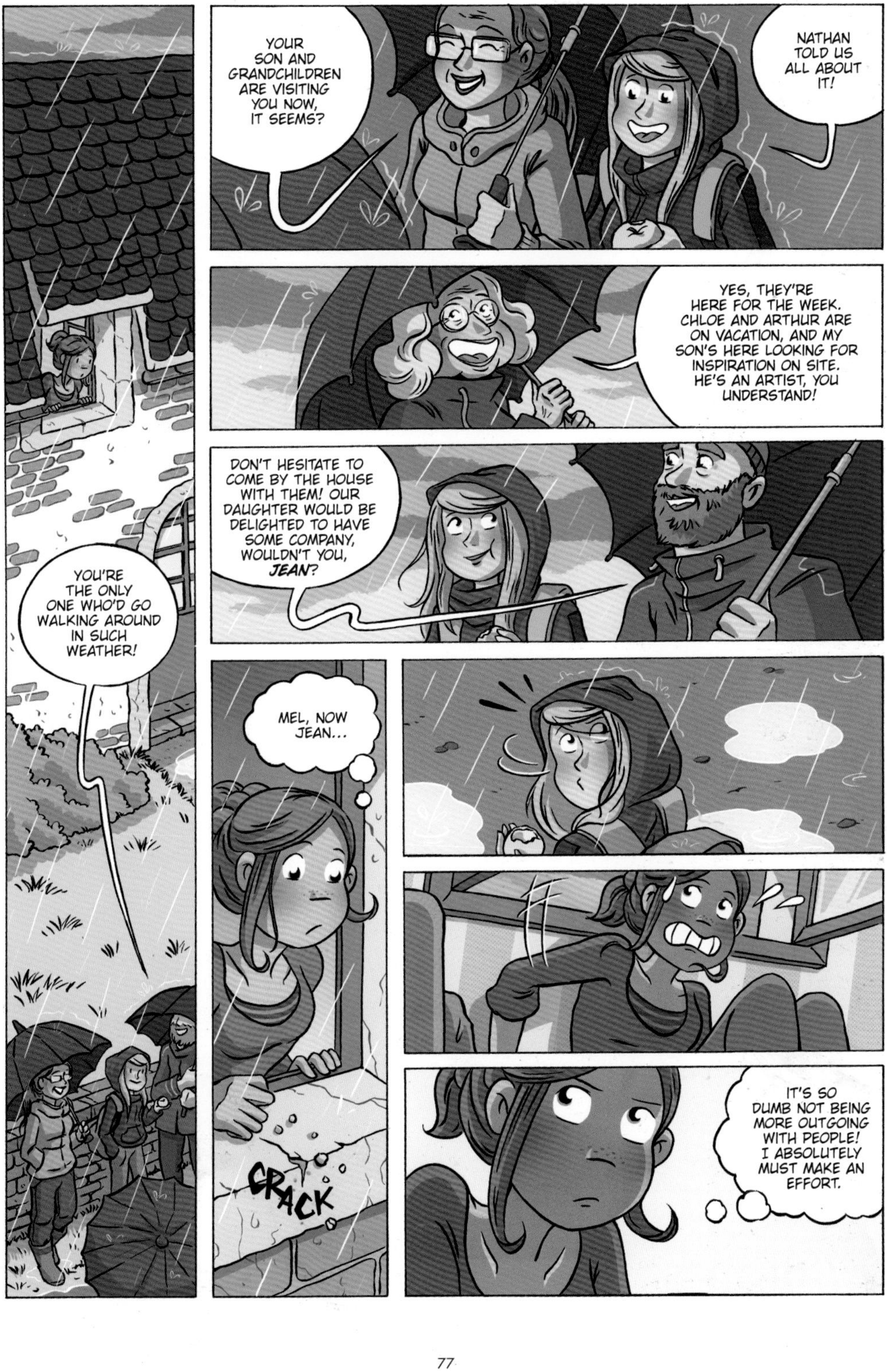
YOUR SON AND GRANDCHILDREN ARE VISITING YOU NOW, IT SEEMS?
NATHAN TOLD US ALL ABOUT IT!
YES, THEY'RE HERE FOR THE WEEK. CHLOE AND ARTHUR ARE ON VACATION, AND MY SON'S HERE LOOKING FOR INSPIRATION ON SITE. HE'S AN ARTIST, YOU UNDERSTAND!
DON'T HESITATE TO COME BY THE HOUSE WITH THEM! OUR DAUGHTER WOULD BE DELIGHTED TO HAVE SOME COMPANY, WOULDN'T YOU, JEAN?
YOU'RE THE ONLY ONE WHO'D GO WALKING AROUND IN SUCH WEATHER!
MEL, NOW JEAN...
CRACK
IT'S SO DUMB NOT BEING MORE OUTGOING WITH PEOPLE! I ABSOLUTELY MUST MAKE AN EFFORT.

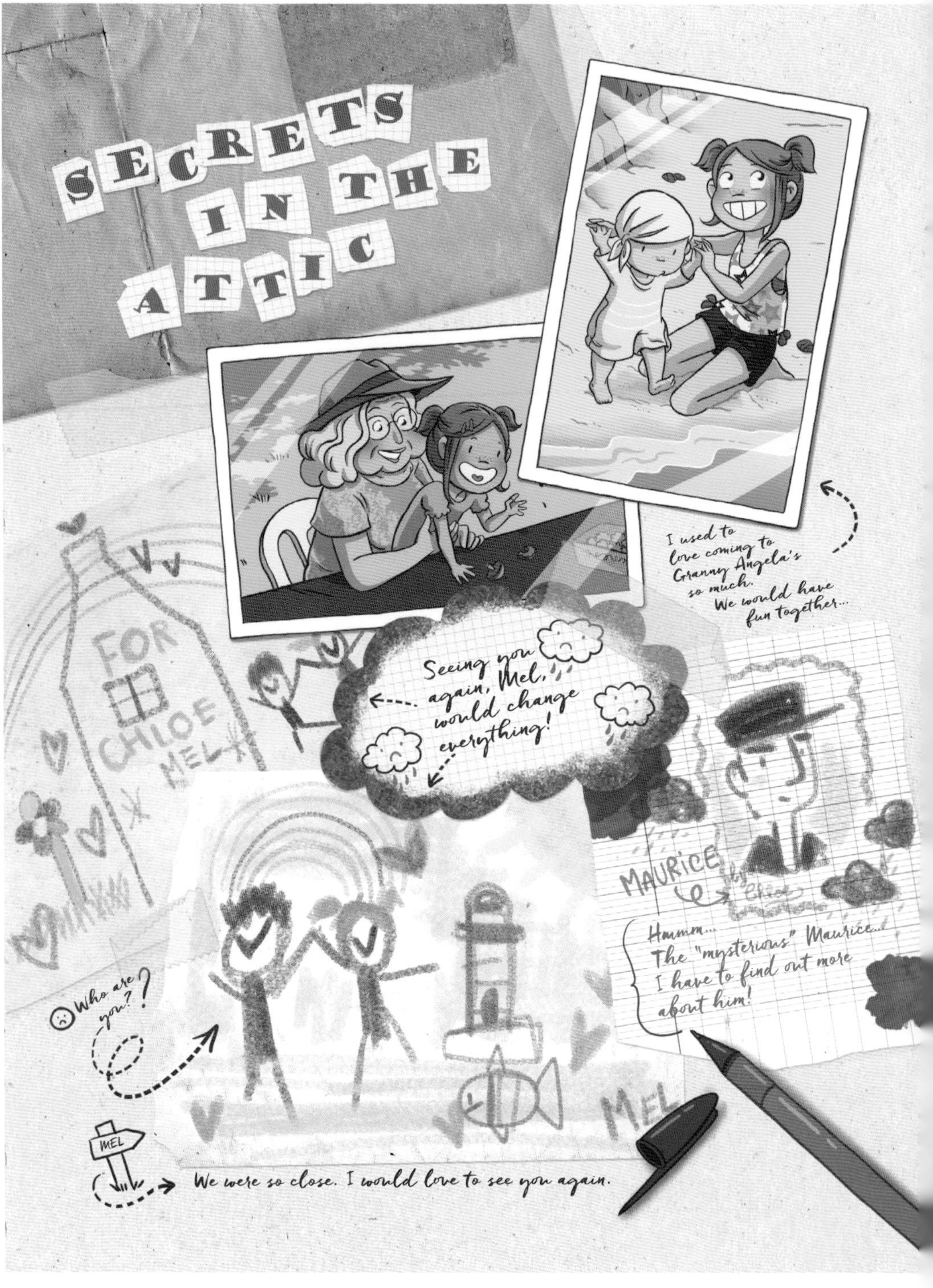
SECRETS IN THE ATTIC
I used to love coming to Granny Angela's so much. We would have fun together...
Seeing you again, Mel, would change everything!
FOR CHLOE
MEL
MAURICE
Hmmm... The "mysterious" Maurice... I have to find out more about him!
Who are you??
MEL
MEL
We were so close. I would love to see you again.

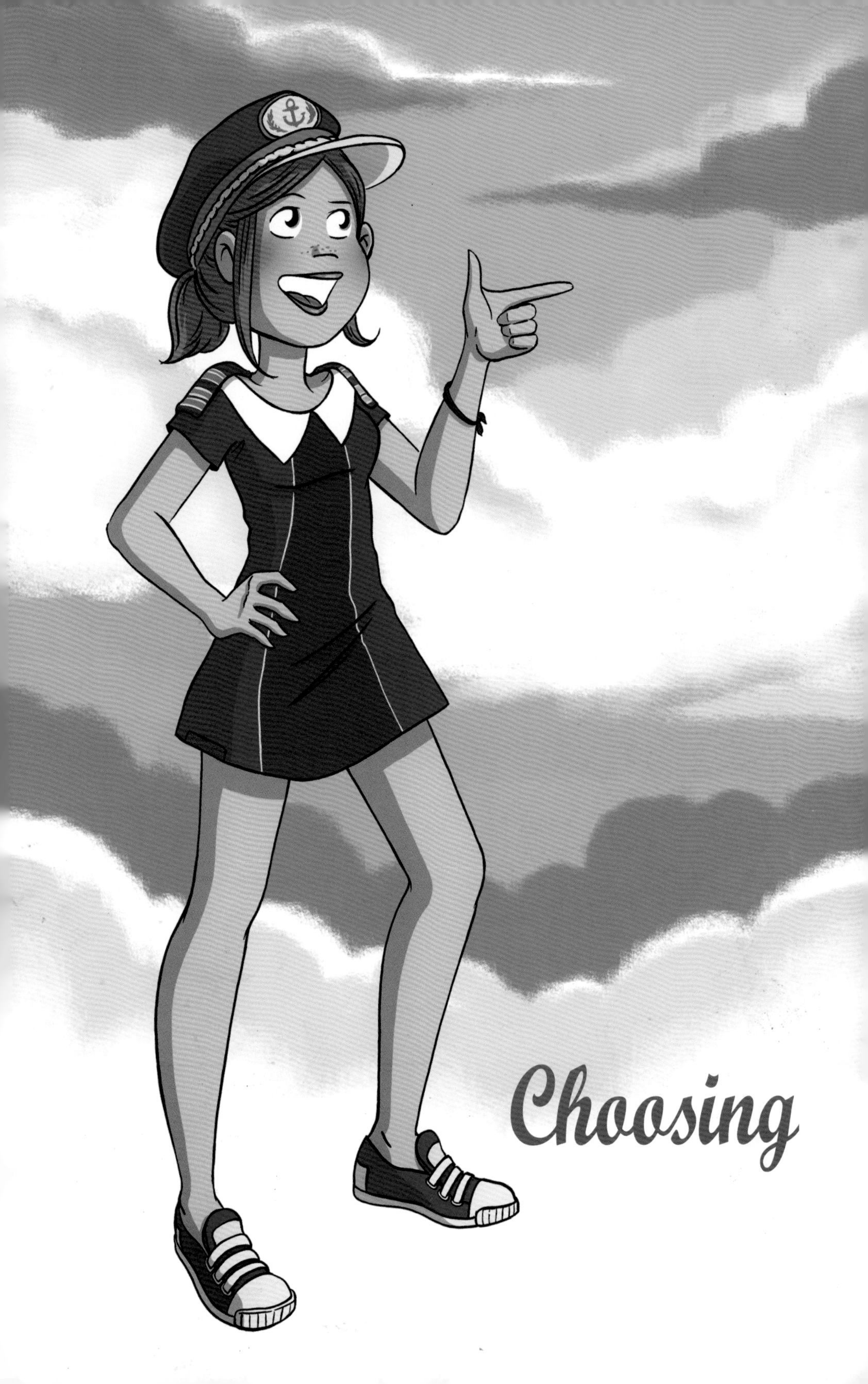

Choosing

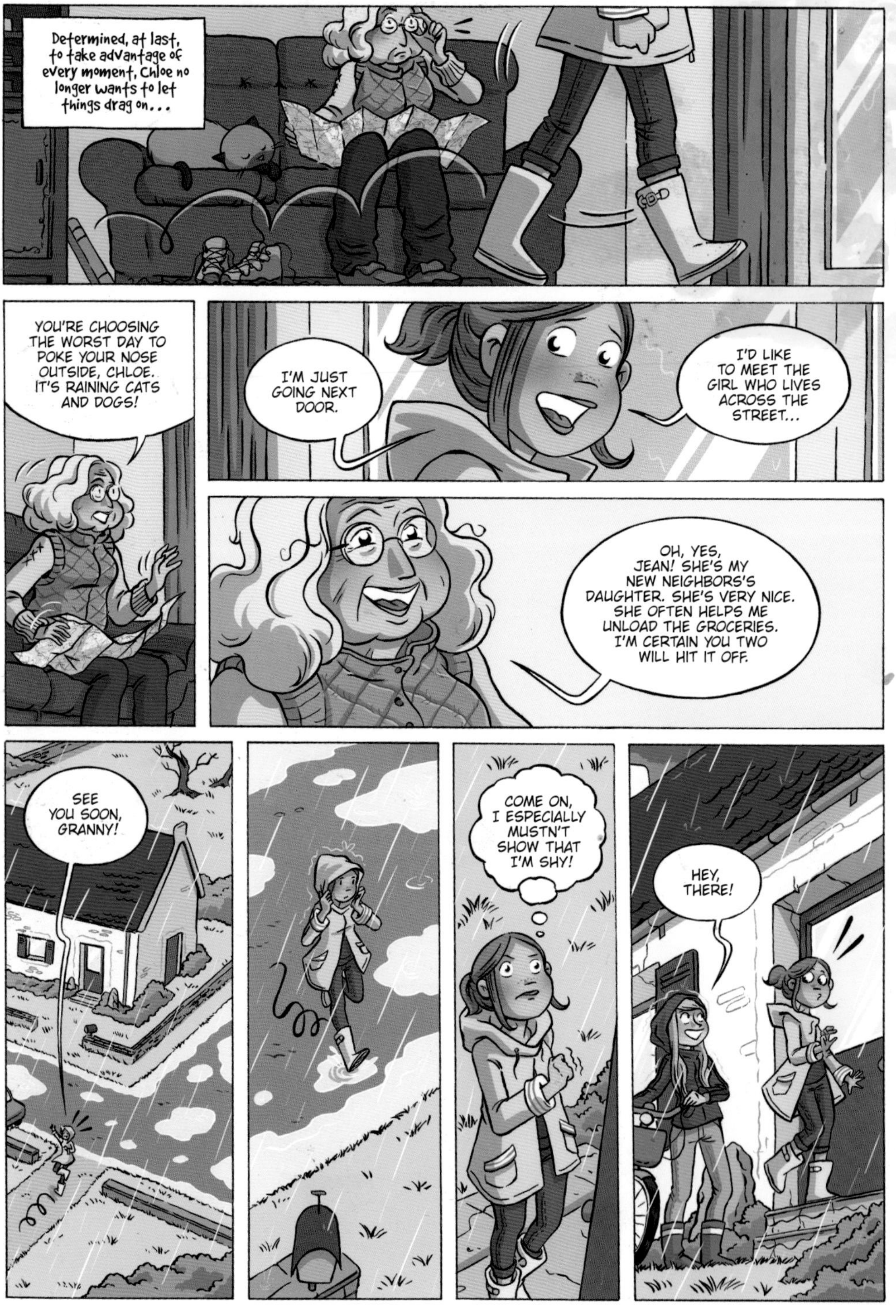
Determined, at last, to take advantage of every moment, Chloe no longer wants to let things drag on...
YOU'RE CHOOSING THE WORST DAY TO POKE YOUR NOSE OUTSIDE, CHLOE. IT'S RAINING CATS AND DOGS!
I'M JUST GOING NEXT DOOR.
I'D LIKE TO MEET THE GIRL WHO LIVES ACROSS THE STREET...
OH, YES, JEAN! SHE'S MY NEW NEIGHBORS'S DAUGHTER. SHE'S VERY NICE. SHE OFTEN HELPS ME UNLOAD THE GROCERIES. I'M CERTAIN YOU TWO WILL HIT IT OFF.
SEE YOU SOON, GRANNY!
COME ON, I ESPECIALLY MUSTN'T SHOW THAT I'M SHY!
HEY, THERE!

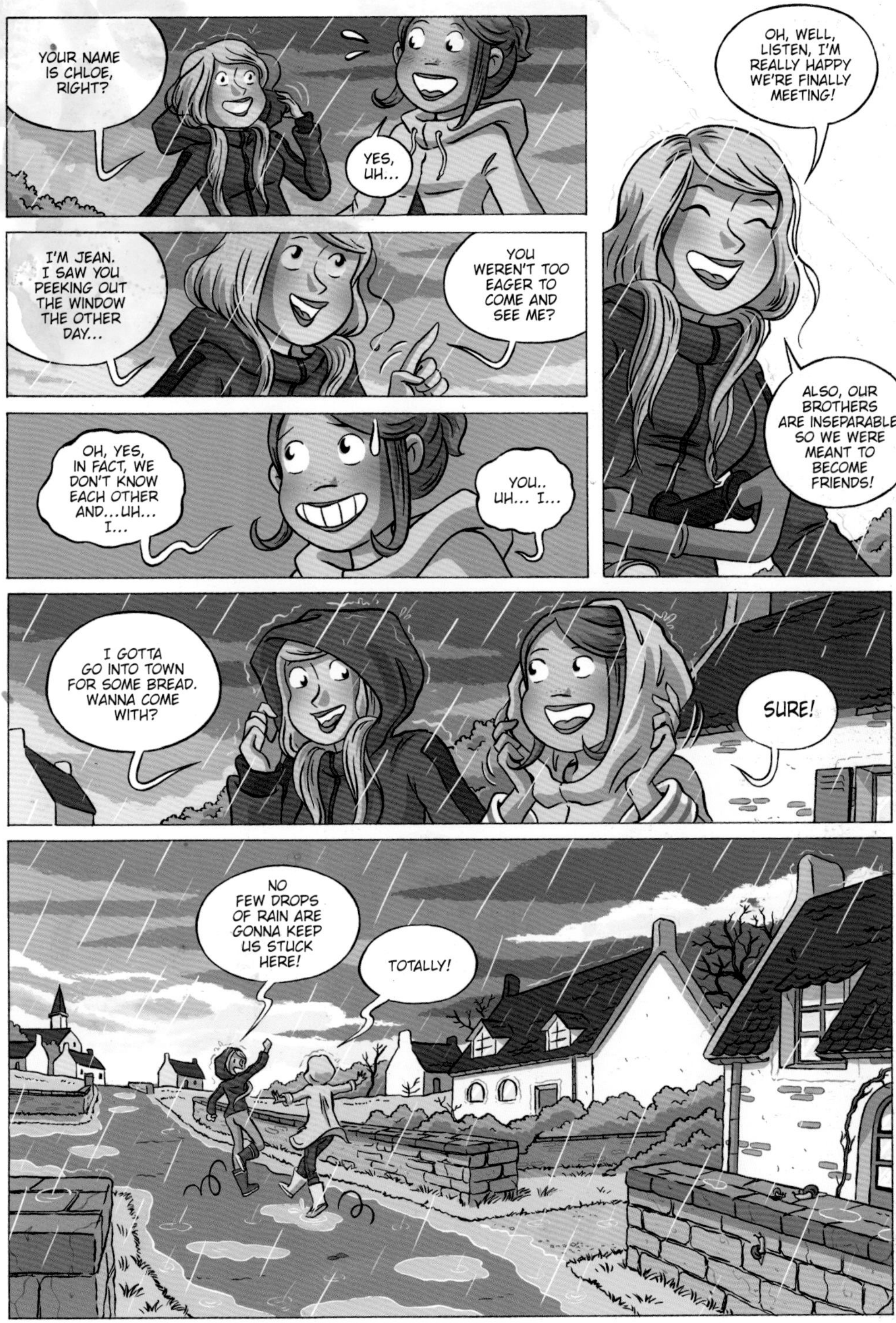

YOUR NAME IS CHLOE, RIGHT?
YES, UH...
OH, WELL, LISTEN, I'M REALLY HAPPY WE'RE FINALLY MEETING!
I'M JEAN. I SAW YOU PEEKING OUT THE WINDOW THE OTHER DAY...
YOU WEREN'T TOO EAGER TO COME AND SEE ME?
OH, YES, IN FACT, WE DON'T KNOW EACH OTHER AND...UH... I...
YOU.. UH... I...
ALSO, OUR BROTHERS ARE INSEPARABLE, SO WE WERE MEANT TO BECOME FRIENDS!
I GOTTA GO INTO TOWN FOR SOME BREAD. WANNA COME WITH?
SURE!
NO FEW DROPS OF RAIN ARE GONNA KEEP US STUCK HERE!
TOTALLY!

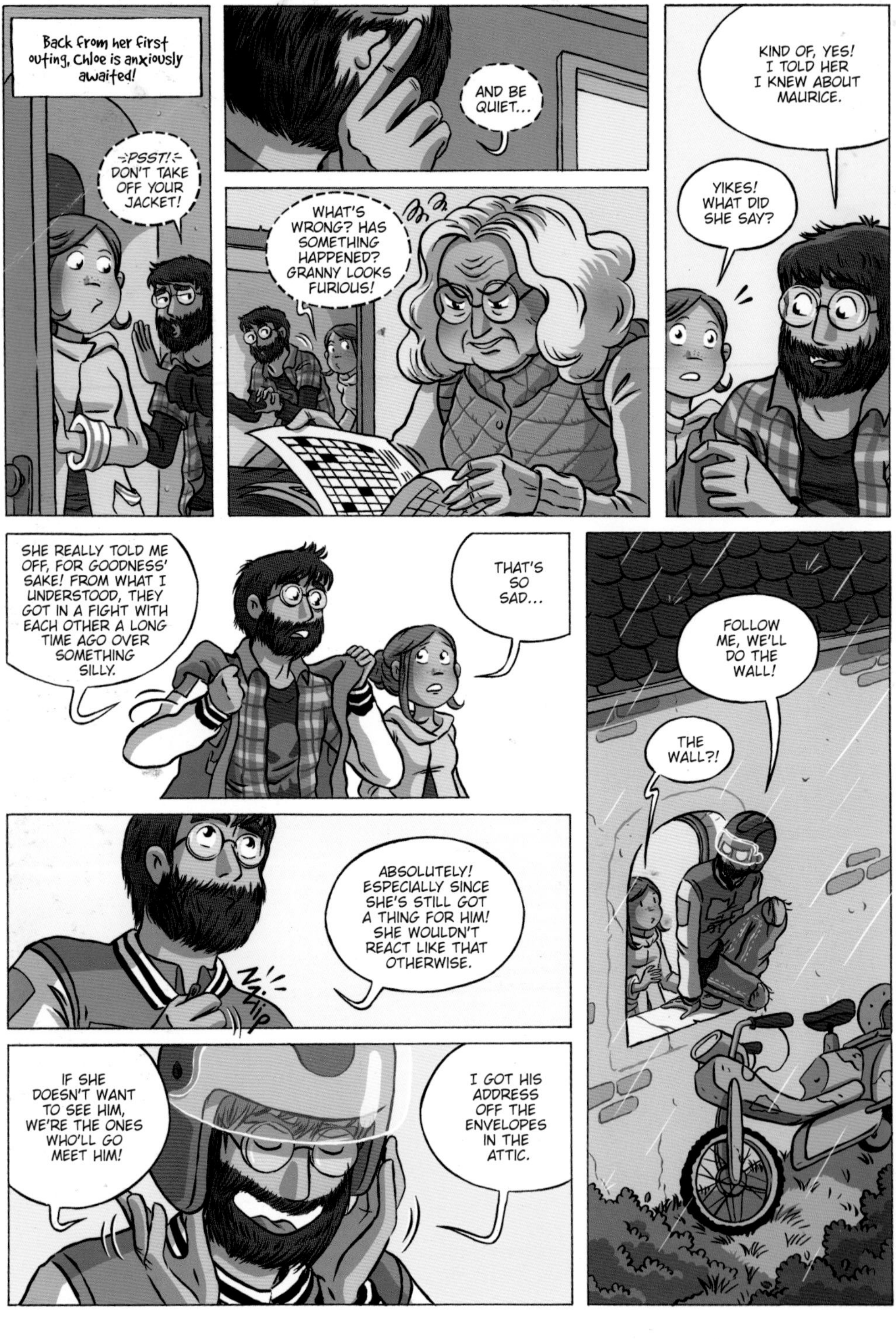

Back from her first outing, Chloe is anxiously awaited!
PSST! DON'T TAKE OFF YOUR JACKET!
AND BE QUIET...
WHAT'S WRONG? HAS SOMETHING HAPPENED? GRANNY LOOKS FURIOUS!
KIND OF, YES! I TOLD HER I KNEW ABOUT MAURICE.
YIKES! WHAT DID SHE SAY?
SHE REALLY TOLD ME OFF, FOR GOODNESS' SAKE! FROM WHAT I UNDERSTOOD, THEY GOT IN A FIGHT WITH EACH OTHER A LONG TIME AGO OVER SOMETHING SILLY.
THAT'S SO SAD...
ABSOLUTELY! ESPECIALLY SINCE SHE'S STILL GOT A THING FOR HIM! SHE WOULDN'T REACT LIKE THAT OTHERWISE.
ZZIP
IF SHE DOESN'T WANT TO SEE HIM, WE'RE THE ONES WHO'LL GO MEET HIM!
I GOT HIS ADDRESS OFF THE ENVELOPES IN THE ATTIC.
FOLLOW ME, WE'LL DO THE WALL!
THE WALL?!

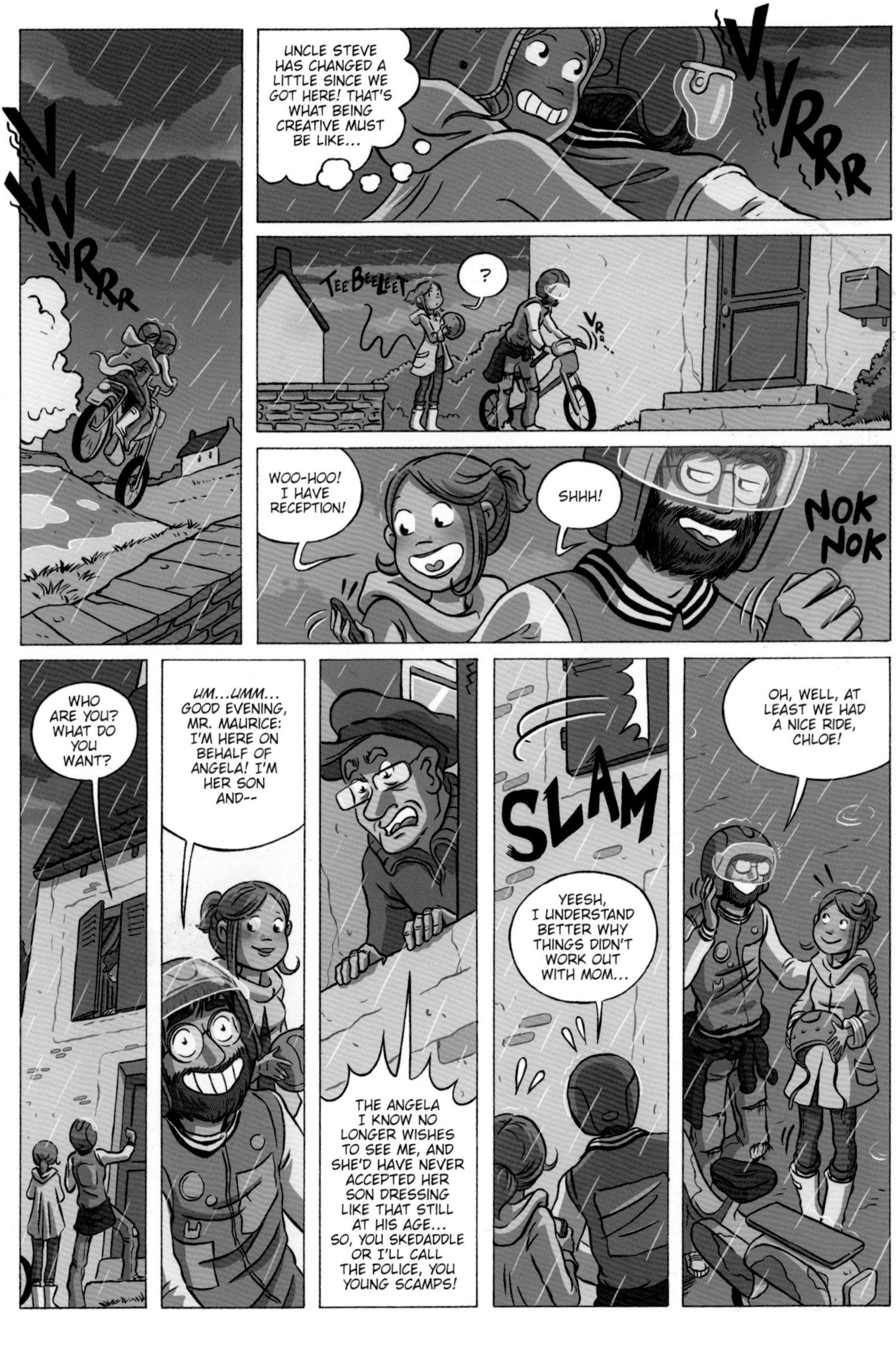
VVVVRRR
UNCLE STEVE HAS CHANGED A LITTLE SINCE WE GOT HERE! THAT'S WHAT BEING CREATIVE MUST BE LIKE...
VVRRRR
TEE BEE LEET
?
VR...
WOO-HOO! I HAVE RECEPTION!
SHHH!
NOK NOK
WHO ARE YOU? WHAT DO YOU WANT?
UM...UMM... GOOD EVENING, MR. MAURICE: I'M HERE ON BEHALF OF ANGELA! I'M HER SON AND--
THE ANGELA I KNOW NO LONGER WISHES TO SEE ME, AND SHE'D HAVE NEVER ACCEPTED HER SON DRESSING LIKE THAT STILL AT HIS AGE... SO, YOU SKEDADDLE OR I'LL CALL THE POLICE, YOU YOUNG SCAMPS!
SLAM
YEESH, I UNDERSTAND BETTER WHY THINGS DIDN'T WORK OUT WITH MOM...
OH, WELL, AT LEAST WE HAD A NICE RIDE, CHLOE!

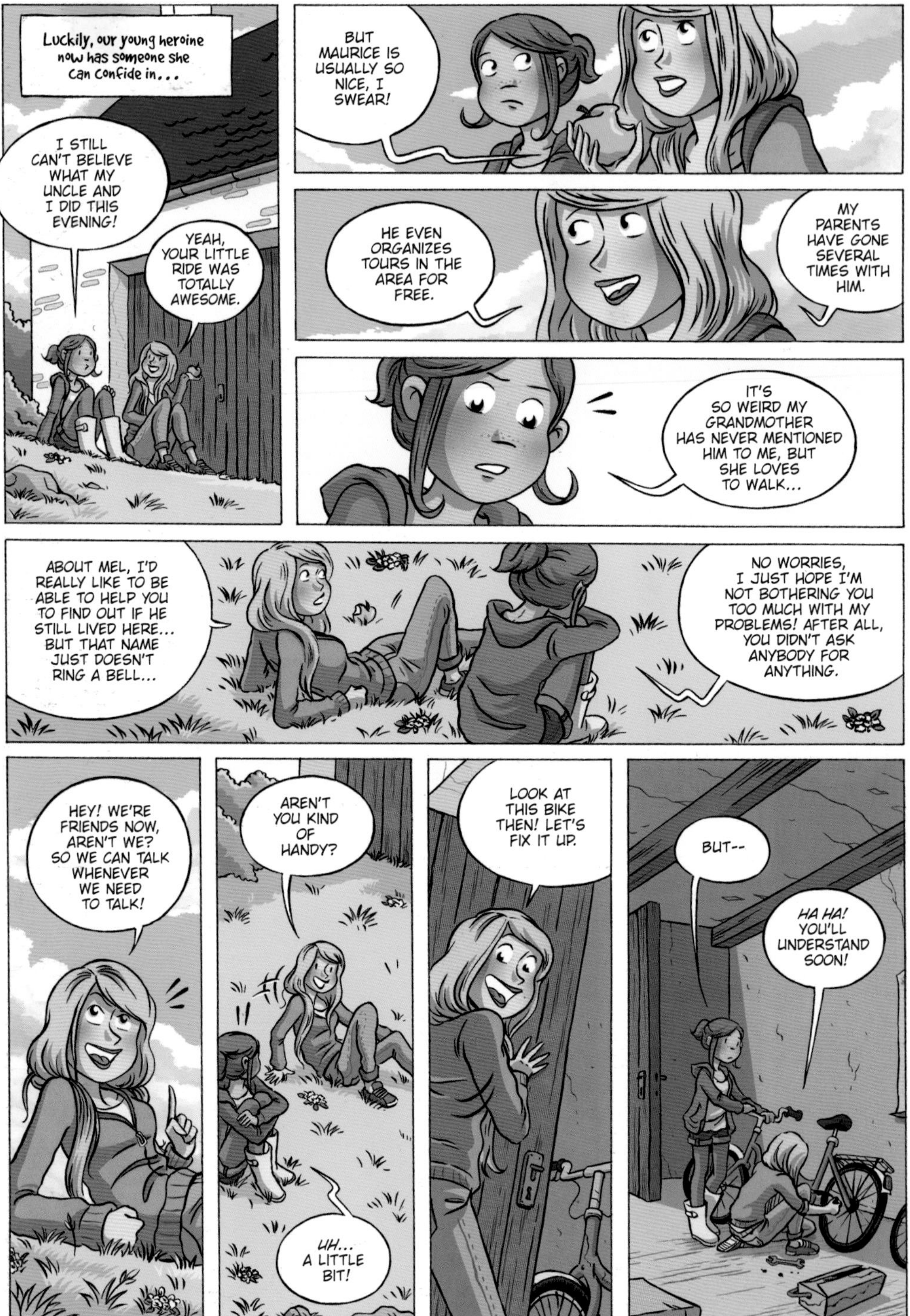
Luckily, our young heroine now has someone she can confide in...
I STILL CAN'T BELIEVE WHAT MY UNCLE AND I DID THIS EVENING!
YEAH, YOUR LITTLE RIDE WAS TOTALLY AWESOME.
BUT MAURICE IS USUALLY SO NICE, I SWEAR!
HE EVEN ORGANIZES TOURS IN THE AREA FOR FREE.
MY PARENTS HAVE GONE SEVERAL TIMES WITH HIM.
IT'S SO WEIRD MY GRANDMOTHER HAS NEVER MENTIONED HIM TO ME, BUT SHE LOVES TO WALK...
ABOUT MEL, I'D REALLY LIKE TO BE ABLE TO HELP YOU TO FIND OUT IF HE STILL LIVED HERE... BUT THAT NAME JUST DOESN'T RING A BELL...
NO WORRIES, I JUST HOPE I'M NOT BOTHERING YOU TOO MUCH WITH MY PROBLEMS! AFTER ALL, YOU DIDN'T ASK ANYBODY FOR ANYTHING.
HEY! WE'RE FRIENDS NOW, AREN'T WE? SO WE CAN TALK WHENEVER WE NEED TO TALK!
AREN'T YOU KIND OF HANDY?
UH... A LITTLE BIT!
LOOK AT THIS BIKE THEN! LET'S FIX IT UP.
BUT--
HA HA! YOU'LL UNDERSTAND SOON!

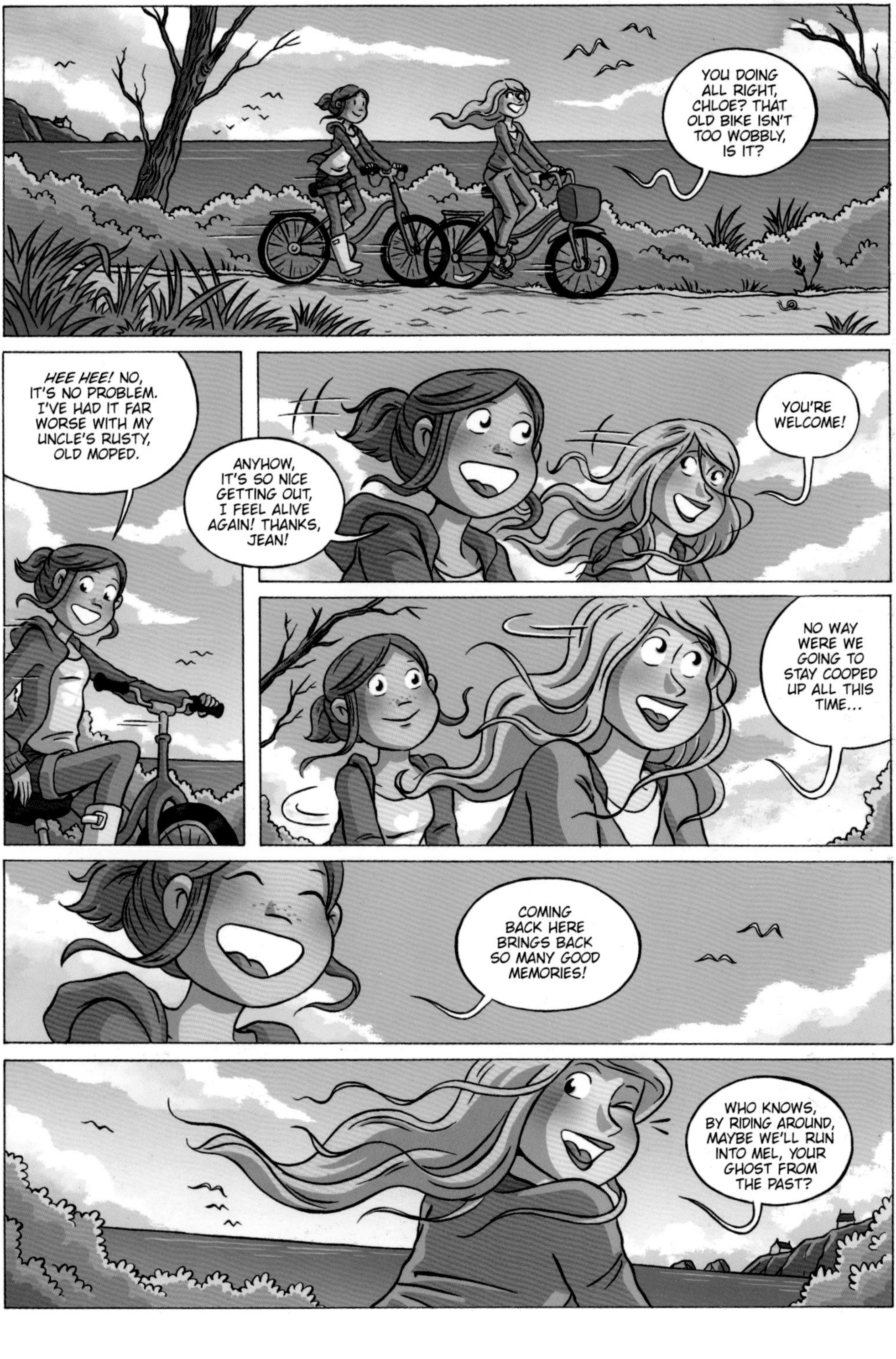
YOU DOING ALL RIGHT, CHLOE? THAT OLD BIKE ISN'T TOO WOBBLY, IS IT?
HEE HEE! NO, IT'S NO PROBLEM. I'VE HAD IT FAR WORSE WITH MY UNCLE'S RUSTY, OLD MOPED.
ANYHOW, IT'S SO NICE GETTING OUT, I FEEL ALIVE AGAIN! THANKS, JEAN!
YOU'RE WELCOME!
NO WAY WERE WE GOING TO STAY COOPED UP ALL THIS TIME...
COMING BACK HERE BRINGS BACK SO MANY GOOD MEMORIES!
WHO KNOWS, BY RIDING AROUND, MAYBE WE'LL RUN INTO MEL, YOUR GHOST FROM THE PAST?

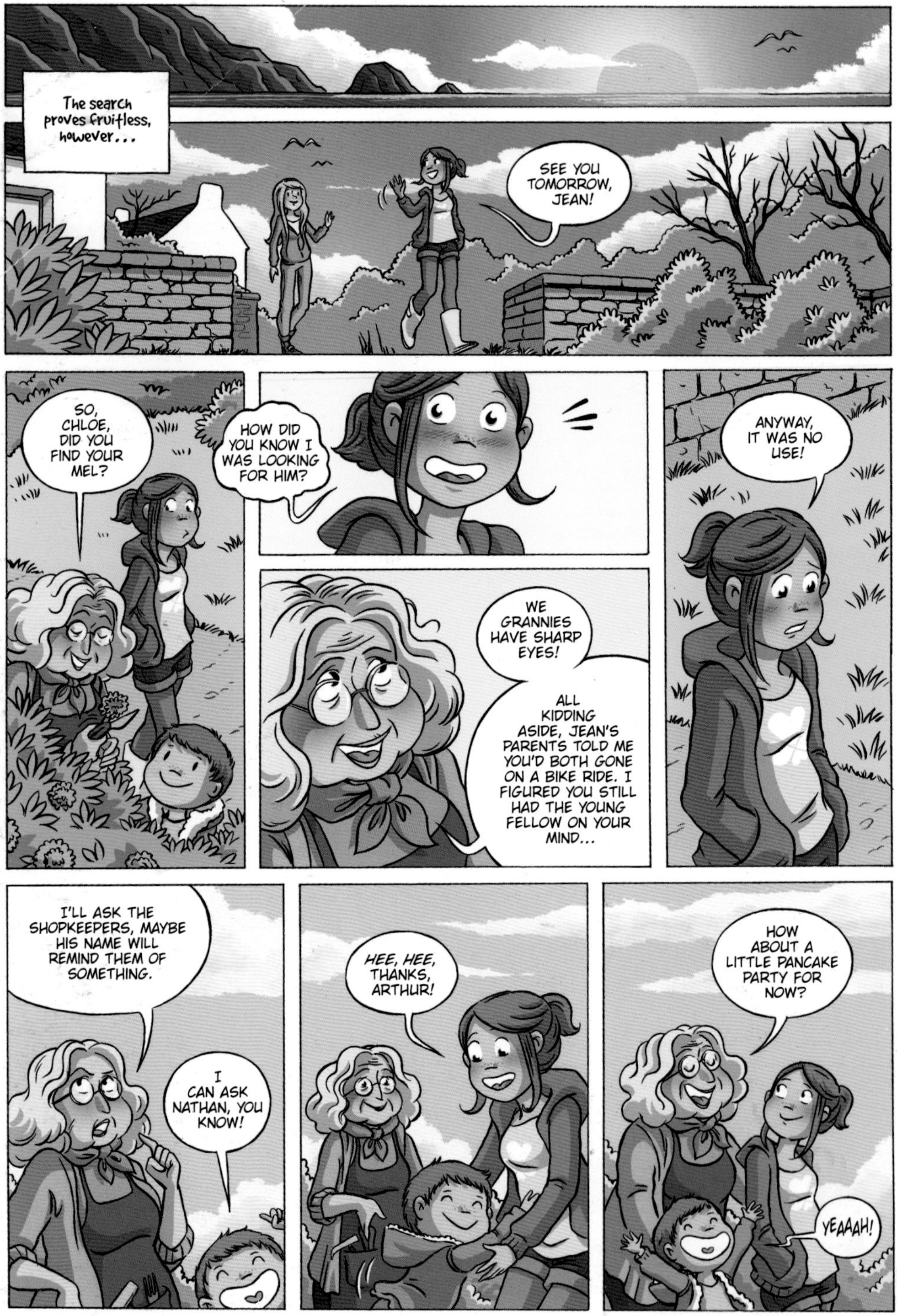
The search proves fruitless, however...
SEE YOU TOMORROW, JEAN!
SO, CHLOE, DID YOU FIND YOUR MEL?
HOW DID YOU KNOW I WAS LOOKING FOR HIM?
WE GRANNIES HAVE SHARP EYES!
ALL KIDDING ASIDE, JEAN'S PARENTS TOLD ME YOU'D BOTH GONE ON A BIKE RIDE. I FIGURED YOU STILL HAD THE YOUNG FELLOW ON YOUR MIND...
ANYWAY, IT WAS NO USE!
I'LL ASK THE SHOPKEEPERS, MAYBE HIS NAME WILL REMIND THEM OF SOMETHING.
I CAN ASK NATHAN, YOU KNOW!
HEE, HEE, THANKS, ARTHUR!
HOW ABOUT A LITTLE PANCAKE PARTY FOR NOW?
YEAAAH!

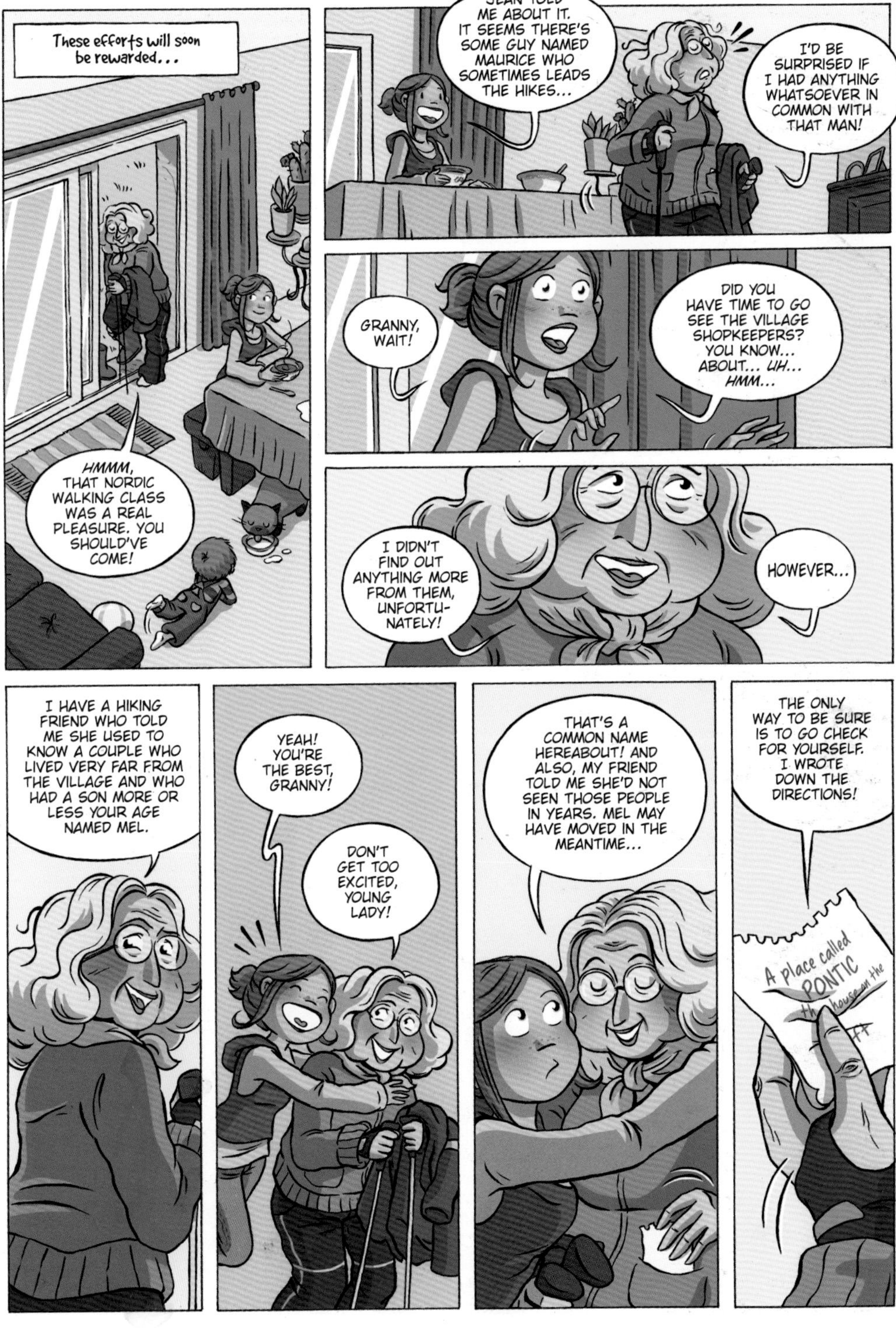
These efforts will soon be rewarded...
HMMM, THAT NORDIC WALKING CLASS WAS A REAL PLEASURE. YOU SHOULD'VE COME!
JEAN TOLD ME ABOUT IT. IT SEEMS THERE'S SOME GUY NAMED MAURICE WHO SOMETIMES LEADS THE HIKES...
I'D BE SURPRISED IF I HAD ANYTHING WHATSOEVER IN COMMON WITH THAT MAN!
GRANNY, WAIT!
DID YOU HAVE TIME TO GO SEE THE VILLAGE SHOPKEEPERS? YOU KNOW... ABOUT... UH... HMM...
I DIDN'T FIND OUT ANYTHING MORE FROM THEM, UNFORTU-NATELY!
HOWEVER...
I HAVE A HIKING FRIEND WHO TOLD ME SHE USED TO KNOW A COUPLE WHO LIVED VERY FAR FROM THE VILLAGE AND WHO HAD A SON MORE OR LESS YOUR AGE NAMED MEL.
YEAH! YOU'RE THE BEST, GRANNY!
DON'T GET TOO EXCITED, YOUNG LADY!
THAT'S A COMMON NAME HEREABOUT! AND ALSO, MY FRIEND TOLD ME SHE'D NOT SEEN THOSE PEOPLE IN YEARS. MEL MAY HAVE MOVED IN THE MEANTIME...
THE ONLY WAY TO BE SURE IS TO GO CHECK FOR YOURSELF. I WROTE DOWN THE DIRECTIONS!
A place called PONTIC

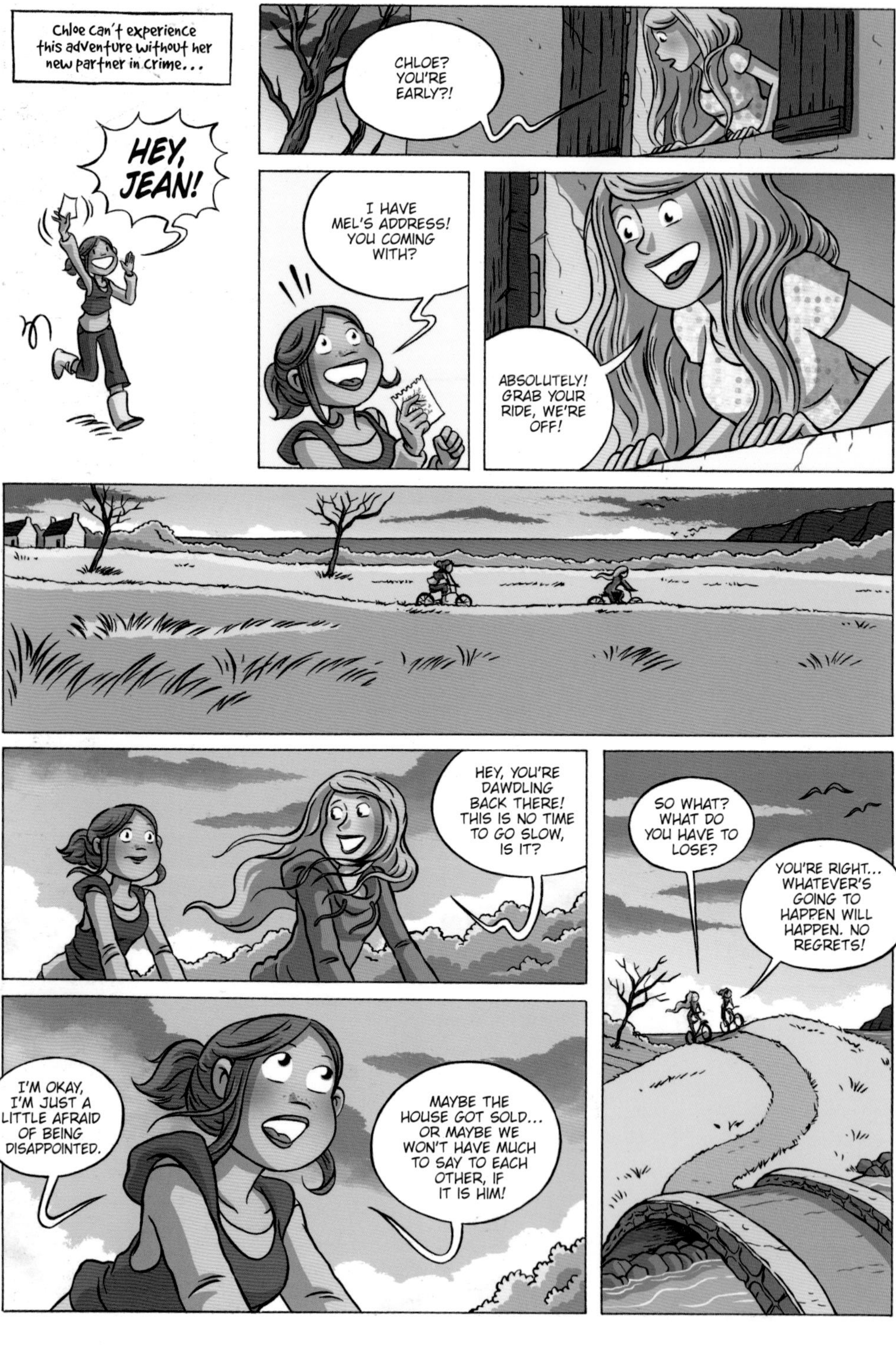
Chloe can't experience this adventure without her new partner in crime...
HEY, JEAN!
CHLOE? YOU'RE EARLY?!
I HAVE MEL'S ADDRESS! YOU COMING WITH?
ABSOLUTELY! GRAB YOUR RIDE, WE'RE OFF!
HEY, YOU'RE DAWDLING BACK THERE! THIS IS NO TIME TO GO SLOW, IS IT?
I'M OKAY, I'M JUST A LITTLE AFRAID OF BEING DISAPPOINTED.
MAYBE THE HOUSE GOT SOLD... OR MAYBE WE WON'T HAVE MUCH TO SAY TO EACH OTHER, IF IT IS HIM!
SO WHAT? WHAT DO YOU HAVE TO LOSE?
YOU'RE RIGHT... WHATEVER'S GOING TO HAPPEN WILL HAPPEN. NO REGRETS!

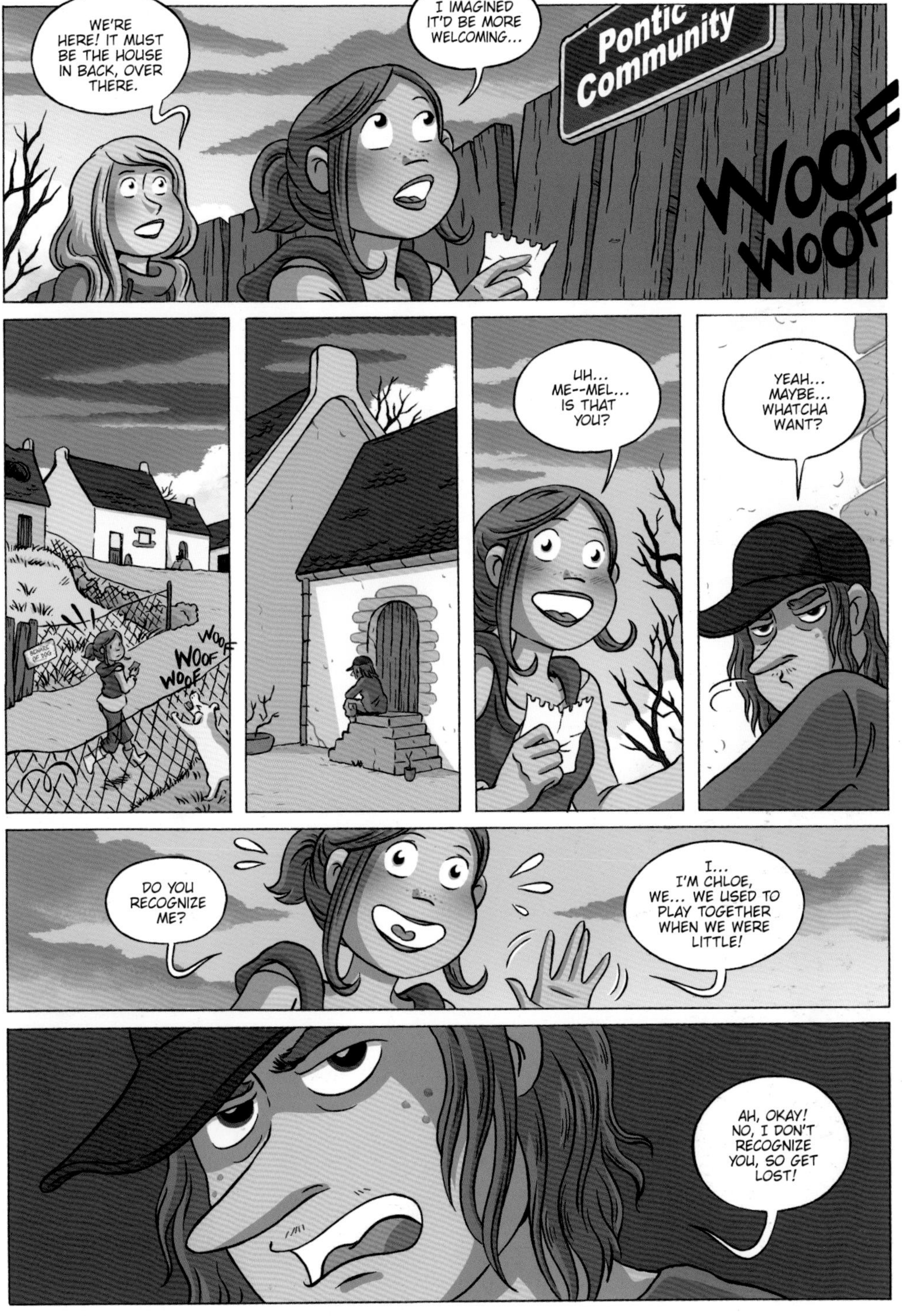
WE'RE HERE! IT MUST BE THE HOUSE IN BACK, OVER THERE.
I IMAGINED IT'D BE MORE WELCOMING...
Pontic Community
WOOF WOOF
BEWARE OF DOG
WOOF WOOF WOOF
UH... ME--MEL... IS THAT YOU?
YEAH... MAYBE... WHATCHA WANT?
DO YOU RECOGNIZE ME?
I... I'M CHLOE, WE... WE USED TO PLAY TOGETHER WHEN WE WERE LITTLE!
AH, OKAY! NO, I DON'T RECOGNIZE YOU, SO GET LOST!

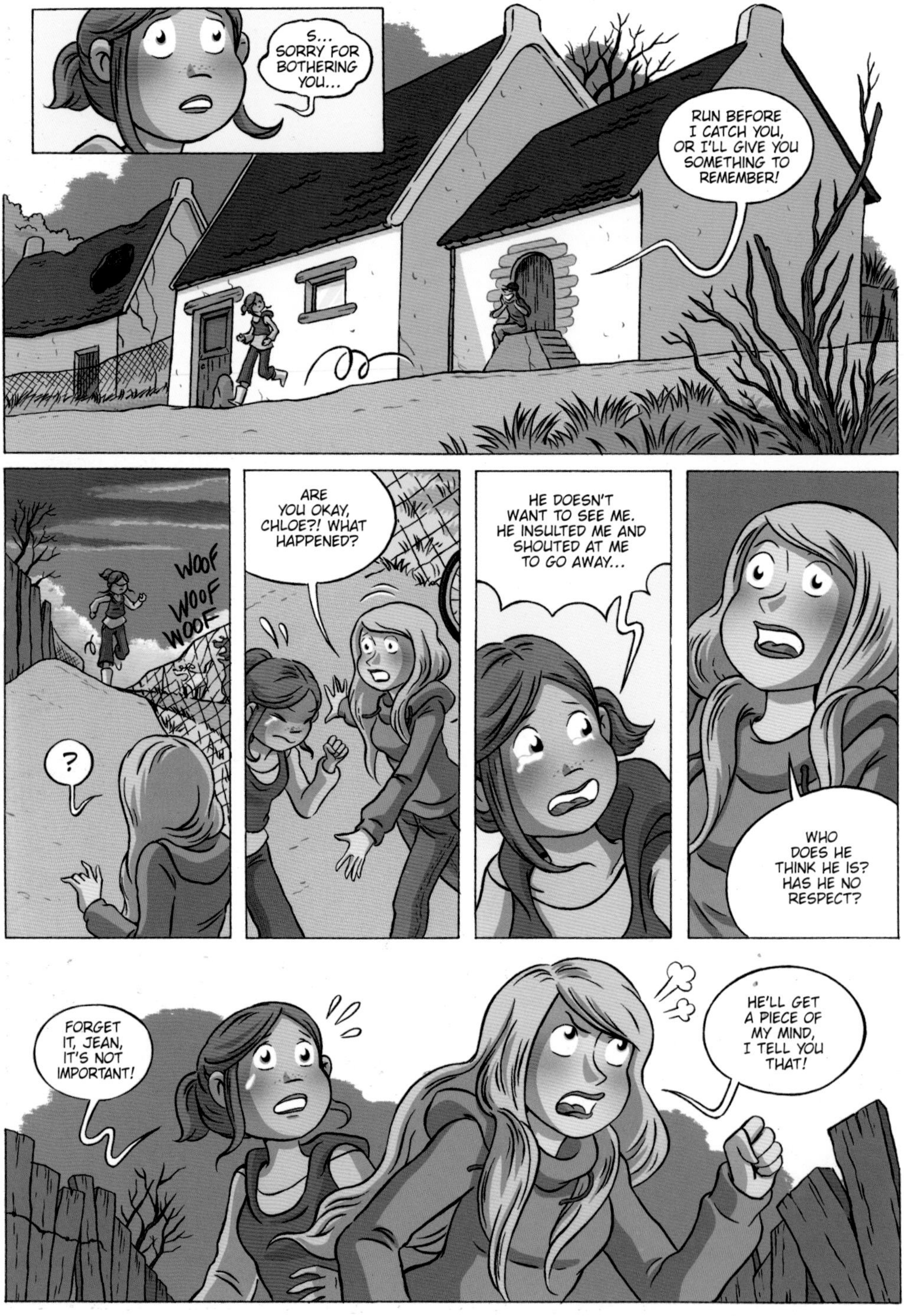
S... SORRY FOR BOTHERING YOU...
RUN BEFORE I CATCH YOU, OR I'LL GIVE YOU SOMETHING TO REMEMBER!
WOOF WOOF WOOF
?
ARE YOU OKAY, CHLOE?! WHAT HAPPENED?
HE DOESN'T WANT TO SEE ME. HE INSULTED ME AND SHOUTED AT ME TO GO AWAY...
WHO DOES HE THINK HE IS? HAS HE NO RESPECT?
FORGET IT, JEAN, IT'S NOT IMPORTANT!
HE'LL GET A PIECE OF MY MIND, I TELL YOU THAT!

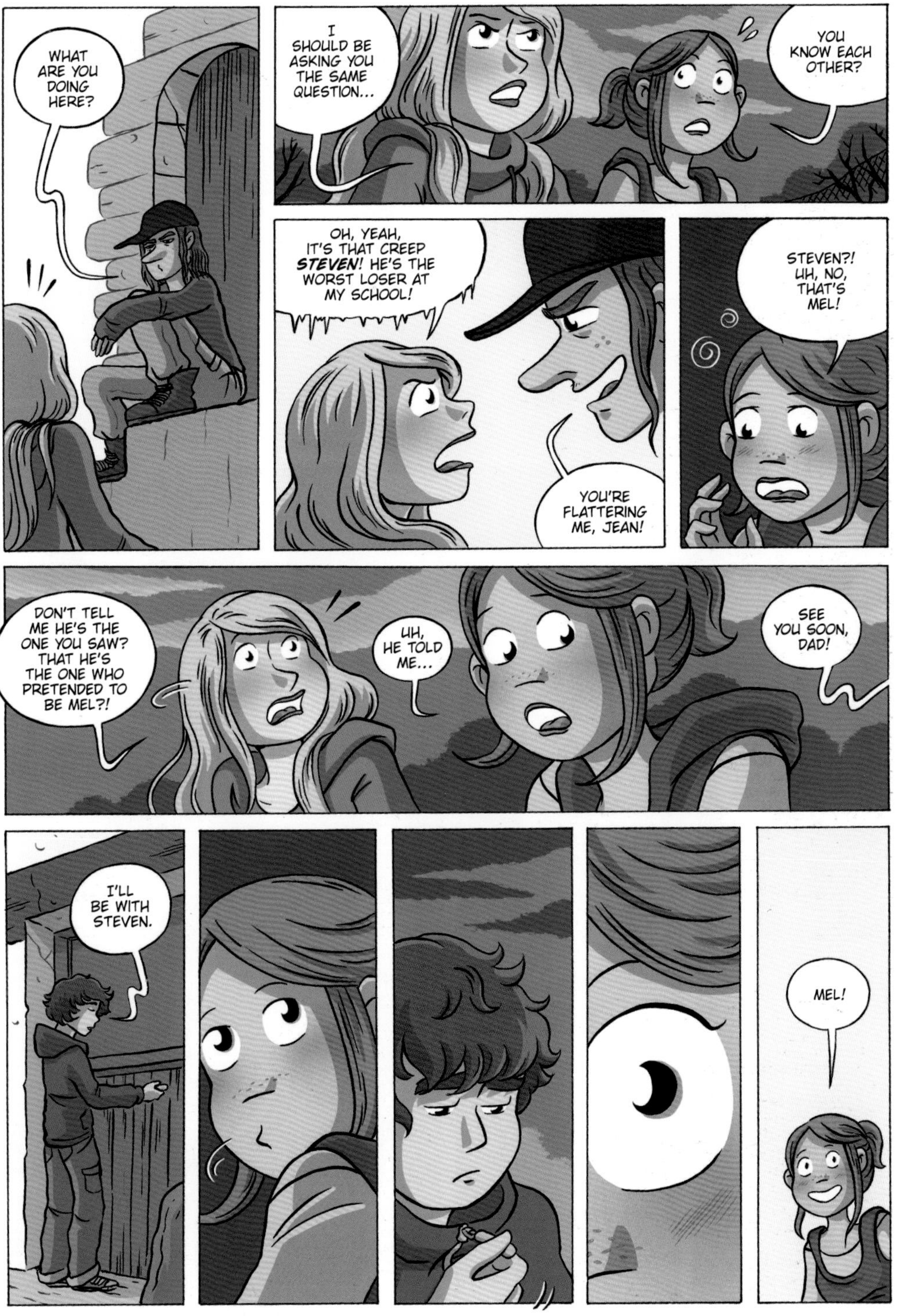
WHAT ARE YOU DOING HERE?
I SHOULD BE ASKING YOU THE SAME QUESTION...
YOU KNOW EACH OTHER?
OH, YEAH, IT'S THAT CREEP STEVEN! HE'S THE WORST LOSER AT MY SCHOOL!
YOU'RE FLATTERING ME, JEAN!
STEVEN?! UH, NO, THAT'S MEL!
DON'T TELL ME HE'S THE ONE YOU SAW? THAT HE'S THE ONE WHO PRETENDED TO BE MEL?!
UH, HE TOLD ME...
SEE YOU SOON, DAD!
I'LL BE WITH STEVEN.
MEL!

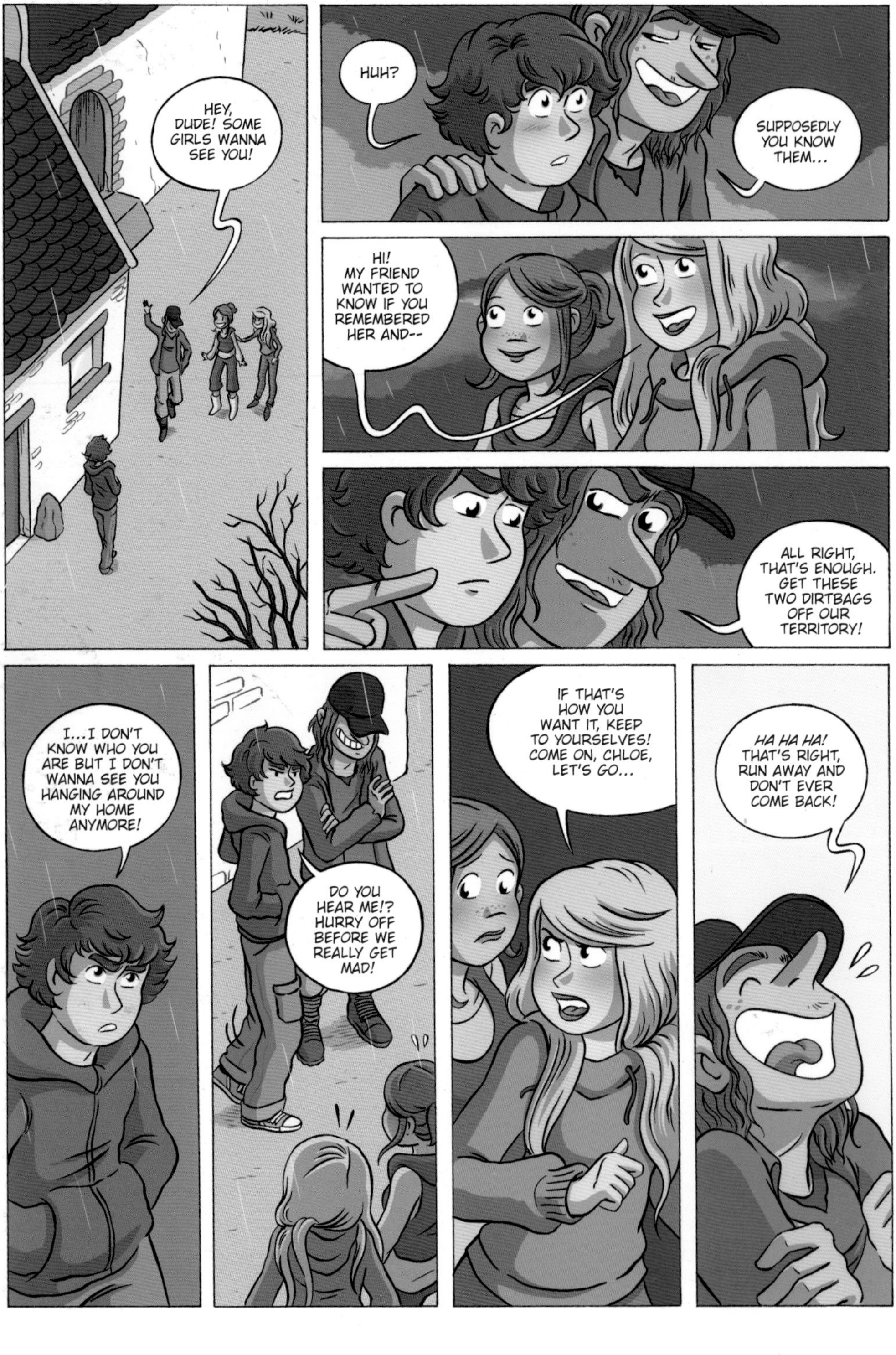
HEY, DUDE! SOME GIRLS WANNA SEE YOU!
HUH?
SUPPOSEDLY YOU KNOW THEM...
HI! MY FRIEND WANTED TO KNOW IF YOU REMEMBERED HER AND--
ALL RIGHT, THAT'S ENOUGH. GET THESE TWO DIRTBAGS OFF OUR TERRITORY!
I...I DON'T KNOW WHO YOU ARE BUT I DON'T WANNA SEE YOU HANGING AROUND MY HOME ANYMORE!
DO YOU HEAR ME!? HURRY OFF BEFORE WE REALLY GET MAD!
IF THAT'S HOW YOU WANT IT, KEEP TO YOURSELVES! COME ON, CHLOE, LET'S GO...
HA HA HA! THAT'S RIGHT, RUN AWAY AND DON'T EVER COME BACK!

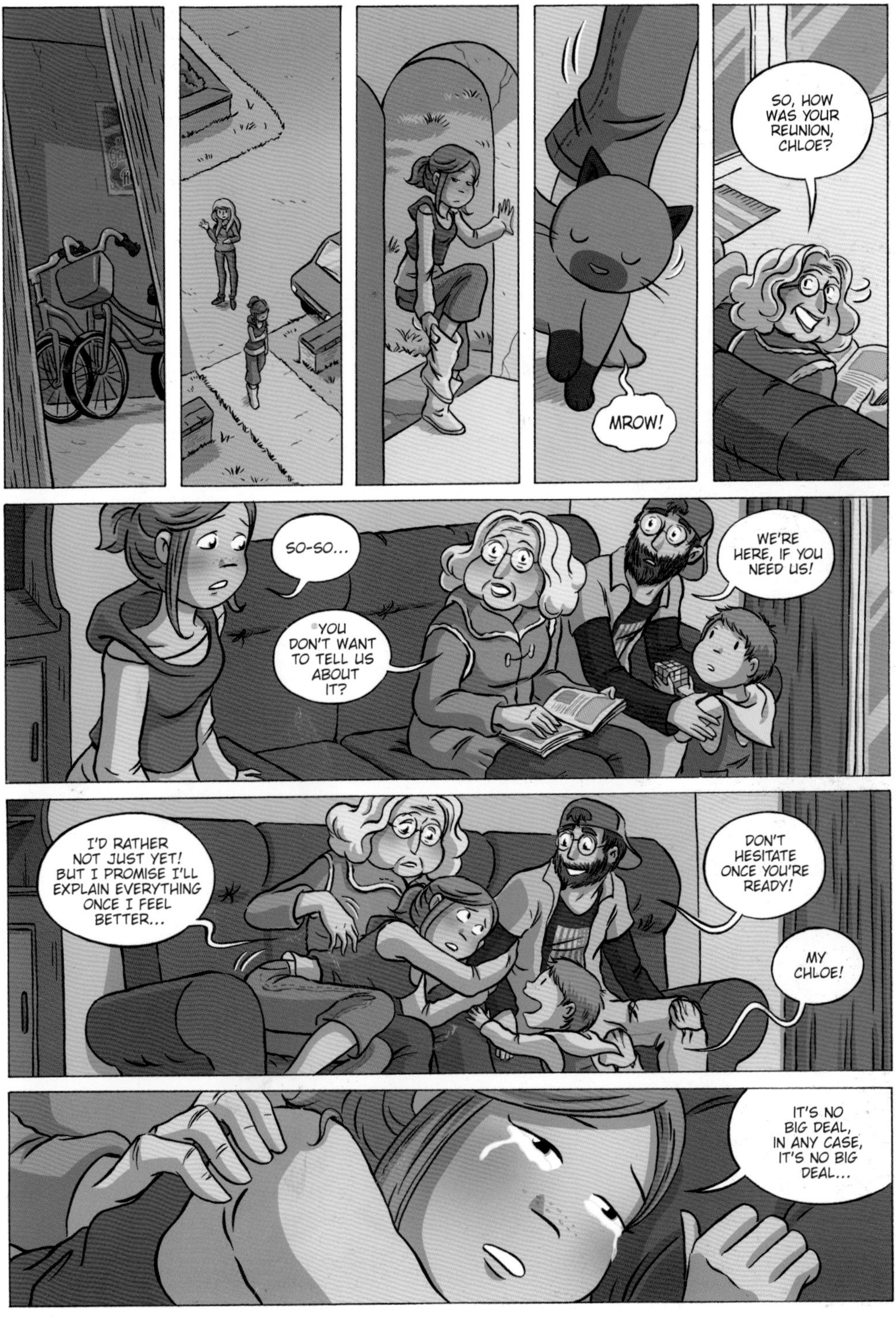
MROW!
SO, HOW WAS YOUR REUNION, CHLOE?
SO-SO...
YOU DON'T WANT TO TELL US ABOUT IT?
WE'RE HERE, IF YOU NEED US!
I'D RATHER NOT JUST YET! BUT I PROMISE I'LL EXPLAIN EVERYTHING ONCE I FEEL BETTER...
DON'T HESITATE ONCE YOU'RE READY!
MY CHLOE!
IT'S NO BIG DEAL, IN ANY CASE, IT'S NO BIG DEAL...

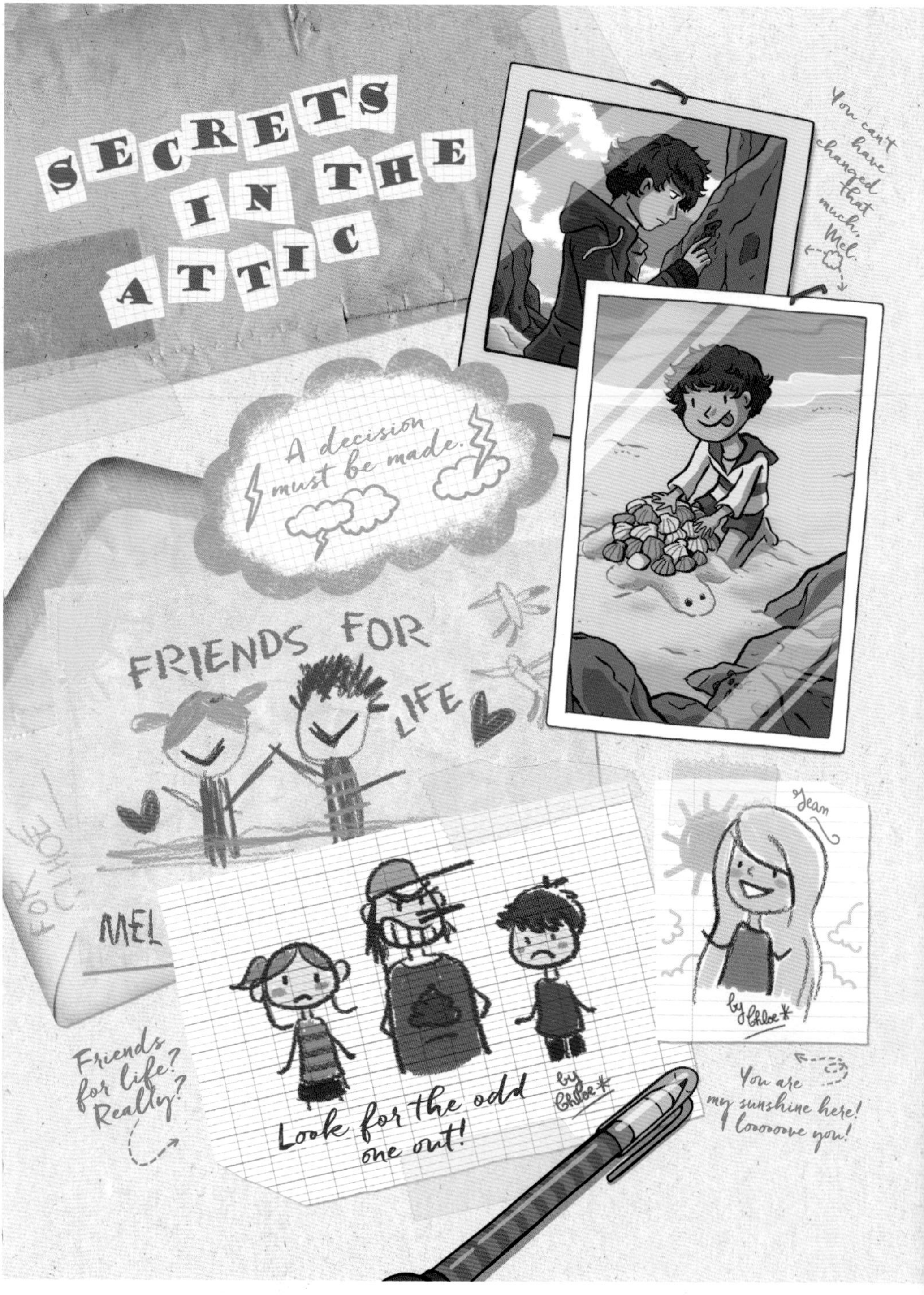
SECRETS IN THE ATTIC
You can't have changed that much, Mel.
A decision must be made.
FRIENDS FOR LIFE
FOR CHLOE
MEL
Jean
by Chloe*
Look for the odd one out!
by Chloe*
Friends for life? Really?
You are my sunshine here! I looooove you!

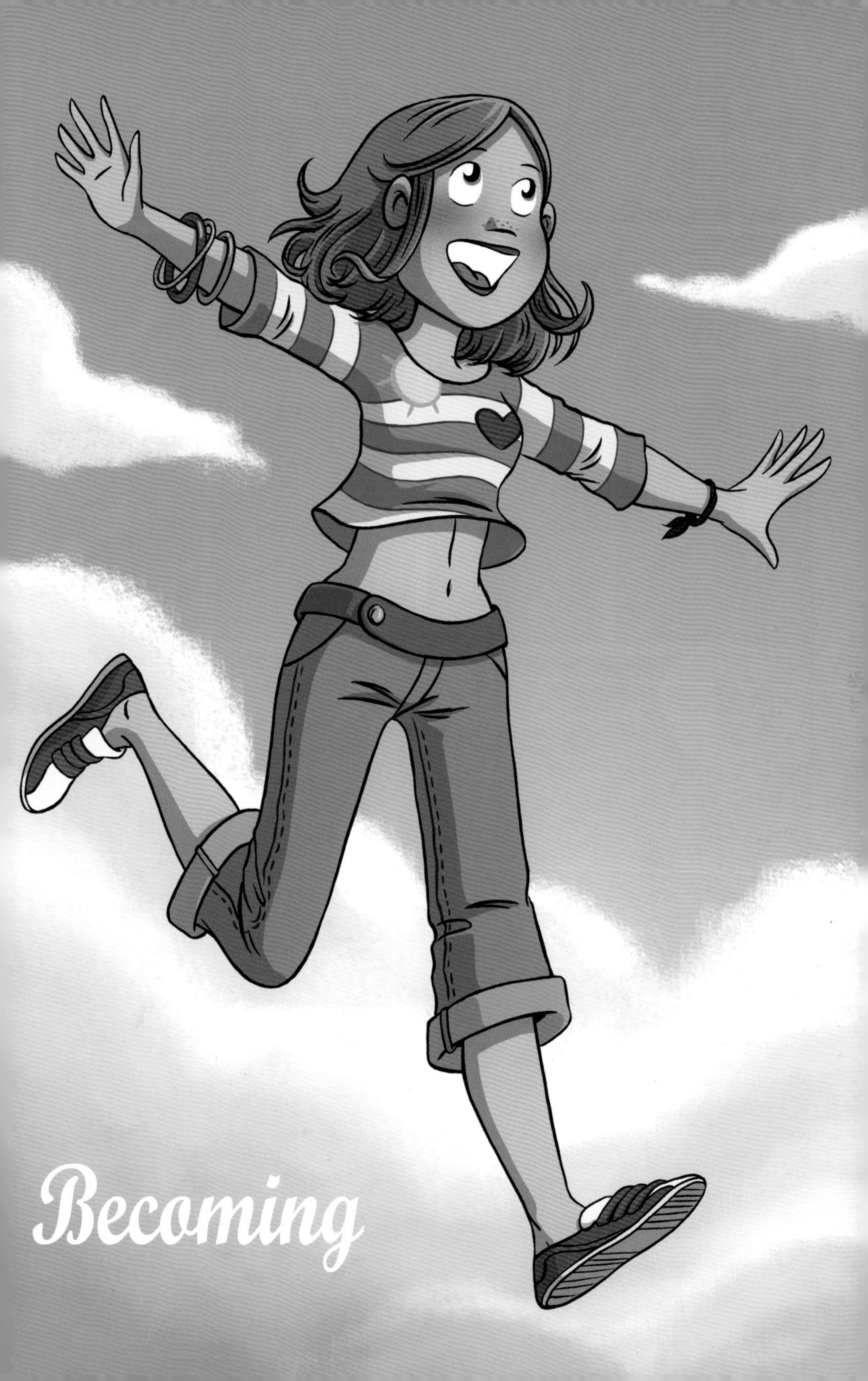
Becoming

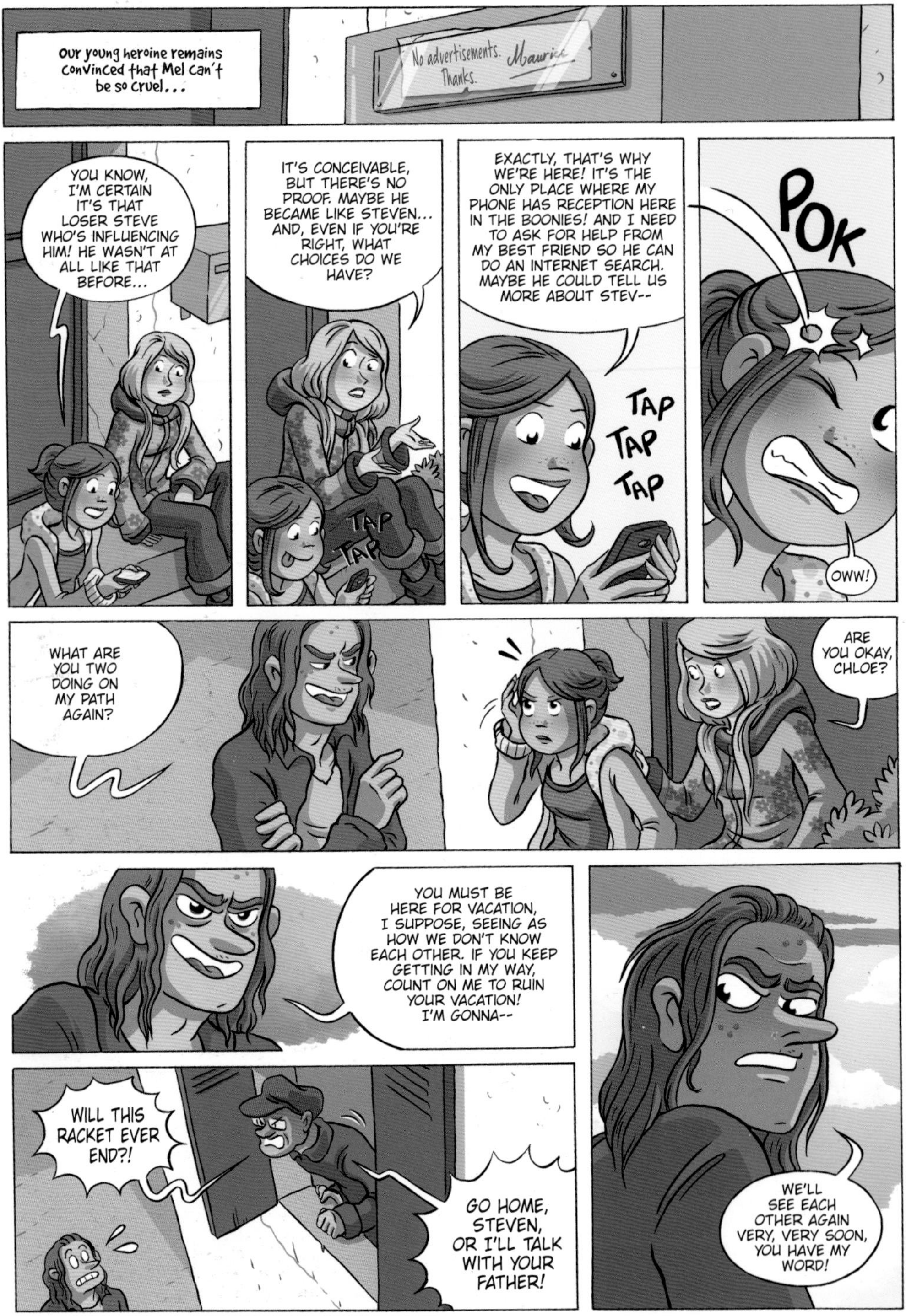
Our young heroine remains convinced that Mel can't be so cruel...
No advertisements. Thanks. Maurice
YOU KNOW, I'M CERTAIN IT'S THAT LOSER STEVE WHO'S INFLUENCING HIM! HE WASN'T AT ALL LIKE THAT BEFORE...
IT'S CONCEIVABLE, BUT THERE'S NO PROOF. MAYBE HE BECAME LIKE STEVEN... AND, EVEN IF YOU'RE RIGHT, WHAT CHOICES DO WE HAVE?
TAP TAP
EXACTLY, THAT'S WHY WE'RE HERE! IT'S THE ONLY PLACE WHERE MY PHONE HAS RECEPTION HERE IN THE BOONIES! AND I NEED TO ASK FOR HELP FROM MY BEST FRIEND SO HE CAN DO AN INTERNET SEARCH. MAYBE HE COULD TELL US MORE ABOUT STEV--
TAP TAP TAP
POK
OWW!
WHAT ARE YOU TWO DOING ON MY PATH AGAIN?
ARE YOU OKAY, CHLOE?
YOU MUST BE HERE FOR VACATION, I SUPPOSE, SEEING AS HOW WE DON'T KNOW EACH OTHER. IF YOU KEEP GETTING IN MY WAY, COUNT ON ME TO RUIN YOUR VACATION! I'M GONNA--
WILL THIS RACKET EVER END?!
GO HOME, STEVEN, OR I'LL TALK WITH YOUR FATHER!
WE'LL SEE EACH OTHER AGAIN VERY, VERY SOON, YOU HAVE MY WORD!

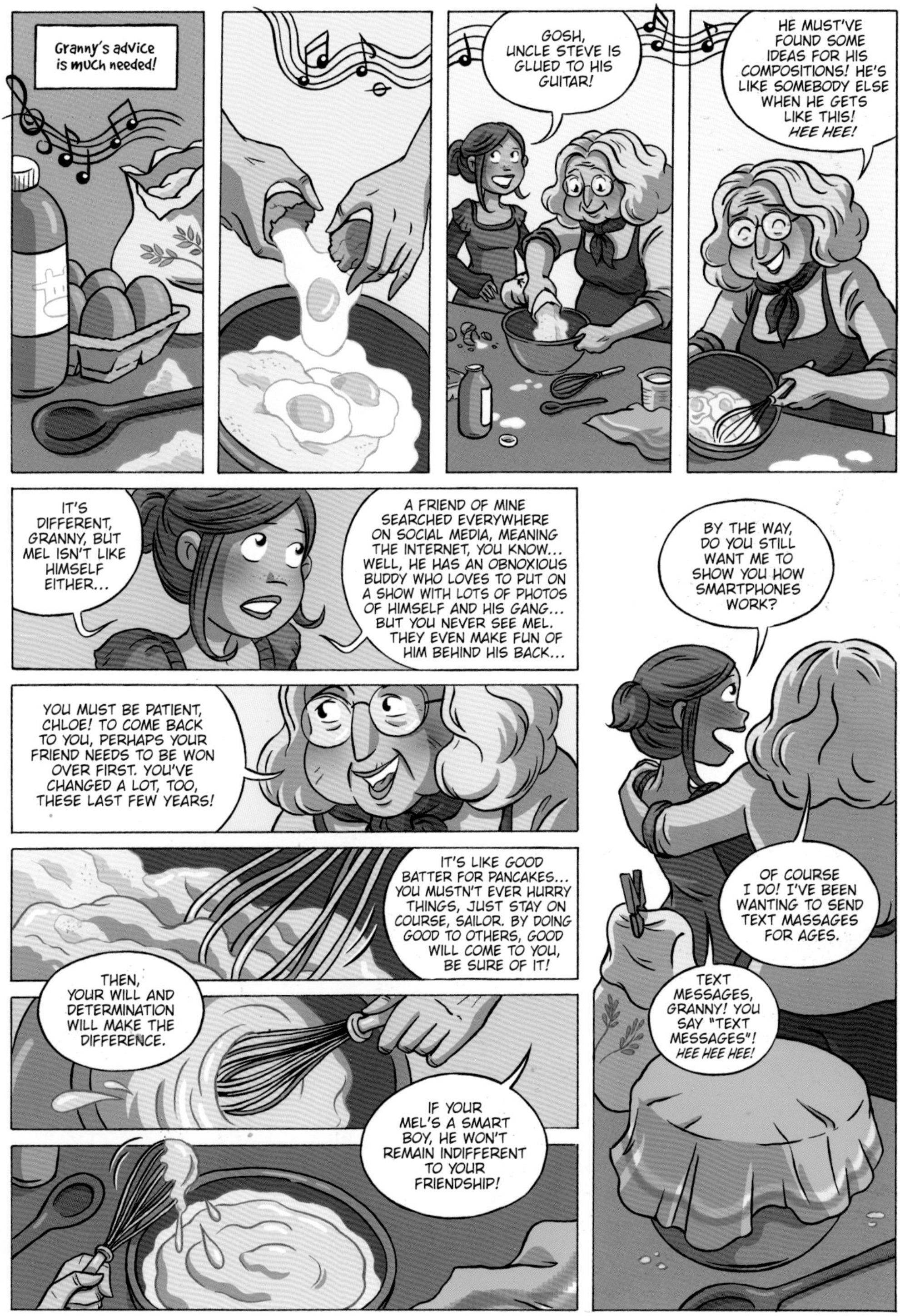

Granny's advice is much needed!
GOSH, UNCLE STEVE IS GLUED TO HIS GUITAR!
HE MUST'VE FOUND SOME IDEAS FOR HIS COMPOSITIONS! HE'S LIKE SOMEBODY ELSE WHEN HE GETS LIKE THIS! HEE HEE!
IT'S DIFFERENT, GRANNY, BUT MEL ISN'T LIKE HIMSELF EITHER...
A FRIEND OF MINE SEARCHED EVERYWHERE ON SOCIAL MEDIA, MEANING THE INTERNET, YOU KNOW... WELL, HE HAS AN OBNOXIOUS BUDDY WHO LOVES TO PUT ON A SHOW WITH LOTS OF PHOTOS OF HIMSELF AND HIS GANG... BUT YOU NEVER SEE MEL. THEY EVEN MAKE FUN OF HIM BEHIND HIS BACK...
YOU MUST BE PATIENT, CHLOE! TO COME BACK TO YOU, PERHAPS YOUR FRIEND NEEDS TO BE WON OVER FIRST. YOU'VE CHANGED A LOT, TOO, THESE LAST FEW YEARS!
IT'S LIKE GOOD BATTER FOR PANCAKES... YOU MUSTN'T EVER HURRY THINGS, JUST STAY ON COURSE, SAILOR. BY DOING GOOD TO OTHERS, GOOD WILL COME TO YOU, BE SURE OF IT!
THEN, YOUR WILL AND DETERMINATION WILL MAKE THE DIFFERENCE.
IF YOUR MEL'S A SMART BOY, HE WON'T REMAIN INDIFFERENT TO YOUR FRIENDSHIP!
BY THE WAY, DO YOU STILL WANT ME TO SHOW YOU HOW SMARTPHONES WORK?
OF COURSE I DO! I'VE BEEN WANTING TO SEND TEXT MASSAGES FOR AGES.
TEXT MESSAGES, GRANNY! YOU SAY "TEXT MESSAGES"! HEE HEE HEE!

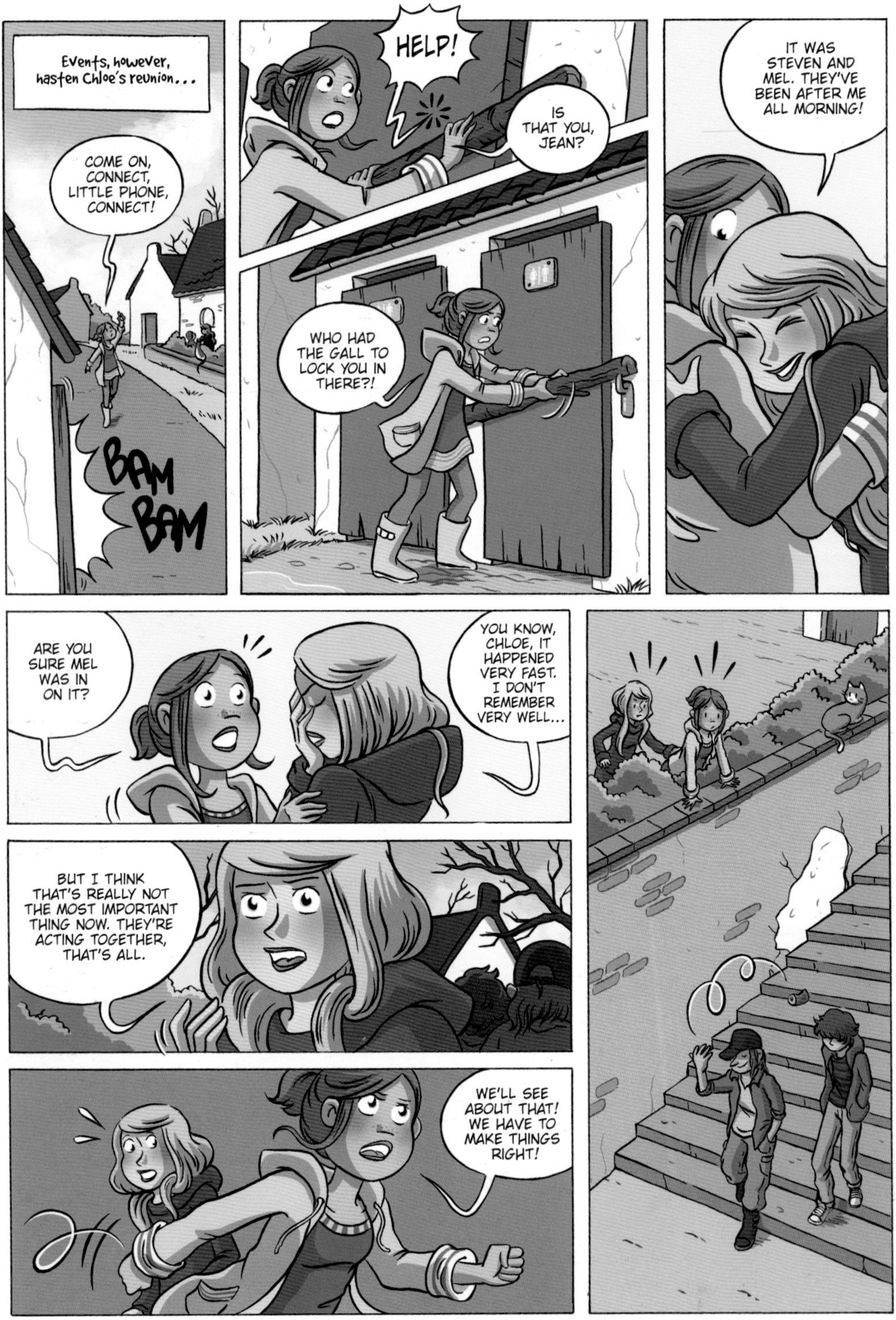
Events, however, hasten Chloe's reunion...
COME ON, CONNECT, LITTLE PHONE, CONNECT!
BAM BAM
HELP!
IS THAT YOU, JEAN?
WHO HAD THE GALL TO LOCK YOU IN THERE?!
IT WAS STEVEN AND MEL. THEY'VE BEEN AFTER ME ALL MORNING!
ARE YOU SURE MEL WAS IN ON IT?
YOU KNOW, CHLOE, IT HAPPENED VERY FAST. I DON'T REMEMBER VERY WELL...
BUT I THINK THAT'S REALLY NOT THE MOST IMPORTANT THING NOW. THEY'RE ACTING TOGETHER, THAT'S ALL.
WE'LL SEE ABOUT THAT! WE HAVE TO MAKE THINGS RIGHT!

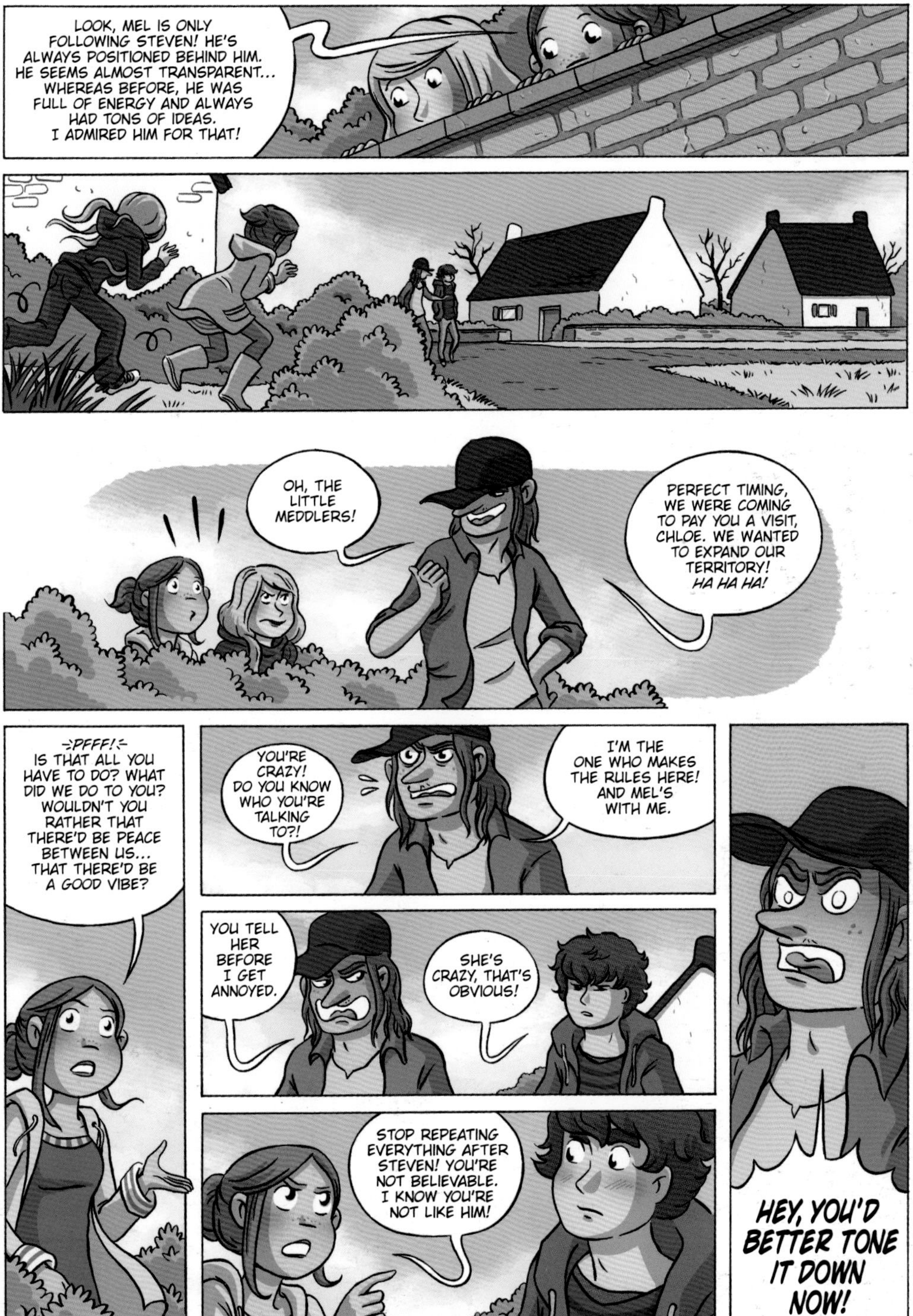
LOOK, MEL IS ONLY FOLLOWING STEVEN! HE'S ALWAYS POSITIONED BEHIND HIM. HE SEEMS ALMOST TRANSPARENT... WHEREAS BEFORE, HE WAS FULL OF ENERGY AND ALWAYS HAD TONS OF IDEAS. I ADMIRED HIM FOR THAT!
OH, THE LITTLE MEDDLERS!
PERFECT TIMING, WE WERE COMING TO PAY YOU A VISIT, CHLOE. WE WANTED TO EXPAND OUR TERRITORY! HA HA HA!
PFFF! IS THAT ALL YOU HAVE TO DO? WHAT DID WE DO TO YOU? WOULDN'T YOU RATHER THAT THERE'D BE PEACE BETWEEN US... THAT THERE'D BE A GOOD VIBE?
YOU'RE CRAZY! DO YOU KNOW WHO YOU'RE TALKING TO?!
I'M THE ONE WHO MAKES THE RULES HERE! AND MEL'S WITH ME.
YOU TELL HER BEFORE I GET ANNOYED.
SHE'S CRAZY, THAT'S OBVIOUS!
STOP REPEATING EVERYTHING AFTER STEVEN! YOU'RE NOT BELIEVABLE. I KNOW YOU'RE NOT LIKE HIM!
HEY, YOU'D BETTER TONE IT DOWN NOW!

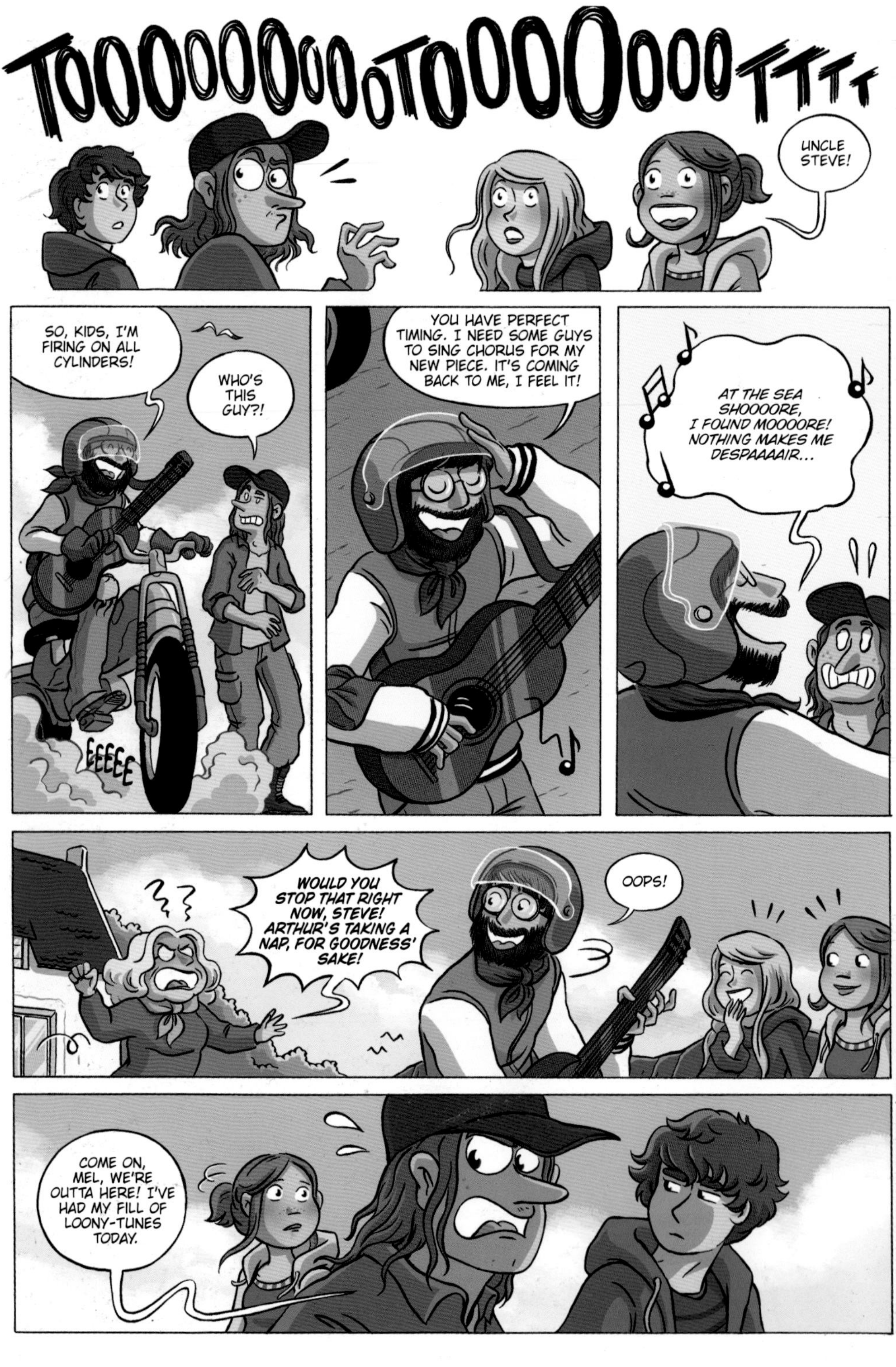
TOOOOOOOOOTOOOOOOOOTTTT
UNCLE STEVE!
SO, KIDS, I'M FIRING ON ALL CYLINDERS!
WHO'S THIS GUY?!
EEEEE
YOU HAVE PERFECT TIMING. I NEED SOME GUYS TO SING CHORUS FOR MY NEW PIECE. IT'S COMING BACK TO ME, I FEEL IT!
AT THE SEA SHOOOORE, I FOUND MOOOORE! NOTHING MAKES ME DESPAAAAIR...
WOULD YOU STOP THAT RIGHT NOW, STEVE! ARTHUR'S TAKING A NAP, FOR GOODNESS' SAKE!
OOPS!
COME ON, MEL, WE'RE OUTTA HERE! I'VE HAD MY FILL OF LOONY-TUNES TODAY.

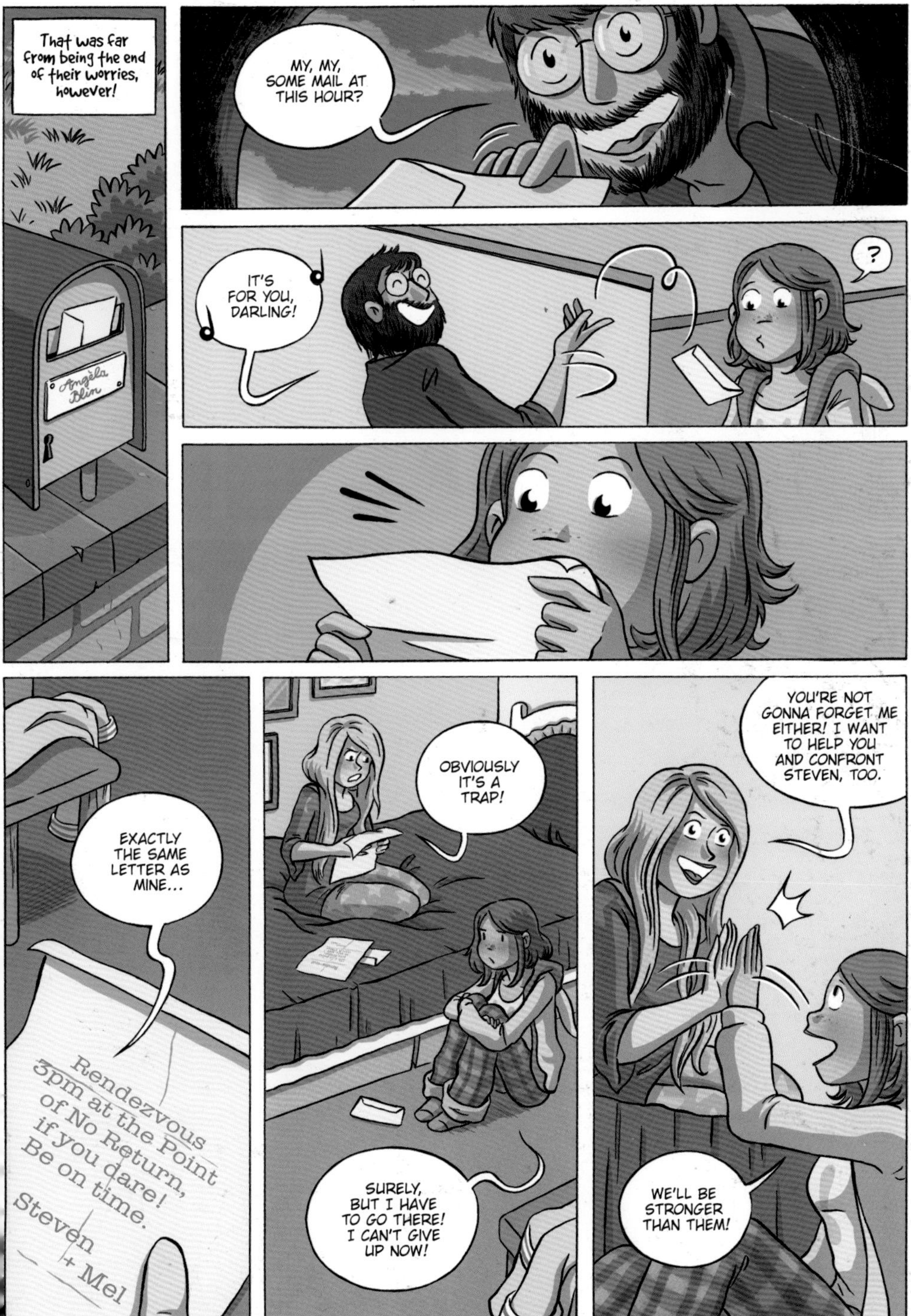
That was far from being the end of their worries, however!
MY, MY, SOME MAIL AT THIS HOUR?
IT'S FOR YOU, DARLING!
?
Angèla Blin
EXACTLY THE SAME LETTER AS MINE...
Rendezvous 3pm at the Point of No Return, if you dare! Be on time.
Steven + Mel
OBVIOUSLY IT'S A TRAP!
SURELY, BUT I HAVE TO GO THERE! I CAN'T GIVE UP NOW!
YOU'RE NOT GONNA FORGET ME EITHER! I WANT TO HELP YOU AND CONFRONT STEVEN, TOO.
WE'LL BE STRONGER THAN THEM!

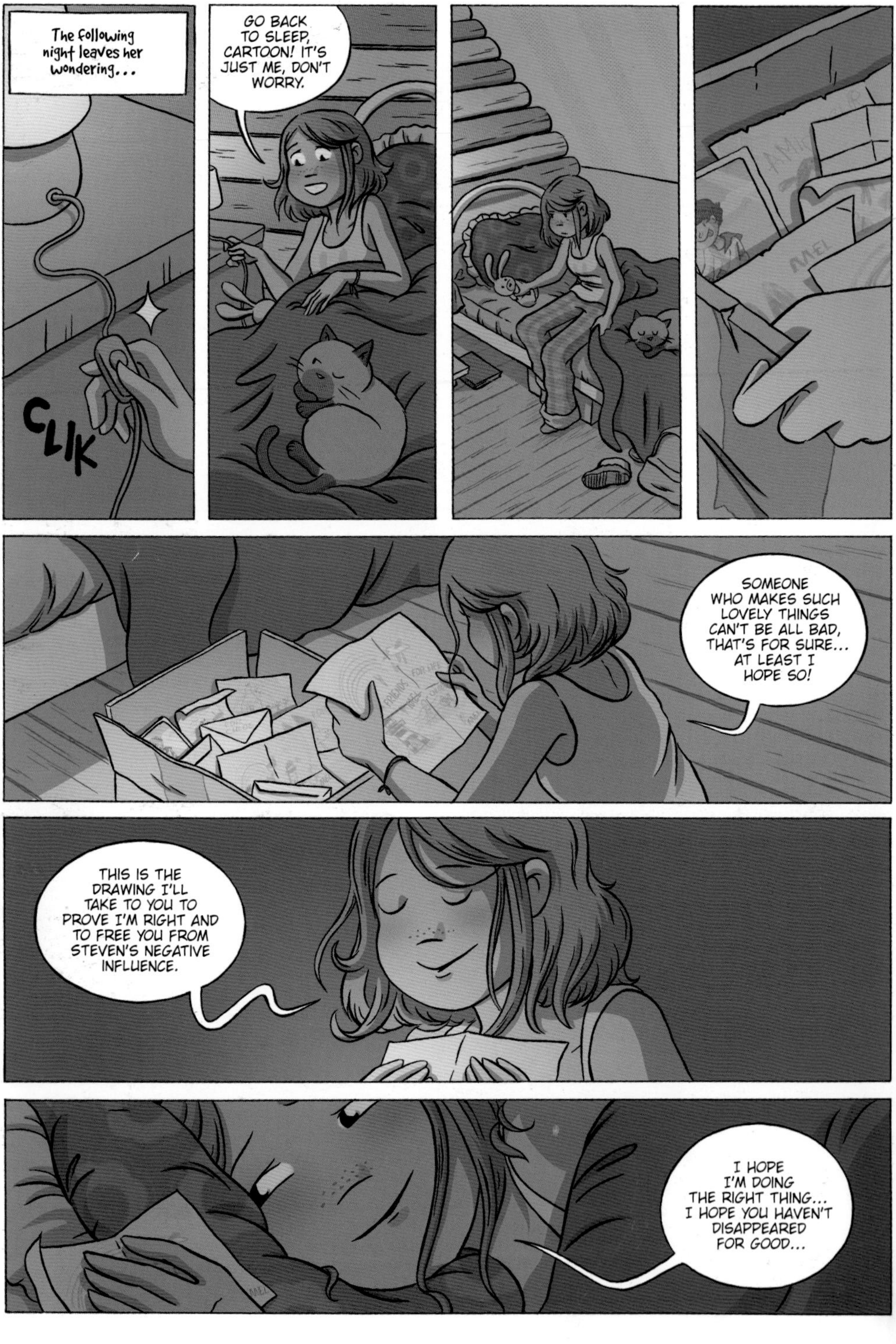
The following night leaves her wondering...
CLIK
GO BACK TO SLEEP, CARTOON! IT'S JUST ME, DON'T WORRY.
SOMEONE WHO MAKES SUCH LOVELY THINGS CAN'T BE ALL BAD, THAT'S FOR SURE... AT LEAST I HOPE SO!
THIS IS THE DRAWING I'LL TAKE TO YOU TO PROVE I'M RIGHT AND TO FREE YOU FROM STEVEN'S NEGATIVE INFLUENCE.
I HOPE I'M DOING THE RIGHT THING... I HOPE YOU HAVEN'T DISAPPEARED FOR GOOD...

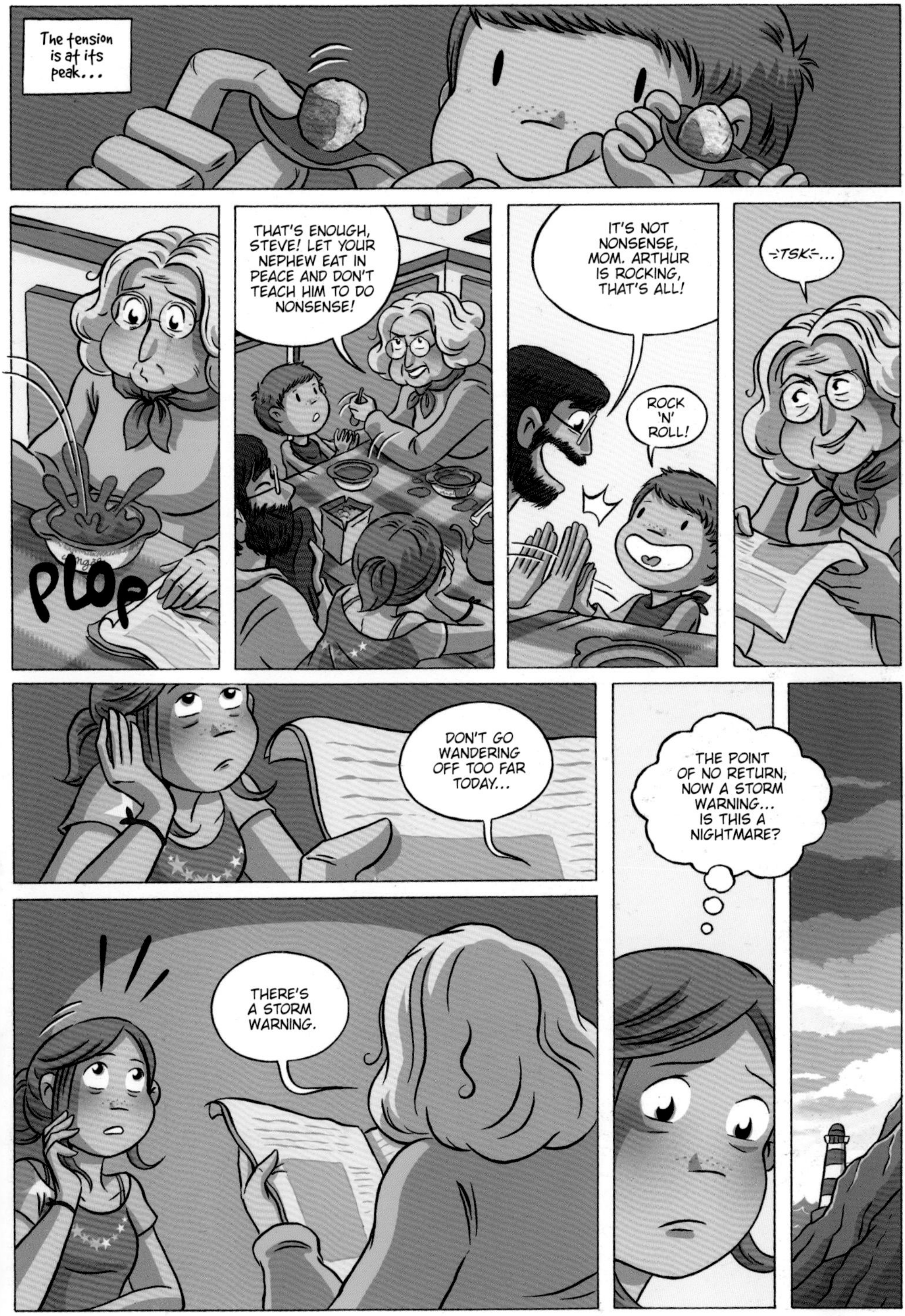

The tension is at its peak...
PLOP
THAT'S ENOUGH, STEVE! LET YOUR NEPHEW EAT IN PEACE AND DON'T TEACH HIM TO DO NONSENSE!
IT'S NOT NONSENSE, MOM. ARTHUR IS ROCKING, THAT'S ALL!
ROCK 'N' ROLL!
TSK...
DON'T GO WANDERING OFF TOO FAR TODAY...
THERE'S A STORM WARNING.
THE POINT OF NO RETURN, NOW A STORM WARNING... IS THIS A NIGHTMARE?

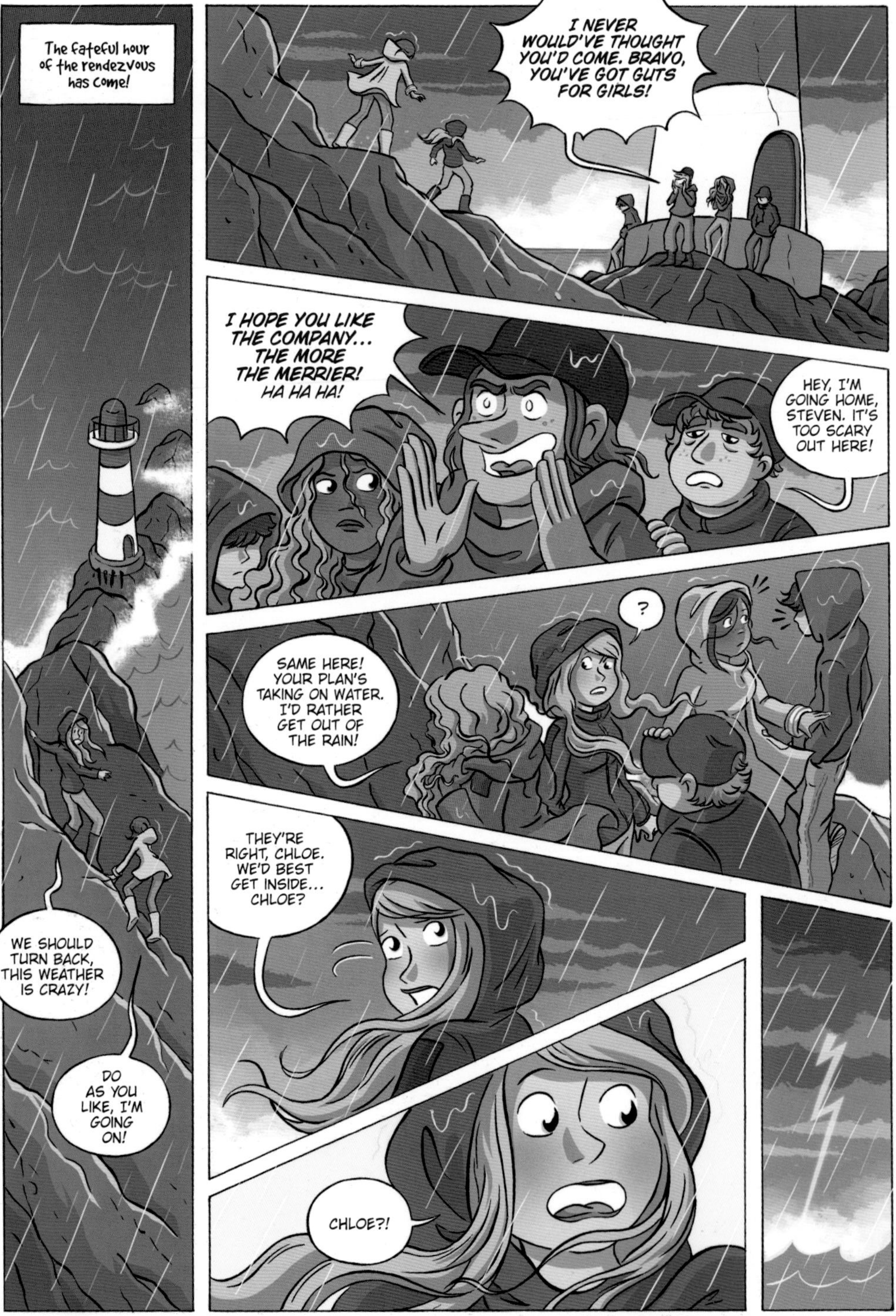
The fateful hour of the rendezvous has come!
WE SHOULD TURN BACK, THIS WEATHER IS CRAZY!
DO AS YOU LIKE, I'M GOING ON!
I NEVER WOULD'VE THOUGHT YOU'D COME. BRAVO, YOU'VE GOT GUTS FOR GIRLS!
I HOPE YOU LIKE THE COMPANY... THE MORE THE MERRIER! HA HA HA!
HEY, I'M GOING HOME, STEVEN. IT'S TOO SCARY OUT HERE!
SAME HERE! YOUR PLAN'S TAKING ON WATER. I'D RATHER GET OUT OF THE RAIN!
?
THEY'RE RIGHT, CHLOE. WE'D BEST GET INSIDE... CHLOE?
CHLOE?!

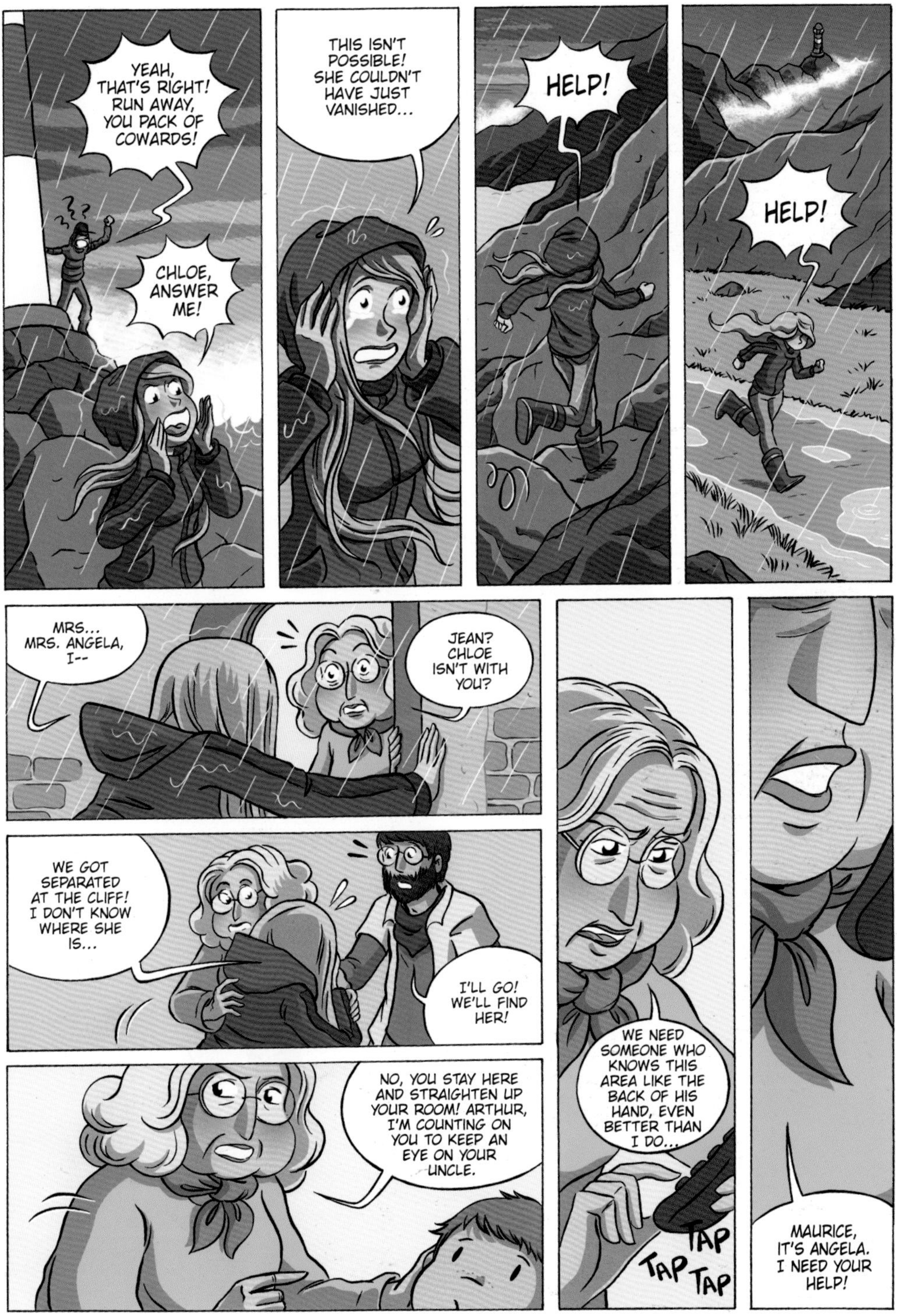
YEAH, THAT'S RIGHT! RUN AWAY, YOU PACK OF COWARDS!
CHLOE, ANSWER ME!
THIS ISN'T POSSIBLE! SHE COULDN'T HAVE JUST VANISHED...
HELP!
HELP!
MRS... MRS. ANGELA, I--
JEAN? CHLOE ISN'T WITH YOU?
WE GOT SEPARATED AT THE CLIFF! I DON'T KNOW WHERE SHE IS...
I'LL GO! WE'LL FIND HER!
NO, YOU STAY HERE AND STRAIGHTEN UP YOUR ROOM! ARTHUR, I'M COUNTING ON YOU TO KEEP AN EYE ON YOUR UNCLE.
WE NEED SOMEONE WHO KNOWS THIS AREA LIKE THE BACK OF HIS HAND, EVEN BETTER THAN I DO...
TAP TAP TAP
MAURICE, IT'S ANGELA. I NEED YOUR HELP!

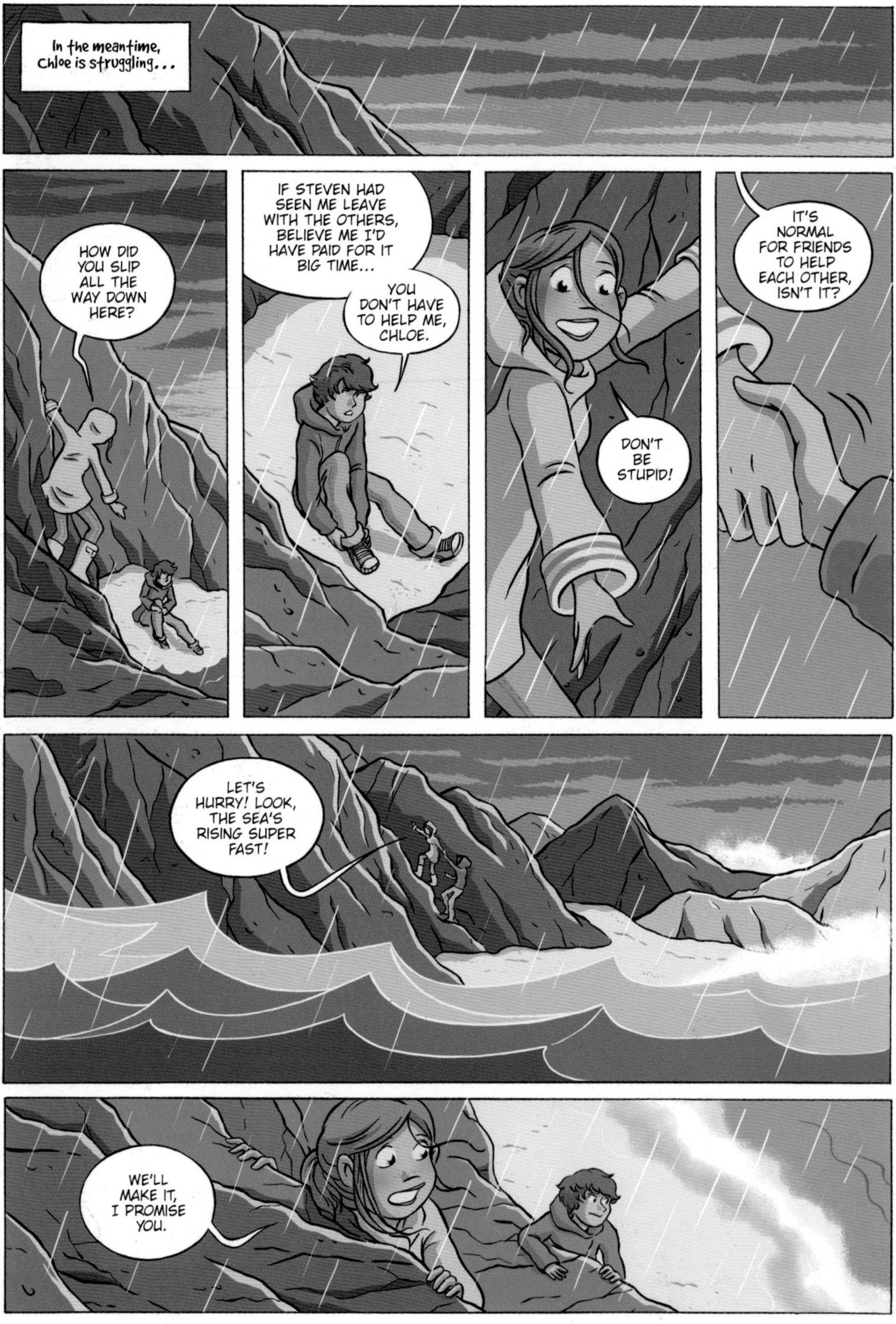
In the meantime, Chloe is struggling...
HOW DID YOU SLIP ALL THE WAY DOWN HERE?
IF STEVEN HAD SEEN ME LEAVE WITH THE OTHERS, BELIEVE ME I'D HAVE PAID FOR IT BIG TIME...
YOU DON'T HAVE TO HELP ME, CHLOE.
DON'T BE STUPID!
IT'S NORMAL FOR FRIENDS TO HELP EACH OTHER, ISN'T IT?
LET'S HURRY! LOOK, THE SEA'S RISING SUPER FAST!
WE'LL MAKE IT, I PROMISE YOU.

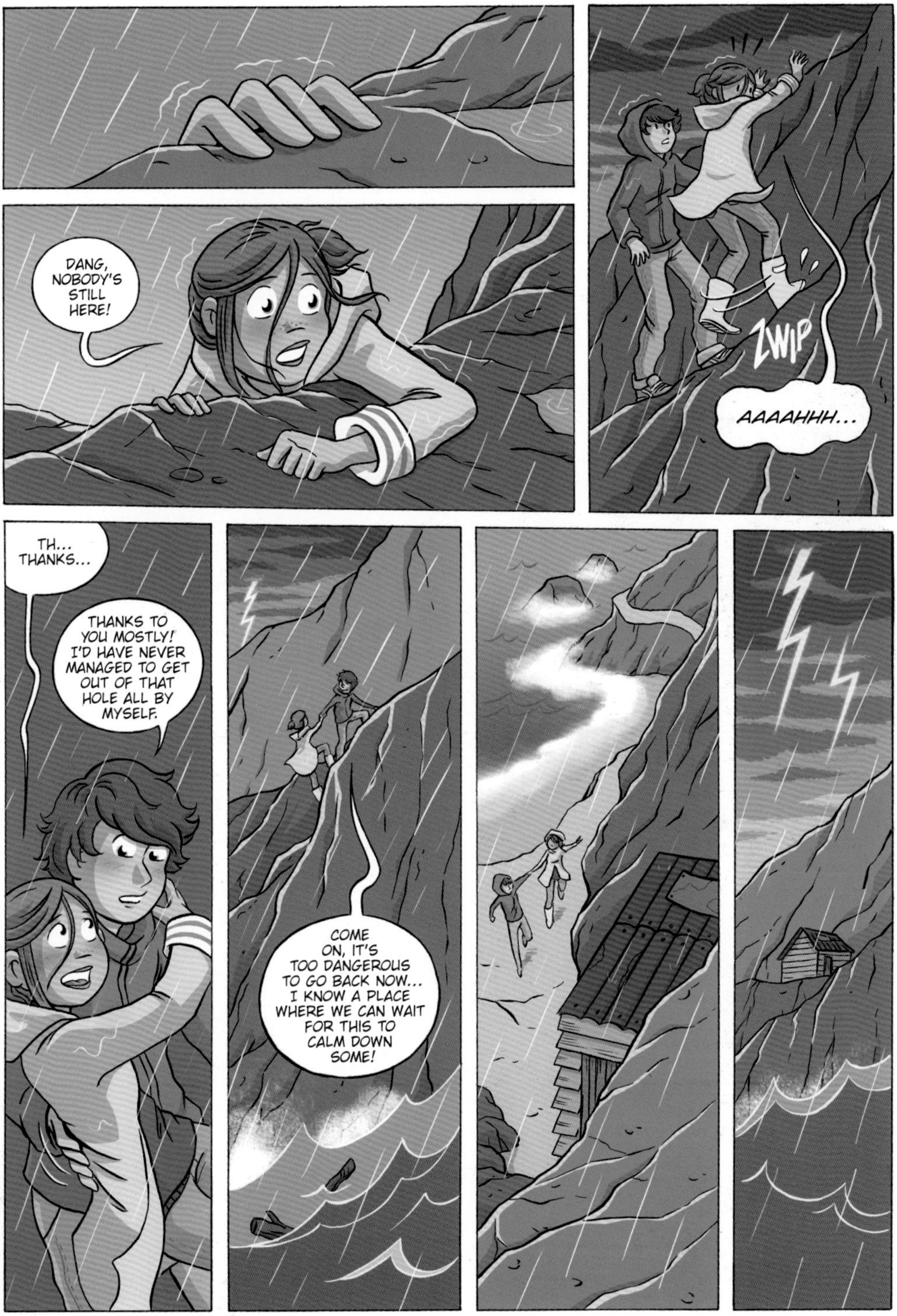
DANG, NOBODY'S STILL HERE!
ZWIP
AAAAHHH...
TH... THANKS...
THANKS TO YOU MOSTLY! I'D HAVE NEVER MANAGED TO GET OUT OF THAT HOLE ALL BY MYSELF.
COME ON, IT'S TOO DANGEROUS TO GO BACK NOW... I KNOW A PLACE WHERE WE CAN WAIT FOR THIS TO CALM DOWN SOME!

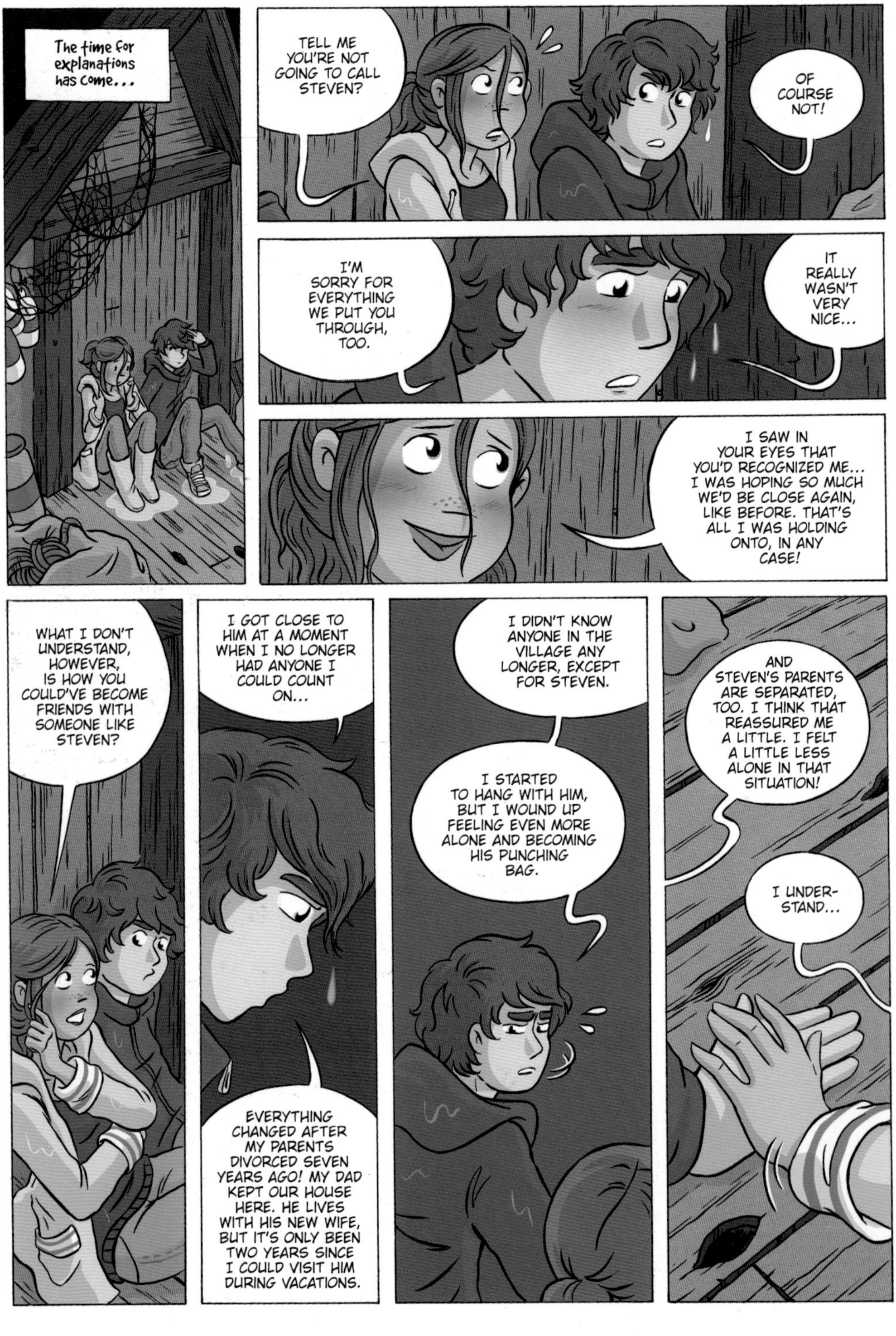

The time for explanations has come...
TELL ME YOU'RE NOT GOING TO CALL STEVEN?
OF COURSE NOT!
I'M SORRY FOR EVERYTHING WE PUT YOU THROUGH, TOO.
IT REALLY WASN'T VERY NICE...
I SAW IN YOUR EYES THAT YOU'D RECOGNIZED ME... I WAS HOPING SO MUCH WE'D BE CLOSE AGAIN, LIKE BEFORE. THAT'S ALL I WAS HOLDING ONTO, IN ANY CASE!
WHAT I DON'T UNDERSTAND, HOWEVER, IS HOW YOU COULD'VE BECOME FRIENDS WITH SOMEONE LIKE STEVEN?
I GOT CLOSE TO HIM AT A MOMENT WHEN I NO LONGER HAD ANYONE I COULD COUNT ON...
EVERYTHING CHANGED AFTER MY PARENTS DIVORCED SEVEN YEARS AGO! MY DAD KEPT OUR HOUSE HERE. HE LIVES WITH HIS NEW WIFE, BUT IT'S ONLY BEEN TWO YEARS SINCE I COULD VISIT HIM DURING VACATIONS.
I DIDN'T KNOW ANYONE IN THE VILLAGE ANY LONGER, EXCEPT FOR STEVEN.
I STARTED TO HANG WITH HIM, BUT I WOUND UP FEELING EVEN MORE ALONE AND BECOMING HIS PUNCHING BAG.
AND STEVEN'S PARENTS ARE SEPARATED, TOO. I THINK THAT REASSURED ME A LITTLE. I FELT A LITTLE LESS ALONE IN THAT SITUATION!
I UNDER-STAND...

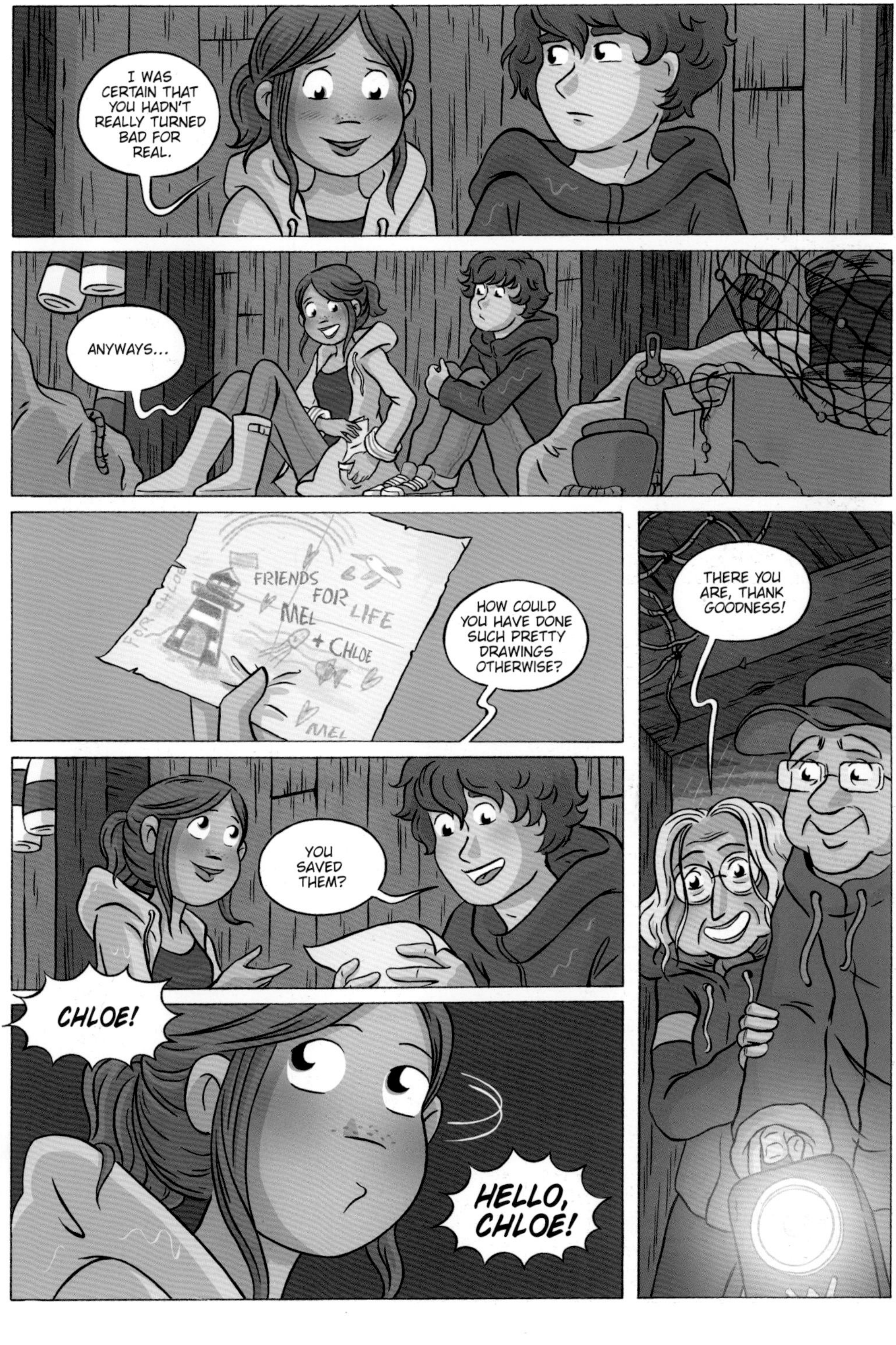
I WAS CERTAIN THAT YOU HADN'T REALLY TURNED BAD FOR REAL.
ANYWAYS...
FOR CHLOE
FRIENDS FOR LIFE
MEL + CHLOE
MEL
HOW COULD YOU HAVE DONE SUCH PRETTY DRAWINGS OTHERWISE?
YOU SAVED THEM?
CHLOE!
HELLO, CHLOE!
THERE YOU ARE, THANK GOODNESS!

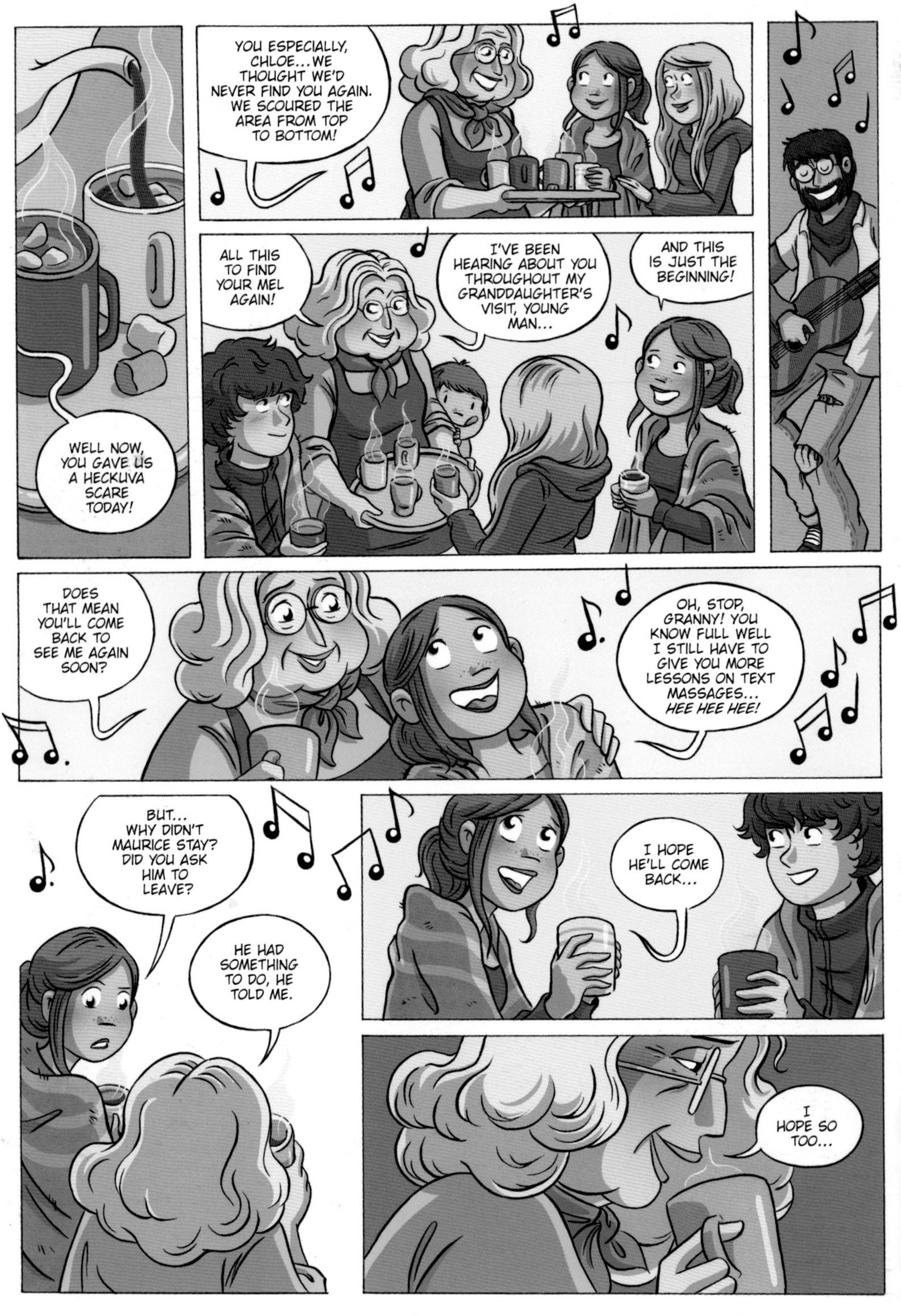
WELL NOW, YOU GAVE US A HECKUVA SCARE TODAY!
YOU ESPECIALLY, CHLOE...WE THOUGHT WE'D NEVER FIND YOU AGAIN. WE SCOURED THE AREA FROM TOP TO BOTTOM!
ALL THIS TO FIND YOUR MEL AGAIN!
I'VE BEEN HEARING ABOUT YOU THROUGHOUT MY GRANDDAUGHTER'S VISIT, YOUNG MAN...
AND THIS IS JUST THE BEGINNING!
DOES THAT MEAN YOU'LL COME BACK TO SEE ME AGAIN SOON?
OH, STOP, GRANNY! YOU KNOW FULL WELL I STILL HAVE TO GIVE YOU MORE LESSONS ON TEXT MASSAGES... *HEE HEE HEE!*
BUT... WHY DIDN'T MAURICE STAY? DID YOU ASK HIM TO LEAVE?
HE HAD SOMETHING TO DO, HE TOLD ME.
I HOPE HE'LL COME BACK...
I HOPE SO TOO...

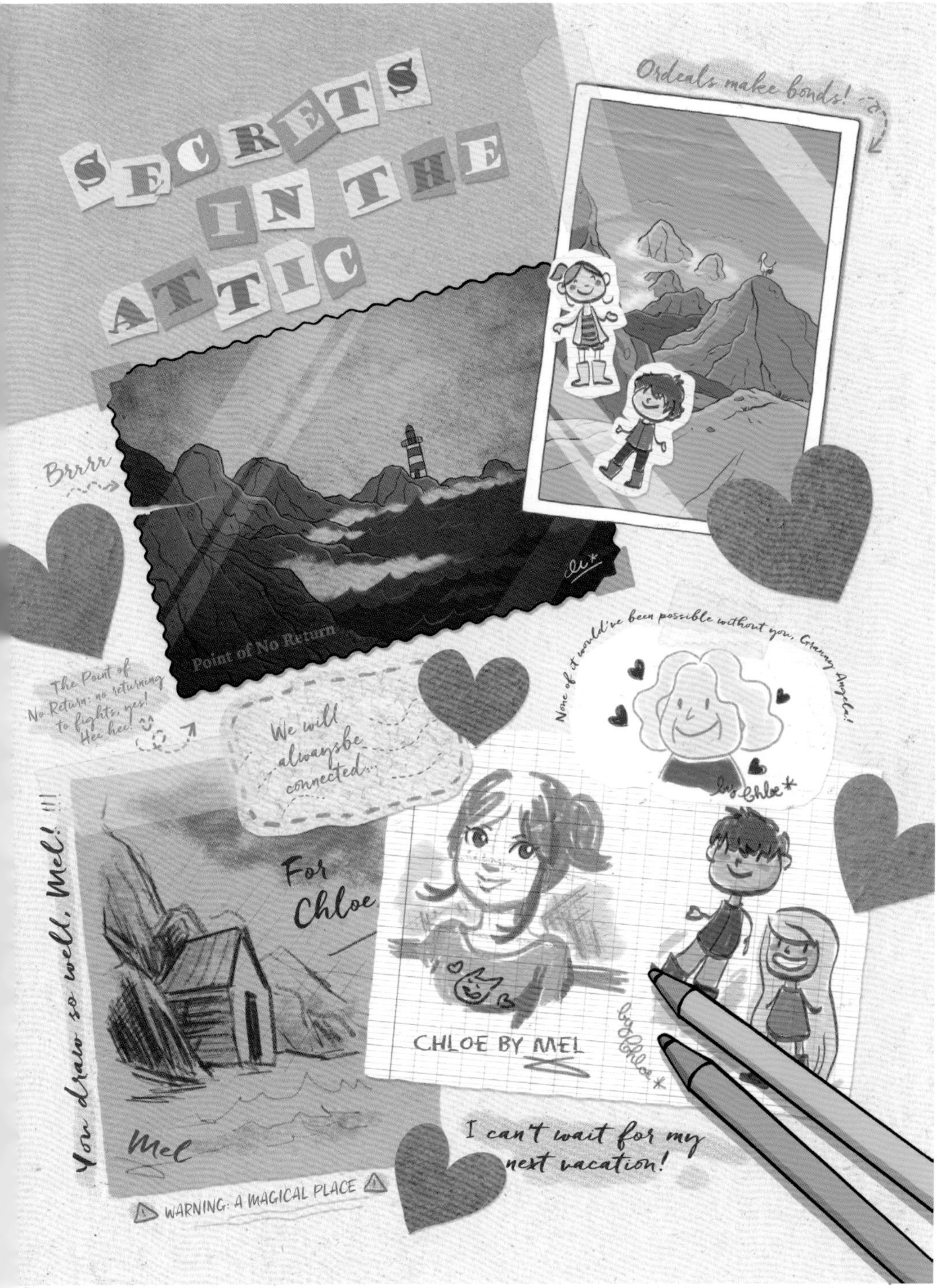
SECRETS IN THE ATTIC
Ordeals make bonds!
Brrrr
Point of No Return
The Point of No Return: no returning to fights, yes! Hee hee!
We will always be connected...
None of it would've been possible without you, Granny Angela!
by Chloe
For Chloe
Mel
You draw so well, Mel! !!!
CHLOE BY MEL
by Chloe
I can't wait for my next vacation!
WARNING: A MAGICAL PLACE

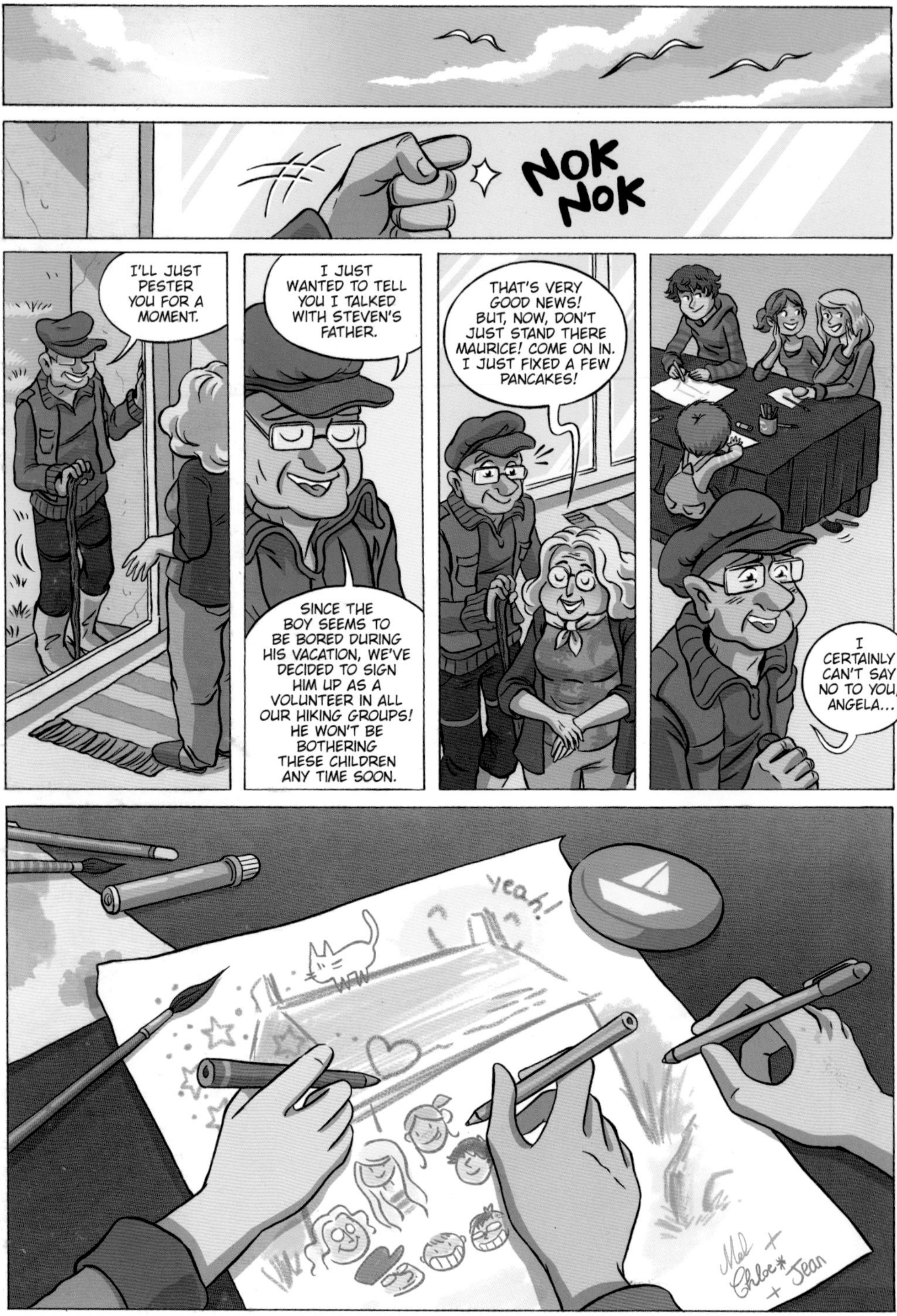
NOK NOK
I'LL JUST PESTER YOU FOR A MOMENT.
I JUST WANTED TO TELL YOU I TALKED WITH STEVEN'S FATHER.
SINCE THE BOY SEEMS TO BE BORED DURING HIS VACATION, WE'VE DECIDED TO SIGN HIM UP AS A VOLUNTEER IN ALL OUR HIKING GROUPS! HE WON'T BE BOTHERING THESE CHILDREN ANY TIME SOON.
THAT'S VERY GOOD NEWS! BUT, NOW, DON'T JUST STAND THERE MAURICE! COME ON IN. I JUST FIXED A FEW PANCAKES!
I CERTAINLY CAN'T SAY NO TO YOU, ANGELA...
yeah!
Mel + Chloe* + Jean